The DEAR WATSONS

Front cover picture:
Author's own photograph of Elizabeth Lancaster.

The DEAR WATSONS

Lynne Birch

BREWIN BOOKS

BREWIN BOOKS
56 Alcester Road,
Studley,
Warwickshire,
B80 7LG
www.brewinbooks.com

Published by Brewin Books 2019

A CIP catalogue record for this book is available from the British Library.

ISBN: 978-1-85858-596-3

Printed and bound in Great Britain
by Bell & Bain Ltd.

Preface
April 1911

From the ranks of ancestors, those sepia tinted stern men with their wives, sons and daughters, all posing stiffly in Sunday clothes, one young woman lives and breathes.

She stands in a doorway, leaning against the frame, arms folded. There is a chill at her back from the hallway, from the wind in the street finding its way around the locked front door. It is somewhere between Sunday teatime and evening, that place where the weekend is drawing to a close and only the night stands between a family and its working week.

The light from the room she is facing falls on the front of her hair, a broad forehead, a stubborn jaw, throwing the rest of her into shadow. Hefty curtains deaden the sound of the squall that is beating the window. She watches her grandmother get to her feet to poke the embers. Showers of red sparks fly up the chimney. She's unsure of her grandmother's age. All old is old when you're fifteen. Her father jumps up from his chair.

"Let me do that!"

He takes the poker from his mother-in-law and lays it on the hearth, squats in front of the fender and, picking up the fire tongs, makes up the fire with gleaming lumps of coal. He drops the tongs back in the brass bucket before returning to his newspaper. It's the Saturday paper. Today is Sunday. Arthur's catching up.

This is home. Lansdowne House, where Gladys Lancaster has grown up with her older sister, Dora, and her younger brothers, Eric and Ralph. Arthur Lancaster, left to his own devices, would never have risked taking on such a place on his clerk's wages when they moved from Birmingham to Worcester, but his wife has always ignored her husband's doubts and the affairs of the big house run smoothly under her direction. With the addition of the lodgers the family lives comfortably and respectably.

It is Sunday the eleventh of April, nineteen hundred and eleven.

"We're going to be part of history after tonight," Gladys says, leaning against the doorpost. She imagines everyone in the country, in England and Wales and Scotland and Ireland, all the people here in Worcester, the family, everyone being accounted for today. "Every single head of the household, sitting down after tea tonight to fill in a census form. We'll all be in the records of Great Britain, long after we've died."

Elizabeth Lancaster looks up from trimming a black straw hat with a fresh ribbon.

"Not everyone'll be doing it. There'll be plenty of folk not as law abiding as your father."

Granny Compson frowns.

"Don't spoil it for her. Let the child think the country is all of a mind."

Elizabeth shakes her head.

"Gladys should know about these things. The world's a changing place. When she's grown up who knows what it will be like. It will certainly be different from now."

"Who would want to spoil the census?" asks Gladys from the doorway.

"They're not all people who necessarily want to spoil it," Elizabeth explains. "There's the homeless, for a start. How are they going to complete a census form? And there's the suffragettes. They don't want to be accounted for, with their husbands as the heads of their families. They're planning a rebellion. They were going to have rallies all around the country today. That's what it said in the paper."

Arthur puts down his paper, giving his wife a warning look.

"I can't see what that's got to do with us."

"And I don't suppose she'll want to go to rallies like those women," says Granny Compson. "She'll want to find a husband and settle down with a home and a family. That's what girls have always wanted, and I can't see it changing."

"Who knows what she'll be doing or where she'll be," persists Elizabeth. "It'll be different, that's all I'm saying. And," she adds defiantly, "I hope by the time Gladys is grown up she'll be able to have a vote."

Arthur is a kind, mild natured man, used to his wife's spirit and so he chooses to ignore her last remark. He can't see that she's right, but if she is and these suffragettes end up getting what they want, he thinks it will cause a lot of trouble in the country. He won't mind himself, but a lot of men won't like it. He can see that coming.

He turns to Gladys.

"Come in if you're coming. Get that door closed. You're letting all the heat out."

"And as far as you're concerned, Arthur," says Elizabeth, "it's time to get going on those forms if you're going to get ours done tonight. Ralph's in bed, Eric's

upstairs finishing his schoolwork and Mr Barker is out tonight. No excuse. The table's cleared ready and waiting."

Granny Compson looks up.

"Where's Mr Barker gone?"

"I've no idea. It's none of our business. I'm his landlady, not his keeper. The paying guests don't have to account to me for their whereabouts." The old woman purses her lips. Sometimes Elizabeth could be very sharp with her.

Arthur puts down his paper.

"You're right, Elizabeth. I'd better get started. The forms look straightforward enough but I need to sit at the table and concentrate on what I'm doing. Gladys, you can help me? We might as well cash in on all this office training you've had. We'll have a go at these forms together."

He sits down at the oak gateleg table and draws the forms from the large envelope. In his slow, deliberate way he unfolds everything carefully, smoothing the folds with his palm.

"Now, let's see … there's me to go first. I'm the head of the household and here …" Arthur stops. "Elizabeth, how long've we been married now?"

"Eighteen years. Surely you can remember that."

"Ah yes. 1893. Thanks, love." He fills in the space carefully with his neat handwriting and the rest of his details. Age: Forty. Occupation: Clerk to Nail Manufacturers. Where born: Balsall Heath, Birmingham.

"Don't we have to put your place of work?" asks Gladys.

"No, they don't want that. Heenan & Froude might be the centre of our lives," he chuckles, "with you and me there in the offices every working day, and I know we think everyone knows about it, what with all the publicity there's been about the work the firm's done for the big tower up in Blackpool and everything, but the folk who've made this form, they're not interested in all that, they just want to know what my line of work is, not where I do it."

"And mine."

"Yes, yours too. But let's get your mother down next."

"Elizabeth Lancaster."

"No, that's not right. Remember your mother's first name is Mary. Then Elizabeth. I know no-one calls her Mary. That's where you're muddled. Born in Birmingham the year after me. There we go, thirty nine years old." Arthur sits back for a break and looks at his wife. "Forty next birthday, lass."

"No need to remind me, Arthur. It'll come around soon enough."

"Now it's your turn young lady. Let's see. Relationship to head – daughter – and look at this, we can put down your occupation." He writes carefully in the

space by Gladys' name. "There we go. Shorthand typist. You should be very proud of that."

"And don't forget where I was born." Arthur looks up from his writing.

"I'm not likely to forget that in a hurry am I. All my girls born in Birmingham."

Arthur's eye is too bright. Gladys looks away. There would be two of his three daughters missing from this census form, one alive but living away from home and one Arthur could not bear to talk about. Gladys makes an effort to fill the room with more conversation, to distract her father with talk of the living.

"I wish Dora still lived with us," she pipes up. Elizabeth relaxes. Gladys has always been good at steering him away from the sadness that engulfs him so easily.

"Well," says Arthur, "Your sister's doing very nicely back in Birmingham, getting a good training in the post office. Amy Parker is an excellent postmistress, and she and her husband have been good friends to us all. Dora couldn't have done better."

"Yes," Elizabeth reflects, "There's a lot of seventeen year old girls would give their right arms to be getting the training that Dora's having..."

Gladys interrupts.

"Don't forget you'll have to put Granny down. And Mr Barker. Everyone who's here tonight has to go on the form."

"Yes, but we'll put the boys next."

And so the moment passes. Granny Compson looks from her daughter to her son-in-law. There'd been the three little girls, each born a year apart. Dora and Gladys and then along came Adeline. Sweet Addy, Arthur always called her, and the apple of his eye. And even when Eric was born the following year – "A son for the new century" they'd all said – even his boy couldn't excite Arthur as much as when he had first held Sweet Addy in his arms.

They'd had a break then, from the babies, until Ralph came along in 1906. Sturdy little Ralph, and the others thriving too. Five lovely children. And then, three years ago – is it really that long – seems like yesterday ... Addy's got a headache, Elizabeth had said. A terrible pain. They'd kept her at home, kept her warm, followed the doctor's instructions. Did all that.

Losing that little one broke Arthur's heart. Even now, you can't talk about Addy, for his eyes fill with tears and no-one can do anything to help him. Upsets the children, Elizabeth has told her mother. Keep him thinking about the living. Which is what Gladys is doing now.

Sensible girl, thinks her grandmother. Just like Elizabeth. Elizabeth keeps things together. Gladys will probably grow up to be the same.

"I think we're done now." Arthur's voice brings Granny Compson back to the present. "That's Eric filled in, and Ralph, and Gran and Mr Barker. We'll just go back to the top and write in the address. Should have done that first, I suppose."

Arthur Lancaster, on that Sunday evening, with the curtains drawn against the wind and the rain on the streets of Worcester, and watched over by his daughter, completes the 1911 Census form for his family, checking it through before giving it to Gladys to put in the large envelope, carefully screwing the top onto his pen, pushing back his chair, rolling down his shirtsleeves, buttoning his cuffs and taking up his customary position once again in the armchair on the opposite side of the fire to his mother-in-law with yesterday's newspaper.

Part 1

1926

Plymouth – November 1926
She stands on Plymouth Hoe under a restless sky. The brim of her hat is pulled low and close to her head, as is the fashion, so that she has to tilt her face upwards to look out at the ocean.

She bends to straighten the cape of her daughter's coat and secure more firmly the scarlet tam o'shanter. But the child wheels away across the grass and the hat flies off in the wind. It is as though an artist has chosen to paint the tumbling brightness of the girl's hair as she streams towards the empty bandstand, chasing the screeching gulls with the energy of a five year old fresh from the schoolroom.

The woman retrieves the child's hat. She would like to take the weight off her legs for a while but, despite the wind that has got up, all the public seating is damp, so she remains standing and watchful. The silver shimmer of the water, stretching to she cares not where, holds no charms for her. She is a Midlander and she longs for her own city, for the cathedral, the familiar winding streets and the gentle banks of the Severn.

She is tired, but it is not so much from the walking but from the weight of homesickness. She has spent the afternoon in the shops, not buying much (though there was plenty that took her fancy), but more to get out of the flat and feel herself to be part of the world. Now they are down at The Hoe, for she has promised Beryl that they could see the sea before they went home.

She is a short, well turned out woman. Her coat, fashionably cut, with its long lapels and low waist, belies the fact that she doesn't have much money to spare, for the skills she learnt from her mother are standing her in good stead and she has turned her hand to sewing for herself and her daughter.

She calls and the child comes back to her.

"Best foot forward. Daddy will be home soon."

She hopes she's right, that Harry isn't going to have to spend another evening out. It's all very well, the job going smoothly, the money and the little car are fine, but he's working long hours and she is so lonely. She knows he enjoys the job, knows he is charming and persuasive enough to be a good salesman, and she hates her resentment.

He is doing his best to keep her cheerful, she knows that, and he's already bought the train tickets ready for the Christmas trip so she'll have something to look forward to.

The summer has been good, she has to admit, with Ralph and Mother staying with them for three whole weeks and Pip coming down with the baby. Ralph, of course, would be the one to bring Mother. Twenty last birthday but still the baby in Mother's eyes. They'd had a lovely time. Trips to the beach – Bigbury-on-Sea at weekends in the Austin – Beryl in the dicky seat, she and Mother in the back and Ralph up front with Harry. How they'd laughed at Ralph in his new boater and blazer.

"Secretary of the rowing club now. Got to look the part!"

That'd given Gladys a few pangs, brought back memories of the long summer evenings in Worcester when she was a girl. She and her friends would leave the office, get down to the boats and off they'd go, rowing up the river without a care in the world. Mother keeping her tea warm for later, never worried about her, knowing how well she handled the boats. Her friends, all from the office. The future stretching ahead, untasted, promising in its vagueness.

Eric hasn't been down to see them this summer, but then that's to be expected after what's happened between him and Harry. He's working hard, Mother has said. Too hard, some of the family would say. He and Pip have been married now for a couple of years. Glad likes her sister-in-law. Sometimes she thinks she has more in common with her than with her own sister. But it's a strange marriage, she has to admit. Eric and Pip never seem to have any fun.

When Gladys and Harry fell in love, folk would say you could see it coming, that it was the way they looked at one another. She doubts anyone has ever said anything like that about Eric and Pip. Eric is always irritable in Pip's company and there's never much in the way of affection between them.

"Your mother's choice," Harry would say. "It's Elizabeth who wanted Eric to have Pip. It's a rebound thing for Eric. He'll never get over his first love."

Gladys doesn't comment when Harry starts. She doesn't like to think about it. She knows he's right, that Elizabeth had been delighted with her pretty young lodger, the gifted pianist, and had decided that Pip would be just the right wife for her up and coming son. And now Pip and Eric have Zena, Elizabeth's second granddaughter and a cousin for Beryl.

Mother and child head to catch the bus that will take them to the first floor flat on Mutley Plain. Beryl licks the back of her hand and tastes the sea. As they pass the lighted windows of the houses lining Lockyer Street, Gladys catches glimpses of other people's lives: mothers setting out suppers; young men and women with long scarves and glowing cheeks coming in from work, laughing together, making plans for the evening; children resting elbows on tables, poring over books, and occasionally, as a front door is opened to let someone in, there is a steamy supper smell. She aches for her family.

* * *

Well, of course, Harry wants her to be happy. Glad in a good mood makes life a deal more comfortable. He fell in love and married a carefree young woman but he's beginning to think she'll be forever in the dumps here in Devon. At times he feels pretty guilty about it all, but what's a chap to do?

They'd started married life back in Nottingham, near to his own family, but then, after they'd had Beryl, Eric had offered Harry a position. God knows Harry tried to make it work in Worcester. Glad was so pleased to be back there with the family, especially with her mother there for her and the baby. And she could see more of Pip. Glad gets on better with her sister-in-law, he thinks, than her own sister. Blood's thicker than water and so she loves Dora but it's Pip and Glad who really hit it off. Eric set him up with one of the vans: *Lancasters, Quality supplies for Quality Bakers!* on the sides in big writing. Harry was to start on the rounds until he'd got the measure of the trade. Given time, Eric had said, maybe make Harry a director. But he never got as far as the selling. Eric on his back all the time.

Harry, you're late back. Where've you been? You're spending too long talking to the customers, and *Harry, you need to clean the van better than that. Polish the wheels up, Harry, before you finish tonight*. It was '*Harry this*' and '*Harry that*' and Harry was supposed to be so grateful to his brother-in-law, six years his junior. Getting Glad roped in had been the last straw. '*Sort out your husband, Glad!*'

Harry thinks about it a lot. There were many things said that would have been better not spoken, but in the end he'd said to Glad, there's no way I can work for your brother. He's not my sort of chap. Okey dokey, he's the business success of the family. Still a young man and got it all sorted with the bakery trade: flour, yeast, sugar, dried fruits, you name it – Eric will supply it. He'll go far, no doubt about that, but I can't stick with him.

Eric the entrepreneur. Doesn't get his talent from father-in-law, Harry knows that much. Old Arthur, good chap, lovely chap, but once a clerk always a clerk for Arthur. It was a big thing for Arthur, moving the family from Birmingham when Heenans started up in Worcester, and of course, they all say the little girl dying had knocked any stuffing he ever had out of him, no doubt about that. She'd been his favourite, Glad always says. Well, there's always one. It was before Harry's time, of course. Harry only ended up in Worcester in the war, chest too weak for fighting so sent to Heenans as an airman mechanic when they realised he'd once been an apprentice.

Mother-in-law is the one in that family with the drive. She's the one who's pushed Eric. If she'd been a man she'd have gone far. Strong woman. Keeps the family going and they all love her for it. Don't blame them either. And she was good to Harry, even after the break up with Eric and the job came up in Plymouth.

"You're a free spirit, Harry, that's the thing. It's the musician in you. It's hard for you to settle." She'd stood at the back of his chair with her hand on his shoulder. "You'll find your niche sooner or later, you see. You've got the personality." Gladys' mother, ever the peacemaker. Always seeing the best in everyone. But Eric, very different from the rest of them. He'd got Ralph roped into the business now and Harry reckoned that'd be a job for life for Ralph.

What had he loved in Glad that made him want to marry her? She'd been different from the girls back home. Nottingham is famous for its lace and the pretty girls, but Harry had fallen in love when he arrived in Worcester in 1916 with a girl who was handsome rather than pretty, a capable girl like her mother, a girl who only came up to his shoulder but could row him down the river as well as any of the men. He liked a girl who was different, a bit unusual. He loved her face, the big eyes and the wide smile and that nose that she hates.

"If you'd been a Roman you'd be royalty with a nose like that," he says. "Anyway, you'd not be the same with a little button of a nose and I may not have taken such a fancy to you." She laughs at that and pushes her hands up through her hair. She has a good brain too, and Harry couldn't have been doing with an empty headed girl. She can add up a column of figures as long as your arm in a flash and she won all those prizes for her shorthand.

"I'm a shorthand typist," she'd told him when they first met. "I take down dictation from the managers and then type it up. It's a good job, much better than shop work." He'd liked that, her pride in her work and the air of independence that the job gave her. She'd nursed an ambition to be a stenographer in the law courts. "That's the tops, Harry," she'd say, but of course once she was no longer Miss Lancaster and became Mrs Harry Watson she'd put away all ideas of a career.

December 1926

Foregate Street Station – Worcester

"Lordy, all this luggage. Looks like you've come for a month and not just for Christmas!" Glad, surrounded by suitcases and boxes, laughs at her brother. There he is, still, in her eyes, her little brother, standing on the platform as the train arrives. He's shaken hands with Harry and given Glad a peck, but he only has eyes for Beryl.

"Uncle Ralph!" She throws her arms around his neck.

"Whoa!" He sweeps her into his arms and lifts her high above his head. "My favourite niece! And you've grown at least another four inches. Must be the sea air!"

"Your face, Ralph, it's a picture!" says Glad. Harry smiles at his wife. Her happiness at being back in Worcester is infectious. Five minutes off the train and she's a different woman. Christmas only two days away and the bonus from his boss in his wallet. The world's a good place.

"Yep, everything but the kitchen sink," he says, "but you know your sister, once she's made up her mind."

"So what is it all, then?" Ralph picks up one of the cases and Harry gathers up the rest of the luggage. Gladys loops the strap of her hatbox over one arm and catches hold of Beryl with her free hand.

"Keep away from the edge of the platform, Beryl." She walks fast to keep up with Ralph. "Well, I've had to pack a lot of clothes. Obviously, if all these parties are going on over Christmas we had to bring our glad rags, didn't we? And my best hat's in this box. On its own. I'll need that for church. And then the presents are in those bags. Some are for Beryl but the rest are for you lot." She stops at the Ladies room.

"I'll just take Beryl in here for a tick, Harry, tidy her up before we get to the family." Ralph watches them go.

"That'll be a long tick, Harry, if I know my sister, by the time she's powdered her nose and fixed her hair." Harry looks sombre.

"She's been planning this trip for weeks. It's the only thing that's kept her going."

"No better, then, Harry?"

"No. I don't think things are going to work out in Plymouth. She's so damn homesick all the time. Hates the sea, pines for the Midlands. I know she's tried to shake it off but she just seems to be getting lower all the time. Somehow, we'll have to get back up here."

"Shame it didn't work out here for you and Eric. That would have been ideal, all of us in Worcester together."

"I know. I feel bad for the way things turned out and for causing trouble in your family."

Ralph shrugged. "Don't worry about it," he says gruffly. He doesn't go in for a lot of family talk and he knows which side his bread's buttered. Besides, Eric's his brother. He likes Harry but he works with Eric. He made sure he didn't get involved at the time of the row between Harry and Eric and he isn't going to get involved now.

"No-one bears a grudge, Harry. Mother knows how Eric can be and she still thinks the world of you. Eric will be civil to you for mother's sake, and for Glad's. Dora's not bothered, she wasn't involved really, was she, and Dad, as usual, never takes sides. Anything for a quiet life as far as he's concerned."

"And Gladys and Pip still get on well. That's a good thing."

"Yes," said Ralph, "Pip might be married to Eric, but she knew well enough when things blew up it was six of one and half a dozen of the other."

"And little Zena's OK, is she?"

"Seems to be."

"Beryl can't wait to see her. And will Dora be coming over? Bringing the children?"

"Yes. They're coming Boxing Day. Dora will come over with Joan and Desmond."

"Blimey! There's going to be a lot of kids. We shall have to think of a bit of entertainment. Keep them out of mischief."

"You know Mother. Got to get the family together whenever there's an opportunity."

Glad reappears with Beryl by her side. Ralph jingles the change in his coat pocket.

"Ready for the off then?" he says.

Harry looks down at his wife and brother-in-law. All the Lancasters are short, unlike Harry's family. *Short and comfortable, Harry,* Arthur Lancaster would say to his son-in-law. *The Lancasters come in small packages but they're from country stock. Strong and stalwart. That's what we are.*

"Yes, Ralph. We're ready. Did Eric let you bring the car or are we getting a taxi?"

"Yes, ma'am, the brand new Morris!" Beryl claps her hands. "Top brick off the chimney for you girls. The carriage awaits!"

January 1927

Elizabeth Lancaster sits at her dressing table. Behind her, reflected in the mirror, Beryl sprawls on the bed sorting through her grandmother's jewellery box. Elizabeth wears her brown hair short and fashionable these days with two forward sweeping curls on her forehead. She is 55 with laughter lines at the corners of her eyes and a face only just starting to age.

She's changed from her morning clothes into a fitted blue paisley dress with tight sleeves and a long front fastening of tiny buttons. She winds the rope of blue beads which Gladys and Harry have given her for Christmas around her neck and lets the rest of it, with its gold tasseled pendant, fall down the bodice of her dress and past her waist. Glad always goes for quality, and Harry would approve.

Christmas has gone off well and they've had a lot of fun. Plenty of people around. Twenty-two on Boxing Night for the party. The family fill the house when they're together, what with three of them married now and the grandchildren. Elizabeth had sat at the piano, played all those carols and then all the favourite tunes. And when they weren't singing along they were begging Harry to do a few solos. Harry, of course, always the life and soul of any party with his magic tricks for the children. She could easily see why Gladys had fallen for him though Gladys' friends say she fell in love with Harry's voice before she even saw him.

Elizabeth had never quite worked out how Glad got to know Harry. She hadn't known Harry existed until Glad asked if she could bring him home to Lansdowne House for tea. Her children were never shy in coming forward and Elizabeth had worried at the time in case Gladys had done the chasing. She'd always imagined her daughters ending up with Worcester boys, maybe Gladys with someone from the rowing club or the office, but in the middle of the war the boys were in short supply.

In the end it didn't matter where Harry came from because they were clearly in love, and she didn't mind when the handsome young man who'd captured their daughter's heart asked Arthur for her hand.

Arthur had given his blessing if that was what Glad wanted. He'd always liked Harry, loves having a quiet drink and a smoke with him after a meal.

Eric wasn't so sure. Arthur had listened to Eric, listened to Eric's opinions over Harry's prospects, but Arthur didn't take too much notice. Eric was young. Clever, yes, and was no doubt going to do well in the world, but Arthur could see that his oldest son might have trouble of his own when it came to matters of the heart. And Arthur may have been right. Eric was married now to Pip and they had little Zena, but they didn't seem to have that same spark about them that Harry and Glad had. Elizabeth sighed. She's so fond of her daughter-in-law. In fact, when Pip had lodged at Lansdowne House it was Elizabeth who had encouraged Eric to court her. And Pip had been glad to be welcomed into the family. But Eric isn't an easy man. Married to the business, Arthur always says.

Arthur had decided that Harry had enough personality and get up and go to make a decent living, and so what if his heart was in his music? Harry knew he'd got to offer Glad security, and that however passionate he was about his singing, it wouldn't bring in enough to keep a wife. So Arthur and Elizabeth were satisfied and Gladys and Harry had married early in the summer of 1918. They just couldn't wait for the end of the war.

But now, with Gladys so homesick, Plymouth so far away, Elizabeth keeps her worries to herself. Enough to do here in Worcester each day, with the boys and the lodgers but in the small hours, when the household is asleep, that's when Elizabeth thinks about Gladys.

"Look at me, Nana!" Elizabeth turns to look at her granddaughter. The low winter sun is shining on the jewellery draped around Beryl's dress and on the string of pearls which she has wound around her head. Elizabeth is careful to look impressed.

"Oh. You're like a princess."

"I wish I was old enough to go to a dance hall."

"What ideas! Whoever do you know that goes to dance halls? You just enjoy being a little girl."

"But I want to be a beautiful lady."

"You're beautiful now and that's enough to be going on with. Now," Elizabeth lifts the big, hinged box off the bed and gently starts to unwind the pearls from her granddaughter's hair, "let's get all these things put away and go downstairs. Grandpa and Uncle Ralph will be home soon."

"Why didn't Mummy and Daddy take me to Nottingham, Nana?"

"Because there are lots of things your Grandpa Watson wants to talk about with them ... grown up things ... and they thought it would be better if you stayed here. Aren't you happy being here with me and Grandpa?" Elizabeth knows the answer.

"Oh yes, there's nowhere in the world I would rather be than with you and Grandpa Lanc and Uncle Ralph and everyone." The child pauses. "I love Granny and Grandpa Watson too and Nottingham's very nice. But Grandpa Watson is a bit stern sometimes."

Elizabeth stays silent. She closes the lid of the box and takes Beryl's hand. "Come on, off that bed! Let's go downstairs and get this tea ready or we shall all starve."

* * *

The house in Nottingham stands auspiciously on the Plains in sought after Mapperley, its solemn, double fronted exterior heralding the prominence of the man within. It is a confident house, a house for a gentleman and a gentleman's family.

And Harry Watson Senior is, indeed, a gentleman, if one listens to the opinions of his colleagues at the Nottingham City Police Force. Now in his fifties and with only a few years left until his retirement, the value of his services as head of the Nottingham Criminal Investigations Department has been inestimable.

During the last eighteen years there's not been a case which Chief Superintendent Watson hasn't solved, and in 1918 he had been honoured with a special recommendation from the Home Secretary for his work in helping to track down wartime spies and aliens.

Today he is at home, preparing to greet his only son and namesake who has arrived from Worcester. He crosses from his study to the drawing room, and settles himself across from Harry and Gladys who sit stiffly on the opposite side of the Persian carpet. His wife fusses around with tea cups and fruit cake. Dorothy, his younger unmarried daughter, helps her mother.

"How was Christmas?"

"Very nice, thanks. Glad's mother made us all as welcome as usual."

"And your family, Gladys? Are they well?" enquires his wife.

"Yes, thank you. Mother and Father send their regards."

"And Beryl?"

"Yes. Beryl's fine."

Emma Watson sips her tea. She thinks Gladys looked tired. "We're sorry not to see her this time." Her husband looks patient.

"I've already explained to you Emma, we have a lot of things to talk about with Harry and Gladys. It's better that it's just the adults."

"I know dear, I know. And Gladys ... how are those brothers of yours?"

"Oh," Gladys brightens. "They're very well. Eric and Pip's baby is doing fine and the business is going from strength to strength." Her father-in-law listens for the first time that afternoon with interest. "They're supplying most of the bakers in the area and Eric's talking about them becoming a limited company."

"That's nice, to hear that little Zena is doing well. And your brother, Gladys, is an excellent businessman," Emma says. "Where do you think he gets it from?"

Next to Glad, Harry shifts uncomfortably. The question sounds impertinent. Gladys is unfazed.

"Oh, my mother. She's always encouraged him. My father's all for the quiet life. It's Mother who's forever pushed us all along."

The room falls silent for a moment. No doubt about it, reflects Emma, Elizabeth Lancaster is the driving force in that family, and they all seem to worship her.

Mr Watson is considering his son's missed opportunity. Why couldn't he have settled down when Eric had offered him a position in his business, he thinks irritably. He could have made a go of it there. Eric Lancaster has got his head screwed on, no doubt about that. A fussy little man but with a fine head for business. Three years after the end of the war he'd started the business from his parents' house. No overheads. Clever move. Yeast distribution. Then built up to everything a baker needs. He could see that the bakery business was going to take off.

And then the brother joining him a year later. Young Ralph, he knows which side his bread's buttered. He sets down his cup and leans forward, regarding the young pair sternly.

"So, I have been making enquiries on your behalf." Harry and Gladys look at one another. "Mother and I feel you shouldn't stay in Plymouth. We would like you to go back next week as you had planned, Harry, but for you to give notice to your employers."

Harry opens his mouth to speak but his father holds up his hand.

"Hear me out. You might think you enjoy selling," he continues, "and I know you've done well. But it's not the right job for you. You can do better. You need to get back to The Midlands too. We all want you to be nearer the family." He turns to Gladys. "And I expect your Mother and Father feel the same."

"Yes," she says. "Mother worries about us being in Plymouth." Her voice falters. Emma Watson turns away discreetly and looks at her daughter.

"Dorothy dear, perhaps you could go and put that chicken in the oven. If we don't get it in soon, it'll never be ready for supper." Dorothy recognises the cue for her to leave them to it. That's fine by her. She doesn't want to get tangled up in their affairs. A quiet life at home with her parents is enough as far as she is concerned. As she leaves the room she sees her brother take Gladys' hand.

"The fact is," she hears him say, "Glad's pretty miserable in Plymouth. She's tried to put a brave face on it all, make a few friends, but she's missing the family."

Emma had suspected as much.

"Homesickness is a terrible thing," she says gently, "and you Gladys, you come from such a close family."

Gladys doesn't trust herself to speak and Harry's father clears his throat to alert Emma not to stray from what he wants to say. Gladys' feelings about Plymouth will make his proposition more attractive than ever.

"I've fixed up an appointment for you, Harry, for the morning." He takes in his son's frown. "I can see you're surprised. It's with Mitchells & Butlers. Good brewers. Good establishments. My force has a lot of respect for Mitchells & Butlers, the way they run things. I know the directors down in Birmingham and they're a very decent bunch. If they like you, they'll offer you a public house to manage. Somewhere here in the Midlands. Somewhere you and Gladys can make a go of." Harry and Glad exchange glances. Emma can't tell whether they are shocked or pleased. "Your mother and I think you could make a success of yourself in the licensing trade. You've got the personality, Harry, and Gladys, you've had some office experience with your employment before you were married. You could help Harry on that side of things." He pauses, waiting for a reaction. Gladys turns to Harry.

"What do you think?"

"Well," Harry pauses, thinking. "It's a bit of a surprise. I don't know. What do *you* think, Glad?"

"I think it sounds a good idea," she says. "I think you should go along and see what they've got to say."

"And you too, Gladys. Go along with Harry tomorrow. They'll want to meet you. They won't offer a married man a licence until they've met his wife."

He knows that Gladys will be an asset at the interview. In some ways his son had disappointed him and Emma in marrying Gladys. He had nothing against the girl, but they would have liked him to have had a Nottingham bride, someone whose family was known to them. But there's no denying, Gladys has get up and go like her mother, and he suspects that she might have her brother's head for business. "You go too. That's what I've arranged."

* * *

Two days later, at Jessops, Nottingham's leading department store, Gladys settles at a table in the restaurant and watches the cashier at the entrance stand up from her desk as Vi walks through.

Vi acknowledges her with a nod and stops on the way to the table to speak to one of the waitresses. The girl reddens, straightens her starched cap and hurries on her way.

Violet May is the senior buyer in Lingerie and Corsetry, a significant part of the Jessops' empire. No-one has an eye for corsetry that could better Miss May's; no-one understands more than Miss May the dramatic effect that correctly fitting undergarments can have on a lady's day and eveningwear; no-one, not even the managers, dares to show anything other than total respect for her. There is only one person in the whole world to whom Vi defers, and that is Gladys.

Vi, at the start of 1927, is thirty four, unmarried and never likely to be. Her father, William, has his own business and he, like Harry Watson Snr, is comfortably settled with his family in Mapperley. He and his wife, Jessie, had two children, Violet and Jack. Then there's Herbert. Little Herbert who is twelve years Vi's junior, who believes he is her brother, but in fact was taken into the household as a baby.

Vi has no idea where Herbert came from and to whom he belonged before he belonged to them, and no-one has ever enlightened her. But what she and Jack have always understood is that Herbert must go to his grave without ever knowing that Jessie May was not the woman who brought him into this world.

It was inevitable, given that the families lived in Mapperley and knew one another, that Vi and Gladys would meet. Gladys was newly married when she first met Vi. They took to one another instantly, Gladys the young married woman, Vi heading for a very different life. For all her professionalism and the respect of Jessops' staff and customers, Vi has a vulnerable side, a shyness when she isn't Miss May of Jessops, and she is devoted to the young woman from Worcester who offered her friendship when they first met, even if Glad does at times dominate her.

After Beryl was born, when Gladys and Harry had left Nottingham for Harry to try his luck with Eric in Worcester, Vi was desolate. Gladys was busy being a wife and a new mother and didn't have a lot of time to miss Vi, but for Vi, the distance between them was painful. Whenever Gladys and Harry came back up to Nottingham Gladys always looked Vi up. Now, across the table, Vi looks closely at her friend.

"Well, look at you, Gladys Watson! Eyebrows plucked and shaped!" Gladys smiles. She knew it would be the first thing Vi would notice.

"I had them done before Christmas. It's all the rage."

"That blue hat suits you, Glad. I'm always telling you that's your colour. But the eyebrows! Whatever did your in-laws say?"

Gladys sits back and looks Vi over, at the cut and quality of Vi's black business suit and her already greying hair, pulled off her face and into a sensible bun.

"You could get a bit more modern yourself. I've told you before. Get your hair cut. And then, once you'd got the hairstyle, you could wear a more fashionable hat too."

"And I've told you Gladys, I'm not intending to cut my hair, not now nor in the future."

"But you in the business, and everyone so fashion conscious these days, you should take the plunge."

"Corsetry isn't fashion. My customers don't come to look at *me*, they come because they know I've got the skill to improve their figures with the right undergarments." And so the two friends start, with a banter that hides deep affection and their pleasure in seeing one another again. Glad folds her hands on the edge of the table and gives a knowing grin.

"I've got some news, Vi."

"Not another baby on the way?" Gladys stares at Vi. The memories of childbirth still haunt her, even after five years.

"That wouldn't be good news, would it. You know that. Not at the moment, anyway. No, Beryl's enough to be going on with."

"So?"

"We're coming back to The Midlands. Harry's got a new job."

"That *is* good news. Tell me more."

"We're going into the licensing business."

"A public house!" Vi's jaw drops and her eyes narrow in disbelief.

"Don't look like that. We came into town yesterday for an interview at Mitchells & Butlers. We met with one of the directors, and he had a long talk with us and then he brought in some of the others to meet us. Lots of questions. And not just for Harry, but for me too. They wanted to make sure I was happy with the set-up. Anyway, they liked us. You could tell. And they've offered us licensed premises."

"Will it be somewhere respectable?"

"Oh, you can be sure of that. After all, they don't want to get on the wrong side of Father-in-Law."

"Ah, no. I suppose he got this fixed up?" Gladys nods. Vi looks thoughtful. "Glad, it could work out well for you. I've never been in a pub myself, neither has mother."

"Times are changing. Women are starting to get out with their husbands. They're fed up of being left behind."

"You'd live on the premises?"

"Yes. There'll be accommodation for us."

"And whereabouts are you going to be?"

"Dudley Port. Tipton." Vi frowns.

"Black Country. Between West Brom and Dudley? That's not a very good area?"

"Well, it's not a wealthy area, no. But it is respectable. And it'll be a start for us. If we make a go of it they'll move us on."

Vi helps herself to sugar, stirs her coffee, deep in thought before breaking into a rare, dimpled smile.

"I think you and Harry could make a go of it. Harry'll pull the customers in and you, you'll be there keeping an eye on things. It might be just what you both need. And you'll be nearer to your folk in Worcester. And not too far away from us!"

Part 2
The Royal Oak, Dudley Port

Autumn 1927
Standing on the busy main street, The Royal Oak at Dudley Port attracts plenty of customers. With the arrival of Harry and Gladys in the spring, business booms. There's always a warm welcome for the locals and the passing trade. Soon after they arrive Harry has the bowling green at the back of the pub restored to its former glory and The Royal Oak team outplay the local opposition all season. He's had the piano in the bar tuned up too, and Saturday evenings always end with a singsong. The regulars look forward to it. The rumour amongst the locals is that Harry Watson had almost gone professional, but then he'd got married at the end of the War and so that'd put paid to his musical ambitions.

Gladys is a changed woman. All the family notice it. She makes her mark when she introduces her 'special lunches'. She has the brainwave as soon as they arrive at the Oak. Harry has said that if she makes a go of it she can keep the profits. She's had the room at the back of the bar cleared out and, at one o'clock each day from Monday to Friday, a two course lunch is served.

Elizabeth and Pip come to visit. Harry embraces his mother-in-law warmly and hugs Pip. He's often wondered why Pip married Eric. He knows well enough why Eric married Pip. To please his mother. Pip used to stay at Lansdowne House for the musical festivals. Ivy Reddal her real name, but Glad decided to call her Pip and the name stuck. Eric had been sweet on that other girl but Elizabeth soon got her out. Not good enough for Eric. Pip was different. You could say she's refined. Elizabeth liked that, and that she's musical. Plays the piano like an angel. Yes, Elizabeth took to Pip and wanted her in the family and that's how Ivy Reddal ended up as Mrs Lancaster.

"We'll be having the lunch!" Glad insists. "Today it's steak and kidney pudding. Aida makes it all fresh. She's very keen for you to try it. We'll have this table in the corner, the three of us, and Aida will serve us." Elizabeth watches her daughter. She can see the pride in her face as she presides over her little enterprise. Soon the room fills with the diners, local shopkeepers, the probate clerk from the nearby solicitors' office, a gentleman and his wife who are passing through on their way to town. Aida brings in the steaming plates, the dark gravy covering the meat glistening under the golden suet crust, and Gladys leaves the table to walk round the room, stopping at each customer.

"Mr Britten, is your daughter feeling better? Such a worry for you and your wife."

"Miss Store, what a lovely brooch! Wherever did you find it?"

And to the strangers: "Ah, you're from Derby. Well, that's a nice part of the world. My in laws come from Nottingham. Not that far away from you."

Elizabeth watches her daughter, sees how animated she is, appearing to take a real interest in all her customers. This dining room, she thinks, is like Gladys' very own little world.

Once they've settled down for the meal, Pip puts her idea to Gladys.

"I've been thinking. You and I could have a day in London. We'll get the train up. You can spend some of that money you're making on yourself."

Gladys' face lights up. Her sister-in-law shares her shopping tastes. No-one better, she thinks, to go with her to London.

"That's a wonderful idea!"

"And I'll have Zena for you, Pip, so you don't need to rush back to Worcester. She can come and stay with us. You can stay the night here, come back the next day," says Elizabeth.

"I shall take five pounds with me!" declares Gladys giddily. "That'll cover the train and lunch with plenty left over to spend."

"It certainly will, my girl!" laughed her mother. Then, more seriously, remembering Glad's misery in Plymouth. "And if anyone deserves to spend five pounds on a day in London, you do."

Summer 1928

They make friends too. There are plenty of customers who would say that Harry and Gladys Watson are their pals, but the real friendship starts when Gladys comes back from church with an invitation for her and Harry to have cocktails with Doctor Gordon and his wife one evening the following week.

Gladys would always remember that evening. It was, Gladys used to say, as though they'd known one another all their lives.

It's been a hot day and they start the evening in the garden. The men are in and out of the house. Harry falls in love with Ian's cocktail cabinet. Ian tells him to go ahead and mix whatever he wants.

Ian is another tall man, so in more ways than one they see eye to eye. Ian runs his practice from his house. The surgery is at the front and the patients are let in by a nurse through the front door. The hall of the house is used as the waiting room. It's a good arrangement.

Nancy Gordon possesses poise which is the result of her years as a ballet dancer. She and Gladys are both as short as their husbands are tall, but whereas Gladys is comfortably proportioned and big bosomed, Nancy is elegantly slender with an oval face and fine features perfectly balanced by glossy, dark hair swept into a ballerina's chignon.

Gladys is entranced. The way Nancy sits, the way she arranges her slim ankles, holds her glass and smokes a cigarette, everything about her is graceful.

Ian brings drinks down onto the lawn for Gladys and Nancy and then he and Harry settle themselves on the terrace, nicely placed for returning to the house for refills.

On that first evening the two women lay the foundations for a long and loving friendship which will only be broken when tragedy takes Nancy away from Gladys years later.

They talk about their children.

"One boy. Everyone calls him Bunny," she laughs. "We've started him at the prep school. We'll be sending him away later. Probably to Ian's old school." Gladys grimaces.

"Won't you miss him?"

"Yes, I will. I'll miss him a lot. He's all I've got."

"Perhaps you'll have some more."

"No, Gladys, no more. We're settling for Bunny. But what about you? Do you think you'll have any more?"

"Not if I can help it," laughs Gladys. Then, more thoughtfully, she says, "That's a wicked thing to say, isn't it. You never know, Nancy. It's just I do enjoy life at The Oak, I love bringing in the business with my lunches and I'm not very maternal." She hesitates. Wonders how far to go with her new friend. Then she reminds herself that Nancy is married to a doctor. "The whole business, giving birth, it's ghastly, isn't it?" Nancy smiles. "Fine when they get older. Beryl's a joy. We wouldn't be without her, of course. But you know what they said of our generation..." Nancy chimes in:

"A Baby Austin and one child!" They say it in unison.

"We're not like you and Ian, we haven't got a car yet," continues Gladys, "but we'll get there. And thank the Lord we can make these choices now about having babies. It's freed us all up."

"Yes, what with not having to have a baby every year like our mothers and everything that happened in the war, the men have to look at us differently now."

"I wonder if we're ever going to get over the war."

"I doubt it. Just think, this time ten years ago, we'd still got another year of it." Nancy hesitates. "Did you lose anyone?"

"No, we were lucky. Eric, he's my older brother, served near the end and came home safe. Ralph, he was only eight when it started. But my sister, that's Dora, she's the eldest, she married a man who's very poorly. He was a silversmith before the War but they don't think he'll ever work again."

"Poor man. What happened?"

"He was discharged unfit for service in 1918. A dreadful riding accident. He's in a wheelchair. But he and my sister still got married. We were married in June and they had their wedding in the autumn." A shadow crosses Gladys' face. "We don't see much of them. It's very sad really. They moved from Birmingham to Worcester. We all thought it would work well, them being near the family. But it hasn't worked out."

"That's a shame."

"My family, Nancy ... my family are squabblers." She volunteers no more information.

"So," says Nancy, changing the subject, "How did you and Harry meet?"

"Ah well, it's a long story."

"Then let's ask the men to get us another drink before you start. And I'll find us some shawls. It's getting chilly."

For years Gladys only had to catch a passing waft of Chanel No 5 to recall that evening in the garden. Women everywhere were basking in the new perfume as they threw themselves into the glamour of the Twenties. Gladys couldn't have afforded such a luxury but it was always Nancy's choice.

"So," Nancy reminds Gladys, "You and Harry?"

"Ah yes. Well, I was a shorthand typist, working at Heenans."

"Heenans?"

"Heenan & Froude. Sorry, Nancy, I always think everyone's heard of them. Their big claim to fame is the Blackpool Tower. They built it, you know."

"Oh yes, of course. I remember now. They used to be in Birmingham, didn't they?"

"Yes, at Aston. My father has been with them, in the offices, all his working life. We moved to Worcester with Heenans in 1903. I was six at the time."

"And that's why you worked there?"

"When I'd got my qualifications, Daddy got me a job there. I loved it, Nancy. I used to get up every morning looking forward to going to work. And of course, in the war, we were working for the Admiralty and War Office. Water pumps, dynamos, all sorts of things."

"And Harry?"

"Harry couldn't fight. You may have noticed, he's very wheezy at times. There's weak chests in the family, in fact he had a brother who died of asthma. So when he signed up they weren't going to want Harry fighting. He was sent to Worcester from Nottingham, that's where he comes from. They made him an airman mechanic because when he first left school he had been apprenticed to an engineer."

"Ah," says Nancy, piecing together Gladys' story, "and I suppose he came to Heenan & Froude?"

"You've got it. But I didn't meet him there. He was in another part of the building, of course."

"So how *did* you meet?"

"I was out with my girlfriends one evening. It was summer, 1916. We were dressed up to the nines in our summer frocks and hats, linking arms, walking up the high street towards the Guildhall." She smiles. "There were so many girls around at that time weren't there, Nancy?"

"Yes. And so few men."

"When we got to the Guildhall we could hear there was a concert going on. The windows were open, with it being so warm. Someone was singing *When I Leave the World Behind.*"

"The Irving Berlin hit."

"Yes. Nancy, it was so beautiful. It made me want to cry. But the girls, they were laughing at me."

"Why?"

"I think I must have just looked different. Blushing, or something. Silly, just at the sound of a voice." Gladys laughs. "So we looked on the board in the doorway, and there was a poster. It said, and I'll always remember it, it said *Harry Watson: Nottingham's Own Baritone.* There was a photograph of him too. And I just looked at those big eyes and, well, I don't mind telling you Nancy, I just melted!" Nancy covers her face in amazement.

"Gladys! You fell in love with a voice!"

"Yes," she chuckles, "I suppose I did. The girls were trying to pull me away, back down the high street. They kept saying I was being daft, that he was probably only in town for a night or two, that he was bound to have a girl back home. I can hear them now, telling me not to waste time thinking about him."

"So that was it, then?"

"Well, back at work I managed to get an introduction through someone who knew of him. It was a bit forward of me, I know, but we hit it off right away. We got married two years later."

"Well, that's quite a story. And is the romance lasting?"

"There's not so much time for it these days. Those first years of married life after the war and before Beryl came along, they were the carefree years. Singing and dancing and Harry trying out a few jobs. We hadn't cared about much, we just enjoyed being young in a world which had found peace."

The next morning Gladys is still thinking about her new found friend. It is only later that she realises that Ian and Nancy, warm hosts as they had been towards her and Harry, had barely acknowledged one another all evening and Nancy had never reciprocated with stories of falling in love with Ian.

* * *

Early morning sun warms the bedroom. Gladys stirs her tea, cup and saucer in one hand, spoon in the other, balancing on the eiderdown. Harry's thinking ahead. It's 1928, July 28th will be the start of the Summer Olympics, in Amsterdam. Harry senses from the papers that the country is getting Olympics Fever. There's high hopes that the English athletes will bring home plenty of medals. Women are being allowed to compete for the first time. Glad thinks that's a good thing, she's all for it, but Harry's told her not to get into any discussions about it. Most of the locals don't think much of women athletes. 'Unnatural' is what Harry has heard a few times in the bar. Glad's a modern woman, and he wouldn't want it any other way, but he doesn't want her upsetting the customers.

What Harry is really thinking is that if folk are looking forward to the Olympics so eagerly, then they could make some business out of it.

"We'll invite them all in for the opening. An Olympics Party. We'll get the bunting up round the front and put up signs telling everyone what's happening. Let them know we'll be making whoopee at The Royal Oak. We'll do an advert, *One on the house at opening time!* That sound OK?" Gladys sips the tea.

"That'll bring them in early," she says, thinking aloud. "And then we'll throw in refreshments later. The cost of a few plates of sandwiches will be worth it."

"And we'll get the brass band along. They said they'd come any time, so we'll ask them for the party."

"That's a good idea. They can have drinks on the house. We'll have the band on the bowling green from eight until nine. People will start coming into the bar later when it gets chilly. We'll have some music going inside too." Gladys' mind is racing ahead.

"I'll get Aida back for the evening. She's always glad of the extra. We'll get some food ready and bring it out. People won't rush off home if they think there's some free food coming along. It won't cost us much and it'll keep the customers buying drinks at the bar." Harry pushes back the blankets and gets out of bed. He stands at the window, sizing up the sky, reckoning on another fine day.

"Right. So all we need is some good weather."

And the weather *is* fine on that Saturday evening. The bunting flutters in the warm breeze. Over the door to the bar Harry has fixed up a Union Jack, as though the customers needed any reminding to be patriotic. Harry's in the bar, serving up the first of his free drinks. People start to move outside onto the bowling green. All the women need are light cardigans over their bright frocks. The men carry out trays of glasses which they set down on the tables whilst they light up their ciggies. There's a lot of chattering about the games, especially about "The Flame". A flame's been lit today in Amsterdam and it'll burn throughout the whole of the Games. Imagine! And if it works out, then they'll do that every four years, at all the games in the future. The old folk stay indoors. The band's too noisy and that swing music they're playing isn't a patch on the old romantic tunes. But the others love it.

Later, when the till is ringing non-stop and people are coming indoors to the warm room, Glad gets Aida to help her hand round the plates piled up with sandwiches and sausage rolls. Under the canopy of tobacco smoke, people are calling for Harry.

"Give us a tune, Mr Watson!"

"Hang on a tick," he calls back. "I'll just get these pints pulled first."

Harry makes his way to the piano, cigarette at a careless angle between his lips and Gladys picks up an ashtray and puts it on top of the piano. He's in his shirtsleeves, with his jacket left behind at the bar. He pulls out the stool, eases the fabric of his trousers over his knees as he sits down, and holds his hands just above the keys for a second. Then he's away.

He starts with the old songs, some of the favourites from the war, and everyone pipes down. Harry Watson always sends a shiver down your spine when he sings. Everyone who hears him is stuck on his beautiful voice and his greatest admirer is Gladys. Now she's allowed herself a drink and she pulls up a chair near to the piano. She never gets tired of watching him bring that piano to life, his long fingers caressing the keys, his eyes half closed. When Harry plays or sings it is as though he travels to another place. Wherever he goes, he attracts attention, even before folk know about the music.

He brings the melodies to a close and starts again with an upbeat number that sets everyone's feet tapping. His hands fly across the keyboard. A few customers get to their feet and then everyone seems to be up on the floor.

The evening has been a big success but Gladys is already thinking about tomorrow and her lunch bookings. And she'll need to get Harry to check the barrels and write up the stock sheets before he goes to bank the takings.

Sometimes we cannot know how happy we are until years later. Such were Gladys' feelings when she looked back on The Royal Oak. Then she was able to say that they were the happiest years.

* * *

Spring 1929

Beryl is mooching along the street, freed from the classroom. Her shoulder aches from her satchel and she has a hole in her stocking. On the whole, it has been a good day. She's made a few friends but they don't live in the direction of the Royal Oak so Beryl, who is going to be seven in July, walks home alone. It is the local school and Mother and Daddy decided it would do well enough. She is perfectly content. When she gets to the pub she is pleased to think that Grandpa Watson won't be there. Everything is quiet.

Granny and Grandpa Watson stayed with them last night. It was a beautiful summer's evening and Beryl had been allowed to stay up late. It was always nice to see Granny. After tea they'd had a game of cards. Granny won. Beryl likes the way Granny doesn't just let her win.

But Grandpa is very different. He is one of the tallest men she's ever seen and she knows he is a very important person in the Nottingham police force. That's no excuse, she thinks, to be so stern and distant. He never plays games, never laughs much, and all he ever really asks Beryl is how she's getting on at school.

He's quite kind in his way, she supposes, and he always gives her something for her purse. This morning he'd put a shilling into her hand with his usual warning not to spend it all at once. And she never does. She is very careful with her money and keeps it safe in a draw in her bedside table.

Beryl frowns. She's tried to work out what is going on. It is something about Grandpa's new idea for them all, and she knows her mother is definitely not pleased. She'd lain in bed last night, trying to catch the conversation, knowing from the tone of their voices that Mother wasn't happy. Sometimes the words came clearly through the wall.

"We like it here. We've made friends."

"We can do better, Glad. This has only been the start."

"What's wrong with The Oak?"

And then Beryl wasn't able to hear Harry's reply. Once, she heard them mention her. About her being settled here. About the air in the city. What city? What air? What did they mean?

She walks round to the side of the building and lets herself into the kitchen. Aida is sorting the vegetables for tomorrow's lunches. Aida's husband, Ted, was killed in the war, in a big battle in Belgium. Right at the end of the War, Daddy says. He's left Aida with three boys to bring up. The oldest is out at work, but Mother always says Aida's had a hard life and it's not much easier now. They have to make allowances. Beryl wonders whether Mother prays for Aida when she is at church on Sundays. Beryl is never quite sure what Mother prays for but she'd have thought Aida ought to have a few blessings, if only to stop her grumbling all the time.

"Ah, there you are, Missy. Your mother says you're to go through and start your homework." Aida's jerks her head towards the door of the living room. "You can take that tray. There's a glass of milk and a slice of the cake your Gran brought with her." Aida sniffs. "I must say, she knows how to bake a decent sponge, does your grandmother."

"Where are my parents?"

"Your father's gone out. I don't know where. He says he'll be back for opening up."

"And my mother?"

"Your mother's gone to Worcester."

"Worcester! She didn't say anything to me."

"Well, that's where she is. She'll be back later."

Aida turns back to the vegetables, a signal that Beryl isn't going to get any more information out of her. She keeps her mouth shut to the child. It doesn't do for the kiddies to know too much. Something is up, Aida knows that much. And it's something that's upset Mrs Watson. Best thing she can do. Get away to Worcester for the day. That Mrs Lancaster has got her head screwed on. Whatever it is, Mrs Lancaster will sort out the missus.

* * *

Elizabeth Lancaster closes a red bound foolscap sized accounts book and stacks the paid household bills on a spike set into a wooden base. Gladys, seated opposite her mother, leans one arm on the table and rests the side of her face against her hand.

"He says we'll be going up in the world. He thinks it's our big chance."

"Well, maybe he has a point," says Elizabeth.

"He sounds like his father."

"And you sound foolish, Gladys, saying that." Elizabeth is ruffled. "Don't start taking against Mr Watson. If it hadn't been for him, you may never have gone into the licensing business."

"Yes, but we're the ones who've made a go of it. And we're happy. Beryl's settled at the school. We've made friends and I've got the lunches to run. I like having that money I make from the dining room. It's mine, just to do with as I please. It makes me feel safe." Elizabeth frowns. Gladys looks resentful. "You don't understand. It won't be the same at The Court."

"Well, Harry could be right. There's plenty in the licensing business would envy you getting an offer like this, to manage such a prestigious place as The Court. As for your friends, well, you're not going to be that far away from The Oak. I'm sure that Dr and Mrs Gordon will love to come up to town to see you both." Elizabeth chooses her words carefully. "You must try and see it as a challenge. And if you make it work, which I'm sure you both will, then Harry will be on his way to having his own tenancy. No more just being a manager. So much more secure. You know that's his dream, and not just for himself, but for you and Beryl."

"I'm worried though, about Beryl."

"What about her?"

"I don't want to bring her up in Corporation Street in the middle of Birmingham. It's not what we're used to. I had freedom when I grew up. I know it's not perfect at The Oak, but there's some fields and fresh air and we've got the bowling green. It's not going to be healthy in the city. The Court is huge. Four floors. And the flat that we'll have. It's on the top floor. No garden. Nothing."

"Have you been to look at it yet?"

"No."

"Well, go and have a look. Give it a chance, Gladys."

Gladys jabbed the table petulantly.

"I don't like the whole business." She emphasises the word "whole". Her eyes flash as she finally says what has been churning through her mind. "It's going to be the death of us."

Elizabeth looks incredulous.

"The death of you! Whatever do you mean?"

"If we go to The Court," Gladys speaks slowly, deliberating on the feeling of dread she wants to impart to Elizabeth. "If we go to The Court, Mother, I feel as though something terrible will happen to us."

"What could happen to you?"

"I don't know, but something that will change everything. For the worse. Forever." She covers her face with her hands, repeating her words. "It'll be the death of us, I just know it. And it frightens me." Elizabeth looks shaken.

"Gladys, you must give it a chance," she persists.

"It's not the life I want. I know that, Mother. It won't be good for us. It doesn't feel right."

"You know Beryl can come to me in her holidays. Maybe she can even stay on here in the autumn. Go to school with Zena. And Mrs Watson is always pleased to see her in Nottingham."

"She doesn't like it much there."

"Why ever not?!"

"She's not that keen on Father-in-law. And as he's about to retire, he's going to be around the house all the time from now on."

"Oh please, don't start thinking like this. That's no reason for her not to go and see Harry's family. They're all very fond of her and you must encourage Beryl to visit." Elizabeth's voice softens. "You must try and support Harry in this. I'll do everything I can to help you out. You know that. We'll all make sure Beryl's all right."

Gladys is trying so hard to trust her mother's judgement. She wants to believe in Harry's dream. She concentrates on the table top. Starts to push her forefinger along the grain of the wood.

"There's something else…" She presses her head into the palm of her hand and massages her forehead. Elizabeth watches her closely.

"Is your head aching?" Gladys waves the question away. The silence hangs around them. "You're expecting another baby."

It isn't even a question. Tears are beginning to prick Gladys' eyes.

"How did you know?"

"I just did. I'm your mother. It's around your eyes, you look as you did when you started with Beryl. Does Harry know?"

"Not yet." Elizabeth drops her gaze, appraising her daughter's body.

"When are you due?"

"December. Some time around Christmas, I think."

"And you're going to tell me it's not the best time for this to have happened."

Gladys wipes her eyes fiercely with the back of her hand.

"No time would have been good. My life is fine as it is." Elizabeth grimaces.

"Gladys!" She takes a deep breath, brings the palms of her hands down firmly on the table as if to steady herself. "You've got to stop this. You'll have to pull yourself together. Stop feeling sorry for yourself. You're being selfish. At the end there'll be a brother or sister for Beryl. That's just what she needs. She's a very solitary child. Your father was only saying so the other day. And you must get behind Harry on his plans. You're still young and healthy. It will all work out. You'll see. And I promise," Elizabeth's voice softens, she rests her hand on her daughter's arm, searches her troubled face, "I promise you, Gladys, I will be here for you."

She gets up from the table. She has said what needs to be said.

"We need lunch sharpish if you're going to get that train. I haven't even done the potatoes and Dad'll be in soon." Gladys gets unsteadily to her feet. She has been shaken by her mother's wrath.

"I'll go and lay up the table." She stands in the doorway of the kitchen. "And I hope you're right, Mother. I'll try and look on the bright side. I promise." Elizabeth looks up from sorting the vegetables.

"That's more like my girl speaking now. Go home and tell Harry your news. You should be sharing it with him. He'll be pleased. And then you tell him you're ready to go and have a look at The Court."

Ten minutes later the sound of Arthur's key turning in the front door brings Gladys out to the hall. His face lights up when he sees his daughter.

"This is a nice surprise. Have you and Mother had a good morning?" Before she can reply, Elizabeth calls out.

"Yes, Arthur. We've been fine. Come on through to the kitchen."

"Something's smelling good."

"It's the stew. It's been on the go for the last three hours."

"Aren't the boys here yet?"

"They'll be here soon enough. Stay here with me and leave Gladys to have a bit of quiet next door." But Gladys has followed her father into the kitchen.

"I'm fine. Daddy's the one who looks tired." Her father smiles.

"I'm not getting any younger. Sixty in July, you know."

"July the ninth. I haven't forgotten." Sixty sounds so old to Gladys. "Are you going to celebrate?"

"Ah, well, Ralph's getting up a river party at the end of June, a couple of weeks early but that'll do me fine. It'll be a good old get together of family and friends." Arthur looks at his wife. "Haven't you told Gladys all about it?"

"No." Elizabeth sounds brusque. "I haven't had time."

"I'm surprised about that. I'd have thought you'd be telling her all the plans." Gladys catches the hurt in her father's voice. To Gladys he says, "Has your mother told you, Ralph's the Regatta Secretary this year?"

"We've had other things we've had to talk about," cuts in Elizabeth. "But of course I was going to get around to telling her all the news." Arthur shrugs and goes out of the kitchen with his newspaper. Elizabeth turns to Gladys.

"Do you think you and Harry will be able to come down for the river trip? It'll be a nice evening. There'll be some music and dancing and a supper."

"We'd love to come. Of course. But we'll have to wait and see how things are going. If we take The Court on it'll be early days at the end of June. I'd better not say yes and then disappoint everyone."

"That's fine. Your father will understand when he knows what's going on. I'll tell him all the news later. You don't want to go through it all again at lunch. And Gladys ..." Elizabeth hesitates, "Stay strong. Think ahead. Think this time in 10 years, where you could be."

It is, of course, beyond anyone's power, even Elizabeth Lancaster's, to know where Gladys could possibly be by 1939.

Part 3

The Court Restaurant, Birmingham

June 1929

The Court Restaurant, given its name because of its proximity to the Victoria Law Courts, as Gladys explained to Elizabeth, is one of The Big Five, a handful of empirical catering establishments in Birmingham owned by Mitchells & Butlers, the Birmingham brewers.

Harry loves it from the start, the elaborate, terracotta four storey building on the corner of Corporation Street, which gives the building its important address, whilst the eighty-five back stairs that the family use to get up and down to the living quarters come out on the other side in James Watt Street, where Beryl waits each day for the tram that takes her to her new school.

At street level the pillared entrance is exactly on the centre of the curve. Over the entrance, carved in stone, is the name: Court Restaurant. At a certain angle, on the pavement opposite The Court, you can view both sides of the building at the same time.

On the ground floor are the public bars. The tall, wide windows stop just above street level so that a man with a thirst and a need for a bit of company might catch a glimpse of the bright interior from the pavement, whilst the stained glass in the windows above gives a touch of grandeur to the first floor function rooms within. The windows on the third floor are arched and form a contrast to the windows below.

High above these three storeys an elaborate balustrade has been constructed behind which is a range of much smaller, gabled windows which are hidden from street view. These windows belong to Harry and Gladys' flat. The kitchens, from where dishes are sent to the first floor dining rooms by means of a service lift, are also on this floor, separated from the flat by hefty doors.

By 1929 Corporation Street has been the principal address in the city centre for over thirty years. The Victorians had dreamt of building a grand Parisian style boulevard, a street as leafy and wide as the great streets of Paris and bustling with life and activity. The shops and arcades were to be unrivalled. Plane trees, poplars and lime trees were to be planted in nearby squares and in other little streets and it was to eclipse the other premier streets of the day.

When the dream of building Corporation Street was finally realised, the architecture lacked a common design, but one thing that the buildings had in common was showiness and status. Some buildings were designed to look like French chateaux, others, like The Court, gave a suggestion of Italian Renaissance.

The most imposing building in Corporation Street is the Victoria Law Courts and Harry sees straightaway the potential for functions that will attract their well-heeled neighbours opposite to the first floor restaurant and function rooms.

Harry wakes every morning with energy and enthusiasm. Once he has dressed and breakfasted, the lift takes him down a floor from the flat to his office. He lights up a cigarette, checks his post. He's on top of the world. The Court is his castle. It has more than lived up to expectations. Glad's settling in a bit too. Bad timing, her being in the family way again now. But heck, everything will be fine. Once the baby comes Glad can get back to being her old self.

As well as his office, the third floor has a games room which houses a large pool table and it seems to Beryl that it replaces Daddy's affections for his bowling green at The Oak. But now, instead of the sound of bowls being played out against the balmy summer evenings when the locals lingered late ("Just one more pint Harry, for the homeward stretch, and something for the missus ..."), now it seems as though the pool room swallows men into its cavernous interior. On a warm evening at The Oak, Beryl could watch all the comings and goings on the freshly mown green from her bedroom window.

Here all she can do is press her face to the metal screen that is stretched each evening concertina style across the top of the stairs and marks the boundary between the family's quarters and the staircase leading down to the third floor. She watches the bar staff carrying drinks up to the games room from the bars below. She sees everything through the endless smoke haze floating towards her.

However thoroughly the public rooms are aired each morning, the family in the flat at the top of the building have to put up with the stale smoke. There's no getting away from it.

* * *

Four miles from the centre of Birmingham and a long way from the glamour of Corporation Street are the Smethwick offices of Mitchells & Butlers, the oldest established brewers in the Midlands.

Summer, as usual, isn't making much of an impression on the factories of Smethwick that loom over the narrow alleys and the sides of the canal. Up on Cape Hill the towering, redbrick Mitchells & Butlers' building casts giant shadows onto the surrounding streets and the area is without sun all year round.

Doug Brown gives his fellow directors a rare, paunchy smile. Lunch has been a long affair and the drinks generous. He's feeling relaxed and pleased with himself. In front of him, on the table, is the first report on The Court Restaurant since Harry Watson's appointment.

"We've got a good 'un there. He's got to know the ropes fast, knows what the punters want. Bar takings are well up and he does very well with the 'nobs."

"Let's face it," chimes in Geoff Woods, "He's Chief Super Watson's boy. Toffee nosed lot up in Nottingham. This chappie knows all about how the other half lives."

"Maybe," replies Doug. "But he gets down in the public bars and keeps an eye on things there just as much as upstairs. Doesn't miss much. The staff like him. And they like his missus. They're both of them fully up to scratch."

"She settling OK then?"says another. "Got a kid, haven't they?"

"A girl. About seven years old. Quiet little thing. Yes, they seem settled OK. And the wife – Gladys I think her name is – she does her bit. She's there in the evenings on the first floor even though she's expecting. Smart woman. Knows what she's doing."

"And I had a drink with Ray Stannage the other day," cuts in Geoff. "The Rotary Chief. He was at the Ladies' Night a couple of Fridays ago. Very impressed. Says The Court's even better now than the Midland."

"Blimey," says Doug, "that's a bit much. Still, it'll keep the other places on their toes."

The other man smiles.

"If Ray Stannage was impressed then things are going well!"

Woods stretches and yawns. "That's The Court taken care of then."

"Until Harry Watson decides to get going on his own one day."

"That likely?"

Doug Brown nodded. "Sure as eggs are eggs. He won't want to be a manager for ever. They'll want a tenancy. You'll see."

* * *

At the start of July Pip comes from Worcester to visit Gladys. Outside the sun is blazing. The window is open but it does nothing to reduce the stuffiness of the room. Gladys hands Pip a teacup.

"I didn't order biscuits, Pip. You said you were trying to cut back."

"Yes, Glad. It's such a struggle keeping my shape and you can't wear the fashions these days if you're bulging all over the place."

"It's not been a good decade for plump women," smiles Gladys. "There's not been anywhere for us to hide our bulges in any of the fashions since the end of the war."

"It looks like waistlines are coming back this winter. That's going to mean we're still going to have to keep slim."

"Yes, waistlines and longer skirts. The flapper's had her day. No more upsetting the old folk with short dresses. It's a shame you can't get to Vi. She'd sort you out." Gladys chuckles. "She's the girdle queen of Nottingham, I reckon."

"I know. But I'm not likely to get up to Nottingham, am I? I must just say no to the biscuits. You're all right for the time being. You can just relax and eat for two now. But keeping trim gets harder. It's ever since I had Zena."

"Four years, Pip."

"I know. I don't know where the time goes. She'll be starting school in September, thank goodness. The child needs some company. She's so demanding. She's not as good natured as Beryl."

"Oh, Beryl. She has to amuse herself. I haven't got much time to give her. The staff keep an eye on her." Gladys fishes up her sleeve for a handkerchief. She holds it to her forehead. "Is it hotter than ever today, Pip, or is it just me?"

"It's very stuffy in here. But you're probably feeling the heat more now anyway."

"I'm only three months gone."

"Mother thinks you're missing having a garden."

"There's the park. And you can get up those back stairs onto the roof. It's cooler up there but it's not very nice. Beryl loves it though. Likes hanging over the railings to watch the people in the street. Makes me dizzy. It's so high." Gladys pauses. What's the point of putting on a brave face to Pip? "You're right, though. Nothing can make up for having your own bit of garden."

Pip places her cup and saucer gently on the table at the side of her chair.

"I'm going to have to disappoint you. I can't stay tonight after all. I shall have to get back for Zena. Your mother was having her but she's not at all well."

"I thought you'd say that. I understand. I spoke to Ralph on the telephone yesterday. It doesn't sound as though Mother's got over that cold."

"It's more than a cold."

"In what way?"

"Well, you know it started after the party on the boat. She was quite feverish a couple of days later. Now it's gone to her chest."

Gladys frowns.

"Why hasn't anyone told me?"

"I don't think anyone wanted to worry you." Pip looks at Gladys' pale, damp face. "You've got so much on your plate. All this," she gestures with an upturned hand around the room, "and you in your condition."

"Do I need to come to Worcester?"

"Oh no, it's not that bad." Pip speaks brightly. "She'll be all right as long as she rests. But I need to get back. Dora's keeping an eye on Zena today as well as looking after Mother but I can't leave her at the house overnight. She's such a restless child. A four year old isn't what you need around you when you're feeling poorly."

"No. You're right, of course. Tell me again, Pip, what happened with Mother." Pip frowns, trying to work out what to say to Gladys. Elizabeth has told her about Gladys' visit to Worcester. Pip knows Gladys hasn't been happy about leaving the Oak, nor about the baby. She doesn't want to add to her troubles. But Elizabeth is poorly. Gladys needs to know that.

"Well, it started off fine. It was a beautiful evening. We all got on the boat in a real party mood. Your mother and father looked so happy. Your mother had on that outfit she made in the spring. Blue and white stripes, long line, very slimming. She'd bought a loose white jacket to go over it and she had on those earrings Ralph bought for her. You know your mother and her jewellery.

"Your father and the boys looked really proud of her. The only thing that was missing was having you and Harry with us. We'd all wished you'd been there. And Ralph laid on the music. Three musicians. Really good jazz players. The boat was decorated with little lights. We danced on the deck. We started with cocktails and a very good buffet supper, then we had a bit of a dance on the deck. When the band finished they got your mother on the piano." Pip smiles at the memory of Arthur's river party. "It was lovely, Glad, really lovely."

"I wish I'd been there."

"It wasn't so nice when the rain started. There'd been some rumblings of thunder. Then the lightning. Then the sky went so dark and just seemed to burst open. Your mother and I had taken shawls. But we hadn't anything waterproof. The forecast had been fine. By the time we got back to the boat club I could feel the wet had gone right through to my skin. It was the same for everyone. There just wasn't any shelter on the boat."

"And when did she start being ill?"

"The next evening. With a sore throat. Then she got feverish."

"I think I should come back with you."

"No. You must stay put. We've got the telephone. I'll keep you in touch. I'm sure she'll be fine." Pip tries to look reassuring and bright. "Now. What are we going to do? It's only halfway through the morning and we've got all day. What are the plans?" Gladys stands up.

"Come on. I'll show you round the flat. And then I want your advice. Bring your tea."

Pip follows her sister-in-law down the long landing to Harry and Glad's bedroom.

"Sit there, Pip."

Everything in the bedroom, the ceilings, the wardrobes and the dark wooden bedstead are high. Pip perches on the edge of a hefty chair covered in green damask. Glad yanks open the tall mirrored doors of the wardrobe.

"I haven't got enough clothes, Pip. It was different at the Oak." Gladys runs her hand along the suits and dresses hanging in the wardrobe. "These things were smart enough to see me through the day and evening. Now I've got to have some evening dresses. For the functions. And I'll have to have some new things soon anyway, now I'm carrying. I've got to smarten up a bit more, Pip. But the cost ..."

"You'll have to get sewing."

"I haven't got the time."

"Tell you what. Lewis's has started a cutting service. You choose the material and they measure you and cut out the pieces of the garment and then all you have to do is run it up on your machine."

"Lewis's! They'll do all that?"

"Yes. I'm surprised you haven't heard about it. People have been talking about it in Worcester."

"Well, I'll be blowed! And there I am, with all that on my doorstep."

* * *

Lewis's, the department store on Corporation Street with the best food hall in the Midlands. Gladys and Pip aren't buying food today, but as they make their way to the ground floor lift they are almost tempted to stop there as they breathe in the mixture of smells, freshly ground coffee and spices and bread from Lewis's own bakers that would have been made this morning.

"Goin' up. First floor: Household linens, towels, silverware, glassware, gifts." The lift attendant looks bored.

"Second floor: Ladies 'n' childrenswear, millinery, bridal 'n' footwear." He is a little wiry man with a low forehead and no neck to speak of. Underneath his hat, beads of sweat glisten on his forehead. He wears his uniform uncomfortably, like a working chap in a wedding suit. He looks like a man who would be happier in his shirtsleeves. At the top he crashes the metal gates open.

"Third floor: Millinery, lingerie, fabrics, haberdashery and the restaurant."

Gladys stalks out of the lift.

"I wouldn't have staff behaving like that, Pip. He wouldn't last five minutes at The Court."

"It's the heat."

"No excuse. We're all hot."

Gladys wanders over to the fabric. She fingers the silk satins and velvets, crisp cotton, fine lawn, and delicate organza. She thinks of all the lovely clothes Elizabeth used to make for her and Dora. It's a lucky man whose wife can sew, Elizabeth always says, and Gladys and Dora learnt as girls how to use Mother's old Singer.

Everyone knows the skill in dressmaking lies in the cutting, thinks Gladys. Clever of Lewis's to start this service.

Pip commandeers an assistant who takes Gladys to be measured up and then they look at the pattern books.

"There's some nice eveningwear, Madam," says the assistant. "This year the length is going right down, just above the ankle. It will suit you well, being petite."

Pip laughs.

"Short, you mean! We're both shorties, aren't we Glad."

The assistant flushes.

"Are you sisters?"

"Bless me, no, Miss," says Gladys, putting her hand on Pip's arm. "This is my sister-in-law."

"Pardon me. You ladies are very alike."

"Yes, a lot of people say that." Gladys rests her hand on a page of the book. "I like this style."

"Yes. I like that too." Pip, who is an excellent dressmaker herself, looks thoughtful. "That dropped waistline with the pouching would do for quite a few months too, until you get big."

"By that time I shan't go down in the evenings, Pip. It'll be too much."

"What about the lace trim? That's what really makes it look good. Can you manage to do that?"

"Yes, I think so." Gladys turns to the assistant. "Do you sell the lace?"

"Yes, madam. We've got a lovely selection. The dress isn't too complicated and you'll find the pieces of the garment will all come marked up. You should be fine."

They choose two lengths of fabric, one in a chocolate brown crepe and the other a black silk. They're guided by the assistant on the trims and buy a cream lace to go with the crepe and a length of sequined velvet for the silk. At the counter the assistant turns over Gladys' cheque and sees the address.

"I'll make arrangements for everything to be delivered for you, Madam. And I'll make sure you have all the necessary threads and haberdashery to complete your garments. I'll write a card for you with my name. If you have any problems please put a telephone call through to me."

"Thank you, Miss."

"Lewis's will value your custom. I hope you'll be satisfied with our service and come to use us regularly."

"I will see how I manage with these two dresses first. We'll take it from there."

"And maybe you would like to open an account with us?"

"I'll think about it." The business of the day completed, Pip and Gladys seat themselves at an airy window table in the restaurant.

"She was impressed, Gladys, when she saw who you were."

"Yes. The Court certainly seems to carry clout."

"And being Mrs Harry Watson."

"But I'd still rather be back at the dear old Oak," murmurs Gladys.

Later, they part outside the store entrance, Gladys to return to The Court and Pip, with some misgiving, to catch the train back to Worcester to see how Elizabeth is faring for, to be sure, Pip has not told Gladys the true state of affairs.

* * *

Gladys catches the train to Worcester. In the taxi she thinks back to last night's call from Eric.

"You'd better come, Glad. She's not good."

"But Pip was only here today saying it was a bad cold."

"Yes, well," Eric clears his throat, "Mother had told Pip she wasn't to worry you."

"That wasn't fair. I have a right to know what's going on."

"Be that as it may, I'm telling you now."

"It's not good enough, Eric."

"We won't argue. The point is, her breathing's got a lot worse since this morning."

"What does the doctor say?"

"Not a lot." Eric pauses. "He's worried though."

"In what way?"

"That it will go to pneumonia. He said we should tell you."

"I'll speak to Harry. I'll come tomorrow. I'll be there after lunch."

* * *

It is Dora who opens the door. Standing in the hall, Gladys kisses her sister cautiously. Dora doesn't always see eye to eye with the rest of the family, even with her mother. Elizabeth makes allowances, knows that her oldest daughter's life isn't easy, but Eric and Ralph can't tolerate anything that distresses their mother.

Dora and Harry Mills had waited until peace was declared in November and then married in December. Dora's wedding couldn't have been more different from her sister's, for whilst she had fallen in love with a fine young soldier, by the end of the war, Dora's Harry was an invalid, a casualty of war.

Harry Mills thinks he's been lucky, he's survived, he's got a life and a wife and children, and he's got his limbs and his eyesight. His life is never going to be the same but he knows he's a fortunate chap to have had Dora stand by him. Plenty of injured men came back to women who'd moved on, taken up with others or just didn't want to know them.

But Dora has stood by him even though she knew life wouldn't be easy. Small wonder then, that sometimes she looks at her brothers and sister with resentment.

Eric and Ralph doing so well in the business, and Gladys landing on her feet at The Court. All of them, she thinks, untouched by the War. And Harry with his chest that kept him out of the action which is why he never got further than Worcester.

"You've come then." Dora takes Gladys' bag and puts it at the bottom of the staircase.

"Well, of course I've come. And it would've been sooner if you'd all told me what was going on."

"How are you?"

"I'm all right, Do'." Dora's name had long ago been shortened to 'Do', to rhyme with dough, and it stayed with her throughout her life. "More to the point, how's Mother?"

"Come in the kitchen. She might be able to hear us in the hall." Gladys stops to hang her jacket and hat on the coat stand. "It's not very good. Not good at all. They're talking about moving her to hospital. And on top of the pneumonia she's got a stomach upset. She can't even keep any water down."

"How's Dad?"

"Quiet. He's very low. He doesn't really know what to do for the best. We sent him to work this morning. He can't do much round here."

"And the boys?"

"Ralph's the one who's most upset. Eric told him not to go into work today."

"He's so close to Mother."

"Both the boys. Even though Eric's got his own family now."

"It's sons and their mothers. They're all the same."

Dora takes the kettle off the gas ring.

"Ralph will be back soon. I sent him out to get a few things from the chemist. Do you want some tea?"

"Thanks."

"Go on up and I'll bring you a tray. Then I'll have to go or I'll miss my bus."

Gladys gets halfway up the stairs before Dora calls up to her. "Don't you go talking too much. You're not to tire her, Glad."

* * *

The day has been slightly cooler and Dora has got Ralph to light a fire. The room is stifling and smells of illness.

It's all wrong, full of unfamiliar things: an oxygen cylinder, like an ugly sentinel at her sleeping mother's side; on the table by the bed Dora has left a jug of water, a glass, several bottles, some pills and a face flannel and small towel.

The only sounds come from the ticking of the mantel clock and Elizabeth's laboured breathing.

Gladys steadies herself. She sits in the wing chair on the other side of the bed and leans forward to look carefully at her mother. Her lips are dry and chapped and a thin line of saliva runs down the side of her chin which Gladys wipes with the flannel.

How has it come to this? Just a chill, they'd said. A cold that her mother caught in the rain on the river. Then it had gone to her chest.

Panic begins to stir in Gladys. She wishes Harry was with her. She rests her elbows on the bed and puts her head in her hands, massaging her throbbing temples.

She thinks of the times she's been in this room with her mother. Elizabeth rifling gaily through her wardrobe, zipping her dress, arranging her hair at the dressing table, chatting all the time to Gladys whilst she chooses a pair of shoes. With Elizabeth's energy gone, the room feels abandoned. Now it seems as though everything else Gladys has done today has ceased to exist: the morning at The Court, the train journey, the taxi, the busy streets outside the window.

Dora arrives with the tea tray and puts it on the table by the fire.

"Here's your tea. And I've brought you some biscuits." Gladys stands up and goes over to the table.

"This is awful. Much worse than I thought. She looks dreadful. You should have told me."

"Well, we didn't." Dora sighs. "We didn't realise how bad things were. Stop going on about it, Glad. It's not going to change anything."

"It's just she looks so ill. Can't anyone do anything more? What are the doctors doing?"

"Dr Spalding is coming back later this afternoon. You'll need to listen out for the bell. He's going to decide whether to send her to hospital."

Gladys tries to steady her teacup with both hands but the trembling defeats her and she gets it back to the saucer with a clatter. Dora's eyes stray down to where the baby's beginning to show.

"For goodness sake, Gladys, pull yourself together. You'll end up sick yourself at this rate. You'll have to hold the fort here now. I've got to catch my bus. I can't leave my Harry any longer.

"There's some cold pork for your suppers and a salad. Dad will be back, usual time. I've done the potatoes. All you've got to do is boil them up. That is, if you can remember how to cook." Gladys winces.

"You make it sound as though we've got servants. You don't know what it's like for me." Dora shrugs and turns away.

"No, Dora, don't walk off. Listen to me for once. All I've got in the flat is a tiny place off the hall where I can make a cuppa and a piece of toast. I'd give anything sometimes to have my own kitchen and be a proper housewife where I could cook for Harry and Beryl."

"And I'd give anything not to have to work my fingers to the bone for everyone day in and day out," Dora retorts, as she straightens Elizabeth's top sheet over the blanket. "Anyway, we're not going to stand over our mother's sick bed arguing. I've got to go. I'll call you later. See what's going on. We've got a telephone kiosk now at the end of the road so I can keep in touch."

"That's useful." Gladys is calmer now. Dora is right, arguing isn't going to help anyone. "You get going Do. You've done enough here for today. I'll make sure everything goes all right this evening."

* * *

That evening Elizabeth is just about awake when Dr Spalding calls. She beseeches him with as much voice as she can muster not to send her to hospital.

The doctor is a thoughtful man in his fifties, growing old alongside the patients he has been looking after for years. He knows Elizabeth Lancaster is not a woman who would want to be parted readily from her husband and children, nor they from her.

Furthermore, there is nothing more that can be done for her in hospital that can't be done here at home, especially now that Gladys has arrived and will be staying at the house.

He gestures to Gladys to come downstairs with him. Arthur and Ralph are in the sitting room, Arthur in his usual chair, staring into the empty grate and Ralph sitting at the table flicking miserably through the evening paper. Gladys sits on the arm of Arthur's chair as he listens in bewilderment, trying to take in what Dr Spalding is saying to them.

After the doctor's visit, Elizabeth drifts in and out of sleep. She isn't in pain, though earlier in the day she'd complained of sickness and had been vomiting. Dr Spalding has diagnosed gastro enteritis and said they must encourage her to drink some boiled water. It seems so unfair, in addition to the pneumonia.

Gladys and Ralph take turns to sit upstairs with Elizabeth or downstairs with Arthur. Around eight-thirty Eric and Pip call. Everyone is subdued, speaking in unnaturally low voices. The evening drifts into night.

On one occasion Elizabeth wakes briefly. Gladys holds a glass of water to her lips, but though she manages a faint smile she has no strength to drink, nor to return Ralph's gentle pressure on her hand. Very soon her eyelids droop and she falls back into sleep.

Her breathing is slow, Gladys and Ralph in a constant state of alarm that each breath is her last. Arthur seems to sleepwalk in and out of the room, helpless and shocked.

Gladys tries to keep him busy. She gets him to make tea. When she feels Elizabeth's feet they are like ice so she sends him to fill a hot water bottle. But no amount of tasks can help Arthur.

At around one o'clock Gladys sends him to the spare room to get some sleep. She and Ralph take turns at sleeping for an hour or two, but neither want to leave Elizabeth. The sun rises at four o'clock.

It is Arthur's 60th birthday. Gladys stands by the window rubbing her aching back and watches as the sky became blue. She's thankful that it isn't winter and that the day ahead, whatever it brings, will be long and light and that Dora and Eric will be coming in soon and Harry will be with her by mid morning.

* * *

St Swithin's Church is silent and empty, save for Gladys sitting in one of the pews to the rear. She is quite still apart from her hands which are fiddling with a wet ball of a handkerchief.

She gazes ahead, down the aisle to the trio of stained glass windows above the altar, but in truth she is not looking at anything much at all. She is thinking about what this has meant to her family. Even after she's left home, she always comes back here on visits, to this bright Georgian church that holds so many memories. She can remember Ralph's christening though not Eric's when she was only four; she thinks of all the Christmas mornings and the Sundays that were part of her childhood. And of course, her own wedding. A wonderful June day eleven years ago, 1918. A year to remember for the world and for Gladys and Harry. The prettiest of weddings. Elizabeth had filled the church with flowers and the rector, who was more a friend than a priest to them, had married them. Gladys had been a radiant bride, had thought then that her happiness would go on forever.

Now she grimaces at her naivety. She thinks about yesterday, so many people in here, the crowded box pews. It had seemed like a terrible dream from which Gladys thought they might wake at any moment. And today is silent, empty, worse even than the previous days. There's been so much to keep them busy. Now there's nothing left to do, no way to delay facing up to it, to the fact she will never see her mother again.

She doesn't know how they will cope. She has no idea how her father will survive. His grief seems to be quiet and helpless, beyond rescue. He joins them for his meals, eats in silence. From time to time he raises his watery eyes and look round at his children as though he's forgotten why they are there.

They've done their best, pulled together, tried to set aside their own shock to help Arthur. There's been so much to do. Gladys never realised. To begin with, of course, Ralph had gone to pieces but by the next day Eric had him helping. He sent Ralph to see the registrar. There was no post-mortem. It was all very straightforward. Gladys' mind didn't seem to be able to absorb the writing on the death certificate. But there it was: *9th July 1929; Mary Elizabeth Lancaster; 46 Lowesmoor; 59 years; cause of death pneumonia and gastro enteritis.*

Eric arranged the funeral. He bought a substantial plot at Astwood Cemetery, a family grave. Elizabeth is at its heart and there will be spaces for everyone else. Gladys thinks it's a good plan. Ralph and Dora aren't so keen but Eric's done it anyway.

Gladys goes over the last week. A week from hell, she thinks. Vi came down from Nottingham, as soon as Gladys telephoned her. Eric and Pip had offered to have her to stay with them but Vi was having none of it. Gladys needs me with her, she'd said. She'd squeezed herself into Lansdowne House, took Gladys to the shops, helped her buy a suit for the funeral.

"I know it's wool, Glad, but it's a very light, summer weight. And this hat is perfect. You need the veil with it. You'll be glad of that with all eyes on you."

She took charge of Elizabeth 's kitchen, being of the opinion that the cure for all ills is to be found in a well cooked meal. Above all, Vi was a solid and constant presence for Gladys, more reliable than her family, more steady than Harry.

The south door of the church creaks as it opens. Gladys watches Harry as he takes off his hat and scans the empty church. He's so tall, always standing head and shoulders above the Lancaster men. She knows Eric envies that. She guesses Eric will never stop minding about his height.

"I'm over at the back," she calls.

"I thought you'd be in here." He stands in the aisle, one polished shoe planted on the step up into Gladys' pew, one hand resting on the back of the pew in front of her. "Are you all right, old girl?"

"Not really."

"We need to be getting along, if we're going to get that train."

"I know."

But she makes no attempt to move.

"Glad, you know I've got to get back for this evening. You need to come too. Beryl will be coming back tomorrow from Nottingham. And I need you." Gladys sighs.

"Budge along," he says. "Let me sit down for a minute."

She shuffles up the pew. He sits with one long leg stretched out into the aisle and his hat on his knee.

"Lordy, Glad, we haven't had a minute to ourselves. This is the first time we've got away from them all."

"Yes." Gladys doesn't look at Harry. She bows her head, twisting the handkerchief.

"Penny for your thoughts." Silence. "C'mon. Get it off your chest." She draws a long, deep sigh.

"I don't know, Harry, I don't know ..."

"What? What don't you know?"

"I don't know why I feel so –", Gladys is struggling, "so angry."

"You're not usually the angry type."

"I know."

"Go on then?" He nudges her gently. "Tell me all about it!" She smiles, despite herself.

"I feel guilty saying it but I'm angry with Mother for leaving me. I feel so let down." She spreads the fingers of her upturned hands in a gesture of helplessness. "She promised me, Harry, she promised she'd help me. I can't manage without my mother, Harry, I can't manage!" Tears start to trickle down her face, her neck, onto the front of her dress.

"Shush, Glad." He takes her hand. "C'mon now."

"And what about God?" She raises her voice. "What's God doing? What've we done, Harry, for this to happen to us?"

"We haven't done anything, Glad. People die. That's life. You know that."

"Yes, but not my mother! My mother shouldn't be dead!" Gladys turns on Harry. "What am I going to do? How am I going to manage when the baby comes?" Her shuddering sobs fill the church. "And Beryl? She was going to have Beryl for the summer. And Dad? Who's going to look after Dad? When this baby comes ... I can't, Harry. I can't do everything! Oh God ... oh God... and she *promised* ... told me she'd be here for me ... and now ..."

Harry sits miserably at Gladys' side. In his world you just got on with things, even the worst things, without trying to think too much about it all. He takes a deep breath.

"Glad, I can't give you any answers. You know that as well as I do. I don't know why your mother had to be taken and I don't know how your dad is going to manage. Eric and Ralph and Dora will have to sort him out."

"That's heartless."

"No, it's what Elizabeth would say. She'd say you've got to get on with your life in Birmingham. We've enough on our plates. You're not going to be able to help everyone."

"My mother managed it."

"Yes, well, no-one's going to try and live up to your mother's way of doing things. That's a fact, Glad." Harry strokes his chin thoughtfully. "And what you're saying about how you're going to get on now, well, I've been thinking about that. What you need for the baby is someone living in full time."

"A nanny?"

"A nanny, a nurse, whatever." Harry waves a hand vaguely. "Someone to look after the baby and keep an eye on Beryl too when we're not there in the evening. And my mother can have Beryl in the holidays. There's enough of them up in Nottingham to help out. And she can go to Worcester too. Pip'll have her to stay. Keep Zena company."

"It won't be the same."

"No, you're right. It can't be the same. But we'll manage. And you'll cope. This is your first real loss and it's a big one. When we lost my brother, when I was still at home, I thought I'd never get over it." Gladys looks up sharply, searches Harry's face.

"Oh Harry, I know. And the way he died. Sleeping in that big bed you shared. Right next to you."

"It was a bad, bad time. He'd had some pretty terrible asthma attacks before, but that night – God, I thought my mother would never recover. But what they say about time healing, well, it's true. Life goes on Glad. It'll be the same for you and your family."

Gladys strokes the back of Harry's hand. "I love you, Harry Watson." All of a sudden she stands up and holds out her hand to him. "C'mon. It's time I piped down. Like you say, we've got to get back to Brum. We can't sit around here all day."

They say farewell to the grieving family, to Elizabeth's freshly dug grave underneath an ocean of flowers. They arrive at The Court with just enough time for Harry to get a bite of supper and change into his tails before he heads downstairs to check all has gone smoothly in his absence.

* * *

Gladys hadn't believed the people who told her time would heal. She'd thought it was a platitude, said by folk who didn't know what else to say to her. But gradually her grief and anger starts to change. One day, to her surprise, she finds she's looking back beyond Elizabeth's death to happier days, to when they were children.

She uses her own upbringing in Worcester as a benchmark and she knows that what she and Harry are giving Beryl is falling short. Gladys doesn't realise, of course, and her mother is no longer here to tell her, that children are more resilient than she imagines and adapt quite easily to the lives they are given.

Thus Beryl, riding the trams each day to school, travelling to the Nottingham relations on the train, secretly exploring the dizzy heights of the Corporation Street roofs, jumping the spaces between the buildings, eating meals cooked by cooks and served by waitresses, thus Beryl is perfectly accepting of her way of life and even wonders sometimes whether the other girls at her school don't lead rather dull lives.

Some things do bother her, but she never mentions them to the grownups. She hates the evenings. There are two girls employed at The Court, 'the maids'. They are supposed to see Beryl into bed and stay in the flat with her. But once the grownups have gone down and they've made Beryl a hot drink from the cubby, they see her to bed and nip off down the back stairs, lured by the liveliness of the staff quarters, and only return in time for the arrival of Harry and Gladys at the end of the evening.

Beryl imagines them somewhere far below in the basement, giggling and flirting in the glare of the electric lights, whilst she lies stiff and alert with her tiny flickering night light casting brutish shadows over the walls, waiting for some bogey man who surely one night will get through the metal gates or come up the back stairs from the street and kidnap her.

July has been a weary month, hot and sad. Beryl's seventh birthday comes and goes. She understands enough to know that Worcester will never be the same now there's no Nana Lanc. She just can't imagine Lansdowne House without her, and she wonders how Grandpa and Uncle Ralph will manage.

No-one has really told her what happened. All she knows is that Nana caught a chill on the river. How can you die just from going on the river?

By the autumn she knows she is going to have a baby brother or sister. Each afternoon, when she arrives home from school, her parents' bedroom door is firmly closed so that Beryl understands she isn't to disturb her mother's rest.

Cook Eleker makes her a beef sandwich and a pot of tea from the kitchen, after which she has to settle down with her schoolbooks and not make a noise.

At least now that she's getting big and tired her mother no longer goes down with Daddy in the evenings to keep an eye on the staff and greet the customers. Instead she stays in the flat, leafing through her women's magazines, crocheting endless coats and bootees and bonnets for the baby that Beryl can't even imagine, and waiting restlessly for Harry's return at the end of the evening.

* * *

December 1929

Nancy breezes in wearing a fashionable café au lait Aquascutum coat with tweed revers and cuffs in the new dropped length. Gladys is lying on the settee, propped up with numerous cushions. Nancy stands over her, hands on hips.

"Good God, Gladys, you're huge!"

She takes off the coat to reveal a matching dress, throws her hat onto the table and drops into the chair nearest the fire.

"You must be going into labour any minute now."

"I hope so. I'm sick and tired of it all. I can't sleep. I feel like an elephant. I can't imagine anyone enjoying having babies."

Nancy fishes out her cigarette holder and case from her handbag.

"Want one?"

"No thanks. I've gone off them."

"Well, you're not much of a smoker at the best of times."

"That's true."

Nancy lights up, gracefully sends a slow stream of smoke into the air.

"I quite like one now and then," Gladys muses, "just to be sociable really more than anything. And of course they keep the germs away, when I'm downstairs with the customers." She nods towards the pile of packages Nancy's left by the door.

"What've you got there? It looks like you've bought up half of Marshall & Snelgrove."

"Just doing the last Christmas bits. The shops are mad. Queues everywhere. But never mind about me, how's life here?"

"Dull," says Gladys peevishly. "Very miserable for me at the moment. Hardly any visitors either. Vi was coming to stay but she's too busy with the Christmas rush at work, and Pip was coming but she's feeling too sick."

"Pip! Sick?"

"Yes, she's expecting too." Gladys smiles wryly. "Seems to be catching, Nancy. You'd better watch out."

Nancy shakes her head.

"No Gladys. Sadly, I don't think that's going to happen. There'll only be our boy. No more, I'm pretty sure of that. Anyway," she brightens, "that's nice news. When's Pip due?"

"Oh, ages. Next summer. She's only a few weeks gone but she's feeling sick all the time. So, to answer your question, there's no-one much around, everyone busy thinking about Christmas."

"It'll be better once the baby's born. You've only got a few days to go now. You'll be back to your old self by the spring."

"I shouldn't complain, I know, but when I think of this time last year, at the Oak, I was so busy all the time. And then I think of my mother." Nancy raises an eyebrow. "Harry's doing his best. He doesn't complain. He could have done with me helping out more these last few months here but I haven't been able to do much."

"Not your fault though."

"No."

"And Beryl?"

"She's fine. She doesn't give us much trouble. Except there is one problem."

"What's that?"

"Well, we've found a nursemaid for the baby."

"That's good."

"She's a woman in her thirties. She's come from The Exchange."

"The Exchange Hotel?"

"In New Street. The couple who manage it, we've got to know them quite well. Harry's in touch with them a lot."

"They're part of the Big Five, aren't they?"

"Yes. Another of M and B's places, quite like The Court. Anyway, their children are now all at school. When word got around that we needed a nursemaid they suggested they send this woman onto us. She's come highly recommended with good testimonials."

"What's her name?"

"Maud."

"Ah," Nancy smiles mischievously, "Your middle name, Gladys."

"Don't remind me. You know I hate it. I used to say to my mother, whatever made you call me Maud? All the servants used to be called Maud. I can't think what possessed her."

"So where is Maud now?"

"She's been in and out, sorting out how she wants the baby's things and her own room. She's very organised. Given me a list of everything she needs. But she won't start living in until the baby's arrived."

"And Beryl?"

"Not very keen, I'm afraid."

"Maud or Beryl?"

"The feeling seems to be mutual. I think Maud's made it clear she's going to be here for the baby and not for anyone else."

"Ah."

"Beryl will get used to her."

"She'll have to, by the sound of it."

"She's used to fitting in around the adults. And she's seven now, old enough to be sensible about it all." Gladys leans forward, pushes one of the cushions down into the small of her back. "That's enough talk about me. What about you? What have you been up to?"

"Well, the usual. A few things going on, shopping, the usual social round, you know the sort of thing. Ian's planning a holiday for us."

"A holiday? Lucky you."

"I suppose so."

"I wish I was having a holiday." Gladys looks puzzled. "But you're not so keen?"

"I'm not. I don't much see the point of us going on a holiday. You know, everyone thinks we look the perfect couple. Doctor and Mrs Ian Gordon. But we don't always see eye to eye."

"Neither do Harry and I."

"Yes, I know, but you two have a spark going between you. Anyone can see that. If I'm honest, we're not in love, Gladys. You must be able to tell. Not like you and Harry. And you have fun." Gladys grunts. "Well … you may not think so at the moment, but you've always had a good life together … the dancing and singing and just enjoying one another's company."

"You've got a good life, Nancy. Your beautiful house, everything you need."

Nancy smiles. Her shining chignon is swept away from her face, and Gladys can see two deep vertical lines above the bridge of her nose on her usually smooth forehead.

"I know. You're right. And don't worry, I'd never leave him." Gladys doesn't know what to say. She tries not to look shocked. "Ian has given me security and I have Bunny to think of. Imagine the boy growing up with his parents living apart. And I'd never do anything to cause trouble. I know how important a good wife is to a doctor. I shan't let anyone down. It's just that at times," she hesitates, looks warily at her friend, "at times, Gladys, I feel so trapped, I could scream."

"It's a woman's lot, Nancy." Nancy's misery gives Gladys some energy. She pushes herself up from the sofa and lumbers across the room to the drinks tray. "Come on, the clock's struck midday. Let's have a sherry. And perhaps I'll have one of those ciggies after all."

* * *

The end of 1929 is stormy and the new decade sweeps in with heavy rains. Hemlines drop, waists come back and the flapper girls' glamour of the '20s becomes fashion history.

A woman called Amy Johnson is planning a lone flight across the world, Adolf Hitler is making news in Germany and people are talking about the real possibility of a trip to the moon within the next few years.

On 12th December Gladys gives birth to a baby girl and Pip and Eric announce that they are moving house. Everyone in the family hopes that the new babies will go some way to heal the pain of losing Elizabeth.

To Gladys, the world outside The Court feels so remote that everyone else might just as well have been on the moon there and then. She calls the new baby Denise and gives her the middle name of Mary. Childbirth has been as ghastly as when she had Beryl, and she vows there will be no more children.

The doctor has ordered complete rest. All she wants to do is get up and get on with her life. She is longing to feel well, to have a routine again, spend her afternoons sewing, the evenings alongside Harry downstairs in the brightly lit rooms, to get back into decent clothes, see her friends, go shopping and get to church.

At least the new nursemaid is doing well. She's devised a military style feeding regime and upset the kitchen staff by insisting on an inflexible morning ritual which involves boiling the nappies and the feeding bottles at the same time as Cook Eleker needs the stoves fired up for the lunches. Harry and Gladys don't interfere. They're confident enough of Cook's devotion to them and Maud's to the baby to know that neither will want to leave The Court, and finally the two women settle on a grudging compromise.

Beryl, for different reasons from Cook, isn't so sure about Maud either. At the beginning of December she'd arrived home from school one day to find her sorting a pile of baby clothes in the spare bedroom, a woman with a sturdy frame, a plain, unlined face, large hands, a navy blue uniform and arms locked firmly across an ample chest at the sight of the child.

"So, you're Miss Beryl."

Beryl had nodded and smiled, remembering her manners.

"I've been wanting to see you. There's some things you and I must get straight before I move in."

Maud crossed the room, stood over her, uncomfortably close.

"You'll need to understand that when your little brother or sister arrives I'm 'ere to look after the baby. If you remember that, Miss Beryl, you and I will get along fine. D'you understand?" Beryl had given an uncertain nod whilst Maud continued. "Just so long as you know I'm not being paid to run around anyone else here. Best get this straight from the start."

It wasn't a good beginning and Beryl had decided there and then she would keep out of Maud's way as much as possible. She can see that Maud's days are given over exclusively to Denise and no-one else seems to matter. It is as though Denise is Maud's baby and not theirs.

At least now Beryl is no longer left alone in the evenings to lie in bed at the mercy of the dark shadows and creaks in the hall. Instead there is Maud, whom Gladys has instructed to see Beryl into bed with a hot drink each evening.

So the routine changes and whilst Beryl washes her face, hangs up her clothes, gets into bed and starts to read, Maud disappears into the kitchens to make the drink. Beryl gets sleepy waiting, thinks she'll just go and get herself a glass of water from the cubby, when Maud shuffles through and bangs the cup down on the little table next to the bed.

"'Here you are. Hurry up with it and get that light out."

Maud goes off without another word, closing the door as she leaves, and Beryl tries to scoop off the greasy skin that is floating on top of the tepid Ovaltine. It makes her feel sick.

Every night Beryl wonders why Maud can't bring her drink through whilst it's still hot. Does she deliberately wait around until it's nearly cold? It feels like spite, but Beryl can't be sure and she has a feeling that if she says anything to her mother, it will end up making things worse.

She thinks about her school friends, imagining their mothers putting them to bed with steamy cups of frothy chocolate, tucking them down into warm beds and waiting whilst they say their prayers before leaving them with a kiss to see them through till morning. For as long as she lives, she thinks, she'll always remember the cold skinny Ovaltine dumped by her bed and Maud closing the door on her each night.

The baby grows and flourishes. Each day Maud calls up one of the barmen on the internal telephone to come and carry the baby down the stone steps from the flat to the street. Then she tucks her into the big black pram which is kept behind the door.

"Off we'll go, Missy," she says to the sleeping bundle, "Off to the park you go with Maudie."

The nearest place for Maud to push the pram is not a park but St Philip's churchyard in Colmore Row. Maud marches past the railings that flank the pathways and, if the weather is dry, she heads for one of the grassy areas and settles her ample bottom firmly on one of the seats that overlook the tombstones. On warm spring days Maud lifts Denise out of the pram and loosen her shawls to let the air get to her skin. By the time summer comes, Maud pushes the pram around the gravestones with the gurgling baby dressed in cool cotton kicking her free legs under the silk fringed canopy.

Denise is christened in the cathedral. Beryl watches the sunlight flooding the richly coloured glass of the windows, casting deep blues and reds onto the cathedral floor. Her father has brought her here often, told her about the man who made the magic windows. She knows he was born in Birmingham and his name is Edward Burne Jones. And he's painted pictures too. Lots of them are in the art gallery.

She wishes Mother would bring her here to the morning service on Sundays so she could look at the windows, but they always have to go to the Methodist City Hall. Nearer to The Court, Gladys says, and more friendly.

In June the telephone call she's been waiting for comes from Worcester.

"Pip's had the baby. Eric's asked me to call and let you know."

"Oh Ralph, that's good news."

"It's a girl."

"Another girl! What are they going to call her? How's Pip? Why couldn't Eric telephone me himself?"

"Slow down old girl!" She can imagine Ralph on the other end of the telephone, holding up his free hand to stop the questions.

"Pip's fine and they're calling her Beverley, Beverley Elizabeth."

"Beverley. That's lovely. And the middle name's the same as Mother's."

"Yes."

"And Eric?"

"Back in the office straightaway after he'd been to see Pip and the baby. He's all right. You know what he's like. He's looking pretty happy, for Eric."

"Well, that's good. Give them my love. I'll get a card in the post to them tomorrow and I'll try and get down next week."

Gladys replaces the receiver. This will be a special baby. Eric's taken losing Mother harder than any of us, she thinks. It'll bring them closer, Pip and Eric. They'll be like us now, a complete family of four. Another new life. Just what's needed in Worcester.

* * *

Christmas 1930

"This is better than last Christmas, when Denise was two weeks old and I was feeling about a hundred."

"You're right there," says Harry. No-one wants to say that last Christmas was also their first without Elizabeth. They want to keep the day upbeat.

"Time for a toast." Harry looks around the table. "Firstly Mother and Father. Thanks for all the support you're giving us."

Emma is happy for her son. Her husband was right, this is just the business for them, even though it's a lot of work, especially for Gladys with the two children. Emma is doing what she can to help, having Beryl to stay for some of the school holidays and trying to be there for Gladys now she's lost her mother.

Eric raises his glass.

"To Mr and Mrs Watson."

Eric gets on with Harry's parents, looks up to Mr Watson, wonders why Harry himself can't be more serious about life like his father.

It's the first time Eric has seen Mr Watson since his retirement over a year ago and he's surprised at the change. Gladys had warned him. Retirement doesn't suit him Eric, she'd said. Time goes slowly for him. He's lost all his drive.

"And to Eric and Pip!" calls Gladys.

"Eric and Pip." They all raise their glasses again. Ralph starts to fidget.

"This is all a bit long-winded, Harry! The dinner'll be cold by the time we've finished." Beryl starts to giggle, nudges Zena.

"Pipe down, Ralph," says Gladys. "Don't be so cheeky. You just let Harry do what he wants."

"Ok then." Ralph gets to his feet. "If we've got to do this properly, here's a toast for you two. Thanks for having us all to stay. You could've just had a quiet time, what with The Court being closed today, but you opened up your home to us." Ralph fumbles for his handkerchief. "It means a lot, us all being together this Christmas."

"You don't have to thank us," says Harry. "We're glad to have you here. And one more toast: to the two new mums. Thank you for giving us two more beautiful girls."

Finally, the family sets about the Christmas dinner. It's been a rush, with the drinkers in the bars last night not clearing out until late. The restaurant, though, closed after the Christmas Eve lunches so Gladys has had time to sort things out ready for the family.

The staff are off duty but Cook has left everything prepared in the kitchen. Good job Harry's mother's here, thinks Gladys, to help sort out the meals with her. Cook's even made them a plum pudding and there's something cold that she's done for this evening.

After lunch, the men make themselves comfortable in the sitting room. Harry sets out four glasses and unstoppers the bottle of brandy.

"Christmas present from the lawyers," says Harry. He nods towards the low table in the centre of the room. "And the cigars. Help yourselves."

"Very nice too," says Ralph.

"A thank you," says Harry. "Nice to be appreciated." He looks towards the door.

"Beryl, what are you doing hanging around out there. Come in. And you Zena. Where are your mothers?"

"Gone to get the babies up."

"Where's Maud?"

"In her room. Finishing her lunch." Harry raises an eyebrow. At Gladys's insistence he'd invited Maud to join them for Christmas lunch, but to his relief she'd preferred to eat alone in her room. She's a good nursemaid but apart from making life easier for Glad she's of absolutely no interest at all to Harry. It's as though she's come from another planet, she's no fun, has no grace, no looks, not a single quality that makes for an interesting woman in Harry's opinion. You'd have thought, he thinks, she might have wanted to go and see her own people today.

He beckons the two girls over to his armchair.

"We'll have a sing song and do some things for you girls when we've had a sit down." Zena's eyes light up. Beryl's lucky. Zena's only five but already she knows that the best person to entertain children is Uncle Harry. More fun than her own father. "Let your dinner go down. Show Zena some of your presents. You can get out that game that Auntie Vi sent you."

Harry Senior wonders what's on the wireless.

"Christmas Day is never much good. You know that," says Emma.

"Yes," agrees Eric, "I don't suppose there'll be much on."

"Have a look at the Radio Times. Look at Boxing Day. There'll be better programmes tomorrow." She turns to Eric. "What do you think of the Radio Times?"

"It's very good. I have it delivered to the house. Pip likes planning what she wants to listen to, likes to tune in to a concert once or twice a week."

"It's been a good year for the wireless," adds Ralph, "especially the football." In April the BBC had made its first broadcast of the FA Cup Final. A thrill still ran through Ralph at the thought of it.

"That was very good," agrees Eric. "I think on the whole the BBC's doing well."

So the afternoon rolls easily on. Gladys sets Denise down on the carpet by the girls. Ralph pokes up the fire, opens a box of chocolates, tells Zena to hand them round.

Beryl hauls Denise to her feet and holds her up by the arms to show how she can manage a few staggering steps.

"Denise isn't at all like Beryl, Gladys," says Emma. "She's going to be quite dark and Beryl's so fair."

"It's not just her looks," says Gladys. "Denise loves being the centre of attention. Beryl's always wanted to keep in the background."

"Denise likes to be the centre of attention because of Maud," cuts in Harry. "Maud spoils her. She's going to grow up thinking everyone will feel the same about her as Maud does."

"Well," chuckles Emma, "it may not be Maud's fault if your daughter likes the limelight. Maybe she takes after you."

Harry has the grace to hold up his hands in a gesture of surrender.

"I admit it. I'm never happier than when I've got an audience."

Emma turns to Beryl.

"You haven't told me yet about your Christmas party. How did it go?"

"Oh Granny, it was wonderful. It was Daddy's idea. He invited all the children who live in the big hotels. Everyone came. And we had the balloon net up in the restaurant. It was just above where we were sitting at lunchtime. At the end of the party Daddy let it down and everyone had a balloon to take home."

"How many children were there?" asks Ralph. Harry rubs his chin thoughtfully.

"About fifty. We sent out invitations to the proprietors of all the big establishments, asked their children and the managers' families. They loved it, Ralph. They all came, even the snooty lot over at The Grand."

"So," says Eric. "Was it a business move, or something you did in the spirit of Christmas?"

"Both Eric, a bit of both. I thought it'd be good to get the children together. They're all scattered around the city centre in these big buildings. It's a funny old life for them. But I thought it would be good for our reputation if The Court got a bit swanky, took the lead in something. It was a great success. I think we'll do it every Christmas. Perhaps make it into a Court tradition for future generations." Eric grasps what Harry is saying, nods approvingly.

"And," continues Beryl, "Daddy got dressed up to do his magic." They all look at Harry.

"Yup," he smiles, "Top hat, tails, the lot."

"And the others didn't know it was my Daddy. He did loads of tricks. They just kept shouting for him to do more and more and more ..." She has to stop to catch her breath. "And then we had Father Christmas. Well, it wasn't really Father Christmas. It was Mr Pendle. But the children didn't know that."

"Who's Mr Pendle?" asks Ralph.

"Edith's husband," says Gladys. "Edith Pendle runs the downstairs bars."

"A woman? Running those bars?"

"You haven't seen Edith Pendle, Ralph," laughs Harry. "She rules down there with a rod of iron. No-one pulls a fast one on Edith. If she has to throw anyone out – you should see her. She frightens them all to death."

"She's also a very intelligent woman," Gladys chips in. "Her stocktaking is spot on and she does it all so fast. Harry doesn't have to worry about the public bars with Edith running things."

"And that's just as well by the sound of it," says Emma Watson. "You've both got your work cut out up here with the restaurant and lounge bars."

Pip appears in the doorway with Beverley and Harry jumps to his feet.

"Now, here's the little beauty! Pip, show Beverley to my mother." Pip crosses the room, loosens the baby's shawl. Emma stares.

"Oh, Pip dear. I had no idea she was so beautiful. She's like a little cherub. May I hold her?"

"Yes, of course." Pip lays the baby in Emma's lap. She is getting used to the wonder that is Beverley. People are always telling her that her baby is picture perfect, like a china doll with her peachy skin and fair curls. Now she lies wide-eyed in the crook of Emma's arm. Zena sits at Emma's feet, knees drawn up to her chin. Beverley turns her head and lets out a gurgle of laughter.

Harry starts a sing song with a few carols. Ralph stands next to the piano and beckons Beryl and Zena to come over. Harry Watson Senior has fallen asleep but the rest join in. *In the Bleak Midwinter. The First Noel. Good King Wenceslas.*

"Beryl can do us a solo now," says Ralph. "What'll it be?"

"I'll do Silent Night. I did it at school for the concert."

She fills the room with the power of her voice. Even Denise, who has been crawling around the carpet, sits herself up to listen. The grownups know what to expect when Beryl sings but still, when she has brought her voice to rest on the last notes, there is a silence broken only by Ralph starting to applaud. They all join in. Beryl drops cross-legged to the floor, as quiet as ever.

"Blimey. She's getting better every time I hear her. Sends shivers down my back when she sings like that."

"See what you've done, Beryl, made your uncle cry," laughs Harry.

"You big baby," teases Gladys. "Do a song yourself. That'll stop your blubbing."

"I'll do this sea shanty, though after Beryl it'll be a bit of an anti-climax."

At the end of the singing Gladys brings in the tea trolley and hands round Emma's home-made Christmas cake. She goes to the window and looks out before she closes the curtains.

"It's not very Christmassy down there. Looks like it's been raining and there's no-one around at all."

Once the children are in bed and everyone's got a drink the evening gets going. Harry's mother and father are the first to excuse themselves and then Eric also decides to turn in. Gladys kisses her mother-in-law.

"I hope you'll sleep well. Let me know if there's anything you need."

Pip, Ralph, Gladys and Harry are left to themselves. Harry crosses to the radio-gram.

"I think we'll have some music to end the evening."

"Put on Bing Crosby," says Gladys.

Harry sorts through the records, pulls the large, shiny disc from its paper cover and sets it on the turntable.

"What's it called?" says Pip.

"It's *Let's do It, Let's Fall in Love.* You'll hear it in a minute. I love it."

"C'mon Glad, up you get. And you Ralph, give Pip a twirl round the room."

So Christmas Day comes to a close with a few dances and few more brandies.

"It's been a good one," says Harry when they're finally in bed.

"The best," agrees Gladys. "The best yet."

1931

People around Birmingham get to know the new manager from The Court. He has presence, they say, fills a room, attracts people, collects friends easily.

Harry's a regular at the Art Gallery. The staff know him. Mr Watson, the chap on the door says, he's in today with his daughter.

There they'd stand, him and Beryl, she in her coat and beret, coming up to his waist, him a head above any other man in the place, looking at the paintings with his arms folded. They'd not say much. She looks like him. Has his eyes.

He takes her to the Pre-Raphaelites, tells her about the Brotherhood, the men who made you feel as though you could reach out and touch the folds of the gowns or the beautiful hair and lips of the women in the paintings, or so it seems to Beryl.

When she gets restless, there's the café, pots of tea, a cake for Beryl, the grand piano in the corner with its top propped open, something special the pianist would come up with to make Mr Watson smile.

Then there's chaps like Gazeeka, the magician.

There's nothing Gazeeka likes better than getting together in the flat at The Court at the end of an evening with Harry to practise a few tricks and drink his whisky. Gazeeka tries a new trick out on Harry before a run at The Hippodrome. Harry always knows what's needed to polish up the bits that are letting the trick down.

Gladys Watson's a good sort too thinks Gazeeka. Lost her mother just when they'd moved. That must've been hard. And The Court's not a good place to bring up kids. But she seems to manage. Don't know what Harry would do without her. She's always around, keeping an eye on things. He might look as though he's in charge but he couldn't manage half as well on his own. He's the personality, she's the brains.

Gazeeka thinks Harry is wasted. Harry's a great musician in Gazeeka's opinion, that voice, and what a showman when he's doing his stuff.

Harry could have gone far in the entertainment business. But marrying Gladys, and then the kiddies coming along. Finish you off, wives and kiddies. You get hitched, and then the little ones arrive and you're done for.

Sometimes Harry's other friends join them. The previous week there'd been four of them in the flat. It'd been two o'clock when Gazeeka got home. Topping evening. Gladys had even played the piano for a bit, before she went off to bed, telling them to pipe down when it got late, Harry singing, then the cards, Harry dealing, always with a ciggie between his lips. He'd even got out that single malt he'd been saving for a special occasion …

* * *

November 1931

The train's so stuffy and the lights above the luggage racks are hurting her eyes. The carriages rattle up the Lickeys, past the gloomy fields, narrow back gardens with straggles of vegetables all darkening in the last of the October afternoon.

The countryside's the worst place, she thinks. Bleaker. Colder. As black as the clothes we're wearing. People come here for a day out. They think it's better than the city. They only come when the sun shines. They wouldn't give it the time of day now.

The chill of the glass against the side of her face helps numb the headache that had started that morning. It will last at least three days. They always do. Not surprising, Harry had said, you waking with a head today, Glad. But really, all Gladys had been able to think in the morning was how Pip and Eric would get through the day.

Every parents' fear …

She is thinking about the day back in June when the sun started to show its strength by early morning, when she'd gone to Worcester for Beverley's first birthday.

The last time we saw her …

Gladys, Beryl and Denise had set off for Worcester. At New Street Station they were glad to get out of the taxi and into the shade. The flower seller was scooping water into his cupped hands from a galvanised bucket, sprinkling his display, pausing to wipe his brow. Once in the train Gladys told Beryl to take off her straw hat and she untied Denise's soft lawn bonnet.

First the rash, then the fever ...

At Worcester they'd had a taxi to Pip and Eric's house. They'd no longer headed for the big red-brick place at Lansdowne. Eric still keeps the tenancy and runs his business from Lansdowne House but their new home, which Eric bought when the business started doing so well, is a far more attractive affair at Lavender Road. Arthur and Zena had been waiting at the bottom of the drive to greet them.

Ralph had taken a half-day and he'd arrived just as her taxi had pulled up. Now, in the train, Gladys smiles to herself despite everything, how they could hardly see Ralph, hidden behind a giant beribboned bear and Zena and Beryl felt as though their chests were bursting, they laughed so much.

They'd toasted the baby's health ... her health ... impossible to think of now ...

The long windows in the dining room had been open onto the garden. Gladys remembers the cut of Eric's wine glass under her fingers; smooth linen; polished silver; the warmed plates; lifting the lids of the vegetable dishes; the minty steam from the peas picked by Eric that morning; tiny shining potatoes under a scattering of bright parsley and later, pale custard over a crisp fruit pie. Even Arthur managing to be jovial, Beverley with her baby talk in his arms.

Beryl and Zena unpacking Beverley's parcels. So many presents.

All her things ... what will they do with them?

The afternoon had slipped away. The two girls flopping on the lawn, taking off their shoes and socks, sliding their soles along the cool grass. Beryl showing Zena how to make a cat's cradle, Ralph in the deckchair and Denise falling asleep on his lap.

She remembers the heat, the perspiration trickling between her breasts. When she got up from the table, her dress clinging to the back of her legs.

The storm had broken as they were travelling home. Thunder and lightning and torrents of rain by the time they got to Corporation Street. She'd told Harry: "Pip and Eric. Happier than they've ever looked."

Only four months ago ...

After all that heat, storms and the tornado. Thunder and lightning and terrible floods; the papers said it was like tropical rain, it was so heavy. And the tornado knocked out roofs and windows and killed that woman in

Sparkhill. Gladys saw it all the next week on the Pathé newsreel at the Gaumont. All so sudden after the beautiful sunshine.

You never know; never know what's round the corner ...

"You're shivering." Harry's voice brings her back. "Are you cold?"

She shakes her head.

"You don't look very comfortable there."

She shifts in her corner.

"I was just thinking." She speaks to the window. "The last time I was on this train was coming back from the birthday party. With Beryl and Denise. On the day of the tornado."

"I know. You said that earlier." He puts down the paper. "Come and sit here, by me."

She levers herself out of the corner, slumps next to Harry.

"I thought then, Harry," she sighs, "how we'd all deserved happiness. I thought we'd had all our suffering, with Mother going like that. And the babies, I thought God had sent them to make up for Mother."

"Glad," he sighs, "God didn't choose for Beverley to get diphtheria. You know it doesn't work like that. And you a churchgoer."

"I can't help it."

"Here," Harry slides his arm around Gladys, pulls her closer. She shakes her head.

"Someone might come in."

"Who cares? We're an old married couple. Anyway, Bromsgrove was the last stop for this train. It's straight on now to New Street." She leans against him, feels his warmth through his overcoat, rests her eyes.

"I've been thinking."

"What?"

"I was thinking ... when Eric bought that plot at the cemetery for Mother with all those spaces ... little did he know ..." Harry pulls her closer. She shudders again. "They shouldn't have to make coffins that small, Harry."

"Don't think about it now."

"I can't help it. And Pip and Eric. Did you see, Harry, they seemed so remote from one another all day."

Pip clinging onto Gladys. Eric standing apart, a small, stony, windswept figure ...

"Yes, come to think about it. But give them a chance. It was a terrible ordeal." She pushes away from him. Sits upright. He sees her eyes are alert now, despite the headache.

"If that'd been you and me. If that happened to you and me –" He can see tears are close. Unusual for Glad.

"Shush. It's not going to happen to us. The girls are fine."

"Yes, but if it did." She is working it through in her mind. "If anything terrible happened, we'd be there for one another, wouldn't we?"

"'Course we would." He can't imagine what would happen to them if they lost Beryl or Denise, but he pulls her back to his side. "You and me, we operate together. We're a team. Always will be. Eric and Pip, well, they're different."

"They should never have got married."

"I don't know about that. But it wasn't much of a love match, was it."

"They say these tragedies can drive a couple apart."

"They've got Zena."

"But Beverley was the apple of their eyes."

"True." Harry absentmindedly rubs her shoulders. "There's nothing we can do, you know. They're going to have to find their way through this, together or apart."

The train has slowed to a cranking rhythm, the lights of Birmingham's suburbs are starting to roll past the window.

"Reach my hat down can you, Harry."

She stands on her toes to see in the carriage mirror, pulls a few curls out from under the brim of her hat and rolls back its tiny veil. She fishes around in her bag for her lipstick, finds her gloves.

They step down into the eternal hubbub of New Street station: the hissing of the slowing trains, the smell of the steam, the smoke, the newspaper vendors shouting the evening's news, porters pushing the luggage trolleys, lights from the station restaurant falling across the platform, the bumping and the running, the calling of greetings and the fading farewells.

"Penny for the guy, Sir!" Harry fishes in his pocket, drops some coins into the cap of the smallest boy standing at the front of the group of children and lights up a cigarette. The air is breathy cold.

"Let's walk, Harry," she says, tucking herself round his arm. "Get rid of the cobwebs. Get ourselves home."

* * *

Harry visits Lewis's, the top floor. He knows what he wants, can't wait to see Beryl's face. Down the escalator, back home along Corporation Street, a tall man with the little cage. Up the back steps, carefully. They're in the living room. He can hear the radio. In the hall he frees the creature from its cage, tenderly tucks it inside his overcoat.

Gladys can see the bulge under his coat as soon as he walks in the room.

"What've you got there?"

This will be the tricky part.

"It's for Beryl." The child jumps up, crosses to her father.

"Let's see, Daddy." Gladys looks from father to daughter with suspicion.

"It's something a bit different, Glad."

She gestures for him to show her.

"Come on, Harry."

And there it is, lifted out of the folds of his coat. Gladys jaw drops.

"A monkey!"

Beryl screams with excitement. Harry lifts the monkey onto the floor, its eyes darting fearfully. Beryl steps forward and it streaks across the room and up the curtain to the pelmet where it remains, frozen with fear. Gladys jumps to her feet, colour rising, hands on hips.

"Harry! How could you be so stupid!"

"It'll be all right. He'll settle down. You'll see." He's beginning to sound lame. "Don't get upset."

"I'm not upset. I'm boiling!" She heads for the door, pushes past him savagely. "It's the monkey or me! Get that thing out now or I'll be gone by the morning." She slams the door behind her. Harry and Beryl look helplessly at one another.

"It's not going to work."

"No, Daddy. She's serious. She's furious. I think you'll have to take it back." She looks up to the pelmet, gives a rueful smile. "He's so sweet."

Somehow they get the monkey down from the curtains and back into the cage. He retraces his steps along Corporation Street, into Lewis's, up the escalator. Harry explains about his wife. The lady in the pet department is understanding. Harry gets a refund and the monkey goes back on sale.

* * *

Daisy England, up close to the mirror, checks her teeth for lipstick and brushes face powder from the lapels of her suit. She always judges a restaurant by the Ladies Room. You can see Gladys Watson keeps her eye on this one. It's not just the quality of the soap and the vase of fresh flowers. Who but Gladys would have thought to put out a box of Kleenex face tissues next to the mirror?

She makes her way back to the lounge bar and joins her husband. There isn't much she can think of to say to him. How she's ended up with a small town manager of a shoe shop she'll never know. He's going to have to buck his ideas up, that's for sure, or Daisy will go stark staring mad.

Desmond knows what his wife is thinking. He wonders what would have happened if they hadn't started their jaunts to Birmingham on his days off. If they hadn't got so pally with Harry and Gladys Watson.

It had begun with a shopping trip, once every two or three weeks, and then one day they'd discovered The Court Restaurant. Now it seems to be routine for them to stay on into the evenings when the shops have closed and have a few drinks in the lounge bar before heading for the station.

He watches Daisy's face light up as Gladys spots them and comes over to their table. Desmond gets to his feet.

"Sit down. Lovely to see you both." She turns to Daisy. "I see you've got a bag there from Walter Austin's."

Daisy picks up the bag, pulls out a layer of tissue paper.

"It's a coat. I'll show you."

Gladys looks around the bar, gestures to Daisy not to unpack the bag.

"Not now. I can't stop at the moment. I've got to see to the restaurant. We've a new waitress in there and I'm not sure she knows what she's doing. I'll come back later, when it's a bit quieter." Daisy's face falls. "I'll be back. Give me half an hour. Harry'll be down soon, we'll have a drink with you then."

Gladys sets off to speak to the barman, to greet other customers and then to make her way through to the restaurant. Desmond watches her, wonders why his wife is so envious. It all looks like hard work to him, but Daisy can't seem to see past the glamour that Gladys and Harry have created.

They make it look easy, of course, as though they're enjoying themselves when they're with the customers. That's the trick. Everyone wants to feel special, and that's why people keep coming to The Court.

Gladys keeps her promise, brings Harry over to Desmond and Daisy's table. Harry tells the barman to bring him a whisky. Gladys has a lime and soda, wishes Harry would do the same and Daisy finally gets to unpack her coat.

"It's lovely, Daisy. I really like the fur collar. Very smart."

"Too smart for Evesham."

"What's wrong with Evesham?" demands Desmond.

"We need to move. Life's passing us by. We need to live a bit." She doesn't add that she'd like to live like the Watsons, but Desmond knows what she's getting at.

"I don't see how moving to Birmingham will make you any happier, Daisy," says Harry.

He starts to look around, his mind on other things. They'd had this conversation many times with Daisy, and he was beginning to wonder why Gladys bothered with her.

Harry thinks Desmond's a good sort but he doesn't know how he puts up with Daisy.

"You don't understand, Harry. You don't know what it's like."

"If you moved from Evesham," says Gladys, "what would you like to do? Where would you like to be?" She knows the answer.

"I think we should do very well in your line, Gladys." Gladys frowns. "We could run a place for Mitchells & Butlers."

"It's not that easy," cuts in Harry. "You're working when everyone else is playing. If the staff let you down you have to turn round and do what you can yourself. It's not all about being down here in the evenings having a drink with the customers."

"And it's not the best place to have children growing up," says Gladys. "We're lucky with Maud. She keeps an eye on things upstairs. Denise doesn't know any different, of course, but Beryl isn't always very happy when we leave her in the evenings. I rush around early evening, trying to get a bit of time with her. Harry likes to keep an eye on her schoolwork but that's not easy either. She's stuck on her decimals at the moment. Harry even woke her up the other evening to try and explain them to her. It was well after eleven."

"That's something that needs to be considered," says Desmond, keen to grasp an opportunity to be backed up. "Think about Joyce, Daisy. What would we do with Joyce?"

"Joyce would be fine," she snaps. "She'd get used to it. Beryl's very independent. It would do Joyce good to be a bit more like Beryl."

"Speaking of Joyce reminds me," says Gladys. "We've got an invitation for her, to our children's Christmas party. It's going to be another big affair." Desmond smiles.

"When does Harry Watson ever do anything in small measures?" he says.

"We thought," says Gladys, "Joyce might like to come on the Saturday if she's free. And she can stay a couple of nights. The girls haven't seen one another since the summer."

"That would be lovely. They got on so well when Beryl came to Evesham."

"And Beryl enjoyed staying with you. It's so different from being at The Court. She never stopped talking about your high street shops and the river walks."

Desmond looks triumphant. "Well, there you are then, Daisy. At least there's one person who appreciates Evesham!"

"Yes," says Harry, "and think very carefully, both of you, before you decide to give up what you've got there."

"I'll pop upstairs later and get Joyce's invitation for you," says Gladys.

"We'll bring Joyce up on the Saturday then, and get her back on Monday," says Daisy.

"What are you doing for Christmas?" asks Desmond.

"It's a bit in the air at the moment," says Gladys. "We're staying put, as usual. There'll be Harry's parents coming, and Ralph, my brother. But we don't know what's happening now with my other brother, Eric, and his family. It's only a few weeks since they lost their baby. They're very low. We hope they will come."

1932

She hears Harry bounding up the stairs to the flat two at a time. Easy for him, Gladys grumbles to herself, with his long legs.

He can hear the trundle of the Singer and heads for the bedroom where a shaft of weak sunlight shows up the dust. He stands over her, waving a printed sheet.

"Glad! What d'you think of this!"

"Hang on, let me finish what I'm doing." Gladys is frowning, hunched over the machine as she feeds the stiff taffeta under its foot with her left hand and turns the handle that makes the whole thing work with her right. No good trying to hurry Gladys when she's sewing.

She reaches the end of the seam, lifts the lever at the back of the foot to release the fabric, pulls it away and breaks off the threads that are still attaching the fabric to the machine between her teeth.

"Why d'you do that? There's a thing at the back there to cut threads."

"It's what I always do. It's how Mother did it." She sits back and looks at him. "Have you come up here to tell me how to sew, or do you want something?" Harry hands Gladys the sheet of paper. She starts to read, her face breaking into a broad smile.

"A railway carriage!"

"They're all the rage. They're called camping coaches."

"I know. I've read about them."

"This one's at Borth. At the station." Gladys looks at the photograph on the reverse of the leaflet.

"It looks splendid."

"One of the customers gave me that leaflet. He's going in a couple of weeks' time. Thought we might be interested. It's all fitted out." Harry sits on the end of the bed. "Trains go direct from New Street. No changing." He fishes a packet of Players out of his jacket pocket. "D'you want one of these, Glad?"

"No thanks. And this dress'll be stinking of smoke before I've even finished it with you puffing away in here." She carries on looking at the leaflet. "This looks like good fun, Harry. And easy to walk to the town and the beach."

"It's free for a week at the end of July, in Beryl's holidays. What d'you think?"

"Let's go. She'll love it and it'll be nice for us all to be together for a week."

"I'll book it then. We'll take Maud."

"Maud?"

"Then she can stay with the girls in the evenings and you and I can go out."

"I'm thinking," she says carefully, "it might be nice to stay in. Cook for ourselves in the little kitchen." Harry bursts out laughing.

"Cook! No fear. We'll leave Maud to do all that. We'll go out on the town."

And so it is arranged. Harry puts in for the holiday with the brewery. A stand-in manager will come to The Court for the week they're away.

Gladys spends the days before the holiday packing.

"Not too much, Glad," Harry reminds her. "We've got to get the suitcases onto the train, don't forget. And it's only for a week."

Gladys nods but puts in plenty of pretty frocks anyway for Beryl and a good selection of summer outfits for herself. Then there are hats and hosiery, beachwear, rainwear, underwear, footwear, toiletries and some bits and pieces of jewellery to fit in.

Maud folds and packs all the baby's things into another bag. She isn't having the missus muddle them all up with her own stuff. Her own things don't take up much space; a change of underwear and spare aprons was all she'd need and she'd travel in her mackintosh and stout shoes whatever the weather.

* * *

Borth

Gladys knows something is wrong. Up until now everything has gone according to plan: the journey from Birmingham and the arrival at the railway station.

There's a porter to help them with their luggage across the platform to the siding where the converted holiday carriage stands. Its livery colours are exactly the same as all the other carriages on the Great Western railway but you can tell it is their carriage because painted down the side, in tall cream letters, are the words "Camping Coach".

Beryl is enchanted with the compartments that now serve as narrow rooms, each with its own function. Maud is to share one compartment with Beryl and Denise. Gladys has got the porter to carry hers and Harry's things to the second bedroom. From the doorway to their compartment Harry watches Gladys undo the straps of their suitcase.

"Blimey, Glad. There's not enough space here to swing a cat. Where are we supposed to put everything?"

"There's cupboards under the bed. But I think we'll have to keep some things in the case."

"And where are we going to put the suitcase?"

"I don't know. Let me get sorted out and then we'll find somewhere for it." Harry folds his arms.

"I don't know, Glad. It's not how I imagined." Gladys sighs. Somehow, if she's honest, the accommodation isn't quite what she'd expected.

It is, as Harry says, very cramped, especially coming from the cavernous Court, and she hadn't realised that they would have to get their water from the station building and use their facilities. And Harry is so tall, he's already banged his head on the ceiling. He just doesn't seem to fit into the place at all.

"I'm going off to think a bit, Glad." From the window she watches him adjust his hat and set off down the path that leads to the town. From the other end of the corridor she can hear the clatter of cutlery and the kettle whistling, followed a few minutes later by Maud appearing at her door with a cup of tea.

"Ah, that's just what I need. I'll come along and have it with you." Maud shrugs and makes her way back up the corridor. Gladys follows and they squeeze themselves into the seats facing one another either side of the fixed table. Maud gets hold of Denise, who is sitting under the table with her doll.

"Up you come, Missy, and sit by me." She holds a glass of milk steady for the child. Through the window Gladys can see Beryl crouched on the ground, carefully arranging stones and moss in a pattern.

"Look at Beryl, Maud. She's in her own little world. I wonder what she's thinking."

"Humph! She's got too much of an imagination, Mrs Watson, if you want my opinion and don't mind me saying." Gladys does mind Maud saying, but the last person she would want to cross is this capable woman on whom she relies and she consoles herself with the thought that her bark really is worse than her bite.

They've been lucky finding Maud and it's worth putting up with the woman's opinions. She adores Denise and does her duty by Beryl. Beryl knows it's all done grudgingly, but still it's better than when The Court staff left her on her own once her mother's back was turned.

* * *

She can hear him whistling before he comes into view and she goes out to meet him.

"Glad, we're off! You and me. We've a taxi coming to take us to The Grand." Gladys glares at him.

"Harry, have you gone mad? We can't just leave. What about the children? It'll break Beryl's heart."

"No it won't. Maud'll look after them and we'll meet up in the day. We'll come over and get her every day after breakfast. I'll make sure she has a good time. And in the evenings it'll just be you and me. We need to be enjoying ourselves too." Gladys looks troubled. She is torn between staying in the comfortable hotel in town and leaving the children with Maud.

"We can't stay here, Glad." He nods towards the carriage. "I can hardly stand up straight in there. I shall end up all bent over by the end of the holiday if I have to stay here." Harry hunches his back, dangles his arms and does a convincing impersonation up and down the platform of an old man with crooked legs. She has to laugh, despite her misgivings.

And he's right. Beryl doesn't complain. She doesn't know any different. Harry is a restless father. She takes it for granted that he isn't like other people's fathers, the men who leave their houses each weekday morning, returning in the evening to suppers, evening newspapers, favourite armchairs; fathers who can put up shelves and mend toys; fathers with garden sheds; fathers who spend Saturdays mowing lawns and Sunday mornings at church, and then reign supreme at the Sunday lunch tables and never change their plans at the drop of a hat.

So now, watching her father carry his bags and her mother's suitcase to the waiting taxi for them to escape to the big hotel on the front, she isn't particularly surprised. She hadn't really believed they would behave like an ordinary family that week. He'd promised he'd be back in the morning. She knows he will make it up to her.

* * *

Her days are filled with donkey rides, sandcastles, ice creams and puppet shows. She decides her father is the tallest, most handsome man on the beach. He is certainly the most popular. Each day there's a little group of children waiting for them.

"Do some tricks for us, sir?" they plead.

"Please Mr Watson! Do the one with the matchbox."

"And the handkerchief one!"

Harry scratches his head theatrically, reaches behind the oldest child's ear and produces a halfpenny.

"How do'you do it?" they clamour. But Harry never tells. Beryl smiles to herself. No-one has a daddy like hers.

Gladys watches them. Occasionally she sets aside her magazine or half-written postcards and heaves herself out of her deckchair to join Maud to walk Denise along the seafront.

One evening Harry is looking through the newspaper in the bedroom, waiting for Gladys to finish getting ready.

"See here. This is about the election they've had in Germany. Looks like Herr Hitler hasn't won after all."

"That's good then?"

"Yep. It says here that he's pretty well done for. He'd have to try and sort something out with the other parties if he wanted power now. Or have some sort of armed revolution."

"I can't see that happening, Harry."

"No. He's done for, Glad. And a good thing too. God knows we've had enough of war to last us a lifetime."

* * *

The evenings belong to her and Harry. Gladys watches from her seat in the cocktail lounge as he orders their drinks, her Martini, his whisky. He towers over the other men, leans easily against the bar, drops into relaxed conversation with the barman. He settles next to her and she listens to him making plans. Things he wants to change at The Court and things they'll do in the years to come. All this time just for one another. It's a luxury.

She stays awake long after Harry, watching him sleeping, and remembers why she fell in love with him. He's so different from the men in her family. He can still dazzle her.

She writes postcards to the family, to her father and to Pip and Eric, to Vi and to her in-laws in Nottingham. To Nancy she writes a letter. She describes the hotel, the shops in the town, having nothing to do for a whole week and being able to spend each day with the family and the evenings alone with Harry.

Nancy, alone, sits at the breakfast table staring at nothing, the letter carefully folded back into its envelope.

"Madam?" Nancy doesn't answer. "Mrs Gordon."

She shakes herself, looks at the girl, standing awkwardly with her tray.

"Have you finished, Madam?"

"Yes, Amy." She smiles. "You can clear these things."

"You've not eaten much."

"No. But I'm fine. Tell Mrs Lawton it was very nice."

Nancy heads for the sunny drawing room, the heels of her shoes tapping on the polished floor as she crosses the hall. She thinks about her friend. Gladys and Harry lead a bizarre sort of life at The Court. She knows there are difficulties, noisy arguments sometimes that leave Gladys drained, but there's something they share, something she can't quite put into words that makes their marriage work.

She stands by the window, looks out onto the shimmering garden and the emptiness of the day ahead exhausts her.

Nottingham 1932

No-one, Beryl swears to herself, will ever know what Auntie Gertie has said to her. Her cheeks burn at the memory, even now, and she thinks it would hurt Mummy and Daddy terribly. She lies on her bed at The Court, finally able to think. How could Daddy have such a nasty sister? How can Auntie Gertie possibly have had kind Granny Watson as a mother?

She's made up her mind, she won't go to Nottingham again, only if she can stay at Granny's. Auntie Gertie isn't nice at all. Beryl pities her cousins, especially Pauline who seems to bring out her mother's cruel side. Olga's the favourite, the pretty one. Pauline can't do anything right. Auntie Gertie boxing Pauline's ears seems to Beryl to be a daily routine.

And Beryl knows a lot more about Uncle Fred than the grownups realise. She's listened to enough of her mother's half whispered conversations that weren't meant for young ears to know about the pans and the crockery that can fly across Gertie's kitchen, that usually hit the wall but have been known to hit Uncle Fred. 'Poor Fred' is what they call him. Beryl can see why.

She tries to piece together how it had started. She'd arrived at Nottingham station to be told by Auntie Dorothy that Granny had been up all night with a sickness. You're to go to your cousins, Dorothy had said. Auntie Gertie will look after you until I've got Granny better.

Two days into the week and everything was fine. Uncle Fred took Pauline, Olga and Beryl to the circus on Saturday and on Sunday he drove Beryl over to Mapperley to see Mr and Mrs May and Auntie Vi. He'd pipped the horn outside Granny's house but no-one heard. He said they couldn't go in, that Dorothy had caught the sickness and was poorly now and the house was a hotbed of germs.

It was after the telephone call from Mummy and Daddy on Sunday evening. She had told them about the weekend, and she'd spoken to Denise too, heard all about the cats and what they'd been up to. And then, alone in the kitchen with her aunt, Gertie had sat herself down, lit a cigarette and eyed her niece across the empty table.

"So, how are they all?"

"They're fine." She had been oblivious to the tone of Gertie's voice which would have alerted the rest of the family that something was about to happen.

"Fine, are they?" Gertie's eyes narrowed as she sent a stream of smoke in Beryl's direction. Beryl remembers that she had tried not to cough. She'd thought it would be rude. "And are they enjoying themselves, do you think?"

"Well, yes, I suppose so. They're all right anyway."

"Enjoying not having you there?" Beryl remembers how she'd felt the heat rush to her face.

"I don't know what you mean."

"Oh come on, Beryl," Gertie's eyes had gleamed, "I think you do. Why do you think they keep sending you up here to us?" Beryl's heart had started to thump, threatening to take over her chest and throat.

"They're – They're so busy," she'd stammered. "And Mummy says it's better in the holidays if I'm out of Birmingham. She likes me to be in the fresh air." She remembers now, she was gabbling, falling over the words.

"Well, you're wrong. I'll tell you why you're here. They don't want you. They just want to be rid of you!"

Auntie Gertie had got up, ground her cigarette out in the sink. Then she'd walked back to the table, towered over Beryl, her face a contortion of hate.

"If they cared about you, Beryl, they'd keep you with them instead of expecting everyone else to look after you."

Beryl remembers everything had gone into a fog in front of her eyes. She'd covered her ears, rushed out of the kitchen and up the stairs, shut the bedroom door. She wasn't going to let anyone see her crying.

Now, from the safety of her own room at The Court, she is quite proud of the letter she managed to post to Mummy and Daddy. Get me home quickly, she'd demanded. Harry had met her at the station. She'd told him she'd been homesick. He'd laughed, took her to the art gallery, let her choose the biggest cake.

* * *

Daisy England finally gets Desmond to move to Birmingham. He swaps shoes and boots for beer and spirits and fulfills Daisy's dream of managing a public house in Birmingham for Mitchells & Butlers. It's a suburban establishment, a far cry from The Court, but Gladys reminds Daisy how she and Harry had started at The Oak.

Beryl isn't so sure she wants the Englands in Birmingham. She likes Mr England but she shares her father's views about Joyce's mother. She overhears him late one evening when she was supposed to be asleep.

"Poor old Des. I feel sorry for him, Glad."

"Daisy only wants what she thinks is best for them all."

"Or what she thinks is best for Daisy! You always defend her."

"I try and see the good in her."

"They were well settled in Evesham. Des was happy there and I don't think Joyce wanted to come."

"I don't suppose Joyce had any say in the matter. But it'll be nice for Beryl, to be able to see more of her."

But Beryl isn't too bothered about having Joyce as a friend at such close quarters. And now she won't be able to go and stay at Evesham in her holidays, which she'd quite enjoyed for a change.

The truth is that Beryl likes being free to roam around The Court and up and down Corporation Street. She is ten now and she just wants to please herself when she's not at school.

Coming home from Nottingham, she discovers Lewis's escalator. The first in Birmingham.

Every day for the rest of the summer holidays she sets off down Corporation Street after breakfast and rides the escalator undisturbed. Up to the restaurant. That's as far as it goes and you still have to climb the stairs to the pets. And then down to the basement. They've got to know her, the staff. They don't mind her, smile at the sight of the bright-haired, big eyed, skinny child from The Court gliding up and down their moving staircase.

Autumn 1933

The consultant is very tall, like Daddy. He invites Beryl to come round to his side of the desk where he remains seated so that he is on a level with the child. Would you like to see my watch? He shows her how it opens, explains how all the little cogs and wheels drive the hands around. She nods politely, doesn't like to say to him that her grandfather in Nottingham has one too, but better, with his name engraved on the case.

Now he feels around her neck. Does this hurt? Here? A little? No cough? That's good. His hands are large and soft and smell of scented soap. When he has finished he tells her to go back around the desk and sit down next to her mother. She puts her hands in her lap, her feet not quite reaching the floor.

He rests his elbows on the arms of his chair, picks up the report and scrutinises it over the top of his half moon spectacles. Then he tosses the paper back on the desk.

"The gland, Mrs Watson, is infected with TB." He watches her face, waiting for the flinch, the panic that crosses the faces of his small patients' mothers when he mentions the unmentionable. No hysterics from this mother. She waits for him to speak. "You were right to seek early advice."

"So what happens next, Mr Ainsworth?"

"I'll have her in the Children's Hospital for a couple of nights for the surgery." He glances at the report again. "I see you're in Corporation Street. I know The Court Restaurant. I had lunch there with the hospital lot a month or so ago. Very nice." She waits for him to get back to the matter of Beryl. He clears his throat.

"I think you should get Beryl out of the city after the surgery. She needs a spell of decent air." Gladys frowns.

"How long do you recommend?"

"I would say if you could take her away for six weeks. That should do the trick."

"Six weeks!" Gladys shakes her head. "I think you should understand, Mr Ainsworth, that I assist my husband in the day to day running of The Court. I can't possibly get away for six weeks."

He leans back, smiling reassuringly.

"Then I'll see what I can do."

* * *

Broadstairs, Kent

She is two hundred miles from home, without Mother and Daddy, without Denise and the cats.

Lilian Alexander marches her round the wide sweep of Broadstairs beach. The walk by the sea has been prescribed as part of the daily regime, but Lilian doubts whether the damp November air that has been hanging around Kent for days will be doing the child much good. The beach is deserted now, the beach huts chained together in a huddle and all the shops and cafes along the front empty and shuttered.

Two nights in the children's hospital to remove her neck gland, and then Beryl's convalescence was fixed up with Mr and Mrs Baker, Dr Ainsworth's kindly ex cook and his wife. They'd moved from Birmingham to be near Mrs Baker's mother. Just what the child needs, a few weeks by the sea.

"No need to worry, Mrs Watson," he said briskly. "I've sent quite a few children to Mrs Baker. She'll look after Beryl."

And the helpful doctor even recommended this charming young woman who takes charge of Beryl each day.

* * *

"She's a good girl, Charles," Lilian Alexander says. "No trouble. Old for her years. Not like a ten year old. She loves the beach. She'd spend all day looking at the sea if I let her. I suppose it's a novelty, being from Birmingham. Not much sea around there."

"So it's working out well?"

"Oh yes. And Mr and Mrs Baker are very kind, as always."

Charles lifts a loose hair from her collar, twists open a couple of buttons and finds her naked breast under the silk of her blouse. A warm flush spreads across her neck, rises to her face. She takes a deep breath, tries to continue.

"They're glad of the money, of course. They're feeding her up well ...". Her voice trails away. She presses herself hard against his body and kisses him urgently, penetrating deep into his mouth.

Minutes later, she lifts his hand away from her breast, pushes him gently away.

"Not now," she says. "We promised ourselves we wouldn't do this here. You're leading me into bad ways."

He smiles.

"I'd better have a look at her. And after that you and I can head out for dinner. I've booked a table at The Albion."

"Is your room comfortable?" He pulls her close again, closes his eyes as he buries his face in her hair.

"You can decide that for yourself later, my dearest Lilian."

She laughs coquettishly, pushes him away, buttons her blouse and smoothes her skirt.

It's a perfect way to carry on an affair. Things were getting dangerous for them in Birmingham, he and his family too well known in the city. Here only Mr and Mrs Baker know the truth, and they are rewarded for their discretion with a steady supply of young convalescents.

When he's not there she thinks how they will spend their stolen time, the long night they will spend together when he next comes to Broadstairs. Not a moment will be wasted. The time they are apart just heightens her longing.

He satisfies her completely and after his visits she is content to fall back into her quiet routine, the retiring young spinster who leads a respectable life in this dignified seaside town.

* * *

Beryl has been at Broadstairs for two weeks, but this is the first time she has been in Mrs Baker's front parlour. One electric bar of the shiny chrome fire has been switched on but the room still feels chilly. Heavy lace encrusted curtains dim what is left of the afternoon light and obliterate the view of the street beyond the bay window. Charles Ainsworth peers at his young patient.

"How are we doing, young lady?"

"I'm all right thank you," she says.

"Are they looking after you?"

"Yes, everyone is very kind." She falters, raises her eyes warily to his. "When do you think I can go home?"

"Well, let's see how things are looking. Come over here, under this light where I can see you."

He moves her over to the floor lamp, reaches under the deep brown fringe of the big velvet shade for the switch.

"Right, just stand here." He adjusts her head gently, scrutinises his handiwork on the side of her neck. "That's healed nicely." He levels her head, feels the rest of her neck. "We've caught that gland in plenty of time. And you're looking a lot better. Mrs Baker says you've put on weight. That's a good sign. I'll write to your mother today, tell her how well you're doing."

At the mention of her mother Beryl looks anxious.

"I think maybe another three or four weeks here, Beryl, and then I'll be satisfied you're strong enough to tackle Birmingham again." He can see her dejection, the droop of her shoulders. "Try and be brave. You're doing very well. Keep on with your walks. Plenty of fresh air and keep taking your Virol." She shrinks further into herself. "It's the best tonic. Full of vitamins to build you up."

* * *

November drags on. Most days the sky is gloomy grey but sometimes they get a morning of crisp air and sunshine. Whatever the weather, her routine is the same.

Miss Alexander takes her to the public library. She discovers new books. She discovers that when you are reading, the world in the book can become more important than the real world. Temporarily she can forget how unhappy she is.

At night Mrs Baker lights a nightlight for her. She's always still awake when it splutters and dies. She lies looking into the darkness, wondering what is happening at home. Will the cats be asleep in the dolls house? Will Mummy still be downstairs? Denise will have been asleep for ages. She realises, to her surprise, that she even misses Maud though not the horrible cold Ovaltine Maud dumps on her bedside table every night.

And then, at the end of that long month, Dr Ainsworth comes to visit and says she can go home. She thinks she will burst with happiness. She'll be in time to help the staff put up the tree and she'll be there for the Christmas party.

Mrs Baker packs her up a lunch parcel for the journey, gives her a kiss and waves her off in the taxi. At Broadstairs station Miss Alexander hands her over to the guard. He stows her suitcase and settles her in the ladies' carriage. It's a long journey, halfway across England, but she doesn't mind. This time the train is going the right way.

* * *

Harry is sent to the station to meet her. Gladys told him to allow plenty of time. Hopeless Harry, on the wrong platform, stands and waits and wonders what's keeping the train.

On another platform Beryl's train arrives. Everyone gets off the train and heads for the exit. There is so much noise and bustle that even when the steam clears no-one notices the little girl with blonde curls and a suitcase standing next to the puzzled guard. He looks at his watch. She tries not to cry.

Time moves on. The father on one platform, the child somewhere else. The station echoes with the announcements of trains coming and going. Then Harry hears his name over the loudspeaker. He is to go to the ticket office. There she is, frightened, tired but above all angry. He eyes her warily, tries to hug her, crouching to her level.

"We can go to the restaurant," he pleads. "I'll buy you a cake." She shakes her head, eyes brimming. "You can choose anything you want."

She won't speak to him. She wants to go straight home, to tell her mother about her stupid father who waited on the wrong platform. All these weeks she'd imagined coming home, falling into his arms when she got off the train.

He picks up her suitcase and follows his flouncing daughter out of the station. Back at The Court no-one will speak to him. Then it starts.

"How could you!" shouts Gladys. "Head in the clouds! You should be ashamed of yourself."

"I am ashamed, Glad. I'm full of remorse." He puts his head to one side.

"And don't think you can charm me this time, Harry Watson! You think that'll get you out of this? Well, you're wrong!!" She folds her arms, her head pounding with exasperation.

He pulls a sad face, gazes at her wistfully, like Chaplin's tramp.

Spring 1934

A light blazing. He is standing over her. Gladys drags herself out of sleep. She turns her head to look at the clock. Ten past two. She groans, rolls over, pulls the sheet over her head.

"What are you doing?"

"Glad!" He rocks her shoulder with a trembling hand. "You've got to wake up!"

"Leave me alone."

"No, Glad. Wake up! I've had a terrible thing happen!" Sighing, her eyes screwed up against the light, she pushes his hand away and props herself up on her elbow.

"Why aren't you in bed?"

"I fell asleep in the armchair." She narrows her eyes.

"Well, that's the whisky. You'll have to stop all this drinking at the end of the evening."

"And I woke up ... just ... a few minutes ago ..."

"Yes?"

"Yes. And a voice ...," Harry is shaking now, "... a voice ... sounded like Tommy..."

"Tommy?" Gladys shakes herself fully awake. "Tommy Chantry?" Harry nodded. "Harry, Tommy's been dead for two years."

"It was him, in the radiogram, speaking to me."

"Speaking to you?" She looks incredulous. She looks closely at Harry, at the sweat pouring down his face. "So, what did he say?"

"He said ..."

"Come on, Harry, what do you think Tommy said to you?"

"He said ...", he takes a deep breath, "he said 'Look after your lungs, Harry'."

Gladys stares in disbelief, then she bursts out laughing.

"You were dreaming!"

"No!" She hears the panic in his voice and tries to compose her face. "I was awake. I know I was awake."

"For goodness sake! Of course you weren't." Harry sits on the bed, takes her by the shoulders, makes her look at him, to acknowledge his fear.

"I *know* I was awake." She knows she has to reason with him if she is to get any sleep.

"Harry, you were tired. You'd had a drink. You've got a cough, a smoker's cough, that's all. Ian's told you it's nothing. But it must have been on your mind. You fell asleep, dreamt that you heard Tommy." Harry listens, calmer now.

"I didn't dream it." He is emphatic. "You know my mother's always said I'm psychic."

"All right." She pauses. "So just come to bed now. There's nothing you can do about it." Gladys pushes up her pillows, preparing to go back to sleep.

"I can't go back in the sitting room. You'll have to get up and turn the radiogram and the lights off."

"Oh, for goodness sake!" She looks at him, exasperated. "We'll be good for nothing in the morning."

She climbs into her dressing gown and goes down the shadowy hall to the sitting room, checks the ashtray is cold, switches off the lamp by his chair, puts the bottle back in the cabinet.

She pauses, looks at the radiogram, sees it is unplugged. She had thought that maybe Harry had fallen asleep and the sound of the machine, on a low volume, had entered his dreams. She is still quite sure that Harry was dreaming. His imagination is vivid. To be sure he has, on occasions, had the odd premonition that could be put down to some sort of psychic powers, but to hear a voice in the radiogram which wasn't switched on. Gladys shakes her head.

Turning to the window, looking down into the shadows of the street far below, she thinks carefully, for the first time, about Harry's cough. It must be worrying him, even if he doesn't say so. She realises now they've been living with the cough for a long time. Harry needs to see someone, get a proper examination, not just take Ian's word for it that he's fine. He'll need a shove, she thinks, to do it. She'll make enquiries. Sort someone out for him to see.

"Glad!" Harry's frame fills the doorway, silhouetted against the shadowy light from the hall.

"What?"

"Come to bed. I can't stay on my own."

She sighs, makes her way back to the bedroom with Harry towering over her, following close behind her.

"Leave the light on," he says.

"This is ridiculous."

"It's no good. I'm all shaken up."

"I can't possibly sleep with this light on."

"You'll have to. There's something strange been going on tonight in this flat. I'm not sleeping in the dark."

Gladys turns to the wall, tries to settle down, pulls the sheets and blankets over her eyes, blotting out the light as well as she can. Harry lies on his back, staring at the ceiling, unable to get the voice out of his head. However much Glad might think he'd been dreaming, he knows he was awake in that room. It'd been so quiet, sitting there, about to get up and go to bed.

He'd been thinking about Tommy, a regular at The Oak, in the bowls team, a good customer and friend, who'd dropped down dead one morning before he'd even had his breakfast. He'd been thinking that it was about three years ago since Tommy died.

He shudders, turns on his side and moves over the bed to the warmth of Gladys. By the time he falls asleep, the dawn light is finding its way into the room.

* * *

Summer 1935

Harry has always enjoyed a drink. Gladys hasn't minded much and often joins him for a snifter at the end of the evening. But things are changing. Now Harry looked like a man who *needs* a drink, and often he'll start the evening with a whiskey in the flat even before he's got downstairs to the bar. He can hold his drink well. Not many people would notice a difference in him. But Gladys, back in the flat at the end of the evening, bears the brunt.

"Flirting! Harry, this is ridiculous. What are you talking about?"

"You know what I mean, Glad."

"No, I don't. Explain yourself."

They were standing facing one another in the sitting room. Harry had gone straight for the brandy. They didn't know Beryl was awake. She wanted to block out the voices but instead she lay in bed, stiff and still, hardly breathing. In the sitting room, Harry eyed Gladys accusingly.

"You've always liked to be the centre of attention. But it's getting worse –"

"Harry –"

"No, I'll say it now I've started. Let's be frank. It's the men. You like it when you get their attention."

Gladys looks stunned. She throws back her head, sets her jaw at Harry.

"How can you say that? Down there," she jabs a finger angrily towards the floor, "down there in the lounge and restaurant, I am doing my job. I am making sure the customers are happy."

"Yes, making sure the men are happy, Glad." He lifts his glass to his lips, stares down at her blearily.

"No Harry. That's not true and you know it!" Beryl lies quite still, hears her father's strangely harsh laugh. "What's got into you?"

"Nothing's got into me. I'm just telling you, Glad, what I see."

Gladys stands in the middle of the room, half her husband's size, feet planted firmly apart, her dress, which she finished sewing that afternoon, shimmering under the electric light. She takes a deep breath.

"I'm not standing here listening to any more of your rubbish, Harry. You don't know what you're talking about –"

"Oh, I think I do," he snipes.

"You're drunk and you're not yourself."

"I'm telling you the truth."

"Well, you're wrong. You sound like a fool. I'm going to bed." She makes for the door but he stands in her way, grasps her shoulders. "Let me go, Harry."

"Glad." She looks up. His eyes are bloodshot. His face looks gaunt. "It's because I love you, Glad. That's why I'm telling you."

She pushes him away, folds her arms.

"Well, it's a funny way of showing you love me. You'd better shut up. Just remember, I never wanted to come to The Court in the first place."

"But you like it now, Glad. You like the life."

"Yes, Harry, I admit it's been more of a success than I thought it would be. But I've given up a lot to be here. We've given up a real family life. And you need to remember, when we're with the customers, we're working, and if I'm helping to keep the customers because they like talking to me then you should count yourself lucky."

She spins away from him, out of the room without another word. On the way to the bedroom she checks on Beryl who, lying heavy hearted in the dark, feigns sleep.

* * *

There comes a day when her heart misses a beat. The voice on the other end of the telephone is gentle.

"It might not be serious, Mrs Watson. But from what you're telling me, I need to see him sooner rather than later. You say the cough's been going on for some time."

"Yes. And he's lost some weight."

"And now the blood?"

"He doesn't know I know about that. Please don't say I told you, Doctor. It was only when I found the handkerchiefs, by chance, pushed at the back of his desk draw."

"Anything else you've noticed?"

She hesitates.

"Well, he's not really himself. He's always been quite easy going, but now –", she falters.

"Try not to worry. And I'll be careful what I say to your husband." A brief silence. She can tell he's thinking ahead. "I'll speak to you again, Mrs Watson. After I've seen him."

"Yes, thank you. I'll ring you when he is out of the way."

"That will be fine. You have my address?"

"Yes. Brearley House, Grange Road."

"That's it. It shouldn't take too long to get to Small Heath from the city centre. Wednesday then, ten o'clock. Ask Mr Watson to ring the bell. My nurse will let him in."

"And after the consultation, please send your bill to me."

"As you wish." She senses the end of the conversation. "Good day, Mrs Watson."

She replaces the receiver, stands very still in the hall of the flat, listening to the distant sounds from the kitchen and working the tip of a thumbnail against her teeth. She knows in her heart it's serious.

* * *

"Flirting!" Nancy looks incredulous. "You, Glad?"

"Yes. He started the other night and he's still going on about it. He's like a dog with a bone. It's when he's been drinking."

"Is this about your jeweller, do you think?"

"My jeweller?" Gladys looks up from taking off her gloves, stares at her friend across the table. "You mean Martin?" Nancy nods. "Gracious, Nancy. There's nothing going on with Martin Langdon. He's not mine at all."

"Well, he always seems to make a beeline for you when he comes into the restaurant."

"But that doesn't mean we're up to anything. Come on Nancy, don't you start."

"No, sorry, I'm just trying to work out why Harry should be feeling jealous."

"It's the drink," says Gladys, with a hint of pique. "I've told you that already."

"Since when has he started all this drinking?"

"Since his cough's got worse. He says he's got a pain in his chest now and the drink helps. Fat chance. Just an excuse." The waitress appears at their table. "What are you having, Nancy?"

"Just a coffee."

"We'll make that two, waitress." Gladys sits back, slides her fingers along the edge of the table and regards Nancy nervously. "He's just not himself. What with the short temper and he keeps going on about his 'psychic experience' as he calls it."

"That was strange though, wasn't it?"

"It's playing on his mind. I appreciate that Ian has told him not to worry, but I've arranged for a second opinion. I hope Ian will understand."

"I'm sure he will. After all, Ian isn't officially his doctor."

"And he hasn't seen Harry for a few weeks. There's quite a change in him. He looks as though he's losing weight. Things don't feel right."

"Men. They make life so difficult at times."

Gladys notices for the first time the dark rings under Nancy's eyes, how drawn she looks. She pushes her own worries to one side.

"How are you getting on then?"

"I'm not so good either. I still feel depressed."

"Have you been back to the doctor?"

"Yes. He's tried me on some different pills but they haven't really helped. I just feel as though I'm living in a fog all the time."

"Are you sleeping any better?"

"No. Ian's moved into the spare room. He needs his sleep and if I'm awake I need to put the light on and read a book. I can't just lie there hour after hour in the dark."

"That's no good. I can't imagine not having Harry in with me." Nancy fiddles with the spoon in the sugar.

"To be honest," she says, "there's not much point in our sharing a bed these days. If you know what I mean." Gladys shakes her head, purses her lips.

"It's a great shame. You like this all the time."

"Some days seem better than others." Nancy tries a weak smile "You know Gladys, whatever the doctors say and however much they make out it's not the case, I'm just so sure all this started after Bunny was born."

"Well, I had the baby blues. I remember it well. It was awful. Especially with Beryl."

"Yes, but this is different. It's like those baby blues never went away for me. And Ian admits I was different before I had Bunny."

"You did say you'd read a book about all this?"

"Yes. There are a few psychologists now who think there is a connection." Nancy smiles. "You'll see, Gladys. One day it'll be different. One day the medics might just have to say that women like me knew what we were talking about."

"And in the meantime you just go on suffering. You and me, we're a glum old pair today."

Nancy looks at Gladys.

"Tell you what. Let's give ourselves a treat. We'll do our shopping and then we'll have lunch at The Grand. My treat. And we'll start with cocktails!"

Gladys' eyes light up.

"You're on! That's the best idea anyone's had for days."

* * *

He greets her in the vestibule that leads off the entrance hall of Brearley House and serves as a waiting room. She looks vulnerable and pale against the deep buttoned upholstery of her chair. She is leafing through a copy of Woman's Pictorial, which his wife reads and then puts out for the patients. He shakes her hand, leads her across the hall to his surgery, opens the door, gestures for her to enter, watching her, weighing her up.

The room has a large bay window which looks onto the front drive and Grange Road beyond. There is a faint smell of antiseptic. The ceiling is high with an eight branched candelabra suspended from an ornate plaster centrepiece.

On one wall hang a set of prints of restful landscapes. Alongside the opposite wall is a high couch with crisp white sheeting and a pillow. The fourth wall, opposite the window and behind the doctor's desk, is taken up with a tall glass fronted cabinet housing rows of pharmaceuticals: boxes, jars and bottles of pills, medicines and ointments.

His rosewood desk takes up the space in the centre of the room. On the desk, in front of his chair, the inkstand gleams behind a neatly arranged leather-framed blotter holding a thick sheet of cream blotting paper.

He is trained, of course, to observe people. He calculates she is about his age. In the waiting room he'd already guessed her height, noticed her feet, her shoes, polished and buckled and hardly touching the floor as she sat in the chair. He watches her as she lays her gloves on her handbag and loosens her jacket. She looks quite calm as she leans back in the chair opposite his desk. He notices her hands. Good skin, he thinks, that won't age much, and the way her hair springs from under the brim of her hat, lightly hennaed, quite becoming.

He isn't fooled. The composure is a show. Just between the eyebrows he can see a puckering. He guesses she is probably suffering with a headache. And the neck and shoulders. He can see the tension there too.

They speak briefly about her journey. She took a taxi, she says. The traffic had been very light. It had taken under half an hour.

Now the room is quiet. The trivialities that pave the way for two people meeting for the first time are over and the business that has brought them together must begin.

He takes a foolscap-sized folder from a draw and places it on his blotting pad. He does everything slowly, leans on the folder, regards her across the desk, notices that her eyes are green.

"How was Mr Watson after my consultation with him?"

She thinks back to a week ago, knowing that she must speak the truth.

"I have to be honest, Dr Eades. He arrived home at lunchtime and he spent the rest of the afternoon drinking." He doesn't look surprised.

"Hit the bottle, did he?"

"Yes." She waits for a reaction but he gestures for her to continue. "By the time he was needed downstairs in our restaurant in the evening he could barely stand up. He was in bed by eight o'clock." She pauses, weighing up how much to explain to him. "I went down on my own to sort things out. We have very good staff. We managed quite well. And it's happened a few times since. It's not easy. We have two daughters. And we live on the premises of our business. My husband, he's quite argumentative when he's been drinking." She falters, her throat too tight to carry on for the moment. Why, she thinks, am I saying so much to a man I've only just met?

"How old are your daughters?"

"Four and twelve. Denise, she'll be five in December."

He smiles, "I have daughters too. Just a little younger than yours. What's your other girl's name?"

"Beryl. She was twelve in July."

"And she's at school, of course?"

"Yes. Amberley Preparatory." She starts to relax a little.

"I've heard of it. At Ward End. Two ladies run it, don't they?"

"Yes, Miss Ainsworth and Miss Major. We've been very pleased with it. Beryl's happy there."

"So, if you're in Corporation Street, how does Beryl go to school?"

"Oh, on the bus. It was a tram when we first arrived but now it's a bus. She catches it just outside The Court, on the James Watt Street side."

"She's very independent then?"

"Very!"

He clears his throat, puts another question.

"How did your husband feel about having an X-ray?"

"He wasn't at all happy. I'm afraid he felt it was an unnecessary expense and he complained about you arranging it for the following day. All in a rush, so to speak."

"Is there anything else you would like to tell me?"

She looks across the desk at the softly spoken, gentle doctor. Oh yes, she thinks. So much I could say. But if I do I'll end up putting my head down on this desk and weeping.

"No," she manages. "That's all really."

He opens the folder but doesn't need to refer to the few papers it reveals. He has read them all, knows what he has to say to her.

"Mrs Watson," he starts carefully, feeling his way. "There is no easy way to say this." He can tell she is bracing herself. "So I'll come straight to the point." He sees the lines on her brow deepen, the hands turn over to grip the arms of the chair. "Your husband has tuberculosis." He pauses. "It is very established."

"Established?"

"Yes. The X-ray shows he has had it for some time."

"For some time?"

"Yes." He waits now, gives her time to absorb what he has said so far. He thinks he knows what she will say next. People want to know about the treatment, never accept to begin with that nothing can be done. But he is wrong.

"He's dying, isn't he, Doctor." It isn't a question and he understands he must respond with honesty.

"Yes, Mrs Watson. There is nothing I can do to cure him. If I'd seen him earlier I could have helped him but both lungs are affected. Badly, I'm afraid."

She leans to one side of the chair, one elbow on the arm of the chair. She rests her head in her hand, massages her temples, her mind racing as she looks straight ahead at him. He waits.

"How long, Doctor? How long have we got?"

"I can't say for sure. But the report on the X-ray seems to suggest that it will be a matter of months."

"Months!"

Now the shock is coming. Any colour she had drains from her cheeks. Her head drops. She holds the edge of his desk with both hands as though to steady herself. He waits for anger, maybe, or disbelief. But he's wrong again. She releases her hold on the desk, presses her palms down purposefully on its smooth top and reunites with his gaze.

"Then I'll have to ask you to help us." She breathes heavily. "Tell me what I must do. I shall have to rely on you." She is in control now. He is the one who is taken aback.

"I will do all I can."

"I want you to take us on. See us through this."

* * *

Maud asks to see "the missus" in private. There's a lurch of panic from Gladys that she is going to hand in her notice. Gladys barely has time to close the door to the sitting room before Maud starts.

"Mr Watson. He's very sick, isn't he." Maud isn't afraid of what she says, isn't going to mince her words just because this is the missus she's tackling. Gladys sighs, searches Maud's broad face, framed in the black, nun-like headdress that she favours as part of her uniform.

"Yes. You're right. He's very ill."

"He looks to me like he's wasting. And he's sleeping a lot in the day."

"Yes. He is."

"And the cough. I can hear him at night-time."

Gladys makes a decision to be honest with Maud.

"Sit down, Maud." She gestures to one of the armchairs. Maud lowers herself squarely onto the edge of the seat, plants her legs slightly apart, feet flat on the ground, the black serge of her skirt falling around her calves. Gladys thinks sadly, Maud has a lap that was made for babies. She dreads what she is about to say.

"My husband has TB. He doesn't know and I want it kept that way. I don't think he could cope if he knew. It's very advanced. And the doctors can't help him." She pauses, waiting for Maud, who seems to be concentrating on the hearth, to absorb what she has said. "I don't know what lies ahead. Our future looks very bleak. If you feel, Maud –," she takes a deep breath, "if you feel you don't want to be part of it, then I will understand."

Gladys can't say any more, sits down shakily on the sofa. She can feel bile burning her throat and her hands are trembling. Dear God, she thinks, let me keep this solid, reliable woman. I need her so much.

Maud's smooth face takes on a thunderous change. She heaves herself out of her chair, squares up to Gladys, her big hands planted on her hips.

"If you think", she starts, "if you think that I'm leaving you and Miss Denise and Miss Beryl too, if you think I'm leaving you now then you've another think coming. I'm not going anywhere." She stops for breath. "I'm surprised you'd even thought that of me. An' that's all there is to it!"

* * *

Sitting alone at Harry's desk, she gives herself a minute. Gladys knows she and the children are heading for catastrophe. If she lets her thoughts get the better of her, the future overwhelms her with dread. Every day she tries to keep her mind on practicalities. She daren't examine her feelings too closely. They lie, full of dread, like a stone in her chest. She can feel the weight of them as she wakes each day and she carries them with her through her waking hours.

To begin with Gladys has kept the grim diagnosis to herself. Harry seems to be convinced that if he rests he will recover. If he ever suspects that he is dying he never speaks of it to Gladys and she isn't going to tell him. But once she has told Maud she knows it's time to face up to things, that she can no longer try and fool herself that things can carry on as normal.

Gradually she tells the people close to her, and especially the people she will need to rely on in the months ahead. She writes to Vi and she meets up with Pip, who returns to Worcester reeling with shock, promising to explain everything to the family.

She takes Daisy England and Nancy into her confidence and agrees that they should tell their husbands. Ian Gordon is shaken. He had been so sure that Harry's cough was nothing. But that had been some time ago. If Ian had seen his friend in recent weeks he might have urged him to take action, such is the change.

The hardest part has been writing to Harry's parents. Now they are coping in the only way they can, by carrying on with their lives in Nottingham and their daily routine. But, like his son in Birmingham, Harry Senior is adding too many extra whiskies to his daily drinking.

Emma Watson comes down to The Court at the end of November to see for herself. One look at Harry and she knows this will be the last time she sees him. She does her best, holds her heartache close, tries not to burden Gladys with her pain, but Gladys isn't fooled. She's already lost one boy to asthma. With Harry gone there will only be her daughters, Dorothy at home and difficult, troubled Gertie wreaking havoc.

Gladys sighs, looks down the ledger in front of her on the desk, enters a few figures. Promptly, at two o'clock, there is a knock at the door. She puts down her pen, crosses the room and opens the door.

"Come in Edith."

Edith Pendle, manageress of the downstairs bars at The Court, is a tall, big bosomed woman who keeps herself well corseted. You could pass a hundred Ediths every day in Corporation Street, going about their jobs in shops and offices, catching a minute to themselves at bus stops with a shopping bag and a ciggie.

Gladys gestures to the one spare seat, Beryl's favourite, the revolving typist's chair. She starts by asking Edith about her daughter who is training to be a teacher. Then she tells her about Harry.

"I guessed something was up. He's stopped coming down to the bar first thing. Now I only see him every few days. I asked him the other day if he was poorly."

"What did he say?"

"That he'd got a virus."

"That's what he thinks, or at least that's what he tells everyone. I'm not going to tell him." Edith frowns. "If he can go along like this it'll be better for us all.

"I've asked you to come up because I want to discuss how we're going to manage. How would you feel about doing some of your hours up here? I know you were office trained and it shows in your paperwork. You're never a penny out on your books nor a bottle short on your stocktaking." Gladys can see interest in Edith's eyes. "I've spoken to Mr Watson and he thinks it's a good idea. He thinks it'll be temporary, of course. If you agree, we'll arrange a rise for you. You wouldn't be expected to take on extra work for the same wages." Edith doesn't hesitate.

"Yes, I'll do it. The extra money will be useful but I'll do it because I want to help. I'll enjoy it too. Like you say, I'll know what I'm doing with the paperwork."

"Do you want to think it over? Talk to Mr Pendle about it?"

"Mr Pendle doesn't need talking to. I've said I'll do it."

And so it is arranged. Edith will work in the office in the afternoons but will still oversee the bottom bars in the evening. No-one runs those bars like Edith, Harry says. She smells trouble before it starts. When she judges a man is too drunk to serve she's never challenged and she can match the toughest of publicans when it comes to turning a troublesome customer off the premises.

Gladys closes the door on Edith, feels satisfied with the interview, knows she can rely on her to keep things going in the office as much as she can leave her domestic arrangements to Maud.

She feels like an army general mustering the troops.

* * *

Do you tell what you've heard? Do you tell what you've seen? Who could you tell anyway? Mother too busy, so tired all the time, only stopping to sleep and to eat and to swallow pills for her headaches, closing the door on her whilst she speaks on the telephone in a low voice. She can't speak to

Mother. She won't tell Maud. There's no-one at school. She's not going to tell at all.

What did she hear? What did she see?

Sunday morning. The Court still and quiet. Mummy at church. Beryl knows Daddy's poorly but maybe, if he's gone downstairs, he's feeling all right today. Maybe, even, there'll be time for some billiards in the games room. She'd like that. They haven't played for ages.

Where is he? Not in his office. Not in the games room. And then she hears him. In the little bathroom next to the office.

She sees him doubled up, gripping the sides of the basin. She edges further round the doorway, smells something sickly. He coughs his rasping cough, heaves again, and it's not sick coming from his mouth but long, ghastly trails of bloody phlegm dropping slowly into the basin.

She turns and runs. Hurls herself back upstairs, slams her bedroom door, falls on her bed. She can hear her heart thumping. She is freezing cold and trembling. She feels sick.

She won't tell. She'll never tell, now she has seen. Something terrible is happening. She'll never say. If she does, someone might explain. She doesn't want to know. She will wait. Someone will have to do something. Sooner or later something will happen. She will wait. And she definitely won't tell.

* * *

January 1935

The kitchens are throbbing with gossip. Summat bad going on. The missus' is running the show. Edith Prendle's got 'er feet under the table, all right. Staying up in the flat now. Not going 'ome in the evenings. An' there's that same doctor keeps calling. Summat bad going on with the master. Summat serious. Any road you looks at it, that's what it boils down to.

They shut up when Cook is there. Cook Eleker keeps her distance from her staff. She's long ago formed a truce with Maud from which a grudging companionship has emerged. So Cook, through Maud, knows what's happening on the other side of the kitchen doors.

What was it Maud said the other day? They all know, she said, but no-one's saying nothing. The missus running herself ragged, even with Mrs Pendle to help, and Miss Beryl flopping around all pale and teary. Good thing the Christmas holidays are over. She's better off at school. Lucky Miss Denise is only five. At least she doesn't know what's going on.

"And Mr Watson? What about him? What d'you think he knows?" Maud shrugs.

"I don't know. He's getting worse. He must know how ill he is. But he still says he'll be better in the spring. And she's definite. No-one is to let on."

Cook and Maud sink into silence. They are sitting in Cook's office. They call it her office, but it's more like a large cupboard with sliding doors off the main kitchen. Cook just has room for a small table where she writes her orders and a couple of old chairs from downstairs upon which she and Maud are now seated whilst on the table is a large flowered china teapot, oddly matched but dainty cups and saucers and a plate of biscuits.

"There's a lot of coming and going," continues Maud. "That Doctor Eades, he's a lovely man. Takes the time to stop and speak to me. Asks how we're getting on. And there's the Worcester lot. Mrs Lancaster's been. She and the missus, they're as thick as ever. Shut themselves away in the sitting room. I never get to hear what's going on."

"I expect the missus gets it off her chest to Mrs Lancaster. They've always been close."

"Yes." She frowns. "But Mrs Lancaster's had a bad time herself, what with losing that lovely little baby. Terrible, that was." Maud stirs her tea, helps herself to a biscuit. "It's over three years now. The time flies."

"Who else comes?"

"Mrs Gordon calls in. She always does Mrs Watson good. Takes her out of herself. And Mrs England. I'm not sure she's much help, but she's sticking by. There's a lot goes on behind closed doors though, that I don't get to hear." Cook sighs.

"Mr Watson. He's in the middle of it all?"

"He's in the middle all right," says Maud, "but that doesn't mean anyone says much about it to him."

"It's terrible. Whatever will the missus do without him? When he's gone?"

"I don't know. He's the life and soul." She takes a second biscuit. "These are nice."

"They're left overs. From the meeting in the lounge this morning. Lot of big wigs from over the road."

"Lawyers?"

"I suppose so. We gave them these with the coffee when they arrived. Then they had a lunch after the meeting."

"I can't see what's going to happen here," continues Maud.

"And what's Edith Pendle doing in amongst it all?"

"She's moved in. She's in the spare room." Cook sniffs disapproval, but Maud puts up her hand to stop her from speaking. "She's all right. I don't know what they'd be doing without her. And she's good with the master. She makes him think he's still in charge. Brings the paperwork up for him to have a look at. That sort of thing."

"And you say Miss Beryl's not right?"

"She keeps herself to herself at the best of times. I've never fathom'd her. And I'm not there for her."

Cook nods but doesn't say anything. She feels sorry for Miss Beryl who isn't any trouble and thanks Cook nicely when she makes something special for her after school. It's always the way. You get a child like that who's no trouble and so no-one takes any notice of her. Maud puts her cup and saucer down.

"Up until now she's always been outdoors roaming around Corporation Street or goodness knows where. You never used to know what she was up to. Or else she'd have her head stuck in a book. But not now. Not any longer.

"Now she's just keeping to her room. And when I look in, she's just lying on the bed doing nothing."

* * *

Beryl comes home from school and finds that yet again her father has been in bed since the morning. Both the Siamese cats are stretched out on the eiderdown, their chins on their front paws, alert to whoever comes into the room. It's as though they are guarding him.

She envies them. She wants to lie down close to him but she's been told she has to make do with the doorway.

"No further, Miss Beryl," Maud warns. "We don't want the two of you to nurse." When Maud has gone, Harry rolls his eyes to the ceiling as if to say what a fuss, and Beryl crosses her arms and does the same thing back.

She leans against the doorpost and watches him. The heat from the gas fire feels stifling and intensifies the sweaty sick room smell which, in future years, always brings her back to this doorway. Her father is muffled under the bedclothes. She can see he is wearing his everyday cardigan over his pyjamas.

"When you're better –" she tails off.

"When I'm better?"

"When you're better, can we go to Malvern?"

"Yes, we can do that."

"We always used to go to Malvern, didn't we? Just you and me. When I was little and we were in Worcester."

"We did." He leans back against the pillows, keeps his hand on his handkerchief. His breathing has changed today from a laboured wheeze to a rattling rasp.

"On the bus?"

"Yes, on the bus."

"Just you and me."

"Just us."

"And we can climb up the hills again? And go to that tea shop?"

"The Kettle Sings."

"Yes. Nice cakes."

"Better than at Lyons?"

She thinks for a minute.

"Different. And we'll go to Lyons too, Daddy. And the Art Gallery."

"Yes."

She eyes him narrowly.

"When are you going to start getting better?"

"Soon."

"Promise?"

"I'll do my best." He closes his eyes for a few moments. The thought of making a promise to her is unbearable. "In the spring. When it's warmer."

He steers her away from talk of himself.

"How's school?"

"Fine."

"Are they still calling you Soapy?"

"Yes."

"Do you mind?"

"Not much."

"It's since people started using Watson's soap."

"I know." She pauses. "But you did say we're not related to the soap Watsons." He smiles.

"No love, it's just coincidence. Ignore them. It's a good name. Think about Sherlock Holmes. What does he call Dr Watson?"

"Dear Watson?"

"Yes. Well, that's what you are. Not soapy at all." The effort of speaking is hurting, the breathing short and shallow. "You, your sister, your mother. You're all my dear Watsons. You're –"

Suddenly he's caught by a violent choking, leaning forward, holding his chest. She can see sweat on his face and tears in his eyes. She turns away. He can't do any more talking now. She thinks the tears are because of the coughing.

* * *

Later that night when Beryl is asleep the phone rings in the hall. Gladys picks up the receiver.

"Gladys. It's Daisy."

There's a silence. Daisy isn't sure whether she is still connected.

"Gladys?"

"Hello Daisy." Gladys' voice is flat. She sounds exhausted.

"You phoned earlier. I'm sorry I wasn't in. I've just been given the message. Are you all right?"

"No. I'm waiting for the doctor. He should be here any minute."

"What's happening?"

"I can't talk." Gladys lowers her voice. "Harry's door's open. He might hear me."

"I'm coming over. I'll get a taxi. I'll be with you shortly."

* * *

Friday 1st February 1935

All night the wind screamed against the window, pulling Beryl awake, muffling the sounds that she was straining to catch. Doors opening and closing. Low talking. At one point she thought she heard someone shouting. Earlier, her father's cough again. Did she dream the crying?

Now she struggles from sleep and pulls her hair away from her face. She cannot recognise the grown-up standing in the bedroom doorway against the light from the hall.

"Your Father's gone."

Far below, from the street, comes the clatter of the early trams. Here, at the top of the building, the world is still. Beryl raises herself on one elbow.

Tries to get her brain to make sense. The person in the doorway is Mrs England. Her chest starts to tighten.

"Gone where?"

"To a better place. No more suffering for him."

"Where's my Mother?"

"Busy. You're not to bother her."

"What's going to happen?"

"They're going to sort out what to do with you later today."

She starts to tremble.

"Can't I stay here?"

"I should think not!" Daisy England folds her arms. She's not going to keep answering Beryl's questions.

Silence. Except for the trams.

"I'm to take you to see him."

"Why?"

"You have to say goodbye."

The electric light snaps on, dangling from the ceiling, thrusting the dawn at the window back into darkness.

"Here's your dressing gown. Don't cry if you see your mother. She's got enough on her plate. You've got to be brave."

Throughout her life, whenever Beryl looks back on that morning, all she can remember is Mrs England standing in her doorway as she woke, and then, in her parents' bedroom, her father looking so small on the high bed. She could have imagined he was sleeping save for the indignity with which they'd knotted a handkerchief round his head to hold his jaw in place.

Beryl puts her hand over her mouth. She thinks she might be sick.

And then Maud brings in Denise. Lucky little sister, thinks Beryl. Being carried in Maud's arms.

She isn't sick. Silently, she follows Maud out of the room.

Her mother is nowhere to be seen.

* * *

At Nancy and Ian's house, very early that morning, the telephone cuts through the peace. This time it isn't a patient needing a visit from Ian, but Edith Pendle for Nancy. She tells Nancy the news and moves swiftly onto practical matters.

"Mrs England's here," she explains. "She's been here all night. But she's very tired, needs to go home really. And –", Edith tries to be tactful, standing in the hall of the flat where everyone can hear, "– and maybe it would be a good thing for Mrs Watson to see *you,* Mrs Gordon."

"I'll come, of course." Nancy looks at her watch. "Give me an hour and I'll be there."

* * *

"Gladys!" Nancy grasps her by the shoulders. The wind howls down Corporation Street, whipping debris across the pavement. Gladys is coatless and bareheaded, her hair flying back from her face. "Come on. Back to the flat."

Teeth chattering, she frowns at Nancy, cradles the zipped case of worn leather close to her chest.

"I have to do the banking –"

"Not now, Gladys. Not this morning. Mrs Pendle will go later. And The Court's closed for today anyway."

Nancy moves one hand to Gladys' elbow, tries to lead her back along the pavement. Gladys looks hostile, gives her friend a hard shove so that Nancy almost loses her balance.

"*I'm* the one who does the banking," she shouts. "Let me go, Nancy. You're in my way."

Passersby on their way to work stare.

Nancy stands her ground, grasps Gladys by both shoulders, forcing her to stand still.

"Gladys dear, look at your feet."

Slowly Gladys steps away from Nancy and looks down at the pavement. She sees her stockinged feet ending in her crimson bedroom slippers. She stares at the pink feathers that trim each shoe, raises her head, blinks at Nancy.

Nancy leads her down Corporation Street, round into James Watt Street and up the back stairs to the flat.

* * *

When Nancy gets home that evening Ian is waiting for her.

"You look done in, old girl. Here, I'll mix you a drink. Martini?"

"Thanks. My head's thumping. I was glad when Eric and Pip arrived. I was ready to come home."

"How long are they staying?"

"Well, a couple of days. They've left Zena with Dora."

"That's a turn up, isn't it?"

"You never know with that family, Ian, who's fallen out and who's in favour." Nancy flops onto the sofa, kicks off her shoes, pulls the cigarette box towards her. "That's a good fire you've got going."

"Yes, Mrs Lawton laid it. I just had to put a match to it half an hour ago. She's left supper too. Cold, so that it would keep if you were late back."

"That's kind."

It seems a long time since the morning when Ian had driven Nancy up to town before his surgery started, dropped her off at The Court.

"So, tell me how you've got on. How's Gladys?"

Nancy inhales deeply, lets a fine stream of smoke escape into the warm air.

"When I got to The Court, Gladys was nowhere to be seen. Daisy England was there, in a panic. Gladys had gone off down the back stairs, coatless and in her bedroom slippers, saying she was going to the bank. And Daisy hadn't been able to stop her."

"Sounds like she was in shock."

"I found her though. In the street. And I managed to persuade her to come back to The Court. It was as though she was in a dream."

"Did you see Harry?"

"Yes, Gladys wanted me to. He looked quite peaceful. They'd tied his jaw up with a handkerchief. Knotted it on top of his head. It seemed so undignified."

"Poor chap." They sit in silence, both staring into the fire.

"Gladys seemed to pull round a little once I got her back to the flat. Then Dr Eades arrived. He'd been there in the night, of course. But he came back again this morning."

"Did you get a chance to talk to him?"

"Not really. He and Gladys were in the sitting room for quite a while. With the door firmly closed." She looks thoughtful. "He's a charming man, you know."

"Yes, I've told you, I've come across him once or twice. He's very well respected locally."

"When they came out she'd been crying, you could see, but she seemed calmer than before. He left her some tablets."

"Tranquilisers, I should think."

"She didn't take them. Said she wanted to keep a clear head."

"Daisy had been there all night?"

"Yes. Gladys told me later, she'd tried to call us first. I explained we'd been at the theatre. So in the end she managed to contact Daisy. She went straight over."

"She's a good sort."

"Once I arrived Daisy went off home and then Gladys wanted to make arrangements for Beryl."

"How was Beryl?"

"Very quiet. She just stayed in her bedroom. I went in once or twice. Sat on the bed. But she didn't want to talk to me. She wanted Gladys really. But Gladys wasn't in much of a state to deal with Beryl."

"So what's happened to her?"

"She's gone to stay with a couple Gladys knows who live near the school. Mr and Mrs Grant. Good customers, I believe. When Glad told them last week what was happening they'd offered to help. They came over to fetch her at lunchtime. Seemed very kind. She's to stay there until the funeral."

"The funeral. What are the arrangements?"

"It's going to be at Worcester. Harry will be buried in the Lancaster plot at Astwood."

"What will Mr and Mrs Watson think about that?"

"Gladys has spoken to them on the telephone. She wants to be able to get to visit the grave easily. She's a lot more likely to be in Worcester than Nottingham. And she certainly doesn't want the funeral in Birmingham. They understood."

"I wonder how they're feeling."

"It's hard to imagine, isn't it. Gladys said the other week that Mr Watson's not at all well so this is going to be another blow. Mrs Watson was very calm on the telephone. And she even managed to talk to Gladys about Beryl. They're going to pay her school fees."

"That's good. It wouldn't have been the right time to move Beryl from Amberley."

"She's very happy there."

"It's the only stable thing in her life, as far as I can see."

"Did you know that Harry had a brother who died of chest problems?"

"Yes. He told me about it once. Asthma."

"And now this."

"Who would have thought it. What's wrong with Mr Watson?"

"Well, it's some debilitating disorder. Gladys isn't really sure. No-one talks about it much. But apparently he looks quite frail and gets very frustrated."

"I bet he does. After the career he had. Retirement's not agreeing with him."

"He's not easy to live with, I gather. He insists on walking everywhere still. He catches the bus up into Nottingham to go to his club in the evenings when really he's not up to it."

"Hmm. Difficult for his wife. And Gladys is still saying none of this would have happened to Harry if they'd stayed at The Oak?"

"Yes. She blames it all on moving to The Court."

"I can remember Harry telling me that Gladys kept on saying it would be the death of them." Ian smiles wryly. "If only he'd known."

"She may have been right. You've said it yourself, Ian. Harry's chest was always weak. And we've often said how bad the smog is in town. It could have made him more susceptible to TB, don't you think? And she didn't want Beryl to be in the middle of the city either."

"You know what, Nancy, I'm not so sure Gladys has done the right thing, sending Beryl to stay with those people."

"Well, that's what's been done. I said we'd have her here but Gladys wants to keep her going to school. It's too far from here, travelling every day. There's nothing we can do about it, Ian. It's up to Gladys."

"Beryl's a little loner at the best of times. This won't help her, sending her to people she hardly knows. First Broadstairs, now this." He shakes his head. "I suppose they're keeping Denise at The Court?"

Nancy gets up impatiently, crosses the room and uncorks a bottle.

"Of course," she snaps. "She's only five. And there's Maud to look after her. It's easy to be critical when you're not involved, Ian. It's no good going on about it. Beryl's gone to stay with the Grants, and that's all there is to be said." Standing by the sideboard, she covers her eyes with a hand. "And poor Gladys, she's got so much on her plate." Her voice breaks. "It's horrible, Ian. Horrible. I dread to think what's going to happen to them. Beryl's feelings are the least of her worries."

* * *

In the dark, half asleep, she reaches for him. Then, as she wakes fully, it crashes over her. The hour hand creeps towards three on the bedside clock. Another forty minutes and she will have got through twenty four hours without him. She starts to panic, then fumbles for the light switch. She can't lie in the dark, letting her mind wander, and she daren't think about the morning.

The room is so cold, she can see her breath. She has a searing pain in her head, bile in her throat. The heaviness in her chest causes her to sag. She presses her lips together hard, massages her temples savagely with her fingertips, fights off the tears. She thinks if she starts to weep now she will never stop.

She gets out of bed, makes her way to the cubby in her nightdress and puts on the kettle. She looks up from warming the pot when she hears footsteps.

"Edith." Edith stands in the doorway, wrapping the two sides of her thick dressing gown round her middle and tying it with a brown tasselled cord. "I'm sorry. I've woken you."

"It's all right. I was half awake anyway."

"Do you want any tea?"

"No. I just wanted to see if you needed anything."

"I'll be all right. I'll take this back to bed. It's too cold to sit around out here. You go along, Edith. Get some sleep if you can."

Edith pads down the hall and Gladys, back in her room, turns the gas tap and strikes a match. The row of little blue flames flicker into life and turn to red as they warm up. She wraps herself in her dressing gown, gets back into bed and props up the brand new pillows in their fresh covers. On Dr Eades' instructions, Edith had called in the cleaners that afternoon. They'd fumigated the room, scrubbed and turned the mattress, made up the bed with clean sheets and new blankets. It feels like a betrayal, thinks Gladys, as though they are trying to eradicate all trace of Harry. But she knows, of course, that it had to be done.

She starts to go over the previous night. Throughout the day she has had to push it all from her, but now she can try to piece things together. Those dreadful hours, they lie around, jumbled and confused.

She knows she was sitting by the bed around midnight trying to keep awake and Harry started choking. He'd turned his face towards her, reached for her hand.

But when were Daisy and Edith standing in the doorway, speaking in low voices? And what time had Dr Eades arrived?

She remembers Daisy taking his coat in the hall. It was raining, he'd said. And that reminds her. The wind. It had howled all night, moaning under the doors and rattling the windows. She'd forgotten about that already. And yet now she remembers talking about it to Edith.

At some point she'd fallen asleep at the side of the bed, with her head on the sweat soaked sheet. When was that? Someone had wrapped a blanket around her. But who was that? And Beryl, crying out? Maud had got up and gone to her, told her she was dreaming, to go back to sleep. It seemed to Gladys that the night had been filled with people, but she couldn't seem to get them into any order.

The only clear memory was of Dr Eades taking Harry's pulse, then leaning forward to listen to his chest. She remembers looking at the alarm clock. It was twenty to four. She knew as he put down his stethoscope and walked round the bed to take her hand. He didn't need to tell her.

* * *

Two women with baskets, turning from a shop window to catch sight of the slowing traffic. Big cars following a hearse, the coffin piled with flowers. People stopping on the pavements, men lifting their hats.

When we've gone past, Gladys thinks, they'll just get on with the business of the day. They'll be thinking they're glad it's not them, in these cars, all done up in black. It's just an ordinary Friday for these people, another grey, winter's afternoon with a few hours to go until the weekend.

She closes her eyes, blots out the strangers on the pavements. Nothing is making sense. This isn't what she and Harry had planned at all. He should be here, with her, in this car, holding her hand. How can he be in that coffin?

Half an hour ago, after the service, Eric had taken her arm and steered her towards the front seat of the car that was to take the women back to Lavender Road. Dora and Pip and Harry's mother already waiting for her. Ian and Nancy standing beside their Ford, talking in low voices to Vi.

"I'll see you later, Gladys," Eric had said. "Pip will look after you until I get back."

She'd stared at her him.

"You think I'm going back to the house *now*?"

"Yes, of course."

"I'm not. I'm coming with you."

"Surely you don't want to come to the cemetery. There's no place for a woman at an interment."

"Of course I'm coming."

"It's not done, Gladys. You can't come. Only the men will be at the cemetery." He tried not to show his irritation. "You've said your goodbyes to Harry, at the church."

"I haven't finished yet. You're not burying Harry, I am." She'd spoken slowly to Eric as though he was from a foreign country and couldn't understand what she was saying, jabbed a finger toward the coffin. "That's my husband and I'll do what I want to do." And then faster, businesslike. "So let's get on with it."

He knew it was pointless to argue, that the last thing he wanted was a scene. Gladys, stubborn at the best of times, stood her ground. Resignedly, he followed her to the car in which Ralph and their father were waiting.

* * *

She stays one night with Pip and Eric. Then she goes back to Birmingham.

It's Maud who points out to her that Miss Beryl has lost weight and goes to the chemist to buy a jar of Virol. She keeps it on a shelf in the cubby and administers a large spoonful of the sticky, brown malt extract each day to build the child up.

No-one talks to Beryl much. The grownups are too busy. Her father has disappeared from her life, leaving a terrible silence. In the dark she lifts out her greatest fear, examines it closely. She turns on her side, curls up, screws her eyes tight to try and block out the things that worry her most of all, the questions that keep going around in her head.

Everything depends on her mother. If her mother were to die, what will happen to her? She'll be an orphan. She would probably have to go to Worcester and live with Auntie Pip and Uncle Eric. And what about Denise? Would she come too? And what if they didn't want them? If Mummy was dying they might promise to look after them, but promises get broken. She thinks of orphans in the stories she's read. Look what happened to Jane Eyre. Could Auntie Pip turn out to be like Jane Eyre's cruel and wealthy aunt?

Every morning she watches Gladys carefully for signs of illness and the first thing she does when she comes back from school is to check that her mother is there. At night she spends long hours awake. She'll never sleep properly again, she thinks. And tomorrow she'll be tired again.

At school the teachers are being extra nice to her. Miss Ainsworth takes her into her office, tells her to be brave, to say her prayers and help her mother as best she can.

She'll never get over that terrible morning. Being sent away. All she wanted was to stay in her own room in the flat, be near her mother.

Mr and Mrs Grant, they'd been very kind. But they hadn't known what to do with her when she couldn't eat. Mrs Grant had tried to make nice things to tempt her, but everything stuck in her throat. She'd managed soup and egg custard and that was what she had lived on. Invalid food, Mr Grant had said.

* * *

The customers are stunned. They'd had no idea. The letters arrive by every post. They just keep coming. Gladys keeps them all, along with the reports from the papers. All of them speak of the 'high esteem in which he was held', of his baritone voice, his interest in art and entertainment, his links with Nottingham.

Death of Birmingham Hotel Manager in the Evening Despatch on the day he'd died. *Link with Nottingham: Funeral of Mr Harry Watson at Worcester* in the Birmingham Post. The description of the funeral and that last awful sentence: 'Mr Watson, who was one of Birmingham's most popular managers, leaves a widow and two children.'

* * *

The largest wreath is from the directors, an expensive looking wheel of unseasonal jasmine and roses with a typed label expressing the sincere condolences of the brewery. A few days after the funeral Doug Brown arranges to see her. It's a bad business, he thinks.

"The Court's on your patch, Douggie. You'll have to go," they'd said at the meeting. "We'll follow up with a letter but someone's got to see her first."

He parks his car, switches off the headlamps. It's one of those February days where the sky is so heavy that, in the middle of the morning, it isn't properly light and evening will creep in halfway through the afternoon.

She is waiting for him in the office. He keeps his overcoat on and declines to give her his hat. He's no sooner seated than a girl appears with a tray. She gestures for her to pour the coffee, seats herself at the desk. She's making it difficult for him. She is quite composed. You wouldn't know what she'd been through.

He thinks about his own wife. If anything happens to him, it won't be like this for Betty. He's made sure she's provided for. And Betty has never worked, not since they were married. Women should be looked after. She'd never cope with anything like this. Mind you, she wouldn't have to. He wouldn't have let a wife of his get involved in the licensed trade. Look where it's landed this woman.

The waitress leaves the room. He hopes Mrs Watson will open the conversation. He opens his mouth but doesn't know what to say. The silence presses heavily in the room. He can hear distant voices and the clattering of plates and cutlery from the floor below.

When he finally finds words they sound feeble.

"The directors send their regards," he stumbles, "their, er, condolences." She nods, purses her lips.

"Thank you."

""How are you, Mrs Watson?"

"I'm managing." She won't say any more. Pointless to tell him The Court is running smoothly, that she has everything under control, that she's just carrying on doing what she's done all these months. Pointless, because it won't change what he's going to say to her. Another silence. She takes a deep breath, exhales a sigh. She's getting impatient now, to get this over with, to get this man out of the office.

"Mr Brown, why not come to the point with what you've come to say?" He bites his lip, runs his hand around the brim of his hat.

"Mrs Watson, you are, I believe, aware of the terms on which your husband took on The Court?" She nods.

"The licence is in my husband's –," she falters, "my *late* husband's name."

"And you understand that it cannot be transferred to you? You can't hold the licence."

"I understand," she replies, "I understand that even though I know everything there is to know about this place, I do understand, Mr Brown, that a woman can't possibly hold the licence to run it on her own!"

"It is the law." He tries to speak gently. She is not making this easy.

"Oh yes, and I know that too." She stops, lets a puff of disgust escape her lips. "I might be a woman, but I know exactly what the licensing law entails. It's ridiculous. People are right when they say the law is an ass."

He starts to feel impatient. None of this is his fault. She's making it very difficult. He wants to get it over with, get away from this unhappy woman in her airless, windowless room. He remembers now what he has rehearsed.

"The directors have asked me to come here to put an offer to you. We know you have dependents –"

"My daughters, you mean."

"Yes, your daughters. The brewery is prepared to offer you one of our off licences."

"An outdoor?" Her jaw drops.

"Yes." He presses on, might as well lay all the cards on the table now he's started. "There's a vacancy for a manager of one of our properties in Nechells. It comes with accommodation. Not what you're used to," he stumbles, "but there's three bedrooms."

"Nechells!" She spits out the word. Ever so slightly she slumps in the chair, drained of all colour. But there are no tears.

"Yes." He tries to elaborate. "It's a good outlet and the people are very friendly. I know it will be very different from The Court –"

"Different! Yes, Mr Brown, it will be very different, to be living and working in the back streets of Birmingham. Why, the only people I know who live in Nechells are some of my kitchen staff. I will be serving them, no doubt, if I take up your offer!" She is angry now. "Oh, how they'll say Mrs Watson's come down in the world!" Her voice is metallic in its bitterness. All the control she has exercised since Harry died rolls like a storm over Doug Brown. "How can Mitchells & Butlers do this?" She breaks off, breathing heavily.

"It is all we can offer you." He's had enough. He stands up. "Think it over. We will be writing to confirm our offer. There's no need for you to make a decision today."

She sits staring at the desk. She wonders bitterly whether they'd have made this offer of Nechells if her father-in-law had still been Chief Superintendent in Nottingham. Being part of his family before he retired had carried weight in the Midlands' licensed trade. Now that's all gone.

"I'll see myself out."

Suddenly she seems to come to, stands up and walks shakily round to his side of the desk. She is so small, he so tall. She holds out her hand, looks up into his face. Now she is once again composed.

"Thank you for coming to see me. I can see it's been hard for you. It would have been easier to write. But cowardly."

She opens the door for him and he stumbles onto the landing. He is haunted for weeks by the failure of his company to do better by this woman. He never forgets her.

* * *

They give her a month. She is to start in Nechells on a Monday, the first of April. That makes sense, she says wryly to anyone who will listen. April Fools' Day.

In the last week of March the new manager starts. He is married, with no children. He and his young wife are going to move into the flat once Gladys and the girls have left. She and Edith start to show him the ropes. She tries to be as helpful as possible. It isn't his fault, she tells herself. Don't take it out on this man. He's so full of hope and enthusiasm, just as Harry had been six years ago.

But sometimes she feels as though she will explode with anger. She knows she is not rational but she is fuelled with bitterness. She watches the customers at lunch in the restaurant and can no longer bring herself to exchange pleasantries with them, making sure everything is to their satisfaction. Now, instead of the glamour of the clientele, she sees overfed men with ruddy faces. Sometimes she feels she could hit them. They are so alive, so comfortable and sure of themselves. She stays in the flat in the evenings. She leaves the new manager to find his feet downstairs on his own. She cannot bring herself to go down there and help him.

She wakes in the night and rants bitterly against the brewery and against Harry, for bringing her here and for leaving her. Then she turns her silent ranting to her mother for telling her to support Harry and to her father-in-law, for getting them into the licensed business in the first place.

And Birmingham. Most of all Birmingham. She will never forgive this city. She will always blame Birmingham.

* * *

Vi and Nancy help with the packing.

"I shan't need those evening dresses, Vi."

"You might one day," says Vi. "Don't just get rid of them."

"There'll be no room for things I'm not going to wear. I shan't take them."

"Then I'll look after them for you," says Nancy. "And when Ian has driven you over to Nechells next week he can come back and load the car with these things."

They make all the decisions, guide Gladys carefully through the sorting and arranging. They try to occupy her with small tasks but after a few minutes she gives up and sits on the side of the bed with her head in her hands.

Harry's wardrobe remains firmly closed. When she'd come back from the funeral she opened it up. She knew she wouldn't be able to clear these things herself, that she would have to leave it to someone else. She'd buried her head in his suits, inhaled the smell of him in the flannel and the tweed, stretched on tiptoe to reach the hats on the top shelf where Harry could easily lift an arm and pick one out. There were plenty of them: snap-brim fedoras, a Homborg and, for the river trips when they'd lived in Worcester, a cream straw boater.

She fingered the brim of his winter hat, stroked the dark band, lay her hand along the perfect crease on the crown. He was always brushing his hats, or getting Maud to steam the brims over the kettle in the cubby.

"You and your hats," she used to grumble. "You're a right old fusspot, Harry Watson." And he would tip whichever hat he'd just retrieved from Maud to one side of his head and smile hopelessly at her. Just like in the films, Beryl would say if she saw him. My Daddy's just like a film star.

No-one, she thought, will want these pyjamas, nor the underwear. She pulled out his shirts, folded and wrapped from the laundry on the side shelves of the wardrobe. Plain or striped, all with modern attached collars apart from the evening shirts with their starchy sheen.

There were the scarves and ties and the good leather gloves she'd given him the Christmas before last alongside his carefully rolled umbrella and, with the shop's soft paper still tucked into its folds, the white silk fringed evening scarf that he'd bought last autumn and never used.

His overcoat was on its original Meakers hanger, next to the suits. When was the last time he'd worn it, the last time he had left the flat? Not in the last month, that was for sure. She remembered when he bought it in the spring of 1932. He'd been to Nottingham for the day and went to the sales with his mother.

He'd rushed back to the flat, pulled it out of the bag, tissue paper flying everywhere. She'd thought it was expensive, even with the reduction. He'd laughed; told her it was an investment. Harris Tweed, Glad. It'll last. I'll still be wearing this when I'm an old man!"

She slipped her hand into the nearest pocket, pulled out two bus tickets, a crumpled Dairy Milk wrapper and a full packet of Players. She regarded the cigarettes thoughtfully. They hadn't helped, she was sure of that. When the cough got worse, she'd tried to get him to cut down. He'd told her not to nag. There'd been a row. Dr Eades told her not to bother. It wasn't worth it, he'd said. Let your husband smoke now if he wants to. In the other pocket she found a handkerchief. They were everywhere, in all his pockets, in all his draws. This one was no different. The blood dried stiff and brown.

They arrange for Edith to pack Harry's things once Gladys has left for Nechells. Gladys agrees they can go to the Salvation Army headquarters next to The Court on the Corporation Street side. Edith will go and see them, make the arrangements.

She wants to be finished now with The Court. It's too painful, and the staff, going about their work the same as ever, are avoiding her eyes. They know all about Nechells and some, as Gladys rightly said, live there. It embarrasses them, the thought of her being there amongst them. They've been a happy crew, working for Mr Watson and his wife. Now he's gone and she's coming right down in the world.

Part 4
Nechells

Spring 1935
Maud is to go with them. She doesn't want paying, just her board.

Beryl is sent to Worcester. Ralph collects her on the Saturday. Gladys wants the child out of the way until she's straight.

Gladys, Maud and Denise move in the next day, the Sunday, the last day of March.

Ian and Nancy Gordon come to The Court straight from church. In the car, Nancy sits in front, Gladys and Maud behind with Denise on Maud's lap. The mood is joyless and after a few attempts at conversation they motor on across the city in silence.

The Mitchells & Butlers' 'outdoor' in Nechells is a red brick building on the end corner of Austin Street. There's a shop window displaying a selection of the brewery's bottled beer. At the top of the window there is a thin row of coloured glass. It's the only pretty thing to be seen, thinks Gladys. A large globe light on a cast iron bracket is attached to the wall above the sign. It dwarfs the door but she can see it will illuminate the shop well in the evenings.

The accommodation that comes with the job adjoins the shop, the front door sandwiched between the shop window and the front window of the house. It's a two up and two down, with a tiny yard and high walls at the back, but, as Doug Brown had pointed out, there's a third bedroom which is, in fact, over the shop which Gladys says will do for Maud and Denise. If you push up the sash window in this room you can lean out and touch the Austin Street sign which is attached to the wall of the building.

* * *

Ian pulls up outside the door. Nancy can see that he is shaken, gives him a sidelong stare to warn him off speaking. Gladys rummages grimly in her bag for the keys.

"Right. Let's get opened up."

She pushes open the door onto the front room.

"There's no hall," she says.

"At least you haven't got all those steps any longer, Gladys," says Ian. Nancy glares at him.

"The furniture we sent over has all gone in all right," says Maud. "The settee and the armchair are fine."

"Yes," says Gladys. "It's a squeeze, but it'll do."

Maud gets out of her coat and heads for the rear door.

"I'll get the kettle on."

"Good idea," says Ian. "And I'll bring in the bags."

"You'll stay for a cup of tea?"

"No Gladys, we'll get going. You need to get on with the unpacking."

She looks at her friend, standing in the middle of the cramped room amongst the clumsy furniture. She hadn't realised Gladys had lost so much weight. Nancy has never seen her looking so defeated. She puts her arms around her but Gladys pushes her away.

"No. Don't do that. You'll set me off crying. Sorry if I sound hard. I don't mean to."

Ian brings in the bags and heads for the staircase. Gladys puts her hand out to hold him back.

"Maud and I can do that."

"We'll go now, then. We've got the phone number. I'll put a call through next week, see how things are going."

"At least I got them to put in a telephone."

"Yes," agrees Nancy. "You'd have been lost without that."

"I don't know what I'd have done without you."

"We're not fair weather friends, you know that," says Nancy. "You have that tea and get unpacked. Everything will look better in the morning."

* * *

On the Monday she has some training for her new job. It isn't difficult, not coming from The Court. The chap from whom she's taking over, an amiable widower who's lived in Nechells most of his life, is going to live with his daughter in Northfield. His son-in-law works at the Austin car factory and they have three bedrooms so there's room for him.

Gladys is at the beck and call of the shop bell. Whatever she is doing in the back room, she has to go through to the counter when she hears that bell tinkle. She hands over the customers' purchases, jugs of beer, something stronger on paydays.

She is closed all day Sunday and Wednesday afternoons. She makes herself a little office area on the back room table and Sunday and Wednesday evenings she settles down with the paperwork whilst Maud clears away the supper things. Sometimes she has a bottle of stout from the shop, just the one, to keep her going, and a couple of cigarettes. Something to look forward to.

The other evenings she's kept busy in the shop. The off licence follows the licensing hours, opening for lunchtime trade and again from early evening, though she doesn't have to stay open as late as the pubs. By nine o'clock she's locking up and hanging the CLOSED sign in the window.

There is a rhythm to the work. Mondays and Tuesdays are the quietest days. Once she gets to Thursday things pick up and Saturdays are the busiest with steady trade throughout the day. If there's a home match at Villa Park the men will be in afterwards and she soon learns to gauge the score by the way they walk through the door.

She keeps the afternoon routine going that she and Harry had at The Oak and later at The Court and has an hour's relaxation upstairs away from it all. By four she's changed ready for the evening opening, no longer, of course, wearing the fetching things she wore in the evenings at The Court, but always with a fresh top or a dress and a row or two of beads.

The customers are a friendly lot on the whole. It's mainly the men, but sometimes the wives call in. They bring back the empties, take the weight off their feet on the chair by the door and chat whilst they wait their turn at the counter. No-one gets close to her, nor to her daughters. She's polite, kind even, to them all, and she earns their respect. You can't really fault her, the women say. But no-one can claim they've really got to know her.

She doesn't want to appear standoffish, but she doesn't trust herself. If she gets too close to them, she might end up on the corner of Austin Street for the rest of her working days. If she starts to care for them, and they for her, she'll lose sight of the goal.

The goal is something she thinks about a lot. It isn't in focus yet, but it's there, and achieving it will certainly mean leaving this little back street shop and house in Nechells.

I'll manage, she keeps repeating. But she can't see how. She feels so alone. In moments of despair Austin Street seems to be swallowing her, and sometimes she can't see how she will ever find a way out. Then she has to force herself to concentrate on the goal.

The talk is all of the King's forthcoming Jubilee. Planning started weeks ago for the street party, and the older women have organised a collection which will pay for the food and drinks. Gladys lets them put up the day's programme on one of the glass panes in the door and she arranges a good discount with the men for a barrel of ale.

She's getting the hang of the barrels. The draught is at the back of the shop. She holds the brewer's measure under the tap at the bottom of the barrel and then transfers the ale to the customers' own jugs. She's learning to keep the measure tilted until the liquid is near the mark to avoid ending up with too much froth.

She's trying to get used to it. People know where she's come from and they talk about her on the street. Beryl stays at Amberley School. She travels each day on the bus, out of Nechells and back to her old routine.

Maud keeps Denise close by her. For the children of Nechells the streets are their playground, their freedom taken for granted. But the missus has insisted that Denise must make do with riding her tricycle between the dustbins and the coal bunker in the yard.

The customers at The Court fade quickly from her life. The lawyers, the businessmen and their well heeled wives. They might talk about Harry and Gladys Watson, the good times they'd had with them, the tragedy that had befallen them. But now there's a new manager and their lives continue uninterrupted.

"Now you'll see who your real friends are," Maud had said. And they were there for her, Nancy and Daisy. Even Vi would come down occasionally, catching an early Sunday train. They'd meet up at the bus station and make their way up Corporation Street to the City Hall for the morning service. Afterwards, they'd find somewhere for lunch.

"My treat," Vi would say. Gladys doesn't remonstrate. She's making ends meet, but there isn't anything left over.

She doesn't want anyone to come to Nechells. I'll see you in town, she says. Do me good to get out. She doesn't want them to see her at work. Even the family she keeps at a distance. Pip comes once and leaves feeling helpless.

There's never a proper time to mourn for Harry and the life she's lost, never the luxury of weeping, but sometimes her grief escapes anyway. It takes her by surprise. A physical pain, a stab in the chest or a prickling that starts in her scalp and runs down her back. The worst is when panic and pain come together, like monstrous waves that pump through her veins and make her heart race.

When Elizabeth died she'd blamed God. This time she can't afford to question her faith. She wakes each morning and prays. It's the only way to get through the day.

* * *

On a day halfway through April the telephone at the back of the shop rings. The operator tells the caller to go ahead.

"Mrs Watson?" That familiar voice. "Dr Eades speaking."

"Oh, Dr Eades." She is flustered.

"This isn't really a professional call." He sounds tense. "I've been thinking about you. Or what I *should* say –", he hesitates, "what I should say is, my *wife* and I have been thinking about you."

"That's very kind."

"We are wondering how the girls are getting on."

"They're managing quite well, thank you."

"Yes, of course." Gladys is puzzled. This is rather unusual, Doctor Eades telephoning out of the blue. He had been the most caring of doctors, all through Harry's last months. But she hasn't needed to call him since they've moved. She'd let his secretary know they were moving, left her address and telephone number for them to change their records.

"And you haven't needed to see me in the last few weeks."

"I'm keeping going."

"The headaches?"

"Well, I'm still getting those. But that's only to be expected." She waits for his reply. He clears his throat.

"We've been thinking about Beryl. She's still at Amberley School?"

"Yes. The bus works quite well from here."

"We wondered whether she would come and have tea one afternoon with our girls. Barbara's only a little younger than Beryl. I'm sure they would get on well."

Gladys is taken aback. "How kind."

"If she comes to us on the bus from school, I'll arrange for the car to bring her home later in the afternoon."

"Well, that would be very nice. Beryl would love to come, I'm sure."

"Then shall we say this coming Thursday?"

"Oh, yes. Thursday would be fine."

"Good. We'll look forward to seeing her. And if it goes well, maybe she would like to come and see us regularly."

"Thank you. Thank you so much. And please thank Mrs Eades for me."

"Goodbye then."

"Goodbye. And thank you again."

Gladys, slightly giddy, replaces the receiver and sits on by the phone. This is something good. A friend for Beryl, and a link with the doctor and his family.

* * *

The corner shop is always chilly, being on the north side of the next street where the sun never penetrates. Ruby Smith tries to think of everything that her customers will need, so as well as all the tins and packets that are lined up behind her on the food shelves, she stocks some fresh vegetables and, down one side of the shop, all the soaps and scouring powders that the housewives of this part of Nechells might ever require to keep their houses clean. These last items give the shop its distinctive aroma. The smells from the blocks of Lifebuoy, the Persil and Vim, mingle with the Reckitt's lavender bath cubes and the Lux toilet soap. Ruby keeps the sweets well away from all the cleaning things so they don't taint.

Ruby's gamble to get in a stock of the Cadbury's Jubilee biscuits in the special tins is paying off. She's been displaying them prominently on the counter for the last month and the customers are buying them. It's more, they say, to have the tin with the King and Queen on the lid to keep than to eat the biscuits.

There are a few sweet jars from which she weighs out the toffees and the mints, but most customers these days want to buy the new wrapped stuff so she's had a shelf fixed in front of the counter to display the chocolate bars in their shiny silver wrappers and the Mars Bars and the Crunchies.

This morning the conversation between Ruby and the two young women she is serving turns to the new woman at the outdoor.

"From what I've heard, she's come down in the world," says Ruby from behind the counter. "Ran a place up in Corporation Street before this. Here's your change, Elsie."

Elsie Porter snaps her purse shut whilst Ruby packs her shopping, a neatly wrapped piece of cheese, sugar, a packet of tea and a large tin of pears. Elsie lingers by the counter, loathe to leave the gossip.

"What's she doing here then?" This from Sylvia, who works in the laundry and has run out of fags.

"Hubby died," says Ruby. Sylvia moves up to the counter and Ruby reaches behind for the Park Drive.

"And I'll have a quarter of those Bluebird toffees." Ruby unscrews the sweet jar and shakes the sweets onto the scales with a clatter.

"You'll get fat, Sylv," says Elsie.

"Speak for yourself." Sylvia fishes in her overall pocket, finds her matches and lights up. "I'm the same sized waist now as when I was married."

"Going back to Mrs Watson. Did you know she and her hubby ran The Grand?" The door opens and a stocky, ruddy faced man comes in with a box of cabbages.

"Not the Grand." Ruby twists the paper bag of sweets and hands it to Sylvia. "Wait a bit, it'll come to me. It's the place by the Law Courts. That big building over the other side of the street."

"That's The Court," chips in Ken Trench. "You interested in these greens, Ruby? Freshly cut this morning from the allotment." He lifts a cabbage from the box, holds it out for her. "See, still wet from the night's rain."

"Yes, I can take those. Put them over there with the sack of spuds. We'll sort a price when I've finished with these ladies."

"Ladies now are you?" laughs Ken.

"We're ladies to you, thanks very much," retorts Sylvia.

"Sound more like fish wives, the way you lot are gossiping," he chuckles. "I'll be back later about the prices, Rube. Got to get some more deliveries out the way this morning. See you later."

"So, this Mrs Watson. What I was going to say was this. That girl of hers, the one that goes to school."

"What about her? Beryl, her name is," says Ruby.

"That's right. Well, on a Thursday she gets driven home in a big car. There's a driver who brings her. Just like they're nobs themselves. Same every week. Around six." Elsie looks as though she's delivered a trump card into the conversation. "What d'you make of that then?"

The others don't know what to make of it, though Ruby has already heard from other customers about the car that comes down Austin Street on a Thursday afternoon. Someone had said it was a Rover.

"Must be friends she goes to, who've got this car then."

"Well, it's all very 'oity toity, if you ask me."

"Nobody's asking you, Sylvia Harris!" The women wheel round. "It's time you girls stopped your gossiping and got back to work."

A straight backed woman standing in the doorway in a tweed suit and dark felt hat looks out of place in Ruby's little shop. Miss Hilda Store is many years retired, but these women still quake at her disapproval.

Elise, red faced, hangs her head, concentrates on a broken fingernail, Sylvia with the zip of her purse. The only one who can do anything to hide her embarrassment is Ruby who takes her time screwing the top down on the toffee jar and placing it back on the shelf.

"You young women, you need to find something better to do than run other people down. I'm ashamed of you. Why not try and make Mrs Watson welcome instead of gossiping behind her back? She's a nice lady and she's been through a great deal. What have her and her children ever done to hurt you?"

Sylvia, red faced, puts her cigarettes and sweets into her overall pocket. Miss Store may not be their teacher now, but she still makes Sylvia feel like she's twelve years old, seated on a wooden form again under her searching gaze.

"Get along with you now. And don't let me hear any more of this nonsense."

Sylvia and Elsie skulk out of the shop, leaving Ruby to face the music. Hilda Store had taught them all, knows about their families, their hopes and disappointments.

"Ruby, you're doing very well in this shop of yours, but you mustn't let it become a place for malicious gossip."

"Oh, Miss Store, they didn't mean anything nasty by it."

"These things can get out of hand if you let them. And Mrs Watson, she's a fellow tradeswoman like yourself. You shouldn't be allowing people to talk about her like that." Ruby looks crestfallen. "She's a good woman. She's a hard worker, Ruby. She's running the off licence well. It's cleaner than it's been for years and she's very obliging. I called on her last week and got to know her a little better. Let's try and show the good side of Nechells to her, shall we?"

* * *

No-one at Brearley House talks about the things that have happened to Beryl. The conversation is steered firmly by Mrs Eades. They talk about school. Sometimes Mrs Eades tells them about her own school days, so long ago when the century was young and there hadn't been a war.

Beryl can't imagine Mrs Eades as ever having been a schoolgirl. She is large and well corseted with a kindly smile on her wide face. Her voice is genteel and soothing. When she leads the children into the dining room Beryl can't help thinking about big sailing ships on the sea.

The routine is the same every Thursday. As she enters the house Barbara comes down the stairs to greet her. She has the same softly clipped voice as her mother, and a mass of fair curls which are cut close to her head so that she is more like Princess Elizabeth than any other girl that Beryl knows.

Tea is served at four o'clock, so by the time Beryl has taken off her coat and washed her hands the grandfather clock in the hall is striking the hour and there is no time to play. Margaret, who is younger than Barbara, follows them into the room and sits down next to her sister. Beryl sits on the opposite side of the table and Mrs Eades at the top.

The dining room, like Dr Eades' consulting room which, of course, is out of bounds, is on the front of the house. The house is set back from the road and the trees and shrubs in the front garden prevent any passersby from glimpsing whoever might be seated at the table. Beryl thinks how strange it would be to live here, so shut away from the world. She has lived amongst other people for so long, at Dudley Port and The Court and now at Nechells, that she cannot imagine what it must be like to live like this.

The table is laid with white china plates and cups dotted with rosebuds and silver tea knives and spoons. Each child has a lace edged napkin that matches the tablecloth. Mrs Pritchard comes up from the kitchen with the large silver plated teapot and lowers it onto the table in front of Mrs Eades who pours tea for herself and the children. The sugar lumps take forever to dissolve because there is so much milk in their tea that it is quite cold.

Beryl never sees Mrs Pritchard's basement kitchen, but the delicacies that she produces from it make her think of it as a magical place. There is always a plate of sandwiches, but not at all like the fat beef sandwiches that Cook Eleker used to make for her at The Court. Doorstops, Daddy called them. These are dainty, crustless triangles filled with egg or ham or creamy cheese like they used to have at Beryl's birthday parties. Sometimes there are scones with butter and jam which Mrs Pritchard makes from the fruit in the garden. In the summer, says Mrs Eades, you will be able to help us pick the raspberries, Beryl.

Just as they are reaching the end of tea, Dr Eades arrives from his rounds. He takes a seat at the other end of the table and helps himself to a leftover sandwich or cake.

"Is there any tea left?" he enquires. Always she tells him it's cold and she will ask Mrs Pritchard for a fresh pot, and always he shakes his head and says it doesn't matter, he's had enough tea for one afternoon. He glances at his daughters but it seems that he has really come to talk to Beryl.

"How are you getting on?" he asks.

"I'm fine, thank you, Dr Eades."

"How's school?"

"School's lovely"

"You enjoy school?"

Oh yes."

"That's good. What do you like best?"

"I enjoy everything. It's nice having a timetable. I know what I'm going to be doing every day."

"Do you mean the routine?" asks Mrs Eades.

"Yes, it makes me feel safe." She feels the heat rising in her cheeks, thinks how stupid she must sound but Dr Eades smiles.

"I can understand that," he says gently. "But you must have some favourite lessons?"

"Games. I like playing games outdoors. And Music. I enjoy music lessons very much."

"And how are things going at home?"

She hesitates. She's not sure that she's been thinking of Nechells much as home. He waits.

"It's fine."

He looks at her with his kindly grey eyes.

"And your mother?"

"Yes. She's all right. She's very busy."

"Well, be sure to send her our regards, won't you." He flicks a few crumbs away from the cloth. "Don't forget."

After tea Barbara is allowed to take Beryl to the playroom. Beryl isn't particularly interested in the dolls' house and the row of dolls lined up in their cots and beds, nor the rocking horse which has pride of place by the fireplace. She prefers sitting at the table in the middle of the room for a game of cards or Ludo or helping Barbara with her latest jigsaw.

Whatever she and Barbara decide to do, there never seems to be enough time. At half past five she has to be ready for Mr Pritchard to drive her home.

Dr Eades' car is a Rover 12 and Mr Pritchard spends hours polishing it. It's the love of his life, and when he drives Beryl home he lets her sit in the front passenger seat and then bores her with details about its engine which, Mr Pritchard says she should understand, has four cylinders. He claims that the car has a top speed of 70 miles per hour, which doesn't mean a thing to Beryl and which Mr Pritchard will never, of course, be able to prove.

When the car turns into Austin Street people stare before they remember their manners enough to look the other way.

When she gets indoors the first thing she does is put her head round the door leading to the shop to relay the doctor's good wishes to her mother.

* * *

Monday the sixth of May, nineteen thirty-five. Gladys can't believe it's twenty-five years. She'd been fourteen and full of excitement for the future when King George had his coronation and now she is thirty-nine and a widow. How she hates that word! Widows are either the careworn women whose husbands never came home from the war or they're old ladies in black who shuffle around their grown up children's homes and are no use to anyone.

She can hear noises already in the street, so she gets out of bed and peers round the curtains to see what's going on. Below her she can see the bunting which the men put up yesterday afternoon, rows of red, white and blue fluttering flags strung between the buildings, and now they are heaving and shoving a piano out of a doorway and positioning it against a house wall about halfway down the street.

Harry had talked about this day. He'd been going to make something big of it. We'll keep going all day Glad, he'd said. We'll be bang in the middle of it all here. Everyone will be coming up to town to see the processions. And we'll have a dinner dance in the evening.

She can hardly bear to think about it now.

When she gets downstairs, Maud is standing at the open front door watching tables being put end to end along the street, just down from the piano. Maud is longing to join in and Gladys suspects that once she and

Beryl have set off for Nancy and Ian's lunch party, Maud and Denise will be out amongst the neighbours.

Denise jumps in and out of the house, pausing on the doorstep to see what's going on and then darting back around the back of Maud's skirt. She's perfectly at home in the street and with her waif-like features and straight brown hair, Denise is starting to look like a Nechells child.

"Maud," instructs Gladys, "bring Denise in, can't you. I don't want her hanging round on the step and you're letting the cold in." But Denise isn't to be defeated so easily, and once inside she climbs onto the back of the settee to get a view through the front window.

Gladys sighs. Is she fighting a losing battle, she wonders? Why doesn't she just give in and embrace life here in Austin Street? The people want to be friendly, want her to be part of their lives. She's lost count of the number of times she's been asked to join them for this party.

By the time she and Beryl leave the house, women are bringing out tablecloths and chairs and tripping over the children who are running round and under the tables. Beryl looks on longingly as she follows Gladys along the street. She would have preferred to stay here, joined in with the neighbours, but she doesn't have a say in the matter.

The programme for the street party looks fun and it would have been a chance to meet up with some of the other girls in Austin Street. But her mother has other plans. It's all organised and Gladys turns sharply into the next street, heading determinedly for the bus stop.

"Uncle Ian and Auntie Nancy are looking forward to seeing you," says Gladys briskly. "Bunny will be home from school, so you won't be the only child." Beryl frowns. Bunny's all right, but he's younger than Beryl and a boy so he's not of great interest to her. "And after the lunch we're going to the park to see the celebrations." Gladys gives Beryl's arm a sharp poke. "There's no point looking miserable. You've done well. You've got that lovely china beaker with the King's picture, and you had the school party yesterday."

* * *

Maud edges the front door open sufficiently to allow Denise to escape onto the street. Maud gives her a minute or two before she runs out after the child by which time Denise has reached the tables where people are beginning to gather.

There's a few women going backwards and forwards to the houses bringing jugs of water to fill the tea urn.

A group of men are standing around discussing the beer barrel and having a smoke. They're not planning on starting drinking until later when the dancing begins but anticipation of the barrel's contents merits early discussion.

The women look up as the little girl from the corner runs towards them with the nursemaid in pursuit. The pair stop just a foot short of the end of the first table, the child beaming up expectantly at the women and the nursemaid breathing heavily from the chase.

Maud, for all her indoor blustering, is shy in company, and now she shields herself behind Denise. The women are hesitant in their welcome. Where's Mrs Watson? She's already made it clear she and the older girl wouldn't be around today. But this little one, and the nursemaid? Wouldn't an offer to join the party be a friendly gesture?

Ruby Smith is the first to find her voice, grasping the opportunity to atone for the gossiping about which she still feels guilty. She is acquainted with Maud from serving her in the shop, so feels it is only right that she should be the one to speak up.

"D'you want to join in? You're welcome to if you like. We've plenty of food."

Maud looks at the other women nodding in agreement and down at Denise, shiny eyed and rigid with excitement. What will the missus say, she wonders briefly.

"Well, if you're sure. I haven't really got anything I can bring."

"Naa, yer all right luv," says a skinny young woman in a flowered overall who is resting an arm on the urn. "Just get a chair an' we'll find space for 'er."

* * *

Gladys is wondering how Ian and Nancy could have let the conversation take such a turn. She listens to what is being said around her and wonders what Harry would have made of these people. Not much, she reckons.

They'd started with a toast to the King. The conversation turned to his ill health and from there to the Prince of Wales. The guests around the table are divided in their opinions as to whether he'll make a good King. Some think he'll be a breath of fresh air, a truly modern monarch. At the other end of the table Ron Underwood, a bullish looking man and current chairman of Ian's Rotary Club, shakes his head slowly and, leaning on his elbow, points his fork at the plump, curly haired lady next to Gladys who had been trilling the praises of the stylish prince. Gladys feels a change in the air.

"The way things are going," he growls, "this country is going to need more from the next King than a handsome face and a well cut coat." The woman's face drops and her husband, seated next to Nancy, looks affronted.

"Steady on old boy. What d'you mean by that?"

"I mean that England's heading for trouble and we're going to need some strong leaders. And the Prince of Wales won't be one of those. It's pretty obvious from what we're hearing about this American woman he's going around with that he's not taking his position seriously."

"The American," says Ian. "She's a married woman. No title. I can't really believe that will come to anything?"

"Who knows? He's a weak man. They say she's got her claws into him. But there's more trouble ahead for us to worry about than the prince's fancy lady."

Nancy laughs.

"There's always trouble somewhere in this country."

"Yes, but what we're heading for, Nancy, is coming from abroad."

"Abroad?"

"Yes." He doesn't explain, seems unwilling to take the conversation further at what is supposed to be a party. Eventually Ian speaks.

"You're talking about Germany, aren't you?"

Ron Underwood fiddles with his cutlery, doesn't look up.

"Surely," says the husband, "You can't be serious. The politicians will never countenance trouble from Germany." He makes an attempt at joviality. "If you don't mind my saying, old boy, you've been listening too much to Mr Churchill and his scaremongering." Gladys starts to feel a tension around the table.

"Scaremongering, sir, is not in my opinion what Mr Churchill is doing! He's the only politician talking sense. They say Germany's munitions' factories are working practically round the clock. Its army is well equipped with immense reserves, make no mistake."

"Mr Churchill wants us to spend all our money on air defences," says Frank sneeringly with an emphasis on 'all'. "It's ridiculous. Lloyd George warned him last autumn not to let his imagination run away with him."

"Well, you wait and see. I'm telling you, there's trouble ahead with Hitler."

"There's a lot of truth in what Winston Churchill says about Hitler," says Nancy, pushing a loose rose stem in the table arrangement back into the foliage. "You only have to read the papers to know what's going on over there." She shudders. "I certainly wouldn't want to be a Jew in Germany at present."

"No, nor in Austria," adds Ian.

Gladys catches Nancy's eye and inclines her head towards the two children who are staring intently at whichever grown up is speaking.

"Right," says Nancy, rising from the table. "Enough is enough. Let's not forget this is a happy day for England. Bunny and Beryl, you're going to love what we've got next. Mrs Lawton has made us a special Jubilee dessert!"

* * *

Gladys and Beryl arrive back in Nechells in good time for the King's broadcast. Denise is standing on the doorstep waving two little flags at them. She has a red, white and blue crepe paper crown pushed down on her forehead. At the other end of the street there's a lull in the proceedings to give the mothers a chance to get the children to bed.

Beryl's face falls. She looks at her mother to see how she will deal with this injustice. But Gladys just brushes wearily past her daughters to tackle Maud.

"I asked you not to let Denise go to the party."

"It was hard to stop her. She slipped out when my back was turned."

"And Maud had a lovely time!" chirps Denise. "She drank lots of cups of tea and they gave her some cake too."

Maud raises her arms and then drops them in a gesture of helplessness.

"Well, I couldn't leave her there on her own, could I? And they were ever so kind."

Gladys goes through to the kitchen. There's a limit to how much she can say to Maud now she is no longer a paid employee. She runs the tap for a glass of water and takes a couple of Aspirin.

She never seems to be free of headaches. There are the stronger tablets, the ones Dr Eades prescribed when she was still at The Court, but she tries to manage without them.

Upstairs she kicks off her shoes, puts her feet up. Ian and Nancy's lunch guests are, she realises, no longer the type of people Gladys would have chosen to spend the day with, and all that business about the way they thought things were going in England had left her feeling low.

What's more, she'd been surprised at how impatient she had felt with those wives, especially the woman whose husband came to her defence when she was going on about the Prince of Wales.

She thinks to herself, those guests of Ian and Nancy's weren't bothered about me. I was invisible to them for most of the time. No-one asked for my opinion. They have no idea what I've been through and what my life is like. And more to the point, they have no idea that I am going to make something of myself.

One day my life will be more interesting than theirs. I just need to be given a chance. I am never going to be anyone's wife again. Somehow I shall get out of Nechells and make something of myself and I'll do it on my own. I just need the chance.

Summer 1935

One Thursday towards the end of August the weather breaks, and there's Ralph running the van slowly through Nechells with struggling windscreen wipers. He's trying to find Austin Street but what with the rain streaming down the windows outside and the steam inside it's hard to make out much. Everywhere he's been today the storm that is marking the end of the heatwave has been threatening. Now it's arrived and the early afternoon sky is as grey and heavy as dusk. Down one of the streets water from the blocked drains has formed a lake which is lapping at doorsteps and distorting reflections from the lights that people have had to put on in the houses. Ralph has to reverse and find another way round.

At the corner of Austin Street he pulls in and makes a dash across the streaming pavement with his hat jammed well down on his head and his raincoat pulled tight across his tummy. The bell tinkles as he pushes at the door and he makes it into the shop on the customers' side of the counter, bringing in more rain on a gust of wind. He closes the door and breathes in the beery smell. The stone floor is pooled with water where the customers have been standing.

Before Gladys appears he has a moment to look around. She's made the best of it, he can see. On the shelves above the barrels she hasn't just arranged the different bottled beers, she's put in a few bits and bobs to add some interest. He recognises the photograph of Mr Mitchell and Mr Butler which had been in the hallway at The Court, and she's done something fancy with some beer mats which he knows they used to have downstairs in the public bar.

On the end of the counter Gladys has positioned the Mitchells & Butlers' blue and gold water jug which Ralph knows for sure was always kept on the lounge bar at The Court. Now it's crammed full of bright daisies with fat yellow centres. He smiles to himself. That's Glad all over.

And then she's there, behind the counter, staring at him.

"Well, I'll be blowed. Whatever are you doing here?"

"I was in Brum, doing some calls. I thought it was time I got to see what you're up to, Glad."

"Well, here I am." A fleeting grimace crosses her face. "Not up to much, I'm sorry to say."

He drops heavily onto the chair by the counter, nods at the flowers.

"I can see the place has got your touch. Looks like you're managing things well here."

"There's not much to manage, Ralph," she says bitterly, "not after The Court. They should have left me there. I could run this place in my sleep. The sales are up on when I arrived, and that's against the national trend, they tell me."

"That means you're doing something right." Ralph tries to find something helpful to say. "Eric was only saying the other day that he'd read beer sales are at an all time low. Some folk haven't got the money, of course, but those that have are spending on other stuff; radios and gramophones and the pools." He frowns. "Seems a funny thing though, if people just give up on a pint of beer. Still, that's what Eric told me."

"And what Eric says goes. We all know that." She smiles for the first time, lifting the hinged centre of the counter. "It's nearly time to close for the afternoon. I'll lock up here and put the sign up. Come through to the back."

He can hardly bear to look at the furniture, a few of her own things in amongst the stuff that was already in the sitting room, all pushed up close. He follows her to the kitchen, which he thinks is more like a scullery. She sets the kettle on the gas ring.

"You've missed seeing Denise. Maud's taken her into town. She needs new shoes."

"That's all right."

"They'll come back soaked. I didn't think the weather was going to break this afternoon."

"How is Maud?"

"I couldn't manage without her. She's not taking any pay, you know. She does all the shopping and cooking. And Denise loves her."

"Even though she's a bit of a strange one."

"Yes, well, she and Beryl don't always see eye to eye. Maud thinks Beryl's a loner. But I haven't got time to worry about that. Beryl's still in Nottingham, you know. She's staying for the summer."

"I knew she was there. Pip told me. How are Mr and Mrs Watson?"

"To be honest, Ralph, I don't know how my mother-in-law copes. From what I can make out father-in-law is in a bad way."

"Still drinking?"

"Yes. He's always liked his drink, of course. Don't we all. But now he's at his club every evening. She has to keep supper ready for him. He's not a very good tempered man at the best of times but Dorothy says it's worse than ever."

"Poor Mrs Watson."

"Retirement was bad enough but he's taken bereavement hard. Losing a child, two children, Ralph. That's worse than anything. Even worse than what I'm going through. And Harry was just beginning to impress his father." She pauses to consider her in-laws' plight. "But Dorothy says it helps having Beryl staying with them. They feel closer to Harry with her there."

"When is she coming back?"

"I don't know yet. I'm waiting to hear from them. Mother-in-law will put her on the bus and Maud will meet her at this end." Ralph watches Gladys moving around the kitchen, filling the milk jug and setting the cups and saucers on a tray. "It's a shame that you've missed them."

"It's all right, Glad. I've come to see you really. And to take a look at Nechells." She looks up sharply and he senses a change in her mood.

"What do you mean by that?"

"Well, since you ask, no-one's been here to see you yet from the family except Pip," he starts, "and if you want the honest truth she said you didn't make her feel she was very welcome. I know you've been down to see us once or twice but you haven't asked us to come up here at all, have you?"

"I don't want you here. I'd rather come down to Worcester or go up to town to see people when the shop's closed."

"Why?"

She slams the filled pot onto the tray and the tea overflows. She jams her hands on her hips and glares at him. He can see the colour rising in her cheeks but the space between them has turned icy.

"Why do you think?"

"I don't know. You tell me."

"All right, since you ask, I will tell you." Her face is ablaze as she squares up on her side of the kitchen table. "I'll tell you exactly why I don't want you lot coming to Nechells. I've come down in the world, Ralph. Everyone knows that, the family, my friends, the people around here. You can see for yourself what it's like." She waves an arm around the cave of a kitchen. "I just want to keep myself to myself and get on with making a living. I've no choice."

"But there's your shorthand and typing. We were thinking, perhaps you could come back Worcester way, get an office job."

"Oh you were, were you!? Is that what they sent you to say? Well that's very kind of you all to be so thoughtful!" The sarcasm is like a slap. "But it wouldn't put a roof over our heads and I couldn't keep an eye on Beryl and Denise if I was stuck in an office all day. So I'm here whether I like it or not." Ralph chews his lip. Gladys' eyes glitter with resentment. "And I don't need folk coming here and gloating over what's happened to me, reminding me of what I've lost."

"Gloating!"

"You heard me." She crosses to the sink, wrings the dishcloth and mops the tea tray. She's trying to stop herself shaking.

"You've no idea how much I miss what we had at The Court." She clears her throat. He can see she is near to tears. "And Harry. I miss him so much. You'll never know, Ralph. And I'd got so used to the life we were leading. All the other businesses knew of us and I could hold my head up high with the best of them."

"You two," he agrees, "you were quite the golden couple."

"I had accounts in all the big shops. People fell over themselves to serve me. It wasn't perfect, I know that, and you know I didn't want to go The Court at all in the first place. But I got to enjoy it and we were really making headway. Running that place was just up my street. Better than being stuck in a house all day. I worked hard but I didn't have to cook, or do housework. Just used to make tea in the cubby. I never did more than toast a piece of bread the whole time we lived at The Court. Now it's different. No staff here, except the man who comes to do the barrels for me once a week and Mrs Parsons in the mornings."

"Who's Mrs Parsons?"

"From the other end of the street. She scrubs through, does the veg ready for our supper, that sort of thing. There's no Mr Parsons so she's glad of the money." Ralph scratches his head, lights a cigarette. "Give me one of those."

"You have this one. I'll light another." He hands the cigarette over.

"And worst of all, having to do all this without Harry." She leans heavily on the edge of the table, chest sagging and head bent with the effort of what she is saying. He makes his way round the tiny table, puts his hand on her shoulder.

"I've put my foot in it, haven't I? I'm too clumsy, that's what Mother used to say. The last thing I wanted to do was upset you." She shakes her head, doesn't trust herself to speak. "Here, let me carry that tray through."

She follows him into the sitting room, grinds the unsmoked half of her cigarette onto an ashtray.

"I'm sorry, Ralph. I didn't mean to shout at you. Here, you have the armchair."

She crosses to the cupboard in the corner of the room.

"Would you like something stronger with your tea? Keep out the damp?"

"No thanks. I've got a good old drive back. I'll wait and have something when I get home."

"You're sure? There's whisky." He shakes his head but she brings the bottle out of the cupboard anyway. "Here. Take the bottle with you. It's a good one. You can see."

"No Glad, I couldn't."

"You know I'm not a whisky drinker. It was a Christmas present from the lawyers' chambers in St James Street. Harry never opened it. Shows how poorly he was."

"Well, if you insist. I'll raise a glass to him when I start on it." He puts the bottle down by the side of his chair. "I still can't believe it. Can't believe he's gone."

"I know. Sometimes I think I must remember to tell Harry something or other. Then it comes crashing in on me that he's not here. It was bad enough after Mother, but this is a thousand times worse."

* * *

At least, says Maud, they'd managed to buy the shoes.

She goes up to change out of her wet things whilst Gladys starts to peel the clothes away from the shivering child. The cotton dress, knickers and socks stick to her skin.

Gladys is tired and deflated after Ralph's visit and she feels ashamed at losing her temper. She leaves Denise's things in a soggy heap on the stone floor in the kitchen and pulls a towel off the clothes horse. Maud comes down the stairs with a flannel nightdress from the winter clothes cupboard under her arm. Denise lets out a wail.

"But it's not my bedtime yet!"

"You can stop that noise," snaps Gladys, "You'll have your tea and then you'll be ready to go up. Keep her warm Maud. We don't want her getting a chill."

"I'll see she's all right," replies Maud firmly.

"We can't be too careful. She's got a cough as it is."

"No need to worry."

Maud knows only too well about the cough. It's a mystery where it's come from. Maud gets off into a deep sleep each night and then the wheezing on the other side of the little room starts.

"I'll rub her with Vick before I settle her down and I'll put a vest on her, keep her chest warm. That should do the trick."

* * *

Next morning Denise has a sore throat and by the evening is heavy eyed and hot. Sweating and shivering, she finally drifts off. Maud creeps downstairs to join Gladys.

"She's gone off. At last."

Gladys, reckoning up columns of figures at the table, isn't listening. Maud starts to sort through a pile of mending, the clock on the mantelpiece and the occasional shifting of Gladys' paperwork the only sounds in the room.

Suddenly, into the peace, bloodcurdling sounds start above them.

Maud rushes upstairs ahead of Gladys. Denise is sitting upright in the bed, head thrust backwards, eyes wide with fear as she gasps for breath. She stretches her arms imploringly towards Maud who sits on the edge of the bed and holds the rigid, terrified child. Maud puts her hand on the little chest and can feel Denise's diaphragm being sucked under her ribs, such is the effort her body is making to try and get some air. The noise is terrible and haunts Gladys for weeks. Great rasping rushes of sound and in between, when she can manage them, strangled cries of panic.

"My God!"

"It's asthma," says Maud without taking her eyes off Denise. "She's having an attack. I've seen one before, years ago. We need the doctor, Mrs Watson." She looks up and Gladys sees the panic in the woman's eyes.

"I'll call Doctor Eades."

"Hurry!"

* * *

He comes home to his sleeping household, drops his bag off in the surgery and in the drawing room he pours himself a drink, meaning to catch up with the evening paper.

If only he could help her. He's done more than enough, he knows, well beyond what a doctor should be doing for a patient.

Is it so wrong, the pleasure he had felt when he first heard her voice on the telephone?

Within seconds he'd regretted that moment of indulgence. Again he was her doctor, calming her, his focus entirely on what she was trying to tell him.

He watches the moths against the glass on the outside of the French windows. Here, in a pale circle of lamplight, he sits on, gently swirling brandy round the glass, going over the events of the evening.

Maud had assisted, persuaded Denise to lie back on the bed, held her whilst he'd given the injection. She'd listened to his instructions and later, when the danger was over, she'd stayed in the bedroom with a chair pulled up at the side of the bed to keep watch over the exhausted child.

Mrs Watson was shaken. He'd followed her downstairs, made her sit down, tried to reassure her. There are new asthma treatments, he'd said. It's not quite as bad as before the war, or even ten years ago. It may be a one off, or the attacks might become frequent. He chose his words carefully.

She'd looked out of place, in that dingy room. She was composed now but her eyes were dull and her shoulders stooped. He guessed by the morning she'd be fighting another migraine.

He knew he should go but he didn't want to leave her. He'd crossed the room, laid his hand over hers for a moment too long.

He sighs, watches the crawling insects against the black night, finishes the brandy.

* * *

Worcester

Ralph is also thinking over his visit to Austin Street. He's not at all happy with what he's seen, but unlike Albert Eades' frustration at his inability to help, Ralph feels there are things that can be done and he starts to form some thoughts which, by the weekend, have turned into what he sees as his brainwave.

On Saturday the weather has settled and Eric takes his garden hat from the hook by the back door and goes out. Ralph gives him ten minutes and then he steps out into the garden, crosses the lawn which has greened up with the rain, and makes his way into the middle of the rose bed where Eric is deadheading the bushes and carrying out a careful check for signs of disease. Eric works on and at the same time explains his plans for replanting the rockery. Ralph isn't listening, absentmindedly he pulls off a nearby leaf, rubbing it into a curl between his forefinger and thumb. As Eric comes to the end of a sentence Ralph takes a deep breath. "I've been thinking." Eric doesn't look up, snips a dying bloom and drops it into his bucket.

"Oh yes. What about?"

Ralph clears his throat.

"Thinking that we're going to have to do something about Glad."

Eric finds another rose that is browning at the edges of its petals, snips again, frowns at the undersides of a pair of leaves on the same stem.

"Such as?" He doesn't look up.

"Well," Ralph starts slowly, not wanting to drop his brainwave too quickly, "it's pretty grim for her where she is."

"Yes. Pip and I have been thinking the same. We're going to see if she can get a week off. M & B must have temporary people who can stand in. And then she can come down here for a holiday. With the girls, of course."

Eric picks up his bucket, moves to the other side of the bed with his secateurs. Ralph trails after him, mopping his forehead, though whether the perspiration on Ralph's brow is due to the strength of the sun or the effort of tackling Eric is not certain.

"I don't think that's enough."

"No? Well, maybe she could get a couple of weeks." He stoops to a full blown rose, dismissing Gladys and his plan for her holiday in Worcester from the conversation. "Here, take a sniff of this. Pip's favourite."

"I'm sorry Eric. I don't want to smell the roses. I want to talk about Glad."

Eric straightens up.

"Why don't you say what you've come out here for, then I can get on in peace," he says irritably. "Spit it out, Ralph, for God's sake!"

Faced with his brother's impatience, Ralph starts to have doubts about his brainwave. Nothing for it, he thinks, but to do as Eric says and come out with it.

"I think we, the family, you and me," he eyes Eric steadily, suddenly confident that he is doing exactly the right thing, "we should get her out of Nechells and back to Worcester."

Eric's face tells Ralph nothing. He picks up the bucket of spent flower heads, crosses the lawn and sits down on the bench by the back door. Ralph follows, thinks he might as well join him. The brothers, side by side, sit in silence and Ralph, for once, is determined not to do all the talking.

"How?" demands Eric, staring ahead. "How do you think that will work exactly?"

"I don't know. I haven't thought that far."

"That's your trouble, Ralph. You never stop to look at the whole picture." Eric feels in his pocket, brings out his Extra Strong Mints, offers them to Ralph.

"No, thanks. I'll have a cig."

So Ralph lights up and Eric sucks mints and they sit together on that Saturday morning, and Eric is slowly starting to think about the whole picture whilst Ralph is wondering what is going through his brother's head.

And thirty miles away in Birmingham their sister is spending her Saturday morning serving the people of Nechells, ringing up the best profits that the shop has ever made for the big brewers, quite unaware that her world is about to change for ever.

* * *

Lavender Road, Worcester
25th February 1936

My dear Nancy

Lovely to get your letter, as always. Pleased to hear that Christmas went well and that you aren't feeling too low, even with the dreadful weather and all this gloom that's following on from the King's death. Lots of people here in Worcester wearing black, even though it's over a month now, and I suppose it's the same in Birmingham.

I've felt everything that's happened this last few weeks to England has been in keeping with my own mood, and all I can say is I am just so relieved to have the anniversary of losing Harry behind me. I shan't go on about it, Nancy. You'll understand, I know.

I hope by the time spring comes people will give up on all these dark things. Pip and I are now just carrying on as normal, and I am sitting writing this at the dining room table wearing the blue tweed suit that you've always liked. What about you? I expect you've kept on in the black. You carry it off so well and it never makes you look dull like the rest of us. We went into black until after the funeral, of course.

Well, life here in Worcester is going on at quite a pace now and I've got exciting news. I can't believe it's six months since Eric and Ralph got me to move here. I still feel bad about Dad moving into digs to make room for us. He doesn't seem very well these days, but he never complains, dear old Dad. And Ralph, as you know, moved out to lodge with his girl's family. I'm not sure how that's working out, because they're not getting on as well as they were and there's talk of another girl on the horizon.

You asked about the girls. Beryl enjoyed her first term at school here. Eric tried to get her into The Alice Ottley with Zena, (big girls' school on the main road, very good reputation) but they were full so she started at a smaller school close to the house here called The Willows. She seemed happy enough, but after Christmas she started with some skin problems, just on her hands, but then the rash spread up her arms and onto her face. She looked terrible and felt quite poorly.

The doctor here in Worcester has diagnosed nerves. He says it's a delayed reaction to everything that's happened to her. Well, I don't know about that, but he recommended a change and a complete rest so she's gone up to Nottingham again to mother-in-law. It means she's missing her schooling, but it can't be helped.

So, here's the big news. We've had a stroke of luck. Eric and I have been thinking about what I should do next. He was keen for me to get a shop here in Worcester, newsagents or something, but I said no. I didn't want to sound ungrateful, but after the Nechells experience I know for sure I'm not the sort of person to stand behind a counter all day.

Then the family started saying I should just go back to office work, even suggesting I apply to Heenan & Froude. Just think, Nancy, going back there with all its memories of dad working there and meeting Harry. That was a carefree time.

And how could I go back anyway, I asked myself, to being at the beck and call of some office supervisor after running The Court? They say never go back, and I never will. There was even talk of me working and keeping Denise here in Worcester and sending Beryl to live permanently in Nottingham. Over my dead body!

Then, just when everyone was getting impatient with me, my prayers were answered (and as you know, Nancy, I've been saying to God for some time that He would have to sort it out, that it was beyond me).

Eric has a customer, Mr De Grey. Eric supplies his bakery in Droitwich with all the usual sundries. Mr and Mrs De Grey have a catering business and a restaurant in Bromsgrove and I'm going to be running it. So my new address will be 58 High Street, Bromsgrove, Worcestershire (make a note, Nancy).

There's a cake shop, supplied from the bakery at Droitwich, and that's up and running, but the adjoining restaurant and hotel premises above have been closed for some time. I've just come back from another visit with Pip and Eric to look round and it's quite run down.

Number 58 is four storeys high, red brick, built when the old Queen was still alive I should say, and it's sandwiched between a shoe shop and a big hotel called The Golden Cross. There's six windows on each of the first, second and third floors, eighteen in all on the front so I shall need a good window cleaner!

There's a cobbled alley between De Greys, as it's called, and the shoe shop which leads from the high street to a yard at the back door of the kitchens and to a small slaughterhouse over the other side of the yard which belongs to the butcher who has the next shop along from the shoe shop.

There's even a garden of sorts at the back. You have to climb up a narrow path towards the library and the cottage hospital and there's this little gate that leads to a patch of a garden. It's better than nothing, and more than we had at The Court. By the way, the butcher is called Mr Partridge which seems appropriate.

On the ground floor is the main room which is the restaurant. It's a long room which runs the length of the building with the kitchens at the rear, and the cake shop is next door with its own shop front and entrance from the street. But there's a connecting door inside, so once the customers have had their morning coffee they can go through to the bakers and make a few purchases there.

Upstairs there's another big room which I think I can really make into something special. I said to Eric, I can do functions in it, but he's as cautious as ever, says let's get you in there first. And then the rest of the place is given over to what will be the bedrooms.

There's a room at the front on the first floor which I've already decided I will use as an office. And the cloakrooms are on that floor too. The rooms on the top floor will do for me and the girls, so after that I will probably have about four rooms to let as hotel accommodation. Of course, there's no big flat like the one we had at The Court.

Things are happening fast, Nancy, and I'm not sleeping, of course, what with everything going round in my head. The place is empty upstairs, not a stick of furniture, and it feels so chilly and echoes as you walk round. The whole inside of the building needs a good airing and decorating and some life breathed into it including the restaurant.

So we have to start almost from scratch. And once it's done, I'll have to advertise for more staff. That'll be the biggest thing, managing the staff on my own. No Harry for people to look up to and adore (there's no doubt about it, lots of the staff loved him), just me, and I only hope I can teach them my ways and that I can get everything to run smoothly.

We take on the lease from 1 April. Coincidence, isn't it, it's the date that a year ago I moved into Nechells. I'll never forget how much you and Ian did for me then. I'll always be grateful. Eric is going to join the board as a director with Mr De Grey and there's a Mr Stenbridge who's another director. He's an accountant. And then there will be me, the managing director with responsibility for running the place. On my own.

Bromsgrove is halfway between here and Birmingham. It's not really a place any of us have ever stopped and thought about, just a traditional market town with a good range of shops and a lovely church up on the hill overlooking the town which I shall join, of course.

There's been nothing in the way of decent catering establishments in the High Street in recent times. Plenty of pubs and a couple of nice hotels. One, The Golden Cross, is next door, and there's Perry Hall which is off the High Street. It's a lovely old building and Eric says it was where Housman, the poet, was born.

But there's nowhere for the ladies of the town to meet for morning coffee or professional people to come in for a light lunch. Those are the sort of people I'm going to make my customers. And De Greys will have a reputation for style and service, right from the start. I'm going to make sure of that.

Bromsgrove is about fourteen miles either way to Birmingham or Worcester so it will work well from the point of view of seeing the family and getting to Birmingham to see you. And of course for you to visit me.

I've been given a chance and I'm determined I'm going to make a success of it, not just for me, but for the girls. Denise's asthma hasn't returned. I'd like to think it was just the one attack, that awful night at Nechells, but I don't think that will be the case and we're watching her carefully. She's started mornings only at The Willows and is quite content. Maud comes down to Worcester on the bus on her day off to see us, brings presents for Denise. Still dotes on her and once I get sorted she'll be coming back to live with us. As you can imagine, she's delighted at the prospect. Not so Beryl, but it can't be helped.

Send my love to Ian and, as always, my love to you, my dearest pal.

Gladys

PS Ash Wednesday today and I went to church this morning. So much to be thankful for. And Pip made pancakes for us all last night!

PPS "My" jeweller, as you insist on calling him, wrote to me. But I haven't responded.

Part 5

1936 - 1943

Bromsgrove

She starts with lists, each one with a heading, and filed alphabetically so she knows where she's got to with carpets and curtains, furniture and kitchen equipment, crockery and glassware. She knows what she wants. Once it's all down on paper, she starts to think about suppliers.

She sorts out people who she needs to get her started: an electrician, a plumber, a painter and decorator and general handyman. Then she takes on three cleaners.

She furnishes a room on the first floor to use as an office and closes her ears to the sawing and drilling and shouting and whistling that echoes around the cavernous building for most of the day.

She keeps her electric kettle close by, drinks endless cups of tea, smokes the occasional cigarette and carries on with the paperwork, checking where she's going, what has been delivered, paying the invoices and always keeping the accountant's budgets in mind.

From time to time she leaves the office and walks round the building, looks at their progress, just so they know Mrs Watson's around and keeping an eye on things. She's fair, they can see that. But, they say, she doesn't look like she'll stand any nonsense.

To begin with, whilst the work is being done to the building and there is nowhere to sleep, she travels back to Worcester at the end of the day. She fixes a good rate with the local taxi company to drive her to Lavender Road at night and collect her each morning. She won't use the bus, even though Eric says it stops near the building and goes straight to Worcester. She's not going to be standing around at bus stops after work. She'll start as she means to go on.

The carpets get fitted, the furniture is delivered. She's ordered square tables; they're the most versatile. You can push them together with a big tablecloth if you get a crowd in, or just lay them up for two without losing much space. Space is business.

Vi comes to stay. She doesn't know much about catering, only shops, but she's full of advice. Together they go to the wholesalers to buy new crockery: cups and saucers, sugar bowls, milk jugs, plates, glassware and two dozen slender little flower vases, one for each table. The tea and coffee pots, the cutlery and salt and pepper pots and the little metal ice cream dishes come from another supplier and Eric orders all the new kitchen equipment through his contacts.

Everything arrives at De Greys a few days later. Gladys supervises the cleaners as they unpack the crates, makes sure everything is washed before it's put away, checks on it herself. At the end of the week Vi tears herself away. Gladys is the person she loves to be with more than anyone and the thought of returning to her life in Nottingham depresses her.

Gladys spends time watching, sees what's going on, who's working hard, who looks interested and who's slacking. That is her way. At the end, when everything is finished, she offers jobs to some of them. So for a start she has the cleaners, one of whom she plans to train for waitressing, and a handyman she can trust.

Whilst the builders are working she keeps the long window at the front of the café curtained so that no-one can see inside from the High Street. The cake shop stays open throughout all the preparations, and curious customers ask what's going on. Joan Blackwood, the manageress who presides over the sale of the bread and cakes, and her young assistant, Doris, smile politely but don't give anything away. They're enjoying keeping the customers in suspense.

* * *

A week before she opens the restaurant she sleeps for the first time in her new bedroom at the top of the building. Early the following morning the sound of the telephone ringing through the house at Lavender Road wakes Pip and Eric. Eric hurries downstairs in his dressing gown.

"Lancaster speaking."

You're through, caller. Gladys waits for the click of the operator's switch. The girl in the Bromsgrove telephone exchange needn't think she's going to have a chance to snoop on Mrs Watson's calls.

"Eric, it's me."

"It's very early. You all right?"

"No, I'm not. I haven't slept a wink."

"I said to Pip you wouldn't like being there alone."

"I was frightened to death. I kept thinking someone had broken in." Eric can't help smiling to himself. "The stairs never stopped creaking. It was dreadful."

"So what's happened to intrepid Mrs Watson? That's what the directors have started calling you."

"I know that," she snaps. "Stop teasing me. It it's not funny." He hears the waver in her voice.

"Isn't there someone can come and sleep in?"

"Don't be stupid. You know there isn't. I don't know anyone here, do I?"

Eric pauses as though he is thinking, though in truth he'd been expecting this call and already had a plan.

"Then it'll have to be Ralph."

"Do you think he'd mind?"

"He won't have to. He'll have to tear himself away from Nancy Williams."

"I hadn't thought of Ralph. It's getting serious between him and this new girl, isn't it?"

"Looks like it. Anyway, when he's finished work at the end of the day he'll have to head over to you."

"It's not going to be for long. Once I've got the café running I'm going to start on the accommodation. When there's people down on the other floors it'll be all right. Even having the girls here will help."

And so Ralph goes each night to Bromsgrove. Gladys rigs up a bed and curtains in one of the empty bedrooms for him. She spends most of her evenings in her office doing her paperwork or, when she can get a break from it all, writing letters.

She's keeping in touch with Nancy and Daisy, and she's written to Dr Eades to thank him for all he has done for her. He replies, says he is happy to keep her on as his patient even though she is no longer in Birmingham.

In the evenings she carries on the routine that started at Nechells and has a glass of stout and a cigarette. She's never liked beer much but she believes what the brewers are saying, that stout is good for you, and especially milk stout with its sweetness and body. As she sits at her desk it's comforting looking out onto the brightly lit pavements and the shuttered shops, and she's starting to relish the thought of the part she will play in the town. She's confident that people will grow to love her De Greys.

Once she hears Ralph letting himself in she starts to relax. She makes a pot of tea and they chat, but soon she starts to yawn.

"Glad, look at you," he says. "You're exhausted."

"It seems a long time since I got up this morning. I'm all right when I keep going, but when I stop then I feel it."

"You've got big black circles under your eyes. You're overdoing it."

"Yes, I am, but I've no choice. It'll be better once we're open for business. It's a strain at the moment, there's so much to think about. It'll be fine, once I get into a routine. Once we get started."

* * *

She sets De Greys going like a machine, and from the day its doors swing open to customers she makes it run smoothly. She has chosen her staff carefully and they work hard, wanting to show her what they can do.

She makes it look effortless, as though she's just letting them all get on with it but she knows everything that's happening. The kitchens, the restaurant, the shop, she sees them all start up each morning, cells of activity and efficiency that together make up the whole.

The delivery vans trundle up the cobbled alley to the kitchen door, the butcher, the fishmonger, the greengrocer and the laundryman. The milkman is there every morning by six and freshly baked loaves stacked side by side in wide wooden trays arrive by eight from the Droitwich bakery.

Crates of lemonade, sacks of potatoes, tea and coffee, soap, polish, everything that is needed comes up the alley. Invoices go through to the office and get paid. And Gladys watches over everything.

* * *

She's doing well, everyone says so, but not a day passes without her longing for Harry. She finds time to go to Worcester, takes flowers to the cemetery, reads what it says on the stone that edges the family grave, sees her mother's name, and Beverley's, and then his, and the date of his death. She talks to him, chides him for leaving her. It beggars belief, she thinks.

On Sundays she goes to the church on the hill overlooking the town, the one quiet hour of her week, and she thinks about him being nowhere but still knows he is somewhere.

* * *

The townsfolk are surprised. Expected something different. Just what we needed, they start to say. Somewhere with style. They come, as she knew they would, different people with different requirements throughout the day.

In the mornings it's the coffee crowd. As spring gives way to summer they walk in coatless, in dresses and skirts of cotton and silk with neatly belted waists, and winter hats are exchanged for cool straw brims or tiny, perched appendages on the sides of their heads.

They plant light kisses that leave lipstick on one another's powdered cheeks, then, when the coffee is ordered, get started on their conversations. There is so much they have to say about their husbands and children, food prices and hairstyles and the problems of keeping domestic help. They smoke cigarettes which they keep in their handbags in elegant cases.

Gladys notices many of them have caught onto the slimming trend, so she slips a range of dainty, less rich cakes and biscuits onto the morning coffee menu. The women weaken and the treats sell well, doubling the morning's takings.

By eleven o'clock the noise has become deafening. There isn't a woman who's not talking. It is as though time is running away and everything must be crammed into the conversations before the clock strikes midday. As, indeed, it does, and then the women call the waitresses, pay their bills, slipping small tips under the saucers and, with conversations still in full swing, gather up their gloves and handbags.

* * *

There is a lull in the wake of the lingering perfume and cigarette smoke and the cacophony of gossip and the waitresses start on clearing the tables and laying up for lunch.

At lunchtime Gladys feels as though she has returned to the days of her little room at the back of the Royal Oak and the lunches that Aida used to cook each weekday. Then they catered for four tables, now it's thirty. But it's the same, she thinks, the people here from the offices and banks are the same, looking for somewhere to relax and enjoy a good lunch to keep them going through the afternoon.

At twelve-thirty Gladys heads for the kitchen to see how things are going. The menu Cook has planned, the supplies that were ordered for today's meals, the cooking that has been going on since the start of the morning, now here it is all ready for the off.

Gladys puts on a white coat and stands outside the kitchen doors, screened from the customers by a partition that separates the entrance to the kitchens from the restaurant. On the restaurant side the partition is covered by a grand, ornately framed mirror which gives the impression of the restaurant being even bigger, but on the kitchen side there is just Gladys, waiting to inspect each dish as it comes out of the kitchen. The soup, the plates of meat and fish, bowls of vegetables and gravies and sauces all are scrutinised by her and returned to the kitchen if she finds something amiss. A mark on the rim of a plate, an undersized lamb chop, an overcooked roast potato, none of this is allowed past Gladys. But she has to search hard for faults. The cook is no ordinary cook, that's for sure.

As the main courses give way to the desserts, Gladys takes her white coat back to the kitchen, checks her lipstick and makes her way through to the customers, cool as a cucumber and smart enough to turn heads. They're nearly all regulars and she asks after their families, takes an interest in their businesses, just as she did at The Oak. She makes people feel special. It's easy for her.

She keeps a mental note of who's who, Victor Powell, with his auctioneer's offices across the road in George Street, Mr Morris, the draper at 118, Mr Bowen from the china shop. She's had to pacify Mr Bowen, realises she should have bought her crockery from him instead of the wholesaler. She promises from now on she will be his most loyal customer, and she keeps to her word. She wins them over as they try to make her out.

If they'd been asked what was needed to get De Greys going again, they would have said it needed a man. There were one or two ladies running businesses in the town of course, the sisters at the wool shop and Babs Luce with her hairdressing salon, and plenty of wives helping their husbands, but Mrs Watson, a woman on her own, taking on this place had been a shock. They'd never heard of such a thing.

They all agree things have got off to a fine start. Now let's see if she can keep it up.

* * *

23rd August 1936
De Greys
58 High Street
Bromsgrove
Worcs

Dear Vi

Sunday evening, and I've got a chance to answer your letter. Pleased to hear you've got over your cold and that Herbert didn't catch it after all. It sounded nasty and you need to keep wrapped up. The weather's terrible here, you wouldn't think it was August. It feels like March. I suppose it's the same in Nottingham.

Well, I've got the girls with me at last, Vi, so that's another big step forward. We can start to feel a bit like a family again, though God knows how we can ever be a proper family without Harry. We chose a Thursday for them to arrive (quieter here what with half day closing, as you know) and Ralph drove them up in the afternoon. Dad came with them for the outing, which was nice. He doesn't look well though; getting very frail. And from what you say, my father-in-law's going downhill too. I'm going to have to try and get to Nottingham to see them at some point, though I'm not sure when.

Of course the girls have been here quite a bit already, so it's all familiar to them, but now they've brought all their things and can call this home it will be different. Beryl doesn't say much but I think she is pleased to be away from Worcester, though she doesn't know anyone here so she's going to be at a bit of a loose end.

You'd think she'd like it in Worcester, what with having Zena there, but although she likes The Willows she's never so settled as when she's up in Nottingham with m-in-law. And she loves seeing you, of course, keeps talking about when you took her to Jessops and bought her that frock. You spoil her, Vi, I keep telling you that.

There's the usual bickering between Pip and Eric and I don't think Beryl copes with that very well. They don't argue out loud, but you can tell they get on one another's nerves and sometimes you can cut the air with a knife. I think I've told you about it before. Zena's being difficult of course, but Ralph and I don't think they handle her very well. Especially Eric. Far too strict, picking faults with the child all the time.

Ralph, on the other hand, is on top of the world with his new sweetheart!

Maud arrived yesterday, came stomping in, still with that old cardboard suitcase, straight off the Birmingham bus. She and Denise are sharing a room so they're happy. Beryl is keeping out of Maud's way, as usual. They still don't see eye to eye, but of course now that Beryl's fourteen she doesn't have to have much to do with Maud which is fine as long as they are polite to one another.

Did I tell you Denise's asthma is back? It's terrible to see. Very frightening and I worry a lot. Maud doesn't panic though.

Denise is so different from Beryl. Beryl has always got on with things on her own. As Maud says, but not very kindly, Miss Beryl's a loner. Denise likes to have people around her, and especially Maud. She's an old head on young shoulders, which is probably to do with being poorly for a lot of the time. I can't believe she's only going to be seven in December. Maud spoils her, I know, but I let her get on with it; she's been so loyal to me through all the dreadful times. She's worth her weight in gold.

Everything's going along well here, though sometimes I am so tired at the end of the day that I just don't know how I drag myself to bed. I'm trying to get a routine going with a couple of hours off in the afternoons. It's the only way, same as at The Court, that one can get through.

Of course, it's all very different now, no evenings, but I still need to keep going after we've closed up. I settle down in the office with my bottle of stout (just the one, that's the Nechells habit I got into) and get going on the paperwork. I'm finding a couple of hours each evening is enough to keep the mountain at bay as long as I set aside time on Thursdays to do the rest, but as soon as I can see the books are looking stronger I'm going to get a secretary. I need to be in the restaurant, amongst the customers and keeping an eye on the staff more than I can at present. Not that I've any complaints, they're a good bunch.

The next thing is to get the bedrooms ready. I've been to a couple of auctions with Mr Cooper, my cook's husband (very helpful chap) and bought some quite good furniture, wardrobes and dressing tables and bedsteads. One of the lunch customers is Mr Morris, the local draper, and I've come to a business arrangement with him. He's going to supply the soft furnishings, one room at a time, without my having to pay until that room is up and running. Then, when the room is paying for itself, I will pay him and we'll move onto the next room.

The local tradespeople are very friendly and they really want to help me. De Greys has a good reputation in the town, and the shop people seem to want to have an association with it. They're a nice lot, but I shall only do business with them. I shall keep myself to myself for the time being, and when the time comes, I shall choose my social circle with care. I have my girls to think of.

All for now.
Love to Herbert and, as always, to you.

Gladys

* * *

Friday 11 December 1936
St John's church clock strikes ten. Gladys turns off the wireless.

"It hasn't sunk in," says Gladys. "We knew it was coming, but still ..." she trails off.

Nancy, standing at the window, presses her face against the cold glass and looks down from the top floor of De Greys to the frosted pavements below. People are indoors, where they have listened gravely to King Edward making his broadcast.

She turns away from the window to the warmth of the room and the reassuring sight of Gladys under the light from the standard lamp.

"I know what you mean. But it's done now. The King is going off with his Mrs Simpson and we're going to get brother George instead."

"Ab-di-cation." Gladys says it slowly, an emphasis on each syllable. "It's a word I never knew, and now it's all anyone talks about."

Nancy draws the curtains and picks up her glass from the small table by her chair.

"I think we need another drink."

"It's too late. We'll have some tea." Gladys pushes herself out of her chair to plug in the kettle. "I'm going to have a headache if I go on with that gin. I'll have to be up early for the Saturday crowd, and there's two couples and a lady on her own staying who will want breakfast before we get to the coffees, whoever's King. I'll need to be there keeping an eye on things."

"The rooms are letting well, Gladys."

"They certainly are. It's all fallen into place. I've got a good person who comes in to do the breakfasts. Tilly Harper."

"Is that the woman who lives in Worcester?"

"Yes. She comes in on the early bus. Does the breakfasts in the upstairs kitchen and serves them up in the function room. Then she does up the bedrooms once people have gone out for the day. She's a good find."

Gladys swirls the boiled water round the teapot, crossing to the basin to pour it away before she spoons in the tea leaves.

"I've got plans now for that big room. I'm going to get it up and running. It's got to earn its keep."

"What have you got in mind?"

"I think weddings will work well. I've got some thoughts, but they're just going round in my head at present. When I get to the New Year I'll start making some proper plans, getting things down on paper. And I'll have to talk to the directors."

Nancy watches Gladys make the tea and wonders what she'd do without her. She has started staying overnight at De Greys when there's an unoccupied bedroom. She tucks her legs up into the chair, as elegant as ever, but Gladys can see she's lost too much weight and her eyes are circled with darkness.

"So, the abdication," she says, "what do you think, Gladys?"

"You know what I think. We're better off without him. He'd have been nothing but trouble." Nancy raises a surprised eyebrow.

"But you used to like him, when he was Prince of Wales."

"Oh yes, when the old King was alive and he had no responsibilities. We all thought he was wonderful. So glamorous. But father-in-law has always said he wasn't steady enough to be King. I thought he was being a killjoy, but I can see now he was right." Nancy smiles.

"Your father-in-law's often proved right."

"More's the pity, Nancy. Here's your tea. D'you want a biscuit?" Nancy shakes her head. "What does Ian say?"

"He's shocked, of course, like the rest of us. But he thinks George will make a better King."

"I wonder how George is feeling. It must be hard, when you thought you'd spend your days being the King's brother out of the limelight and then suddenly, overnight, you've got to be King. And that stammer of his. However is he going to manage when he has to make speeches?"

"And what about Princess Elizabeth? She'll be Queen one day." Nancy sips her tea. "You know, Gladys, I don't suppose it's the right thing to say, but there's something very romantic about giving up the crown of England for the woman you love."

"Hmm, I can't agree with you on that one, not at all. He's let the country down. But it will be for the best, especially if the newspapers are right and things are going to get worse with Germany. We'll need someone reliable and steady on the throne."

The friends fall silent, finishing their tea, and then Gladys gets up and puts the cushions straight on her chair.

"I'm off to bed now, Nancy. Don't forget to turn the fire and lights off when you're finished in here. I shouldn't sit around too long on your own. You'll only start feeling low again."

"I'll be up soon."

"Night, dear."

Nancy looks up at her friend, standing with her hand on the handle of the door.

"Gladys."

"Yes?"

"Thank you."

"What for?"

Nancy pauses, searching for the right words.

"For being here. You're so busy, but you always make time for me. I don't know what I'd do without you."

* * *

Her free time is precious and, apart from her regular attendance at the parish church for eleven o'clock matins where she is starting to get to know people, she keeps herself to herself. She's friendly to everyone and uses their shops and services as much as she can but still the local tradespeople think she and those girls are different.

Beryl travels back to Worcester to school each day. The 144 bus trundles its regular route between Birmingham and Worcester and picks Beryl up on the high street outside De Greys.

A Miss Wilkinson, who runs a friendly little school in New Road, is recommended for Denise, but at the first sign of colds or an outbreak of flu at the school Gladys keeps her away for fear of another illness which will exacerbate the asthma. Denise has to get used to amusing herself. For Christmas Ralph gives her a book of smooth, blank paper bound in blue leather. She writes her name on the first page, and underneath the words "My Diary". It is the start of a lifetime of keeping a journal.

The townsfolk never get to understand much more about Gladys than the day she arrived. She's an enigma, they say. They know she and her late husband ran a big place in Birmingham and that she has family in Worcester, including a brother who's involved in the business. But no-one's complaining. De Greys is beginning to attract people from outside the town and then those same customers are using high street shops. She could have landed from the moon for all they care.

One exception to the people Gladys keeps at a distance is Babs Luce, whose husband is a partner in the local estate agents, Luce & Silvers. Their offices are on the ground floor of Tudor House, a magnificent black and white building on the junction of New Road and High Street and not far from De Greys. Upstairs, Babs has her own business, the Tudor Salon, which is, according to the ladies whose hair she coifs and whose faces she pampers, the only salon in Bromsgrove worth patronising. So Gladys' customers are also Babs' clients, and the two women grow close from the status in the town of their establishments and their admiration of one another's businesses.

Babs, like Nancy Gordon, is a restless wife, though it's Nancy's depression that gets the better of her whilst Babs Luce is looking for more excitement. She thinks married life is a humdrum sort of existence and when she's not at her salon she'd rather be out than stay at home with her husband, who bores her. So Babs, in the evenings, often leaves him to his armchair and newspaper and calls on Gladys, who welcomes a chance to share a gin and while away an hour or two of gossip up in her sitting room.

* * *

Spring 1937

True to her word, Gladys has the long function room and the kitchens on the first floor up and running and there is a steady stream of bookings: meetings, private parties, weddings and funerals. Gladys sorts out extra staff to call on when needed. Cook Cooper trains up an assistant to take over in the main kitchen on these days and, when the restaurant is crowded downstairs and a function is in full swing upstairs, everyone pulls together to keep things running smoothly. Gladys puts up Cook's wages and those of Alice and Rose. She tells the sisters they are officially the two senior waitresses. She doesn't intend losing good staff to anyone else in the town, though she's pretty sure there's nowhere else that they would wish to be.

Denise decides she wants to grow some flowers in the little garden and Mr Cooper says he'll help. He shows her how to get the patch ready and one day he arrives with plants wrapped in damp newspaper that he's dug up from his own garden for her. When they are all planted he gives her strict instructions to remember to water them, and to his surprise they start to flourish.

* * *

The party has been the talk of the coffee set for days and people bought their tickets well in advance. You couldn't just turn up. Mrs Watson wasn't going to let anyone in off the street. There are celebrations going on all around the town, street parties and jamborees, but at De Greys they have been promised something more sophisticated.

Weeks ago, Gladys had thought to herself what would Harry say about the forthcoming great day? Get some business out of it, Glad. Don't leave De Greys idle. Folk'll be fishing around in the afternoon for something to do. And get a licence. The men won't want to sit around with cups of tea all afternoon.

Coronation Day is a public holiday. De Greys is closed in the morning because people won't be coming out for coffee. They will be in their homes, tuned in to wireless sets to hear the service actually being transmitted from Westminster Abbey as it is happening. But Gladys knows that once the broadcast finishes, people will be looking around for somewhere to keep the spirit of the day going.

So she dresses the upstairs room with red, white and blue bunting and fills tall vases with enormous lilies and ferns. When the guests arrive she greets the ladies with boxes of chocolates decorated with elaborately tied patriotic ribbons and the waitresses carry pots of tea, sandwiches and cakes out to the tables. She's got Mr Cooper to arrange a bar down one side of the room from which he starts dispensing drinks.

Gladys has brought in Chas Brown's Swing Band from Birmingham, people Harry used to get to come to The Court, and soon there's hardly enough space on the dance floor at the end of the room for all the couples who've got up for a boogie. They have to shout to make themselves heard above Charlie's sax, but no-one seems to care.

Some of the ladies are beginning to look quite warm under their face powder and hats and the men are mopping their brows. Cigarette smoke swirls around the room and the scent from the flowers is overpowering, so she opens up the windows that overlook the cobbled alley.

To one side of the room, resplendent on a table draped with red, white and blue garlands, sits a mountainous cake, decorated with curls and scrolls and tiny flags, one for each guest, and as the afternoon draws to a close, Mr Cooper uncorks the champagne.

At a pre-arranged signal from Gladys, Charlie proposes a toast to the King, the guests rise to their feet to sing the National Anthem and then Gladys cuts the cake. She has stage managed everything, and the afternoon has run a perfect course.

Reluctantly, the guests start to gather up their belongings, handbags and jackets and the little gifts and Gladys stands at the door and bids each couple farewell. Her arms ache from the hearty handshakes of the men, but she doesn't have trouble in smiling at the compliments that are heaped on her and her staff, nor at the thought of the afternoon's profits.

Mrs Watson, they say as they come down the stairs and out onto the pavement, certainly knows how to put on a party.

As she goes back up the stairs to supervise the clearing up, she can hear Harry. Told you so, Glad.

* * *

21 November 1937

As Gladys thrives in her new life, her father is fading. She gets down to Worcester as often as she can to see him but, in truth, he is quite content to be on his own. Having refused Pip and Eric's offer of returning to Lavender Road, he is quite settled, he says, in his digs. He's taken nicely to his rented room and he likes Mrs Griffin, a thoughtful landlady who keeps house well and he's enjoyed her cooking, though these last few weeks he's had no appetite. Truth to tell, he really didn't want to return to his son and daughter-in-law, where the atmosphere is not always restful.

Arthur never interferes or speaks his mind to his family, but he often talks to the photograph of Elizabeth that hangs over the fireplace in his room. In the picture she is smiling, but not at him because she is seated sideways to the camera. She is looking beyond Arthur. In her left hand that is furthest from the camera she is holding a Japanese parasol and the backdrop is a rock face which gives the impression that Elizabeth is at the seaside. Arthur knows that the photograph was taken in Worcester but he likes the rocks, reminds him of days spent on the beach at Weston-super-Mare.

It's one of those dark November afternoons. The door's ajar, so Mrs Griffin can hear if Arthur calls. He hears the clock in the hall downstairs striking four. Is that all? He's lost track of time today and doesn't think he'll bother trying to get dressed now. It's all such an effort. He's too tired and it doesn't seem worth it.

Eric looked in earlier and Arthur told him not to come back this evening. He doesn't want Eric's fussing. He's quite comfortable and very tired. Can't be bothered with talking.

If he was still at work he'd be sitting at his desk, getting things up together for the post. All the overhead lights would be blazing and everyone would be busy. You wouldn't notice the dark and the weather outside the high windows. You'd just be getting on with the job and the time wouldn't drag.

Hennan & Froude has been his life, that and his family. He sees himself as he once was, a young man in Birmingham, cycling through Aston each day to work, walking past the factory floor and up into those offices. Mother and Dad were so proud of him. You're doing well, Arthur, they used to say. The night classes are paying off. You've got a job for life there.

And then, with the new century, a fresh start, in a lovely riverside city away from the noise and smoke of Brum. They fell in love with Worcester. Do you remember, he says to her picture, when we first got here, we felt like we were on our holidays?

He gazes at the picture of his wife, looking serene against the rocks. It's as though she's waiting for him. Arthur frowns, would like to protest. I was thinking, he says to her, I'd hang on here for a bit, see how things work out for them all. I want to see how Gladys fares at De Greys. And Ralph. I've got hopes for him with Nan Williams. Might be a wedding there. You never know.

But the light in the room starts to fade. All he can see now is Elizabeth, smiling steadily, slowly turning her head to him as she beckons with her free hand.

* * *

They bury him next to their mother and Beverley and Harry.

At Lavender road, Eric has put out all the letters on the dining room table.

"Here, read this one. From Mr Woolley, at Heenans."

While Gladys reads, Eric stands at the French window looking glumly at the wet leaves that are smothering his lawn.

"All this about him being kind, taking the trouble to help people out. It sounds like Mr Woolley is very upset."

"There's a lot like that. Everyone speaks highly of him."

"Well, he was that sort of man." She holds out the letter. "Dear old Dad. I hope someone will write letters like this about me one day."

Eric grunts, turns away from the window.

"You're not as soft hearted as Dad. You're more like Mother."

"And she was the one with the drive. I suppose I've got that too."

"Dad was never going to set the Thames on fire."

"They had a good marriage, didn't they. What do you think made that work so well, even though they were so different?" Eric refuses to meet her eye. He doesn't want to talk about marriages.

"Do you want to read some more of these?"

"Not now. Later, perhaps. I'm going upstairs to have a freshen up."

"I'll get some drinks going. Can you manage a gin?"

"Can ducks swim!?"

* * *

Spring 1938

Thursday 24 March

Emma Watson stands in the hall and frowns at her husband as he buttons his overcoat and lifts his stick from the stand.

"Do you really need to go up into town again, Harry?"

"I told you earlier. I've got a couple of people I want to see at the club."

"Whatever do you find to talk about with all those people?"

He doesn't answer. She doesn't understand how his only pleasure these days is the conviviality of the members of his club, some of whom are his old colleagues.

They sit, these old men, in the comfort of the lounge where the steward keeps the fire well banked up, deep in the old leather armchairs, going over the state of the world. Herr Hitler taking over Austria, declaring it part of Germany, the British Minister being recalled from Vienna, all these things which bewilder him when he reads the newspapers. It weighs heavily on him, the thought that Europe could be heading for another war and he prefers to discuss these things in the company of men.

"But it's so cold and dark. Why don't you telephone and put it off? Meet them for a lunch instead of this evening." He ignores her, takes his hat from the table under the hall mirror. "At least," she coaxes, "order a taxi."

"I'm fine. Don't fuss." She hears the irritability. "The walk to the bus stop will do me good."

"It won't, Harry. It might be March but it's so cold. And I don't like you walking out at night when it's dark. Not since ..."

"Go on," he snaps, "say it. Not since I got so slow and had to use this damn stick. You think I'm decrepit, don't you?"

"No, not decrepit. I don't think that." She sighs, knowing that there is no use in trying to argue with her restless husband. She lifts down his camel scarf from the rack, puts it round his neck and tucks it into his coat.

"I give up." She pats his chest, reaches up and kisses his cheek. "Just go carefully."

"I'll be fine. You go onto bed when you're ready. I don't know what time I'll be back."

"Promise me you'll get a taxi to come home?"

"Yes, Emma. I promise I'll get a taxi at the end of the evening."

Friday 25 March 1938

"Hair?"

"Yes."

"You want to be a *hairdresser*?"

"Yes. Well, not just a hairdresser."

"What then?"

"I want to be a properly trained stylist and beautician, and then run my own salon."

She should have known Beryl was up to something, breezing in first thing in the morning with a tray of tea and ruffling the peace of her bedroom. The only time, thinks Gladys, that I get a chance to have some time to myself.

"What's brought all this on?"

"Well, you keep telling me to make up my mind about what I want to do."

Beryl opens the curtains onto a bright March morning. The sun lights up the buildings on the other side of the High Street. Gladys can see from the way she has taken up a position against the wall with her arms folded and her mouth set determinedly that this is serious.

"Well, I'll have to think about it."

"Why do you always have to say you'll think about things?"

"Don't answer me back. And don't just stand there. Pour the tea."

Beryl shakes her head in exasperation.

"I'll have to speak to your uncle about this."

"What's Uncle Eric got to do with it?"

"He'll be upset if we make any decisions about your future without speaking to him."

"Why, though? He's not my father."

"No, but he's the only man we've got who cares about us."

"Zena wouldn't think so."

"Don't start bringing Zena into this."

"Why not? He's awful to her. She thinks he doesn't care about her at all!"

"That's enough," says Gladys sharply. "I've heard enough. Don't push me, Beryl. And you'd better be getting along or you'll miss the bus and be late for school."

Beryl leans against the wall and, clearly with no intention of moving, starts to nibble the edge of a fingernail, fair hair falling onto her shoulders, the huge brown eyes looking too big for her face. Harry's eyes.

"And how exactly are you going to set about being a hairdresser?"

"That's easy. Mrs Luce has offered to take me on." Gladys' mouth drops.

"So you and Mrs Luce have got it all planned have you, Miss?"

"That is," adds Beryl, "if you agree."

"I'm not discussing it any more this morning. Go and get your coat on and get down to the bus stop. Leave me to have my tea in peace."

Beryl understands it's time to retreat. She heads for the door with a toss of her head.

"Come back here. Let me give you a kiss before you go."

Beryl leans over the bed, catching sight of the bedside clock.

"Oh gracious! The time!"

"I told you to get a move on."

She is gone in a flurry. Gladys goes back over the conversation. No doubt about it, Beryl has got to get a job when she leaves school in July and if this is what she wants to do, well, Babs would be a good employer and she'd see Beryl would get a good training.

Gladys isn't sure whether Beryl would ever have much of a head for business though. Still, that's for the future.

The telephone on the bedside table starts to ring, cutting across Gladys' thoughts. She leans over, picks up the receiver, puts it to her ear.

"Operator speaking. Trunk call from Nottingham."

"Thank you."

"Go ahead caller."

"Gladys? It's Dorothy." Gladys frowns. Her sister-in-law isn't in the habit of making telephone calls. The Nottingham family are letter writers, not telephone people.

"Oh hello. This is a surprise. I wasn't expecting it to be you. Is everything all right?"

"Bad news, I'm afraid. I'm over at The Plains, with Mother." What now, thinks Gladys. "Father's had an accident."

"Oh Lord, how is he?"

"It's not looking good."

"What's happened?"

"He went out yesterday evening to catch a bus up to his club in the city. It was very dark, and Mother said she thought he should get a taxi. You know, he's so slow and unsteady, shuffling along on that stick."

Gladys imagines her father-in-law, making slow progress along the The Plains, stopping frequently to get his breath, leaning heavily on his stick.

She thinks about the last time she saw him, at Dorothy's wedding the previous autumn. She'd been shocked at his frailty. Harry Watson had not taken kindly to retirement. With his career at an end, it was as though he had lost his way in life.

"He was going to catch a bus at the Bennett Road stop for the city when he was knocked down. The driver, a Mr Thorpe, he was in a dreadful state apparently. Just kept saying he never saw anything. They took Dad to the General Hospital. His leg's broken in several places, but it's his head that's worrying the doctors."

"How bad is it?"

"Very bad." Gladys can hear the trembling in Dorothy's voice, imagines her in the hall of her father's house. "Dad's not conscious. But Jack's been there all night, just waiting to see if there's any change."

"He's a good man, your Jack."

"Yes. I don't know what we'd do without him."

"And how's your mother?"

"Not very good. She just seems to be in a daze."

"It's not surprising. I can understand that. Do you want me to come up?"

"No thanks. It's good of you to offer but there's nothing you can do up here and you've got enough on your plate. Just keep us in your thoughts. And your prayers."

"Of course. Give my love to your mother. And let me know if there's any change."

* * *

He dies three days later of his head wounds. The sister in charge of the ward that morning makes a note of the time. Eight-thirty.

Jack Millington goes to the inquest. Dorothy stays with Emma. No point, he says to his wife, in putting your mother through it. She'll need her strength for the funeral.

He can't shield his mother-in-law from the newspapers though, and the inquest is reported in detail. Nottingham folk, the editors know, will want to read every detail of how the Chief Superintendent met his end.

Emma sends Dorothy away, sits at the dining table alone and spreads out the newspaper. Slowly she reads, sees in her mind a Mr Austin Thorpe, driving along the dark road, not seeing Harry close to the offside mudguard trying to cross the road and Alfred Stone, the witness, coming along in his car behind Mr Thorpe, who says he first saw "...a gentleman's hat lying in the road...", then a "...bundle of something black."

She feels a rising nausea in her throat, gets up from the table and opens the window that looks out onto the lawn at the front of the house. The magnolias are starting to open and she finds herself thinking about the weather forecast, which is for a cold spell. I hope, she thinks, the frost won't taint the blooms. The fresh air is helping her.

Mr Austin Thorpe. She frowns as she reads. At the inquest, according to the newspaper, he said he is a lace curtain manufacturer. There are thousands working in the lace industry in Nottingham. Why does there have to be a Mr Austin Thorpe, a man who set off in his car last Thursday evening from wherever he had been to go to wherever he was going and turned into Bennett Road as Harry was stepping onto the road? Mr Austin Thorpe. A man, she conceded, whose life, like her own, would never be the same again. *A bundle of something black.* She shudders, thinks however long she lives she will never get those words out of her head.

This ignominious end! *If only*. Two more words she can't leave alone. She can't rail against her dead husband, she wishes she could, but there is no anger in her, just this numbness.

If only you'd listened to me, Harry.

* * *

Thursday 31 March 1938

"Mrs Watson will appreciate that you made it to the funeral."

"She did well. So composed."

"No more than you were when you lost Harry."

"Yes, but I was prepared. Can you imagine the shock of what has happened to father-in-law, Vi. And she's much older than I was. Anyway, I think she was glad to see me."

"You're the link with Harry. You and the girls."

Gladys kicks off her shoes and puts her feet up on Vi's fat, velveteen pouffe.

"You just never know what's round the corner."

"No. Everything's been going along so much better for your family recently, hasn't it." Vi stoops to light the fire that she'd laid earlier, before they'd set off for Parliament Street Chapel. "What with Ralph and Nan getting married."

"That was a lovely day."

"It sounded like a very happy wedding. You brought it all to life in your letter."

"Nan's such a nice young woman. Just what we needed in the family."

"Yes." Vi tries to look serious but the sobriety of the entire day has been tinged, for Vi, with an elation that has been with her ever since Gladys telephoned a couple of days ago and invited herself to stay for the night.

"Are you sure you're warm enough, Gladys?"

"I'm fine."

"Shall I get you a rug?"

"Don't fuss." Gladys swats Vi away impatiently. "Just bring in that tea you've been talking about for the last twenty minutes."

Vi pins up a clump of grey hair that's come loose and grumbles her way to the kitchen. Gladys watches her, thinks to herself that Vi looks like a proper old maid. She comes back, trundling a tea trolley into the room, puts a little table next to Gladys.

"You can be Mother, Gladys."

Gladys heaves herself up.

"Where's that cake you were talking about?"

"I thought you said you were full up with what you ate at the wake."

"I am. But that doesn't mean I don't fancy a bit of cake. Go and get it."

At last they are settled with the cups filled and slices of Victoria sandwich set out on the Royal Albert. Gladys starts to go over the day.

"You know, Vi, when we were at the service, I kept going over this last ten years, thinking about what's happened since 1928."

"There's been a lot of water under the bridge. Let's see, you were still at The Royal Oak then."

"Yes. Nice cake." She steadies her plate on the side table, stirs her tea thoughtfully. "When I think of the people I've lost since then. First Mother, then Harry, now both the fathers."

"And Eric and Pip's little one."

"Yes. Beverley."

They fall silent. Gladys gazes at the freshly lit fire, at the smoke and a few flames drawing up the chimney.

"My poor mother-in-law. Just think. She's lost two sons, and now this."

"The whole of Nottingham is shocked. It's been in all the papers."

"Well, he was so highly thought of up here."

"Even though he's been retired for quite a few years. People still remember him."

"He never took well to retirement. His mind was too active. He couldn't just settle down at home. That's why he was always at his club. I think he just felt like he'd been put out to grass."

"I wish someone would put me out to grass," sniffs Vi. Gladys looks surprised.

"I thought you liked your job. You're so good at it."

"Yes, I am. But still, some days I get up and think there must be something else in life for me to do. And I do get very tired."

"We're not getting any younger, Vi."

"Nothing I can do about it anyway. Changing the subject, how are Beryl and Denise?"

"They keep me going. If it wasn't for the girls, I'd have had nothing to live for when Harry died. You know that. And talking of ten years ago, I never dreamt then that Beryl would have a sister."

"I'll never forget you telling me you were expecting again. You weren't at all pleased."

"It was a shock at the time, I admit, but once we'd got her, we were thrilled."

"Of course."

"I knew in my heart it was better not to have an only child. It was just at the time things had been going so well at The Oak and the thought of another baby just didn't fit into how I saw our lives. Then Harry sprang the news on me about going to The Court. I took a bit of time, Vi, to come round to it all." Vi tops up the cups, lets Gladys carry on talking. "And then losing Mother. If only she could have lived to help me through all these years."

Gladys has been through this so many times. Vi finds the best thing is to get Gladys back to the present.

"How is Denise getting on at Miss Wilkinson's?"

"Not very good. It's not the school. It's a very nice little set up and Denise loves it. But she's too delicate. If there's a cold going round she catches it and then the asthma starts up again. She's missing a lot of days. Weeks even."

"That's no good."

"I'm going to have to have a rethink about Denise." She leans back against the cushions that Vi has put at her back, closes her eyes for a moment or two. "And now Beryl's decided she wants to be a hairdresser!"

"Really?" Vi looks thoughtful. "Well, Gladys, that's not a bad idea."

"I know. She wants to be apprenticed to Babs."

"Babs Luce?"

"Yes. But Babs isn't proving to be very steady at present. She's got marriage problems. I think there may be another man."

"Well, that's not the place for Beryl, then."

"On the one hand no, but on the other hand, Babs runs the best salon in the town and will give Beryl a good training." She breathes deeply, lets out a slow whistling sigh. "It's so hard, having to make all these decisions on my own. Eric thinks it's a good idea, for her to have an apprenticeship. Though Albert feels very strongly that she should come into the business."

"Albert?" Vi looks up sharply. "You mean Dr Eades? What's he got to do with it?"

Gladys examines her hands, picks at something imaginary under a fingernail. She is cross with herself for mentioning him.

"He's proving to be a good friend. I do see him occasionally, if I ever manage to get up to Birmingham." She looks her friend squarely in the eyes. "But I see him at his house, usually for lunch, and usually with Mrs Eades present."

Vi picks up the tea things, sets them on the tray. *Usually*, thinks Vi. Usually Mrs Eades is with them. The word isn't lost on her.

Gladys watches Vi head for the door with the tray, her back stiff with disapproval. Vi knows, thinks Gladys, that I'm not telling her everything.

* * *

Gladys creates a new office for herself at the back of the cake shop. She gets Mr Weaver, the builder, to partition part of the dark, stone corridor which everyone calls the back alley and which runs the length of the building, so that now, from the cake shop, you take a couple of steps up into the corridor and on your left is a door into a little square room. There is no outside wall but Mr Weaver installs a window in the new wall overlooking the alley to try and give a feeling of space. However, it doesn't lift the gloom or the chill so, regardless of whether the sun is shining outside, the electric light and a bar of the electric fire are on all day.

Past the newly created office, further along the back alley, there is another door on the left that leads into the restaurant and then a third door leading into the kitchens. The alley is a useful place to store crates and boxes and provides extra cool storage for Cook, especially when she's preparing for a function.

With the agreement of the directors, Gladys advertises for a secretary. Miss Primrose Mitchell is streets ahead of the other young women who apply for the position. Not that Gladys lets her think she's indispensable, but Prim, as she likes to be called, with her fast typewriting and bookkeeping skills and quick brain, is exactly what Gladys needs. She hands over the day to day running of the office to Prim and gets on with managing the business.

What Gladys and Prim do not foresee in the summer of 1938 is that they will one day share a secret that they will take to their graves, and that years later, when Prim leaves Gladys's employ with enough money to set up a business with her new husband, their unspoken vow of silence to one another as they go their separate ways ensures that the dangerously twisted threads of the web they have created stay unbroken for the rest of their lives.

* * *

Summer 1938

The summer is making things worse for Denise. From the window she looks down onto the bustle of the high street, the women's bright frocks and straw hats, people stopping for a gossip, mothers struggling with prams, calling to the older children to keep up, keep away from the kerb. She recognises the young man with the bad skin from the solicitors on Worcester Road who comes in for his lunch, striding past Woolworths, a leather document case tucked under his arm. Mr Morris is standing outside his shop, looking at his window display, greeting a huge lady in a primrose yellow linen coat and matching hat. They disappear into the darkness of the shop's interior.

Everyone seems to have a purpose to their lives except her. Beryl, now that she is at the Tudor House, seems to Denise to be part of another world which Denise cannot share. In the evenings she only stays in long enough to change and have something to eat before she's off out again, to the tennis club or a get together at someone's house and now she's got a boyfriend.

She breezes in from work, sings as she sprints up the stairs, closets herself in the bathroom for ages and comes back downstairs ready to go out again on a cloud of perfume with her hair catching the light as it waves around her face and her nails painted pink. Denise feels as though Beryl is completely beyond her reach.

She finds her mother in the new office. There are papers stacked in two trays marked "In" and "Out" on the desk and files piled up on the spare chair.

Gladys is writing cheques, and Denise stands and watches her filling in the spaces and putting her signature in the corner. She can never read her mother's writing, which just looks like lines of squiggles and loops. She likes the office, the smell of coffee and carbon paper and the desk with the telephone and the big black typewriter with its rows of keys and "Imperial" written in gold on the front.

She waits for her mother to stop writing. Then, when she has her attention, she explains that she is depressed. Gladys swings her chair round and glares.

"Whatever are you talking about?"

"It's how I feel."

"I've never heard anything so ridiculous." Gladys is exasperated. "Who put such a word in your head?"

"No-one. I read it. In a book."

"Well, you'd better snap out of it. I haven't got time to listen to all this whining."

"I'm not whining."

"All the attention you get, with Maud here running around after you. You don't know how lucky you are."

"I can't help it if I get asthma."

"No, but you can stop feeling sorry for yourself."

"All I really want is to be able to go back to school when the new term starts."

"Well, you can't. Look at you. You're so pale and as thin as a rake."

"I miss the other children."

"You may not be going back at all. I might look into having you taught on your own, here at De Greys. What with picking up all the infections at school and then the amount of time you have to miss –"

"No, Mummy. Please, you can't do that," she implores. "It's not just lessons. I want to be able to play with my friends."

"You're to have a rest from school. I've told you. I've spoken to Doctor Eades. He agrees. And if you do go back you can put all ideas of being allowed in the playground out of your head. You're not like other children."

Denise's eyes start to fill.

"I don't want to be different."

"Don't argue with me." Gladys sighs, puts down her pen. "Your chest will never be strong," she explains for the hundredth time, trying to be patient. "We need to build you up, ready for the winter. You are just going to have to get used to being on your own. It's for your own good."

"But Mummy – ," Gladys cuts her short.

"I haven't got time to go through all this again. I'm trying to run a business. It's the middle of a Friday morning and I've got a lot to do. Go and find something to keep you occupied. Something quiet."

If her mother won't listen, she knows where she will go. She stalks through the kitchens, her face no longer pale but flaring. She ignores Cook Cooper and the two women working at the sink, even though she has been told always to be polite to the staff, and she heads out to the little garden.

The tree must have been there for years. She clambers furiously over the flowers and presses the side of her face against the rough old bark until it hurts. The tree is big and constant and as she whispers her account of the conversation with her mother her anger and frustration leave her. It is as though the tree absorbs it.

The child who comes back through the kitchens is calm and composed. She wanders down the empty restaurant which is slumped between coffee time and the lunch rush and climbs the stairs to her bedroom where, later, Maud finds her sprawled across the bed asleep with the book she had been reading fallen to the floor.

* * *

April 1939

On Thursdays, when most of the shopkeepers in Bromsgrove close at lunchtime and take a half day's break, Gladys gets a few hours to herself.

Sometimes she gets out of Bromsgrove, to see Pip in Worcester or back to Birmingham, and sometimes she corners Beryl or Denise to tackle whatever might be on her mind. This afternoon she's caught up with a few jobs, sorted out her summer clothes and now, at five o'clock, she is ready for a showdown.

Beryl breezes in from the salon and takes the stairs two at a time to the first floor. Gladys is waiting on the landing and ushers her into her bedroom.

"Where were you last night?" starts Gladys ominously. "You didn't come in until ten?"

"I was with Terence."

"What were you doing?"

"He let me have a spin in the car early on."

"Then?" Demands Gladys.

"Then we went to the meeting."

"What meeting?"

"At the tennis club. The AGM." Gladys sighs.

"You know I don't approve."

"Approve of what? The tennis club or my learning to drive?"

"Don't act as though you don't know. It's Mr Hall I'm talking about. He's kind to let you loose on his motor car and I don't doubt his intentions are honourable, but he isn't suitable for you." Beryl raises her eyes to the ceiling. "You can take that look off your face. We've been through this already. He's too old for you."

"I'm seventeen in July..."

"... and he is nearly thirty. I do business with Mr Hall, he's a nice man and a good chemist, but he's not right for you."

Beryl tightens her mouth, biting back what she would really like to say to her mother.

"You don't trust me. Is that it?"

"I'm not prepared to discuss it any longer. If Mr Hall wants to teach you to drive that's one thing, but you are not to stay out all evening again without telling me exactly where you are going and with whom. That's all I have to say on the matter."

* * *

Gladys is not the only mother that day to be arguing with her daughter. Coughton Court is an English manor and one of great houses of neighbouring Warwickshire and Lady Throckmorton's life is as far removed from Gladys' as is possible.

The Catholic Throckmorton family has owned the house for over six hundred years and today's problem, Lady Throckmorton supposes, is somewhat less of a drama than their ancestors' role in the gunpowder plot, or of an even earlier Lord Throckmorton who assisted in the divorce of Henry VIII from Catherine of Aragon.

She is trying to keep calm, to think clearly about things and not let her judgement be clouded by her feelings.

She came to Coughton Court some twenty-five years earlier when she married Courtenay Throckmorton, a hero of the Boer War. It had been a fine marriage until war was declared on Germany. When Lord Throckmorton left for France in 1914, he had led his battalion to what he was certain would be a fast victory. But two years later, on a beautiful April morning similar to today, the news had arrived. Lilian had never for a moment imagined the death of her husband. She'd taken it for granted that he would return.

Elizabeth, their oldest child, had been ten at the time of her father's death. Richard, the heir, two years younger, suffered the loss bravely, his future responsibilities already shaping his thoughts and behaviour. But Anne was too young at five to understand the impact of the day in 1916 when the dreadful news was brought to Coughton.

This morning, facing Anne across the breakfast table, Lady Throckmorton knows she will have to admit defeat.

"I keep telling you, he doesn't see himself as German. He's Bavarian."

"Please don't shout, Anne."

"You don't seem to understand, however many times I say it."

"I know Ludwig is from Bavaria. Of course I know that. And I know he thinks of himself as not being German, but when we go to war –"

"*If* we go to war!"

"It's not a case of if, you know that. You're not stupid. You read the papers. There may be people in the country still wanting to believe that it's not going to happen, but listen to Mr Churchill. He knows what he's talking about. And when it happens, if you are Ludwig's wife, you'll be over there in Germany and you'll be caught up in it. Ludwig will have to play an important part, for sure, whether he likes it or not."

"No Mama. You know he and his family aren't at all happy with what Hitler has been doing."

"Be that as it may, Ludwig will have no choice in the matter. He'll be snapped up by the military. His title, his position. They'll give him a key role and he'll have to take it. There'll be no choice."

Anne pushes back her chair, throws down her napkin. Lady Throckmorton tries to stay calm.

"Anne, let's not quarrel again. Hear me out, please."

Mother and daughter, across the table, both strained and deadly serious. Lady Throckmorton takes a deep breath.

"I like Ludwig. He is descended from one of the great Roman Catholic families of Europe. The von Twickel name is as old as the Throckmortons and it could have been a good match. You would be a baroness. There would have been no objections at all in normal circumstances."

"Meaning?" Anne's face is set hard.

"It's quite irresponsible of him to put you in this position as things stand in Europe."

"But we love one another. I keep telling you."

"I understand that. But these are going to be dangerous times, Anne. How can I give my blessing to this marriage, to losing you to Germany?"

"You won't lose me. I'll be all right there. As you say, the von Twickels are an old and respected family. I'll be safe."

"Your title will be no guarantee for your safety."

"I think you are exaggerating."

"No, I'm being realistic. And what about here in England, and at Coughton itself?"

"What about it?"

"All the hardworking patriotic people here on our estate, the staff, the tenants. What will they feel?"

"Now you're sounding bourgeois."

"So many of them, who have already been through one war against Germany. Some who fought, and mothers and fathers who lost sons."

"It's irrelevant. You're going to bring up Father again next, aren't you?"

"No." She puts down her napkin by her untouched coffee, pushes back the heavily carved Jacobean chair. "No, I'm not going to speak of your father and I'm not going to prolong this fight with you. I've said everything I wish to say and I shan't stand in your way any longer."

She looks grave, standing across the table from Anne, steadying herself on the back of the chair.

"I have decided to give you my blessing, because I don't want you to turn against us and because I know you and Ludwig are very much in love, and of course you will be married here at Coughton."

Lady Throckmorton waits. When Anne composes herself and raises her head she is fighting back tears.

"Mother, I will never be able to thank you enough for this."

"We're going to have to give some thought to the best way of going about this." Lady Throckmorton shakes her head. "We haven't got the staff any longer for a big wedding. I'm not sure how we can cope."

Anne fails to notice the stoop of her mother's shoulders as she walks away towards the door, the slight tremble of her hands.

"Leave it with me now, Anne. I need some time."

* * *

The telephone on Eric's desk rings shrilly. "Lancasters. Eric Lancaster speaking."

"It's me."

"Gladys. Are you all right?"

"I've had a shock." Possible catastrophes flash through Eric's head.

"What's wrong?"

"Nothing's *wrong*. You'll never guess."

"Go on then, tell me."

"I've had a telephone call."

"Yes?"

"From Lady Throckmorton's secretary. At Coughton Court."

"Lady Throckmorton's secretary. Are you sure?"

"Course I am, you donkey."

"What's she doing telephoning you?"

"One of the daughters is getting married. In June. They want De Greys to do the catering." Gladys' excitement seems to be coursing through the telephone wires to Worcester.

"Are you quite sure?"

"Stop asking me if I'm sure."

"Sorry. How has this come about then?"

"I don't know. They've heard about my weddings and the private catering we've been doing. They want to meet me. There are some things, apparently, that have got to be explained. I'm to go over to Coughton tomorrow morning."

"Blimey. This is wonderful news."

"Yes." There's a pause on the line. "Are you still there?"

"I'm thinking. You don't think it sounds fishy?"

"Fishy! What an idea. The aristocracy don't do fishy things."

"They certainly do. But hopefully it's not the case with Lady Throckmorton." Eric sits down, pulls his book of telephone numbers towards him.

"I'd better tell the other directors. Mr De Grey will be over the moon."

"Best wait until I know more. Leave it a day or two."

"All right. As you wish. But if this works out, it's going to be a big feather in your cap."

"Yes, I know. I'll ring off now then. I've got a rep waiting to see me."

"OK. I'll wait to hear more. And well done!"

* * *

In the office, Gladys pulls a chair round for Cook.

"It's all clear in my head now," she says, flicking open a spiral bound notebook that she has taken from her bag. Cook can see that the pages of the notebook are covered in Mrs Watson's shorthand. "I met the housekeeper, a very nice woman, and she explained everything. The wedding is on the twentieth of June. They haven't got the staff they used to have, so they're going to need to bring in extra help.

"We're going to keep to cold dishes. I thought those would be easier to transport. I've suggested various savouries, they'll be served before the meal, and then we'll do some of our big platters of dressed salmon and there's quite a few desserts on the list. I've got it all written down here and I'll get Miss Mitchell to type it up for you.

"We'll take four of our waitresses. Alice and Rose, of course, and two others. And they want us to provide some crockery."

"Crockery?"

"Yes, it will make it easier for them."

"I'd have thought they'd have enough of their own at Coughton Court."

"They're not using all the valuable stuff, only for the main guests."

"For the top table, I suppose? The bigwigs."

"You've got it. There'll be plenty of those. The Archbishop of Birmingham is going to marry them." Cook pulls a face.

"Catholic?"

"Of course. The Throckmortons are a very old Catholic family. And Sir Anthony Eden will be there."

"The Member of Parliament?"

"That's right. At Leamington Spa. But he's an old family friend."

"He's the one who's been in the papers about the Germans?"

"Yes. He's like Winston Churchill. Well, like most people now, I suppose. Quite convinced we're heading for another war."

"God forbid."

At the mention of Germany, Gladys bites her lip. She eyes Cook warily, knowing that she might not be so keen on the idea of helping when she knows about the groom.

"There's something I should mention to you." Cook looks up sharply, catches the uncertainty in Mrs Watson's voice.

"What's that then?"

"Miss Throckmorton's fiancé is a German baron. Well, Bavarian actually is what I've been told. But that doesn't seem to make much difference to people here." Cook rubs over her forehead as though she is trying to get this information into her brain.

"A German! Whatever does the family make of that?"

"Well, I don't know. No-one was likely to gossip to me about it."

"Where are they going to live?"

"In Germany."

"Heaven help her! All that we're reading in the newspapers, and she's going to go and live there." Cook folds her arms, broods for a minute. "Well," she says eventually, "it's all a bit rum, as Mr Cooper would say, but it doesn't make much difference to us, does it. Business is business and it's not every day the aristocracy crosses our path."

"No. You're right," replies Gladys, relieved. "I'm just wondering what else we need to be thinking about."

"Well, all these things they want us to bring, how are we going to get them over there?"

"Ah, I've thought about that. I'll rope in everyone I know who's got a motor car and we'll take it all over, all in one go, on the morning of the wedding."

"And the crocks? We can't use our stuff. We can't spare our own, especially on a Saturday."

"No. I know. I'm going to ask Mr Bowen to loan me some things. He can pack everything in his van and come over with the rest of us on the day."

"I suppose," says Cook, "they're busy over at Coughton then?"

"They certainly are. I met a Mary Thompson, Lady's Throckmorton's ladies' maid. Such a nice woman. Been there for years. She's flat out making the wedding dress and dresses for the six bridesmaids."

"Six!"

"Yes. And there's a page boy. But I don't think she's doing his outfit. She's making the trousseau, though, on top of all that. Imagine."

Cook couldn't imagine. Put her in a kitchen and she can work miracles, but her sewing stops at darning Mr Cooper's socks. And she's not very good at that.

June 1939

The grandeur of the wedding leaves a big impression on the De Greys waitresses. Mr Bowen, driving back to Bromsgrove at the end of the day, can hardly concentrate with all the chattering and giggling.

Buck Jones could have taken some of them in his taxi, he thinks, instead of the four women having to be squashed up in his van with the boxes of crocks in the back rattling away.

The taxi's up front, carrying Mrs Watson who is sitting in the back on her own. He guesses she's just needing some time to herself. What a day it's been. Quite a triumph for Mrs Watson and it will certainly put De Greys on the map.

* * *

Gladys is exhausted but she supposes she'd better put a call through to Eric. He'll be waiting to hear.

"It's me."

"How did it go?"

"I couldn't have wished for better. They were so pleased with us."

"You got everything over there all right?"

"Yes. I've plenty to tell you. But look here, I'm too tired to talk now. Come over tomorrow if you're free. Have some lunch with me. Bring Pip. Come up to the sitting room at 12.30. We'll have a sherry before we go downstairs."

* * *

At the far end of the restaurant, near to the kitchen service doors, there is a table in an alcove on which is placed a permanent reserved sign. New staff are instructed never to show anyone to that table, that it's Mrs Watson's. It must always be kept free for her or her daughters.

She leads Eric and Pip up the restaurant to the alcove, stopping to ask after some customer's sick mother, someone else's house move, to admire a new hat, ensure the gentlemen from the bank are enjoying their lunch. It's second nature to her.

Pip is reminded of lunchtime at The Royal Oak. Gladys seems to have been doing this for ever. She never oversteps the mark, but it's a genuine interest and not just for show. The customers love it.

Charm itself, though she's seen the other side of Gladys too, the side that she has had to cultivate. When staff first tried to challenge her, when tradesmen thought they could swindle her, when she found smeared cutlery or marks on freshly laundered cloths, then she started to show how tough she could be.

Everyone knows Mrs Watson doesn't tolerate shoddiness and has no time for insolence or anyone who challenges her authority. She abhors sulky staff and weepy waitresses and only the other week Pip, walking into Gladys' office, saw her pouring scorn on a sobbing girl. Snivelling, she says, never got anyone anywhere.

Now the three of them settle at Gladys' table and Eric picks up the menu.

"Try that fish," says Gladys, "it's the dish of the day. Cook's made a lovely sauce this morning. Something a bit different."

Once the orders are taken Gladys gets down to reliving the day.

"We went over in convoy. Buck Jones led with me in the front of the taxi. I had Alice and Rose in the back. They wore their black dresses but I got them to keep their aprons and headdresses back to put on at the last minute. We took spare aprons too."

"Good idea," says Pip.

"Yes, just in case. I wanted them to look spotless. Victor Powell turned up with his car and took the others. I think he quite enjoyed driving the young women. And then there was Mr Cooper. He and Cook got all the food into the cars. She'd got it well organised."

"Did the big bread trays work out?" asks Eric.

"Yes. She'd packed everything up into the trays with greaseproof paper. She took the cooked meats whole and carved them when she got to Coughton. And then there were ten big serving dishes with the salmon."

"Ten!"

"Yes, Pip. Ten salmon. All beautifully dressed. They looked marvellous. And then there were the five hundred cocktail savouries. She did a wonderful job.

"Mr Bowen brought up the rear of the convoy with all the crockery and we fitted in a couple of the bread trays with him too. We drove off up the High Street. Beryl was walking to work. She was saying last night, we looked so funny. It was early, of course, but quite a few people were about and watched us leave. We had to go slowly, what with all that food balanced in the cars. Like a funeral procession, Beryl said."

"So," says Eric, "what happened when you got there?"

"We had to drive up the back drive, of course, and then we got everything unloaded through the tradesmen's doors. The kitchens are huge. We were given our own area to work in, a smaller kitchen off the main one.

"Their cook was very pleasant, and the rest of the staff. One of the youngsters had been put on kettle duty, kept everyone going with plenty of tea. Very welcoming. Of course, they were all working flat out. Had been for days."

"I'll bet," says Pip. "This fish is very tasty, Gladys." She waves her knife over the plate. "As you say, it's the sauce. What is it?"

"It's one of Cook's secret concoctions. But I know there's real cream in it."

"Well, it's delicious."

"Back to what you were saying," interrupts Eric. "What happened next?"

"Patience, Eric."

"Not his strong point," says Pip cuttingly.

Gladys ignores the tension.

"We were all ready, the morning had gone well and I was upstairs with the waitresses. We were getting the measure of the set up when who should walk into the room but Lady Throckmorton!"

"Gracious," says Pip. "What is she like?"

"Oh, she was very pleasant. She knew who I was, came straight up to me and thanked me for stepping into the breach. Those were her words."

"That's the upper classes for you," observes Pip. "They're not ones who put on airs and graces."

"No. No need to. She was dressed ready for going to the church. In a long silvery grey dress and coat with a fur stole around her shoulders. I suppose you'd call the colour of the outfit dove grey. Her hat matched. It had a beautiful diamond brooch that was holding up one side of the ruched brim. It was dazzling."

"She sounds very imposing," says Pip.

"She's not very tall. Only about my size. In fact," laughed Gladys, "the waitresses were funny. They said she looked a bit like me. Imagine that!"

"And?" Says Eric.

"And what?"

"What did she want, Lady Throckmorton? When she came up to you."

"She asked me if I would mind staying in the Blue Drawing Room when they were all at the church. All the wedding presents were displayed in there. She said someone needed to keep an eye on them."

"What an honour. She must have thought you were trustworthy."

"Well, I hope so Eric! I mean, it was all well and good feeling honoured, but I'd not really got the time. I needed to be with my staff in the last hour before the guests started arriving."

"But you couldn't say no?" says Pip.

"Well, of course not. They were very impressive, the gifts."

"You'd expect that."

"Yes Eric, I know. I felt it was a big responsibility. I sat there, surrounded by this great display, feeling quite nervous. Apart from a mass of very expensive looking glassware and silver and porcelain, there were quite a lot of oriental looking presents. Rugs and things. Very exotic. And a chiming clock, looked French, so pretty, in a glass case and a big carved elephant with ivory tusks standing in the middle of it all. I just kept thinking, supposing something goes missing. I'd get the blame."

"And when they all came back from the church?"

"Oh, well. Where do I start? This Miss Thompson, who'd made the dresses, well, she'd made them all look like something out of a fairy tale."

"What colour were the dresses?" asks Pip. Eric gives up. Resigns himself to having to listen to the women.

"They were all in white, Pip. Everything was white apart from the flowers. And the page boys, they were in white too. The bridesmaids had circles of flowers on their heads and carried little posies of rosebuds and carnations that picked up the pink of the roses in the bride's bouquet. She's so clever, Miss Thompson. I spoke to her at the end. It had taken her six weeks to get everything made. Including the trousseau."

"And the groom?"

"He was a good looking man. Looked very pleasant. Of course, I didn't actually speak to any of the guests. Obviously."

"So," says Eric, "how did the food go?"

"Oh, fine. I could hear guests discussing the savouries, very appreciatively, saying how unusual some of them were. There were so many people. Beautiful clothes."

"Did you see anyone famous?"

"Well, one of the butlers pointed out Sir Anthony Eden. Apparently he's quite a regular at Coughton. Very close friend of Her Ladyship's.

"They all went through to the dining room eventually. You should have seen how it was laid up. Massive silver candelabra all down the tables, gigantic vases, big colourful flower displays, fruit bowls on pedestals in amongst it all. It's given me some fresh ideas to use here.

"Cook's salmon and meats were all laid out on the cold tables ready to be served up. They looked really good."

"She's done a fine job." Gladys turns to Eric.

"Yes, she certainly has. I wonder, what do you think about a rise in her wages?"

"Good idea. We'll put it on the agenda for the next board meeting. And you can do a report on the wedding."

"I've already thought about that and made a few notes. I'll get Prim to type it up."

"Your new secretary," says Pip. "That must be a help, having someone to do all the office work."

"Yes, it's made all the difference. You can come round to the office and meet her after lunch."

"How's she getting on?"

"Fine. I'm very pleased with her."

"And the office?"

"That's been a good move. Better than being stuck upstairs. Much more room. You'll see for yourself."

"Your days of being a secretary are well and truly over."

"I just haven't got the time these days to be doing everything."

"Mind you keep your eye on the ball in the office. Never let staff take over, however much you need to rely on them," says Eric.

Gladys, tight lipped, shakes her head.

"No-one's going to get the better of me. I've got my finger on the pulse, don't you worry. No need for you to think you have to tell me what to do, just because you're my brother and a man. I'm older than you and don't you forget it!"

* * *

August 1939

Each weekday morning Prim Mitchell lets herself in, picks up the post and heads for the office via the cake shop where young Doris is stocking the shelves with fresh loaves and Joan is arranging the day's cakes in the glass display cabinet.

She hangs her coat on the back of the office door, places her hat on top of the metal filing cabinet that takes up one corner of the room and locks her handbag into the bottom of the filing cabinet because, as she is often heard to say, you can never be too sure.

She says it several times a day, about anything from the freshness of the meat delivered to the restaurant to the assurances of Prime Minister Chamberlain that England won't have to go to war with Germany.

Prim lifts the green fitted dust cover off her typewriter and starts to open the post. All the envelopes are slit open with a brass paper knife and their contents unfolded and smoothed out. The envelopes she keeps to one side for her nephew who collects the stamps.

Amongst today's post Prim sees something familiar. It is a folded sheet entitled Public Information Leaflet No 2, with closely printed information on the two inside pages and on the back.

Everyone in Britain has already been sent Public Information Leaflet No 1, *What to do in the Event of War*. The leaflet today is a different colour and has two sections, one of which is information about gas masks, but it is the second section, *Masking your Windows,* which causes Prim some concern. Ten minutes later she goes in search of Gladys who tells her they can meet up at coffee time.

"Come through to the café at 10.30," says Gladys. "and we'll discuss it then."

* * *

"I'll need to talk to the other directors about this," says Gladys. "It's going to be a big job. There's sixteen windows over the four floors on the front, before we even start on the shop front and down the sides."

"That's the problem, isn't it," says Prim. "It's all an 'If'. You're going to be asked to spend time and money on all this and we don't even know if it will be needed."

Gladys isn't listening. She seems to be staring at a space on the wall. Prim waits. After a few minutes Gladys pulls down the pen that's lodged behind her ear.

"We've got to think ahead, Prim. The news on the wireless is serious. It's all well and good Mr Chamberlain trying to keep in with Hitler, but if he's wrong then things will happen quickly." She frowns, shakes her head. "Hitler's a nasty piece of work, whatever the Prime Minister says, and if war comes and we can't black out our windows we'll end up having to shut until we're sorted out."

"And everyone's going to be trying to do the same," says Prim. "There'll be a shortage of material, for sure."

"Look at what this leaflet says: *Do not leave things until the last minute.* It says you could put up sheets of black paper or paint the windows. Can you imagine how depressing that would be? If war comes, Prim, De Greys is going to have to look more welcoming than ever to people."

Prim listens, doesn't attempt to interrupt, knows Mrs Watson well enough to understand that just because she's talking it doesn't mean she wants an answer.

Gladys presses her hand down on the leaflet as though she is getting the better of the problem, taps her fingers thoughtfully.

"Phone Mr Morris. Do it now, Prim, before other people get in first. Arrange for me to see him. He's the man we need."

* * *

Mr Morris comes over in person to do the measuring. He enjoys doing business with Mrs Watson, knows where he stands.

He smiles to himself when he thinks about the way she set about those bedrooms when she first arrived, how taken aback he was when she'd first made her proposal. You supply all the soft furnishings and linens, one at a time, she'd said, and I'll pay for each room once it's earning its keep.

He'd taken a gamble agreeing, but she'd kept her word and he did all right out of it. The rooms are always let, often for weeks on end to the same people, young clerks from the banks who come to the Bromsgrove branches for training. Clever move of hers, to get in with the banks. There's a steady flow of respectable young men staying at De Greys and she's not having to rely on travelling salesmen and the small amount of passing trade that comes the way of the town.

A couple of days later he sends his assistant over to Gladys with the estimate for blackout blinds for De Greys. Gladys picks up the telephone receiver, asks the operator to connect her. He's been expecting the call.

"Mrs Watson. Good morning. You've got my estimate?"

"Yes. It's too expensive."

"Well, I did say yesterday that the glazed Lancaster cloth is of the highest quality."

"I know that. I phoned to say we need to give more thought to the entrance. We'll have to have something to block out the light as people come in and out of the building at night."

"A light trap."

"Is that what they're calling it?"

"Yes. It would work well with curtains. And during the day you could tie them back against the wall. I could make them look good."

"Well, I've already told you I think your estimate is high. So how about including these door curtains in the price?"

He agrees. No use in arguing with Mrs Watson and besides, once Mrs Watson's blackout curtains are up at De Greys and her customers find out who supplied them, that will bring in more orders for him.

* * *

Beryl dismisses the idea of a war, and even if it happens, she's sure it won't change anything much in Bromsgrove. Ladies will still want to have their hair done at the salon and Carton Millage, star of the local operatic society and the best looking member of the tennis club, will continue to court her. Gladys, it seems, had worried unnecessarily about Terence Hall whom Beryl had given up long ago, even though he had given her every attention possible and taught her to drive his MG, his pride and joy.

All summer Carton and Beryl have been together and she has won the hearts of his family, who, being musical themselves, are enchanted by Beryl's singing and piano playing. Mr Millage in particular, long since retired as a member of the Gilbert and Sullivan Operatic Company, has, like his son, fallen for this fragile looking girl who happily joins in the family's musical evenings.

This morning, as Beryl busies herself at the salon, she might feel her ears burning. Barbara Millage has been entertaining at home, and the ladies are lingering later than usual over the coffee cups and the last of the cakes.

"I expect," says Madge James, "She likes coming here, being part of normal family life."

"Yes. There's that. It's such a different life that she's had from Carton. But of course, she's very musical, so they've got that in common."

"Didn't they meet through Iona?"

"Yes. She palled up with Beryl at the dramatic society. Then she brought her back here to meet Carton." Betty raises her eyebrows.

"Matchmaking for her brother?"

"It's possible," agrees Barbara.

"And Mrs Watson. Does she approve?" This from Betty Wheeler.

"Oh, well, of course she approves," retorts Barbara. "Why shouldn't she?"

"Why indeed," laughs Madge. "Carton is a good catch. Good looking, good prospects."

"I was just curious," explains Betty. "I hear she's seen off one or two young men before Carton whom she didn't think were suitable."

"Well," says Madge. "She can't say that Carton is unsuitable and it certainly looks like he's spoken for now he's met Beryl. That'll break a few girls' hearts in Bromsgrove."

* * *

Sunday 3 September 1939

"This morning the British Ambassador in Berlin handed the German Government a final note stating that, unless we heard from them by 11 o'clock that they were prepared at once to withdraw their troops from Poland, a state of war would exist between us.

I have to tell you now that no such undertaking has been received, and that consequently this country is at war with Germany."

Neville Chamberlain, Prime Minister

* * *

Gladys doesn't know immediately what's going on, doesn't hear until she gets back from church that broadcasting was interrupted at a quarter past eleven. She knew it was coming, they'd all known it was only a matter of time once Germany had got into Poland.

* * *

Beryl is late waking. From the warmth of her bed she watches the way the sun is lighting up the pattern on the drawn curtains and thinks about last night's party at the tennis club and the day ahead that she'll be spending with Carton.

* * *

At Lavender Road, until half an hour ago, it had been just another Sunday morning.

"What does it mean?" demands Zena.

"It means," says Eric, "What Mr Chamberlain says. We are now at war with Germany."

* * *

Beryl clatters down the stairs and into the little sitting room on the first floor. Gladys looks up sharply.

"Have you only just got up?"

"Yes."

"You're too noisy on those stairs."

"It's my sandals."

"It's those heels. They're very high. You mind you don't sprain your ankle."

"They're fine. These straps across the top give a lot of support."

"If you've only just got up, you didn't hear the broadcast?"

"What broadcast?"

"That Hitler hasn't met the deadline." Beryl throws herself onto the sofa opposite Gladys.

"You mean, to leave Poland?"

"Yes."

"So are we going to have a war?"

"War has started. An hour ago. War with Germany." Gladys puts her head in her hands. "Again."

November 1939

With the blackout arrangements complete and all the space in De Greys that she can possibly muster ready for what she is sure will be an exodus of people seeking safety away from the cities, Gladys is prepared.

But the war doesn't start with a bang in Bromsgrove. At the beginning children are evacuated from Birmingham to people's homes, but then, when things seem quiet and the children get homesick, many of them return to their parents. London's getting it, the Brummies would say. That's where Hitler's hitting.

It is only a matter of time. London might be Britain's capital but everyone knows that Hitler will get round to the Midlands pretty soon with an aim to try and destroy the factories that will give Britain the arms to defeat him. And they know that the nights will be the time to fear.

By the beginning of 1940 there is a steady trickle of people coming out of Birmingham, trying to find somewhere safe to stay overnight. At De Greys, once all the bedrooms are occupied, Gladys arranges for people to sleep on the floor of the restaurant. They are young men, happy to push back the tables once the "Closed" sign goes up on the front door and unroll a motley selection of mattresses and sleeping bags. It's a novelty, an adventure, and takes them back to the camaraderie of their days in the Boy Scouts.

They wake each morning to the sound of Tilly Harper telling them to get a move on, to put back the tables and chairs, open the windows to let some air in and to get upstairs to the bathrooms. By eight o'clock they've eaten a hearty breakfast, picked up their hats and bags and set off up the high street in good spirits to the bus station.

The 144 bus takes them into Birmingham and along the way they pass the Austin factory. Plenty of the young men have family members and friends working in there, and the bus goes quiet as it passes, all eyes looking to *the works*. It's still all there, they say.

* * *

Alice Wheeler stands at Gladys' table in the restaurant, explains about the lady and gentleman who she's left waiting at the front door.

"They've come out from Birmingham. I've said there's no rooms left here. They've asked to see you anyway. Well, they asked to see the manager. I told them, there's no manager here."

"Who did you say I was then?"

"The Lady Director." Gladys smiles to herself but to Alice she says what are they like, this couple? "Well turned out. They don't look short of a penny. She's in a two piece with a fancy hat. And they've parked a car outside."

Gladys pushes her tea cup away, gets to her feet.

"I'll come," says Gladys.

* * *

They're grateful, he says, for her taking the time to see them. They're not brummies, thinks Gladys. Not by the sound of them.

She's nearly as tall as her husband, wears her clothes well. Smart shoes. Gladys can see she is anxious.

He's nice looking, in a kindly way. An amiable man, she imagines. He tells her that his wife can't sleep. It's been going on for weeks. They don't want to be in Birmingham any longer.

"Your waitress says you're full up. But we wondered, maybe you know somewhere else that might have a vacancy?"

"Just the two of you?"

"Yes. Most of the time. We've two sons but our eldest has already joined up. Our youngest is just seventeen. He's on watch duties at night in one of the city parks. So he won't be here much."

"And in the daytime?"

"I'll be going to Birmingham. I'll use my car if they don't cut the petrol ration any further. I'll give a lift to anyone else who needs to get in each day."

"You work in Birmingham?"

"I'm in business. We distribute parts to the motor trade. I'm a director. We came to Birmingham from London. Sixteen years ago. Our son also works with me."

Gladys thinks quickly. She's got one room left she saves for Nancy or Vi when they stay. From now on, she thinks, they'll just have to share with me.

"I have got one room I could let you have. It's at the top of the building, I'm afraid, and it's not big." She turns to the wife. "And there's a small room leading off which you could use as a sitting room. If your son needs to stay sometimes, we could put a folding bed up in there for him."

He turns to his wife.

"What do you think, dear?"

"It sounds perfect. Can we see the room?"

"I'm sorry, we'll need to get it ready first. Maybe you could come back in a couple of days' time?"

"No," he says. "We'll take it unseen. What are your rates?"

"Five guineas a week. That will include breakfast and an evening meal."

"And if we return occasionally to Birmingham and don't need the room or the meals?"

"There wouldn't be a reduction. Accommodation here is in such demand."

"Yes. Of course."

"I'm sorry."

"No, we understand." He turns to his wife. "Are you happy to come here, Lily?"

"Absolutely. She reaches out, rests her hand lightly on Gladys' arm. "I'm so grateful. I feel I will be able to relax here. It feels as though it was meant to be."

Gladys nods. She hears it all the time. She gestures to the reception desk.

"I'll have to take a deposit. And I need some details for the records. Firstly, can I have your names?"

"French," he says. "Our surname is French. I'm Stanley. And this is Lily."

* * *

Christmas 1939

Beryl knows nothing is forever, learnt a lesson for life on that stormy January morning in 1935 when Daisy England stood in the doorway of her bedroom with the terrible news.

So when Babs Luce leaves her husband and the Tudor Salon closes, bringing Beryl's apprenticeship to an end, and when at night she lies in bed waiting for the ghostly wail of the air raid sirens or has to go to Worcester to sleep at Lavender Road in Zena's room when Gladys lets her room, Beryl just accepts what has come her way.

De Greys is full to bursting but she steers clear of the residents, especially the young men who sleep in the restaurant each night. Not so Denise who revels in talking to everyone so that Gladys has to tell Maud to restrain her from pestering people.

* * *

Babs Luce moves into De Greys, temporarily, so she can sort herself out. Beryl knows exactly what 'sorting herself out' means, has gleaned enough from whispered conversations to understand what's going on.

She arrives one morning in time for coffee with four coats over her arm and several hat boxes. The suitcases are delivered later. Everything is crammed into the tiny box room on the second floor. Gladys gives her a discount of half a guinea a week on the usual room rate. "As you're my friend," says Gladys, "and because it's not one of the best rooms. But you'll have to pay in advance, Babs. Like everyone else."

* * *

Spring 1940

One afternoon Gladys summons Beryl to their table in the restaurant.

"You can pour, Beryl. Do you want a cake?"

Beryl shakes her head.

"What is it you want to talk about?"

"I'll come straight to the point. We've got to think about your future. You can't just languish."

"I'm not languishing."

"You are. You're just wasting your time. And I can't afford to have you around here doing nothing."

"What am I supposed to do? It's not my fault Mrs Luce has let me down."

"She hasn't let you down. The circumstances were beyond her control." Beryl pulls a face. "I know you're missing the job. Every time I see you you're down in the dumps. But you've got to pull yourself together and get on and do something."

"What sort of thing?"

"Eric has something up his sleeve, but I'll come to that in a minute. First of all, I've made an arrangement for you to be a volunteer."

"Doing what?"

"They need someone up at the police station in the evenings."

"The police station? What am I going to do there?"

"They've set up a Report Centre. They'll teach you how to work the switchboard and you'll get calls coming through when the Germans are flying this way."

Beryl looks at Gladys in alarm.

"How do they know when they're coming?"

"It's all to do with radar. I don't know how it all works and you don't need to know either. You'll just take the messages and pass them on."

"So, what do they want me to do? Tell the Germans to steer clear of Bromsgrove?"

"Don't try and be clever."

"I wasn't. It was a joke."

"It's no joking matter. It seems you have to answer the telephones, write down the messages you're given and then pass them on. Then the air raid sirens can be switched on."

"I don't know whether I want to do that," frowns Beryl. "I've never worked a switchboard."

"Now's the time to learn. You'll be fine."

"Wasn't there anything else I could have done?"

"No. That's what's been arranged. And as it will only take up some of your evenings, not enough to keep you occupied, Uncle Eric has found you a job for the mornings."

"What sort of job?"

"A paid job. Driving. You'll enjoy it."

"What sort of driving?"

"One of the vans. It's like this. The bakery is losing the van drivers. They're joining up. So you'll do one of the bread rounds. Uncle Eric will send a boy with you to do the carrying. You'll drive, the boy will do the delivering."

Beryl brightens up. Ever since Terence Hall took her out in his car, she's been longing to get a chance to drive again.

"How much is he going to pay me?"

"That's to be arranged. You'll have to get going early to get over to the bakery at Droitwich to pick up the van, but you'll be finished by lunchtime." Gladys looks at her watch. "I've got to go. Stay here and finish the tea. And here's a leaflet for you. It tells you all about the Report Centre."

Beryl concentrates on examining her fingernails, makes no effort to pick up the official looking piece of paper.

"Go on. Take it. You need to understand what you'll be doing before you start. You're to go up to the police station at six o'clock tomorrow evening."

"I can't possibly go tomorrow. I've made arrangements with Carton."

"Then you'll have to unmake them. You'll be at the police station at six o'clock. Don't be late. Wear something sensible and try and make a good impression. Don't let me down."

* * *

It's the end of a warm July afternoon and Ralph is passing through Bromsgrove on his way home. In the kitchen Gladys and Cook are staring at the meat delivery.

"It's not much, is it," says Cook. Gladys pushes away the butcher's paper wrapping, gives the joint a poke.

"You're sure it's beef?" she says.

"I'm sure."

"What else could it be?" interrupts Ralph.

"Horse," says Gladys.

"Blimey!"

"This is definitely beef," says Cook, running her finger over the grain of the meat. "But I don't know how many portions I can get out of it. It'll have to be sliced very thin. It's about half of what I usually have to work with."

"I thought," said Ralph, "that they weren't rationing restaurants yet. I thought there were just restrictions on how many courses you could serve."

"They're not rationing caterers," explains Gladys, "but that doesn't mean it's easy to get hold of things. Shortages are shortages, and if there's not much meat to be had then the butchers have to share it out around the hotels and restaurants as best they can."

"I bet," says Ralph, "they don't allocate it fairly."

"They don't," says Cook bitterly. "I can tell you that for sure. There's some places getting favours done for them. I suppose they're the ones in the know somewhere along the road." Ralph shakes his head, turns to Gladys.

"How about a cuppa', Glad?"

"Good idea. Time I stopped and had a break. We'll go into the restaurant and they can bring the tea through." Ralph holds his hand up to stop her.

"Let's have it upstairs. In your sitting room."

"What's wrong with down here?"

"I've got something I want to talk to you about and after seeing that bit of beef it's none too soon. But we need some privacy."

* * *

"You've made it nice in here."

Gladys kicks off her shoes.

"This is my new chair. Do you like it?"

"Bit flowery for my taste."

"My feet and legs are killing me." She settles in the chair, half heartedly massages one leg and then the other. "We've had to make some space in Mr and Mrs French's sitting room for an extra bed. That's why the chair's in here."

"More people to cram in?"

"I don't mind. Their son's come for a few days. He's most likeable. Quite a charmer and very good looking."

"The girls will be onto him then?"

Gladys leans back in the chair, stretches out her legs and crosses her ankles.

"You're looking well, Ralph."

"Yes. I can't complain. How are things going here?"

"All right. We're getting by. We're full, of course. Bursting at the seams."

"That's good. Pity you can't fit in any more."

"Ah, well, funny you should say that. I've got some news. There's a big house come on the market, at the top of the Alcester Road. It's a whopper, Ralph, and it's got acres of garden and more accommodation outside, a cottage and a couple of chalets that I could let."

"So? How can you possibly take that on?"

"You know Pip's been left this money?"

"Yes, Eric told me. Quite a tidy sum, isn't it?"

"Certainly is. She's coming in with me. She's going to loan me half the asking price and I've been to see the bank."

"Blimey. You don't waste time then."

"We had quite a chat. I did my sums before I went, gave him all the figures, told him how much I thought I could make out of it."

"And what did he say?"

"He's going to let me have a decision by the end of the week."

Ralph rubs the back of his neck, looks thoughtful.

"You're sure you won't bite off more than you can chew?"

"I know what I'm doing. I'll let most of the rooms and give them breakfast at the house. They'll have to come down here at lunchtime for their main meal."

"And the money? How're you going to pay back the money?"

"I've worked it all out." Ralph shakes his head, can't quite believe what he's hearing. "Don't go on about it now. I'm trying not to think about it. I shan't know anything until the end of the week."

She flicks her hand dismissively.

"Change the subject. Tell me how things are going in Worcester."

"Pretty quiet. Well away from the troubles by and large."

"That's good. Have you seen much of the others?"

"There's trouble with Zena."

"What sort of trouble?"

"I'm not sure really. I think she and Eric aren't getting on. You know how he can't bear anyone to cross him. He lays the law down, things he'd do better to let go, like telling Zena she can't paint her fingernails. And she's fighting back."

"She would. Eric's too petty at times and Zena's a spirited girl."

"Not like Beryl, Glad."

"Beryl has her moments. But no, she and Zena are different. Mind you, Beryl paints her nails. I don't mind but Vi got a bit upset when she was staying."

"Vi's an old prude."

"What does Pip say?"

"She's in the middle of it all, trying to keep the peace. She doesn't back Eric up as much as he'd like."

"I don't blame her. He can be so difficult at times. Always so sure he's right." Gladys sighs. "Things have never been right since Beverley died."

"That's a long time ago now."

"I'm telling you though, that's where the problems started. Zena's not a bad girl, but Eric and Pip have let losing Beverley take them over. Zena's got everything she wants in one way, but in other ways she's being neglected."

"You surprise me. I've never heard you speak like that before."

"Well, you mark my words. Things won't work out well for the three of them. What about Dora? Any news?"

"Nothing of Dora. I called round a couple of weeks ago but there was no-one in. I pushed a note through the door but she's not been in touch." Ralph shakes his head. "It's not right, Glad, these rifts. Mother wouldn't have liked it at all."

"I know. It's hard to know who's at fault. I think Dora and Eric were at loggerheads and it's just gone on from there."

"What do you think started it?"

"I think," says Gladys slowly, feeling her way through something that's bothered her for some time, "I think that Dora feels she hasn't had much help from the family. With her Harry."

"I don't understand that."

"Well, Eric's given me a lot of help. There's no denying it. Having us all to live in Worcester and then getting me set up here."

"True." Ralph smiles wryly. "But you know as well as I do, Eric doesn't do anything in life that's not going to suit him. Don't forget he's part of the business arrangement here. The more you make a success of the business the better for Eric."

"Still," argues Gladys, "if it wasn't for him I would probably still be in Nechells. Or maybe I'd have found a job in an office somewhere. Anyway, we can't keep going over it all. What is it you want to tell me that's so private?"

* * *

When he's gone, she goes upstairs to her bedroom. This is the hour when no-one must disturb her. She can't relax today, not after what they've discussed, but she still stays lying on the bed as Dr Eades recommended. All women, he insists, would have a lot less trouble with their health if they put their feet up every afternoon for an hour.

It's nothing short of a bombshell. She's never been dishonest, never imagined she could be. Not in the ordinary run of things. But they're no longer living in ordinary times.

She thinks it could work. It makes sense, seeing as he's in touch with the farmers. There'll be more meat than you can use, he'd said. We can sell on. Decide who you can trust. Get them on your side Glad. Whatever you do, don't tell Eric.

* * *

"You must invite him."

"Why?"

"Because it's polite. He's sitting around the place twiddling his thumbs. He's at a loose end."

"It's not my fault." Beryl frowns. "I don't even know his name."

"Yes you do. It's Basil. Basil French." Gladys presses on. "He doesn't know anyone here. All his friends are in Birmingham."

"I know that. But I'm going with Carton. He'll be in the way."

"Nonsense. It's a party, Beryl. You'll ask him and that's all there is to it. I'm not discussing it any longer." Gladys ignores Beryl's scowl.

"Also," she continues, a slyness slipping under her words that Beryl doesn't notice, "I can't see you'll have to worry about him once you're there. He's such a good looking young man. I expect there'll be plenty of girls willing to take him off your hands."

* * *

He's waiting in the front hall of De Greys at seven forty-five sharp, wearing a navy blazer and grey slacks. The top of her head is level with his shoulder. She hasn't really noticed him properly before. She looks up, sees the way his hair is neatly parted. It is thick and wavy and as dark as hers is fair.

Now she comes to think about it, she quite likes the look of him, the wide eyes and symmetry of his face above a perfectly knotted tie nestling against the gleam of his white collar. She looks at the raincoat he has folded over his right arm.

"It's not raining."

"The forecast isn't good." He smiles down at her. She has, he thinks, a vulnerability about her, something that makes him feel she needs looking after. "I'm just a cautious sort of person."

She shrugs, sees now he is also holding a trilby hat with a green feather tucked in the band. No one here in Bromsgrove has got a hat like that. He clears his throat.

"It's very good of you to ask me. I hope you don't mind my tagging along."

"It's all right."

"I won't get in the way. I promise."

"We have to wait for Carton."

"Is he your boyfriend?"

"Yes." He wonders about her life, and he wonders about Carton.

"Are you engaged?"

"No. Not engaged." He sees a flush pass across her cheeks.

"I'm sorry. That was rude of me. It's none of my business."

"N-no. It's fine. And there's the doorbell."

Carton arrives, looks puzzled.

"Who's this?"

"This," she says, waving her hand in Basil's direction, "this is Basil French. From Birmingham. He and his parents are staying here. He's at a loose end so my mother's suggested he comes out with us."

Carton rallies, remembers his manners and extends a hand to Basil.

"I hope you don't mind," says Basil.

"Not at all," replies Carton rather too brusquely. "You're welcome."

Carton bustles towards the door, holding it open for Beryl to step into the street. She holds back, frowning.

"I've forgotten my torch," she says. "It'll be pitch dark by the time we walk back."

"I've got one," says Carton gallantly.

"So have I," adds Basil.

* * *

She stays at Carton's side, but out of the corner of her eye she watches him. When they'd arrived she'd introduced him to their hosts, Barbara Davenport and her sister Sally, and his offer to help with the drinks was a good move. Now he's looking completely at ease as he circles the room, offering to refill glasses as he tells people his name and where he's from and why he's in Bromsgrove. People are taking an interest, particularly the girls, as her mother had foreseen. He's a new face, handsome and charming, and a welcome change from the usual crowd.

Upstairs, at the end of the evening, the bedroom is full of chatter as the young women sort through the layers of coats on the bed. You kept quiet about him, they say to Beryl. She shrugs, puts on her fur jacket and stoops to the dressing table mirror to check her hair.

Outside there is no moon to help them on the walk home. The darkness of the blackout clings to the three young people as they make their way back towards the town. Carton's torch, dimmed with a covering of paper, lights the way. He takes Beryl's arm to guide her.

At the top of New Road, by the Cottage Hospital, Basil feels for her free hand. His daring takes her breath away. What cheek! But she leaves her hand in his.

Summer 1940

Denise longs to be a Girl Guide and wear a blue shirt and a hat with a brim and a badge. The Guides and Brownies in Bromsgrove are busy every weekend collecting salvage and some have even been helping the council men paint the kerbstones in the high street. She'd watched enviously from the window as they carefully daubed white paint at intervals onto the kerbstones to make it easier for people to find their way in the blackout.

She long ago gave up hoping she could ever join them. All her pleading to her mother has been in vain and she knows she's pushing her luck. Maud reminds her that she is lucky even to be allowed to remain at school.

The school, however, is collecting paper, a precious wartime commodity, and so Denise gets organised. She keeps a log book and records the names of all the residents and staff at De Greys. Everyone is pushed into her scheme and on Friday mornings she sets off on her rounds.

She starts in the kitchens where Cook has let her keep a large box by the back door for staff to fill with their old papers. There's a few in the box, some evening editions of the locals and some copies of The News of the World.

Once she has ticked off the kitchen in her book she makes her way to the office.

When she's collected all the office paper and thanked Miss Mitchell, she decides to start on the residents. Gladys has given her strict instructions not to bother the cake shop staff in the mornings so she'll come back later in the afternoon when the shop is quiet.

She climbs to the top of the building slowly so as not to get out of breath and knocks on Mr and Mrs French's door. They are the newest residents, the people with the son who stays sometimes and who is getting friendly with Beryl, and their details will need to go in the book. Denise will have to explain to Mrs French what is expected and how the scheme works. She's noticed already that Mr French often comes back from Birmingham with the Evening Mail and she knows they read the Sunday papers, so they will be a useful addition to the scheme.

Part 6

Mount Pleasant, Bromsgrove

Shaded by thick hollies and tall pines, there is a bend in the drive which hides the house so that, coming out into bright daylight at the end of the drive, the visitor is taken by surprise.

Its architect, mindful of the success of the Edwardian businessman for whom the house had been commissioned, had ensured that from every angle Mount Pleasant was an imposing building with its double gables, wide bay windows and steep pitched roofs.

Standing in the summer heat with Victor Powell waiting to show her round, Gladys knows, even before she goes inside, that this will be her house. She visualises days like today with the French doors open onto the tree lined lawns that sweep around two sides of the house, the deck chairs, afternoon tea.

At the far end of the lawn she can see one of the two chalets which are listed in Victor Powell's particulars. She can make something of those and she knows there is the cottage at the rear of the house which she will let. Her mind is racing. There's room for croquet, maybe even a tennis court. She's not imagining herself in one of the deck chairs. This is going to be a business venture, though the thought that it will also be a proper home for her is a thrill.

Mr Powell unlocks the front door and she steps into a square hall the size of her sitting room at De Greys, from where the staircase rises and gives way to a galleried landing. I shall get a gong for this hall, she decides, to summon the residents for their meals.

Ahead of her are double doors that lead to the main dining room and to her left is a high ceilinged sitting room with an ornately carved mahogany fireplace and the French windows leading to the lawn. She visualises winter evenings, knows exactly where she will put up a Christmas tree.

Beyond the dining room is the shady, stone flagged kitchen, the butler's pantry and a back door to a small yard and outbuildings, the coalhouses and the laundry. In the opposite corner of the yard there is the small cottage with its own front door which Victor Powell thinks may originally have been lived in by a member of staff, a gardener or a housekeeper. Already she is calculating how much rent it will bring in.

Gladys likes the feel of the polished dark oak of the stair rail as they climb to the first floor. She inspects all ten bedrooms, or almost ten, for one room is a tiny angled space sandwiched between two larger rooms which will just about house a bed and a single wardrobe.

Seven of the rooms are on the first floor, and three, accessed by a narrow, winding staircase, are on the top floor in the gabled roof. All the bedrooms, except the smallest, are fitted with wash basins and fireplaces. There'll be no fires upstairs, thinks Gladys, unless someone is ill. And she also decides which will be her room, the big sunny one overlooking the drive, and she will have a gas fire installed. It will double as her sitting room, the place of refuge and privacy for her and whoever else she may choose to entertain there.

A deep porcelain bath, surrounded by black and white tiles and supported on white iron feet, takes up a large part of the first floor bathroom. Gladys frowns at the green linoleum.

"That'll have to go. I don't like green. It's bad luck."

Victor Powell raises an eyebrow. The way Mrs Watson is making all these plans, he thinks. There's a lot of water to go under the bridge though probably, knowing her, she'll end up with what she wants.

* * *

Lily French is surprised that she rather enjoys her new life at De Greys. Stanley has done the right thing, bringing them out from the city to this quiet little market town. She knew she could rely on him, when he said he would find somewhere safe for them.

Away from the thunderous noise of the night bombings, Lily is sleeping better and finds she isn't missing her usual ordered routine as much as she'd imagined. She worries about her sons, of course, Geoffrey already in the thick of it and Basil will be next, she knows, but at least for the time being Basil is able to get away from his reservist duties in Birmingham and come and see them for a night or two now and then. Mrs Watson puts him up. So helpful.

Over coffee one morning in the restaurant she finds out more about Mrs Watson. When Stanley comes back that evening she can hardly wait to tell him.

"You'll never believe it. She came here from Birmingham. She and her husband used to be at The Court."

"The Court?"

"Oh you know. That big place opposite the Law Courts."

"What! The Court Restaurant in Corporation Street? Are you sure?"

"Yes. Mrs Baker told me all about it this morning. We had coffee together."

"How does Mrs Baker know? She's been staying here no longer than us."

"She got it out of Mrs Watson's daughter." Stanley looks up.

"Beryl?"

"No, not Beryl. She doesn't give much away."

"Not to most people. But she and Basil seem to have a lot to say to one another when he's here."

"Yes. I know." Lily loses track of her gossip for a moment, then shakes her head. "But Beryl's spoken for. There can't be anything in it."

"Lovely girl, though."

"Stanley French! You can put any thoughts of matchmaking out of your head. We mustn't upset anyone here. And anyway, it's Denise who's been talking. The little chatty one." Lily leans forward. "There's no Mr Watson. Mrs Watson's a widow."

"She's very young."

"Mrs Baker thinks he died of TB. When they were in Birmingham." Stanley stirs the sugar into his tea, two spoonfuls, he looks thoughtful.

"So how did she end up here?"

"No-one seems to know. She's a mystery, Stanley. That's what Mrs Baker says. Fact is, though, she's not short of money." Here Lily sits back, working her way up to impart the cream of the morning's gossip. "Guess what."

"What?"

"She's buying a house on the edge of the town. Up the hill on the road to Stratford-upon-Avon. Huge, apparently." Stanley looks startled. "Can you imagine, running De Greys and then taking on a big house?" Stanley can't imagine. Mrs Watson is a woman beyond his understanding of women. "The plan is, she's not only going to make it a home for her and her daughters, she's going to let rooms there to more people coming out from the city."

"As well as all the rooms she's letting here," says Stanley thoughtfully. "That's a clever move."

"I don't know how she does it. She seems quite an ordinary woman in lots of ways, but really, when you come to think about it, she's really quite extraordinary."

Worcester

Despite the heatwave, Eric's neck is wrapped up in a woollen scarf and he refuses Pip's suggestion to take the drinks into the cool of the garden. He sits on the opposite side of the empty fireplace sipping whisky and hot lemon. All this stifling day, nursing his cold, he has been thinking about Gladys and Pip's plan to buy Mount Pleasant.

"This house," he croaks, "I'm not sure about it all."

"It's a big, solid looking house. Well built. She can't go wrong with it."

"It's all happening in a rush though. I haven't even been sent any particulars to read."

"There aren't any. The house came on the market, Mr Powell told Gladys about it immediately and he hasn't had to draw up any particulars."

"I'll have to go over to Bromsgrove, see for myself."

"There's no need. You're not well enough to go this week and Gladys needs to get a move on. We know what we're doing."

"Look here," sighs Eric, "you've come into this money that your mother left you. It's the first time in your life you've had some of your own. You've no experience of financial matters. I want to make sure you know what you're doing."

"Oh shut up Eric!" she snaps. "Don't speak to me as though I'm a child. I know what I'm doing." Eric shakes his head. "I'm making an investment. And I've got complete confidence in Gladys."

"All right." He sneezes hard, several times, shakes out another clean handkerchief. "So let's say you pay for half of the house. How is she getting her half?"

"How many times do we have to go over this! She's having a loan from the bank. It's already agreed."

"And then, when she's bought it – if she buys it – where's the money coming from to furnish and equip it?"

"She's having a lot of the furniture in with the price. The bedrooms are furnished, there's a linen cupboard full of stuff that's being left, the kitchen has a built in range, the owners are leaving the refrigerators and everything in the laundry room. It's just the main rooms downstairs, the reception rooms as Mr Powell calls them."

"Hmm," Eric manages a smile. "Well, all I can say is that if Victor Powell is involved I pity the poor chap selling the place. Victor Powell's loyalties certainly won't lie with the vendor."

"Gladys has always looked after Mr Powell well at De Greys," says Pip, "and now he will look after her. Tit for tat. Simple as that."

"So you'll buy half the house and then she will pay you back eventually?"

"Not 'eventually'. Over four years. She's got it all planned out, had to do that before she went to see the bank manager. I'll get my loan back, plus the interest."

"And you say the bank manager thinks it's a good plan?"

"Absolutely. With so many people wanting somewhere to stay away from the cities for however long the war lasts. And there's certainly no sign that it's going to be over soon."

Eric grunts, gets to his feet, fusses with winding the clock on the mantelpiece, and replaces the key in the silver snuff box. When he's finished, he runs his finger over the top of the clock case, holds it up for Pip to see.

"See, this new woman. She's not dusting properly."

"Don't change the subject, Eric. Are you going to give the plan your blessing or not?"

"If it's what you want to do, Pip, you'd better go ahead. I suppose Gladys knows what she's taking on."

"Gladys knows exactly what she's doing. It will work. You wait and see. Mount Pleasant will be another of her successes."

* * *

"You're driving a van?"

Basil's voice echoes round the kitchen, still and empty of the usual clatter and steam, whilst upstairs Gladys, and many of the residents, are lying on top of their beds trying to keep cool on this heavy, sticky Sunday afternoon. Only the presence of the two young people stirs the air in the kitchen. Basil, in shirtsleeves, loosens his tie and props himself against the marble pastry counter.

"It's good fun. I've always enjoyed driving."

"So tell me about it."

"There's not much to tell." Beryl frowns, slops the water from the kettle into the pot, feels the back of her neck. "These thunder flies, they're horrible."

"Just ignore them."

"I can't. They're driving me mad. Where do they come from?"

"I don't know. They only appear when the weather's like this. Tell me about the driving."

"Hang on until I've got this tray sorted out, then I'll tell you. I can't concentrate on two things at once." She swipes her brow with the side of her hand, hooks damp curls behind her ears. "It's so hot in here."

"I don't mind about the tea if it's too much trouble."

"No. I'll do it. I've started now."

"Can I help?"

"I'll manage. It's just I'm not used to the kitchen. I'm all right upstairs with the kettle in the sitting room, but I don't come in here much." She flounces around the kitchen, opening and closing cupboard doors. If this is an attempt to impress Basil with a show of domesticity it is certainly failing.

"What are you looking for?"

"Cake. Or biscuits." She shrugs irritably. "Oh, I don't know where Cook hides these things."

He ambles across the kitchen.

"These tins look hopeful. Here, how about this?"

"Fruit cake. Well done."

He carries the tray through to Gladys' table in the hot, still restaurant. Beryl follows with the cake tin.

"Now, come on. Tell me everything about your new job. From when you get up in the morning to when you've finished."

"I have to be at Droitwich by eight." She catches his look of puzzlement. "That's where the bakery has its depot. The van's already loaded up and they give me the list of addresses that I've got to drive to. Then Davey gets in the passenger seat –"

"That's the boy?"

"Yes. David Spencer. Everyone calls him Davey. We do five villages. That's a full round. He gets out at the houses and delivers the orders and we're finished by lunchtime. Except on Saturdays. It takes longer then because we have to collect the money."

He watches her across the table. She seems so slender, so fragile. He can't imagine her driving one of the lumbering delivery vans.

"Are you really enjoying it?"

Her eyes lights up. "Absolutely. And Davey's good company, very bright, and he makes me laugh. He's not got a very happy home life. From what I can make out his father is a pretty awful man. A drinker, I think. His mother is working nights at the Austin factory."

"Poor kid."

"Yes. He's just fifteen. Not much of a life. But he's so cheerful, Basil. I know I didn't have a very happy childhood, but nothing like that."

"Your troubles were very different. From what you've told me, you've been through a lot."

Beryl shrugs. "You know, when my father died I used to watch my mother the whole time, making sure she didn't have any signs of illness. I lay awake every night worrying myself sick, wondering what would happen to Denise and me if she died too."

"That's probably quite natural for a child in those circumstances."

"Do you think so?"

"Yes, I do."

"You're the first person I've ever told. I've always felt guilty about it. I thought I was selfish, when my mother was going through so much, and all I was bothered about was whether I'd lose her too."

"I don't think you should feel guilty."

She leans forward, rests her chin in her cupped hands. She's looking at him but her thoughts are far away. "Just think," she says, "whilst I was at The Court with all those things happening to me, you were only a few miles away, in the same city, at school in Moseley." She toys with a slice of cake. "I wish I'd known you then."

He smiles, takes her hand, steers her back to the present.

"And so, when you go to Droitwich, you drive yourself there?"

"Yes. I still can't believe my mother's bought a car."

"She doesn't drive though, does she?"

"She's never driven. But when we move up the hill the plan is that I'm going to be running her up and down to De Greys." Beryl gives a wry smile. "I think it's another of her ploys to keep me busy, that and the van driving and going up to the report centre in the evenings. My mother can't bear to see people sitting around doing nothing. It's laziness in her eyes."

"Not in yours though?"

"When I was a child Maud always used to say I was a dreamer. And that wasn't meant as a compliment, I can assure you. I've never been able to win where Maud's concerned. As for not having a lot to do at the moment, it's not my fault if the salon's closed. I loved working there."

"Maybe you can carry on your training somewhere else. Not now, of course, but when the war's over."

"Whenever that may be. You've said yourself, you and I, we're going to be called up. Then we'll really be in the thick of it. Who knows how old we'll be when it's all over. All my plans to get my qualifications and open a salon. Will they ever come to anything now? It feels as though our lives have ground to a halt before they've even got going, as though everything has been swept to one side to make way for war."

Basil lights a cigarette, pushes back his chair.

"Come on." He holds out his hand to her. "It's too hot to stay inside and it's no good feeling sorry for ourselves. Let's get out. We'll have a walk along the high street. You can tell me all about the people who run the shops here."

* * *

Carton whispers through the darkness.

"Can't you keep still?" He hands her the box. "Have another chocolate. And stop fidgeting."

"I'm trying."

"Well, try harder."

Usually, the minute the lights are turned down and the music starts, she is hooked. Tonight is different. Ever since they arrived at the picture house there's been an atmosphere and she's dreading what will happen when the film ends.

A couple of hours later they step out into the gloom of the evening and start walking back to De Greys. He puts a restraining hand on her arm.

"Slow down, Beryl." She hunches her shoulders, crosses her arms tight to her chest. He shakes his head. "What's wrong with you?"

"Nothing," she says airily. "Nothing's wrong."

Carton stands still in the middle of the pavement. She, a little ahead, turns round to face him.

"You might as well tell me."

"Tell you what?" Her voice is all innocence, but colour suffuses her face.

"What's going on?"

"I don't know what you mean."

"For God's sake. Do you think I'm stupid? Or blind?"

She presses her palms together and brings her hands to her lips in a prayerful gesture to stop herself from speaking. He waits, hoping his silence will force her to say something, but it's all too much for him.

"It's Basil, isn't it?"

She keeps her head down. Carton will stand there all night if necessary, until she speaks. Basil's name hangs between them.

"What makes you think that?" She doesn't look up, keeps her head bowed over her hands.

"It's obvious. Even that first night when he came to the party with us. You tried to hide it but you couldn't take your eyes off him. And he was interested in you from the start. Anyone could see that. But I didn't think he'd do the dirty on me," he says bitterly.

Now she looks up, her eyes huge and tearful.

"It's not like that."

"How is it then, Beryl?" he demands. "I'm baffled. You need to tell me. How does he compare with me? You and I, we have so much in common. Everyone says so. And my family, they've treated you like a daughter. Is this what they get in return?" His voice falters. "Tell me what's going on then. It's the least you can do."

Beryl shakes her head, spilling tears onto her cheeks.

"Please don't shout."

"What do you expect me to do? Come on Beryl, explain to me what's happened."

"I know everything you're saying about us is right," she says. "I'm just so sorry and I can't help what is happening. Honestly, it's not his fault. He didn't mean to break us up. I'll swear on the Bible if you want."

"Don't be silly."

"I want you to believe me, it hasn't been like that. We really just started as friends."

"Friends?" Carton shakes his head.

"Yes. He hasn't done the dirty, as you call it. Hasn't even tried to kiss me."

"So?"

"It's as though I've known him for years. We just talk a lot."

"Oh, right." Carton gives a short, bitter laugh. "So you talk a lot. And I suppose you and I never talk?" He stops, takes a deep breath, tries to keep a snarl out of his voice. "What else? What else do you do with him that you can't do with me? Come on Beryl, put your cards on the table."

"He makes me feel safe."

He didn't expect that.

"Safe!"

"Yes. Safer than I've felt since I was a child."

He doesn't know what to say. She looks beyond him, into nothing in particular, trying to find the words to explain her feelings. Carton waits. Finally, she speaks, slowly, thoughtfully, selecting each word with care.

"He makes me feel as safe as before my father died. And I'd never thought my life could be like that again." Her eyes meet his, calm and honest. "And that is the truth. I'm sorry, but that's all there is to it. There's nothing else I can say."

She has never seen a man look so unhappy, so defeated. She can't believe she could hurt someone so much, but her guilt is mingled with relief. There is nothing more she can say. She shakes her head, turns from him, makes her way alone along the street to De Greys.

* * *

In England there is a new breed of lawbreakers, honest, respectable citizens in peacetime, and Gladys and Ralph, Cook Cooper and Prim Mitchell are amongst them.

It starts with Ralph, the late evening calls, a few bags of sugar, some butter and, of course, the meat for the restaurant. But Gladys soon realises there are greater possibilities.

And so it begins. Tucked snugly amongst the names of the flesh and blood residents who eat and sleep and breathe the air of De Greys, there are other names that swell the numbers on the forms, names of non-existent people who will never need a share of government food rations. On the papers that Gladys and Prim complete in triplicate, the lengthy forms headed *Ministry of Food and Agriculture*, sixty residents may be listed as well as the non-residents who frequent the restaurant each day.

The recipient of these forms is a Mr Harold Manning, His Majesty's Food Inspector, Bromsgrove and District Division. Should he ever choose to search De Greys for sixty residents, whether in the public rooms or the bedrooms, he'd find it hard to find all of them. But Mr Manning won't be looking, because Mr Manning has succumbed to the charms of Mrs Watson, and particularly to the charms of the little parcels she regularly puts into his hands. Something for your wife, she says, and do give her my regards. And your lunch today, Mr Manning, is with the compliments of De Greys. Any day that you'd like to eat here, with our compliments. She smiles on him graciously, Lady Bountiful, fully understanding the risks, but knowing that Mr Manning is firmly entangled in her web.

The deliveries arrive in daylight, all accounted for on the forms, to be carried up the alley where Cook will sort what will be needed for the kitchens.

Cook then puts up a few parcels for Mrs Watson, small enough to fit in a lady's handbag. Gladys keeps these in a separate fridge upstairs, well away from the staff, and during morning coffee she presses them into the hands of special customers in the restaurant, the wives of men of influence in the town who might be of use to her.

The rest of the delivery goes back down the alley under cover of the blackout, to be collected later by local shop owners who will stow the parcels under counters in the shops along the High Street.

They pay what Mrs Watson asks of them, wouldn't want to argue with her, those shopkeepers who call in the dead of night for their parcels, who creep back to their shops as though they are carrying gold, knowing that the next morning their wealthy customers, the ones in the know, will be shopping early and paying handsomely for whatever is stowed under their counters.

Gladys and Prim supervise the money. There are no accounts to be kept, of course. People leave the alley with their parcels and Prim pushes the bank notes into the back of the bottom draw of the filing cabinet. By lunchtime the next day the money has gone, leaving only Prim's handbag under lock and key because, as we all know, says Prim, you don't know who you can trust.

* * *

"It's been a shock. And a disappointment."

Beryl feels as though her face will never stop burning. Mrs Millage should never have come. What does she think she can change?

"We're just all so sad. Carton, of course," Mrs Millage breaks off, opens her hands in a gesture of helplessness, "is inconsolable." She looks across the table at Beryl. "He had such hopes, such plans for you both. We all did." Beryl concentrates on the tablecloth, on the coffee pot, the untouched plate of biscuits. "Of course, if you never really cared for him." Beryl jerks her head up in astonishment.

"Oh! How could you think that of me?" Mrs Millage shrugs. Beryl presses on. "You must know I didn't mean for it to be like this." Mrs Millage sits back, takes time to collect herself, searches Beryl's flushed face.

She can see that the girl is being honest and all of a sudden it's her turn to feel embarrassed, to see herself as she must appear to Beryl. What, she thinks, did she hope to achieve by coming to visit Beryl at De Greys? Did she really think she could turn back the clock, make everything right for Carton?

"I'm sorry. I should never have come. I can see you're upset too. I suppose I just wanted you to know how sad we all are. We wanted so much for you to be part of our family."

"And I'm grateful to you for being so kind to me. You and Mr Millage. I shall miss you."

Mrs Millage smiles thinly, straightens her hat, picks up her bag and gloves.

"I must go."

"Would you like more coffee?"

"No thank you. I've some shopping to do before lunch."

"I'll come to the door with you."

"I'm fine." She holds up her hand. "You stay here."

Beryl gets to her feet, feels she should make some sort of gesture, take Mrs Millage's hand, plant a kiss on her sad, powdery face even, but the moment passes and anyway, she has absolutely no idea how to start to say a satisfactory farewell, let alone kiss her.

So she stands at her mother's table and watches as Mrs Millage makes her way out of De Greys and onto the street.

* * *

The one thing that doesn't keep Gladys awake at night is worrying about the war. Even when the eerie wail of the sirens breaks into the night. She doesn't underestimate it, of course, listens daily to the news on the wireless, but she has put her faith in God and Mr Churchill and she doesn't imagine for a minute that either of them will let her down. Even when the sirens wail and the planes are overhead, Gladys isn't afraid. Hitler isn't interested in Bromsgrove. The barrage balloons, floating high over the Austin works to distract and confuse the planes, are clearly visible from high points in the town but still, to Gladys, the danger feels remote.

It's not that she is burying her head in the sand. You can't escape the wireless broadcasts. Italy's now at war with Britain and the Germans have got as far as the Channel Islands. That's bad. Very bad.

She's much happier now that Churchill's Prime Minister, didn't much like Mr Chamberlain. Mr Churchill is stronger, more confident, gives the people hope when he talks on the wireless.

And every day she prays, of course, for the soldiers and the sailors and the pilots and the poor people in the cities, every morning and every night, and especially she prays for Dr Eades and his family in Birmingham.

Still, at four in the morning it feels to Gladys as though all the parts of her life are clamouring for attention. It starts with Harry, where they would be now if he'd lived, whether they would still be at The Court. What would Harry think if he could see her now? What had Ian Gordon said to her the other day? You're building a little empire now, Gladys.

Ian and Nancy. Poor Nancy, Gladys feels as though she is losing her. She fears for her friend who has everything that she hasn't got, and yet is full of despair. She tries not to think of the terrible things Nancy tells her. The things that keep Nancy awake at night, the demons that drag her downwards, away from hope, away from any desire to carry on living. Gladys can't understand it. Tells Nancy to count her blessings.

It would have been so easy to give up. She thinks back to the lonely days and nights at Nechells. Now she's safely established in this town, no longer a nobody and with a successful business. Her staff know she doesn't suffer fools gladly, her suppliers know she will never let them get away with overcharging her or delivering poor quality goods and her customers know that her arrival in the town has made quite a difference to their busy market town.

St John's clock strikes the half hour. She thinks of the alley, the eager shopkeepers, the web that she has woven. Everyone, Ralph, Prim, the food inspector and the chosen people in Gladys' life who gratefully receive their little parcels from her, knowing she may well call in a favour one day but all of them happy to be firmly fixed inside her web. It's not like real law breaking, she thinks. She's doing everyone a favour. They're all respectable, most of them in church with me every Sunday.

Sometimes, lying in bed but far from sleep, she lets her mind run away with the consequences if it all goes wrong. She'd lose everything, her position and her money and she would probably go to prison.

But it won't come to that. There's not one person in the know who can speak out without implication. The cash is piling up in the safe in her wardrobe. She'll use some of it to furnish the new house and she'll shove some along the line to Pip to help pay off her loan. She's up to her eyeballs financially, she knows, but if she can keep De Greys and the catering ticking over and fill Mount Pleasant with paying guests, then in a couple of years she'll be clear. And the business on the side, she thinks, however long they can keep that going for, that's her bonus.

She doesn't think for too long, takes deep breaths, tries to relax as Dr. Eades has advised. She knows from his letters that he is flat out in Birmingham. It seems a long time since the afternoon he and Mrs Eades had surprised her, turning up unannounced at De Greys.

Tea and cakes at Mrs Watson's table. Gladys presiding, cool as a cucumber and no-one except Albert Eades himself knowing how she was really feeling. She cottoned on to what he was doing by bringing his wife, establishing a friendship between the two women, keeping everything honest and open. Nothing underhand.

Now they have started a correspondence. She searches for some sign, something to remind her of the way he was that night in Nechells. She knows she wasn't mistaken. But the letters don't give anything away. "Dear Mrs Watson", "Kindest regards", "My dear wife wishes to be remembered to you".

Mrs Eades writes too, and the visits become more frequent, short respites for them from the bleak, bombed city. She likes Mrs Eades, the large, softly spoken, well-bred woman. She doesn't want anything to upset her, doesn't want him to stop loving his wife, but lying here with the dawn light pressing against the window, what she thinks she'd give now to have him with her, just to be given an hour of him.

She gets out of bed, pulls on her dressing gown, goes through to the little sitting room and plugs in the kettle. She needs to pull herself together. She draws back the curtains and looks down onto the deserted street, waiting for the people who work in the shops and offices to set it in motion, bring it to life. She wishes summer would last longer, hates the thought of another winter in the blackout, long, dark nights stretching into morning without being able to open a curtain or raise an inch of blind.

Maybe, she thinks, once we are settled at Mount Pleasant. I'll be able to invite people, entertain properly. I shall invite Dr and Mrs Eades, and their daughters. It won't seem strange, she reasons. I'll be returning their kindness to Beryl when we were in Nechells. There'll be space to do these things.

* * *

It doesn't take long to complete the purchase of Mount Pleasant. By early September she is back to making lists.

Vi comes to stay. The vendors are leaving a lot of furniture but it's not enough for Gladys.

"We need some special bits and pieces, antiques. I want big old pictures, nice bone china, that sort of thing. I've cash to spend and I want Mount Pleasant to look established. I don't want anything that looks new and brassy."

"Where are we going to get all these things then?"

"We're going to go to house auctions. Not round here, though, where people know me. There's a lot of well-to-do people in Birmingham selling up their big houses and that's where the good stuff will be." Vi thinks through what Gladys is saying.

"I've read in the paper that there's a lot of people who've been getting fed up with those big houses," she says. "They can't get the servants any longer, couldn't even before the war started and now it's impossible."

"It's been a problem for years. All those folk who used to be in service, they've seen the light, realised they could earn more in the factories. They don't see people in big houses as their betters any longer just because they've got more money. And now, with all the danger in the city, people just want to get out. Even though they're not going to make much money out of it."

"So when do we start?"

"Next Tuesday. There's an auction at a big house in Edgbaston." Gladys picks up a foolscap sized booklet from her desk. "Here, have a look through this brochure. There's some nice looking stuff. Porcelain, brassware, silver. Just what we need."

* * *

14 November 1940

The picture house crowd spills out of the Regal Cinema into the dark, clear early evening. The moon is so bright it could be daytime. In the distance they can hear the sound of the planes. The blackout, thinks Basil, is a waste of time on a night like this.

Beryl buttons her coat, pulls the collar up round her ears. Tomorrow, she thinks, she'll look out her gloves and hats.

"That was just about the strangest film I've ever seen," she says.

"Were you really scared?"

"It was so frightening the way he convinced her she was going mad."

"Maybe we shouldn't have gone to see it."

"Oh no, it was marvellous. I wouldn't have missed it and I'll never forget it."

"Your mother says you've got a terrible memory."

"My mother," she says, "shouldn't be saying things about me to you. It's not fair."

"Nothing will change my opinion of you."

"Oh yes?" She looks up at him. "And what is your opinion of me?"

"You're not going to trick me into saying sweet nothings," he laughs. "You know how I feel." He looks at his watch, then up at the sky. "Come on. Let's get a move on. I don't like the sound of these planes."

They turn the corner into the High Street and stop in their tracks. Her hand flies to her mouth, as though to stifle a scream. Basil pulls her towards him.

"What's happening?"

Basil stares at the distant sky, a hellish, red panorama, and tries to work out what's going on.

"It's fire somewhere and it looks as though it's pretty big. Some poor blighters are getting it badly. It's to the east. It must be Coventry."

"But surely we wouldn't be able to see it from here?"

"I don't know. I can't think what else there is over there."

"But Coventry's nearly forty miles from here." She is incredulous, sure that Basil must have got it wrong.

"Come on, let's get you home."

* * *

Maud is standing on the pavement, looking anxiously up and down the High Street. When she sees them she beckons urgently.

"Hurry up! Where've you been?" They catch the panic in her voice. "They're looking for you, Miss Beryl. You're needed up the police station. You've got to get there double quick."

"What's going on, Maud?" asks Basil, trying to calm the woman.

"They're bombing Coventry. It's bad. Very bad."

"Just as I thought." He turns to Beryl. "I'll come with you."

"I'll be all right."

"No. I'm coming. I'll walk up with you. Let's get a move on."

* * *

Coventry's bombing knocks the stuffing out of the country, and particularly out of the Midlands. In Bromsgrove vicarage, Thomas de la Hay has spent most of Saturday trying to write his sermon. He's still not satisfied, but it will have to do.

St John's church is packed on Sunday morning. They pray for the people of Coventry and for the King who'd come down from London yesterday to see the wrecked city for himself. They pray for the people left homeless and for the rescue workers, they pray for the wounded and they pray for the souls of the dead.

Gladys sits in her usual pew on the north side of the aisle, Beryl and Denise alongside her. Looking around, she can see there are quite a few here this morning who aren't regulars. People always end up in church when terrible things happen, she thinks.

She knows there are plenty of people in Bromsgrove with a Coventry connection. She's got one of her waitresses off, the poor girl trying to find out what has happened to her brother. News is slow, phone lines are down all over Coventry, everything dead.

She is wondering what the vicar can possibly say to them. People are in no mood to be told to love the enemy, and woe betide him, she'd heard more than a few say that morning, if he starts on forgiveness.

He knows all this. He knows they expect him to give answers. He tells them God understands them, that today no-one can be expected to feel anything but anger. He entreats them not to let it get the better of them, assures them that good will triumph over evil. He tells them to bear up, to keep listening to Mr Churchill, not to lose heart and to carry on praying for victory. He keeps away from forgiveness.

At the end of the service people leave quietly. Today no-one feels like lingering; there is no passing the time of day or sharing of gossip.

He has done his best. He can't see what more he could have done. He hopes they've found some comfort.

* * *

Birmingham is raided all through November and on the third of December the German planes start on the city early in the evening. The bombing goes on all night and next morning people climb out of the shelters, not knowing what will be left standing.

In Bromsgrove things are up and running at Mount Pleasant and the residents are starting to settle into a routine. Cook Cooper agrees reluctantly to manage without Tilly Harper at De Greys so that Gladys can move her up to the hill to do the breakfasts and suppers and to come in on a Sunday to cook lunch.

Every day except Sunday the residents walk down the hill in twos and threes to De Greys for lunch. They're a familiar sight, the motley little group of people brought together in circumstances they could never have imagined. Mr and Mrs Baker are old and slow so they set off before the others and arrive last. Mrs Owen, as short and plump as her son is tall and thin, walks down on his arm and Arthur Butterfield, stopping now and then to get his breath, slopes along on his own. Patrick Cory leaves last and overtakes them all. George and Winnie Price are out at work during the day so they don't make the lunchtime trip.

The residents are a mixed bunch but they all agree on one thing, that they've landed on their feet at Mount Pleasant. The ordered pattern of their days has become a blessed routine in an unsteady world. And it's hardly a refuge, they say, more like country house living.

At De Greys Gladys gets going on the Christmas decorations and the public rooms take on a festive air. Paper bells and streamers smother the ceiling of the upstairs dining room and the walls are strung with assorted fairy lights. Downstairs the decorations are more restrained. Mr Cooper brings in a pile of mistletoe and great branches of holly from heaven knows where, and Gladys knows better than to ask.

The restaurant is busy and the function room is fully booked. There are daytime parties given by employers for their staff and in the evenings all the local societies are keeping on with their Christmas dinners and dances. Everyone is out for a good time. Live for the day.

1941

Patrick Cory looks forward to Sundays. In the mornings the house is quiet, most people having taken themselves off to various churches around the town, but by a quarter to one Tilly Harper bangs the hall gong for the residents to gather in the drawing room. Mrs Watson greets them and, unless they are joined by Mr Lancaster, the professor supervises the drinks tray. Then it's time for lunch.

The residents often find there are extra guests and it is the one meal of the week when Mrs Watson joins them. Today, seated at the opposite end of the table from her, Patrick Cory has a good view of today's diners.

In addition to the regulars, Dr and Mrs Eades have joined them. The young people are all girls today. There's Beryl and Denise and the doctor's two daughters. And Zena Lancaster, she's here again. Three years younger than Beryl, but looks about twenty. He's heard there's a problem between her and her father. From the look of her she's probably a bit of a handful. Patrick Cory regularly thanks heaven he hasn't had children, or he would if he believed in heaven.

"Isn't that right, Professor Cory?"

"I'm sorry." He turns to Mrs Owen. She sighs, thinks to herself he might be a clever man but when it comes to conversation he's very inattentive. "I was miles away."

"The doctor here, I was explaining to him about your arrangement in the garden."

"Ah!" He livens up. "I'm renting the chalet on the lawn."

"As your studio?" asks Dr Eades.

"Yes. The piano was delivered last week. It's a bit tight. Just about fits."

"And your students? They're happy to come to Bromsgrove for their lessons?"

"Not exactly lessons, Doctor. They're mostly postgraduates. I'm their supervisor."

"So they don't need to see you too often?"

"Exactly. They work independently at the university, and come to see me from time to time. Of course, there's a great deal of disruption at present. Some are getting special dispensations to complete certain areas of research before they're called up. It's all very unsatisfactory."

"You're fortunate, Professor, that you can carry on your work away from Birmingham."

"I certainly am. Not so easy for you, Doctor."

"I can't leave Small Heath. It's a treat just to get away here for a few hours."

"I do realise how fortunate I am. Mount Pleasant is like a haven. We've all settled in here very well." Patrick Cory hesitates. "You're right in the thick of it."

Dr Eades looks beyond the diners to the bare dripping trees and the mist which has been hanging over everything all day.

"We've had a rotten time of it for weeks and a terrible lot of damage has been done. We lost count of the number of raids months ago. We get the wailing banshee nearly every night, but we don't take much notice unless bombs fall. Last week, just to keep us awake, they dropped two land mines and knocked down some fifty houses." He looks at his wife. "Isn't that right, Babs?"

"Yes. Fifty." She turns to Gladys. "You would be so upset if you could see Small Heath. Two thirds of the people have gone. They've had enough. Hundreds of houses are knocked down, and the factories."

Mrs Owen shakes her head. Even though she keeps up daily with the news on the wireless, the doctor's account brings everything closer. Sometimes, here at Mount Pleasant, she can almost forget the war is being fought so ferociously only a few miles away from them.

"How could they do this to us?"

"I'm afraid," says Dr Eades, "our chaps are doing terrible damage in return."

"But of course, the difference is we never wanted this war," says George Price.

"And didn't start it," says the Professor.

"In Birmingham we call the bombs the beasts. Some of the incendiary bombs explode and injure the people trying to extinguish them. I've had four patients permanently blinded that way and many more with injuries to the eyes. Some can still manage to see or are blinded in one eye.

"Now I tell everyone tackling an incendiary bomb to put on their gas masks first to cover their eyes and hold the lid of a dustbin in front of them while they put sand on the bomb. Then they're safe."

"How terrible it all is." Mrs Baker, in a flutter of distress, crosses her hands on her chest. "Those poor people. And what would they do without brave doctors like yourself?"

He shakes his head, smiles wearily.

"I'm not brave. I have no choice. I'm the medical officer in charge of our First Aid Post. I'm just doing my job, like hundreds of others."

"Don't you worry about your family?" asks Mrs Owen.

"Well, we have had a hit on the house."

"But," explains Mrs Eades, "we decided the girls should stay with us. We just push on as best we can."

"Just like our dear King," murmurs Mrs Baker. "He has the Queen and the princesses with him in London. Such an inspiration!"

"A hit on your house?" Mrs Owen ignores Mrs Baker. Bromsgrove is so quiet, the enemy planes flying over the town but with no interest in destroying it. She cannot imagine what the doctor and his wife are going through. "Was it badly damaged? Was anyone hurt?"

"No, thank the good Lord. Nobody was hurt." He sits back in his chair and rests his hands on the edge of the table as though to steady himself. "I came home about four-thirty in the morning and I found a lot of clay in front of the house. When I got in the family and the maid were all safe and they'd got five strangers with them who'd rushed in for shelter. All fine. But there'd been an enormous bomb dropped near the house. I couldn't see it in the dark, but it had blown a large hole in the side of the house. Part of the roof off, all the windows and frames blown in and the foundations are driven in."

"That's going to take some putting right," says George Price, a steady, practical man who often tries to imagine the years it will take to rebuild the cities.

"I've had an architect in to give me a quote but the District Valuer hasn't agreed the figure yet. The bomb crater was one of the biggest in Birmingham and measures seventy feet across." Dr Eades shakes his head. "It goes on and on. Since then I've been within eight yards of a small bomb but I was lying on my tummy round the corner in the vestibule of the First Aid Post. They keep trying to bomb that place. It's been set on fire seven times."

For once, Tilly Harper's carefully cooked meal goes cold on the plates of the people gathered there as they listen intently to the doctor's story.

Gladys can hardly bear it. When he had walked into the house she'd seen at once the change in him, the weariness in his eyes, a stoop that had never been there before. Now, seated at the head of the table, she looks composed, but inside she feels sick as he relates his tales of death and danger.

* * *

He survives. So far they're all surviving. Everyone she knows.

Basil and Beryl celebrate their eighteenth birthdays, he in June and she in July, though as Beryl points out, there's nothing much to celebrate these days about reaching eighteen.

Basil joins up, leaves for Leicestershire.

"I've chosen Ordnance Corps," he explains, "seeing as I've spent two years in the motor trade." Beryl looks doubtful. "Don't worry, it'll be fine. I'll enjoy it."

Three weeks later he writes to her.

I've come to realise I'm at the wrong end of the war, and I'm not going to spend however long it goes on for being sworn and shouted at by an ignorant reservist Sergeant Major.

Last Friday on the parade ground, standing miserably in my gas cape with the rain running down my face, we were all suddenly halted and told to face the front. This young lieutenant emerged from a building across the park and came towards us in an elegant greatcoat with a smart peaked service cap and leather covered cane.

I don't mind telling you it was a moment of revelation. I tried to look as though I was concentrating on orders but, as the lieutenant muttered a few words to the Sergeant Major and retired once again indoors out of the rain, my mind was whirring with possibilities.

And the long and the short of it is I have decided to go for a commission, preferably in the Royal Artillery. I'm not going to spend the war marching up and down in the rain in a gas cape. I intend to be in a nice dry building, smartly dressed as an officer.

* * *

"Nursing!"

"It's all organised."

"I don't think I'll make a very good nurse. I'm not sure that's what I want to do."

"You've no choice. You've been accepted. Dr Shepherd is sending you a letter confirming everything. You'll get it in a few days' time."

"But I haven't even had an interview."

"It doesn't matter."

Beryl regards Gladys through narrowed eyes.

"Dr Shepherd. The one who comes into De Greys with his wife."

"Yes."

"I suppose," says Beryl slowly, "you've been pulling your strings again. No doubt he gets some of your little parcels sent his way."

Gladys jabs a warning finger at Beryl.

"Don't ever let me hear you talking like that. You have no idea what's going on. Do you understand?" Beryl rolls her eyes, concentrates on the ceiling. "You should be grateful. Working at the hospital means you won't have to go away from home. You can still live here and cycle up and down each day. It's only a mile or so to Barnsley Hall."

"The lunatic asylum?"

"It's still got those patients there, but you know perfectly well it's been made into an emergency military hospital. I didn't realise there was quite so much going on up there. Three wards have been taken over in the main building and there's thirty new temporary wards been put up in the grounds. They're taking men from the Front and air raid victims. And Dr Shepherd is the Chief Medical Officer."

Beryl looks doubtful.

"How am I going to learn to be a nurse?"

"You'll be fine. Look what a go you've made of messaging up at the police station. You didn't think you'd be any good at that but you know how pleased they've been with you. Have a bit of confidence in yourself. And anyway, you're not making a career out of it. You'll be a wartime nurse, a Red Cross nurse, so you won't be doing a very long training. You'll do it at a hospital in Dudley. It's a six week course. You'll go to the hospital each day and you're going to stay with Ian and Nancy."

"It's all planned then?"

"Yes. And it's very kind of Uncle Ian to have made the arrangements."

"I suppose he's been pulling strings as well." Beryl lets out an exaggerated sigh. "And that's the end of the driving as well as the police station. I hadn't banked on being a nurse. I'd actually have preferred to be a driver in the army."

"Those drivers' jobs, they're going to the university girls. And anyway, I don't want you taken you away from us. You'll make a good nurse."

"When do I go?"

"Beginning of next month. It will be good for Nancy to have you around in the evenings. I'm worried about her. You'll cheer her up a bit and you'll be back in time for Christmas."

* * *

February 1942

Beryl tries to remember everything they're teaching her. Frequently, during those six weeks in Dudley, Uncle Ian isn't able to make head nor tail of half the things she's learning. Don't ask me, he laughs. It's all coughs and colds and varicose veins in my surgery. I don't come across bones smashed to smithereens and gunshot wounds and, once she gets going at Barnsley Hall, she realises she doesn't need to know either.

Her days are endless routines of bed making and feeding, toileting and sluicing, bed baths, bed pans and dressings, cleaning and sterilising, taking temperatures and serving of meals and everything to be got ready each morning for the arrival of Matron's visit.

Nothing must interfere with preparations for Matron's rounds: books and magazines are whisked out of the men's hands and stowed in lockers. Everything and everyone, patients and staff, must be in the correct place and the ward must be spotless and calm.

New patients come in batches and at short notice. One day everything will go smoothly and she'll get off duty on time, then the next day there'll be a whole intake arrive and they're rushed off their feet.

The routine is always the same. Line them up on arrival ready for doctor to do the injections, the walking wounded standing and the rest on stretchers and in wheelchairs. Doctor jabs everyone and there's always a few who faint: big, brave men from battle who fall at the sight of a needle.

She can see that what she really needs to keep in her head and do well are the things that most please Sister. Getting on the wrong side of Sister would be the worst thing. She's already seen it happen to some of the other girls.

As far as Beryl can make out, making beds is an exceptional priority, way at the top of Sister's list of things that must be done well, so she concentrates hard on getting it right, remembering to take each corner of the top sheet sixteen inches up from the foot of the bed as she's been taught and getting her hand in the centre of the fold so that the two sides fall back down to the mattress at forty-five degree angles. There will be trouble if Sister runs her hand along the top sheet and finds wrinkles. That means she's got the corners wrong and the whole thing has to be done again.

Back in the freshly made beds, the men complain that the sheets are too tightly tucked in but it can't be helped, she tells them. It's what Sister wants and that's an end to it.

And then there's the perils of the kitchen. At the end of night duty she makes the breakfasts and if she's on days it's the suppers. She must slice and butter twenty slices of bread from each large loaf for the breakfasts and again in the afternoon. It seems impossible to cut the bread so thinly. It's not good enough, grumbles Sister, viewing Beryl's piles of uneven slices, and grudgingly she sends staff nurse into the kitchen to demonstrate.

Staff Nurse is so much more encouraging than Sister.

"Just let the knife do the work," she says," don't hurry it along. And butter the loaf before you slice."

Easy, thinks Beryl, when you know how. She gets the hang of it and plucks up courage to ask Staff Nurse about boiling the eggs.

"They all want them done differently. Some like them soft, some hard. It's very tricky."

"Put them all in together, Nurse," laughs Staff Nurse. "Bring them to the boil and give the whole lot four minutes." Beryl looks doubtful. "Those men, they're giving you the run around. You need to be firm. Just dish everything up and let them get on with it. Tell them they're lucky to get eggs at all!"

* * *

Spring 1942

There they are, with their stupid cocktails, all four of them at the end of the lawn with the sun going down behind the trees, and Denise knows Beryl's not going to welcome her butting in.

They've been out there all afternoon, the sound of the croquet mallets smacking the wooden balls tormenting her. She couldn't catch what they'd been talking about but there'd been a lot of laughter and occasional shrieks of protest from Beryl or Zena as their games were won or lost.

Now they're making the most of the daylight. Basil and Beryl side by side in the deck chairs, Beryl gazing at Basil as though he's been away for years instead of only a few weeks, and Zena, stretched out cat like on the grass, making eyes at Maurice. Denise wants to scream.

She knows everyone is amused by her. Ridiculous, says her mother. How can a twelve year old know about falling in love? You're making a fool of yourself. Leave Maurice alone and behave.

He's Basil's oldest friend. They were born on the same day in the same year and spent all their schooldays together. He is as fair as Basil is dark, his eyebrows almost white, and he's very sporty, loves jazz and fancies Zena madly as far as Denise can make out. Beryl says he's not as thoughtful as Basil but she wouldn't mind that.

The first time he comes to the Mount, he arrives with flowers for her mother and talks to Professor Cory all through lunch. Denise tries to find something to say that might engage his interest. She doesn't understand anything about sport. It is beyond her. Music, though, is easier.

And then one wonderful day he arrives with a record under his arm. He sits her down in the mahogany framed armchair by the French window. You'll like this, he says, and her hopes fly.

He winds up the gramophone, slowly slides the record out of its brown paper cover and places it on the turntable. He flicks the switch to get the record turning and gently brings the needle down onto its edge.

"Now," he instructs, "see if you can hear that tritone. And you'll pick up the chord based improvisation if you listen carefully."

He sits opposite her. She watches him closely, not the slightest bit interested in the complexities of *Salt Peanuts*. She, the awkward, dreamy, dark haired twelve year old. He is completely lost to her. There is just him and Dizzy Gillespie. He keeps his head low and moving in time to the tempo. He is completely oblivious to her, giving up his whole self to the music.

And she makes up her mind. One day she will marry him.

* * *

Summer 1942

Basil completes his six week pre-Officer training in Kent and transfers to Catterick in Yorkshire. Beryl barely has time to miss him. She starts to feel as though her life doesn't exist outside the hospital.

It's her twentieth birthday. At breakfast the residents were kind and gave her cards but really it's just like any other day. Old Mrs Baker stands by the bedroom window looking down on the drive.

"She's off again. She told me she didn't get in until after midnight yesterday."

"That's war for you."

Mr Baker, seated in the wing chair by the fireplace, is hidden behind The Times.

"These young people," she frowns, "they've lost their youth to the war."

He lowers the paper, looks across at her sternly.

"Without the youngsters doing their bit you know perfectly well we'll never win. It was the same for us. It's happening all over again, just as it did for us in 1914."

"You don't need to tell me that. I know we're relying on them, of course. They're our only hope. But there's nothing to stop me feeling sad for them."

He waves the paper in her direction.

"It's looking quite good in the Atlantic anyway. The Germans have given up their coast positions. They're withdrawing the U-boats."

"That is good news. I don't know what we would have done without the Americans."

He shrugs, gives the paper a shake and turns to the crossword. She knows better than to carry on. He is, she knows, just another proud Englishman who can't bear to admit how much hope is pinned on Mr Roosevelt.

* * *

In addition to the wartime patients in the emergency wards, the rambling red brick building still houses the hundreds of patients who, as far as Beryl can make out, live permanently at the hospital.

When she arrives to go on duty she has to be taken by the caretaker through a labyrinth of corridors and wards where the regular inmates are housed. Progress is slow. Her escort is weighed down with keys. Each door that they arrive at has to be unlocked and locked again when they have passed through.

The smells and the sounds make her squirm. She tries not to think about the stories that are going round about these wards. Sister tells the young nurses not to take any notice, that they're all rumours, but Beryl knows for a fact that some terrible things have happened and that only recently one of the patients really did stick a spoon into someone's head. It sickens her to think about it and she's dreading starting nights. She never gets used to walking through those wards and she often thinks that even if you weren't ill when you arrived at this place, you would certainly end up going mad in a very short time of being incarcerated here.

Sometimes, at the end of a shift, she is so exhausted she can hardly muster the energy to cycle the mile and a half home through the dark and the silence. There never seem to be any cars around, just the occasional glow from another bicycle coming towards her. Unless the moon is shining, you can't see who it is. You could pass your own mother, she thinks, and not be any the wiser.

She gets up some speed as she turns into Alcester Road, pedals fast uphill and plunges down the drive. In another minute, through the trees, she can see the house looming and then, as it comes into full view, the smallest of night lights, which Gladys leaves on the windowsill of the drawing room, a tiny, defiant pinprick of light in the blackness to welcome her home.

* * *

Christmas Eve 1942

Driving rain has turned the earlier snow to slush, spoiling all hopes of a white Christmas. Basil steps out onto the dark platform, trying to avoid the people who are splashing through the icy puddles as they make a dash from the warmth of the waiting room to the train. Buck Jones is waiting for him.

Twenty minutes later he swings his kitbag out from the back seat of the taxi and steps up into the porch. Beryl is working so he doesn't expect to see her until later this evening. It is Maud who opens the door.

"Come in quick. Don't let the heat out. We've been all day trying to get this place warm. The wind's finding every crack."

She doesn't change, he thinks. The day Maud cheers up they'll know there's something wrong.

She looks him up and down, standing in the middle of the hall in his greatcoat, the traveller smelling of the cold and the smoky train. More handsome than ever in that uniform, though she keeps her thoughts to herself.

"Get that coat off."

She takes it from him.

"Thanks, Maud."

"I don't want it hanging up in the cupboard, making everyone's things wet," she grumbles. "It can go in the kitchen to dry out. Give me that hat too. And leave your bag in the corner." She opens the door to the drawing room and he inhales the mingled fragrances of pine and wood smoke. "I'm to let Mrs Watson know you've come. She says you're to make yourself at home."

Left alone, he crosses to the banked up fire, his outstretched hands smarting as they start to warm and he smiles to himself at the swanky silk poinsettias and gold painted cones on the mantelpiece. Exactly what you would expect at Mount Pleasant, he thinks. All the picture frames and wall lights and even the pelmets above the windows are weighed down with holly and mistletoe and the Christmas tree, taking up a large space at the end of the room and almost touching the ceiling, is festooned with scarlet and gold bows.

"Hello Basil."

"Mrs Watson!" He crosses the room, extends a hand to her. "Happy Christmas."

She doesn't quite reach his shoulder. She is wearing grey, a fine woollen dress with a draped bodice caught at one shoulder with a pearl and diamond brooch that he's never seen before. Her hair, hennaed redder than ever, is brushed up from her high forehead in a mass of waves. He wonders what his mother thinks of it all, for although she admires Mrs Watson she probably doesn't quite approve.

She steps back and he feels as though he is being inspected.

"You're looking well," she says. "I think you've put on a bit of weight."

"We have some jolly good meals at Catterick."

"That's good to hear. We all thought you were beginning to look a bit gaunt the other month. I suppose this is officers' fare now."

"Well," he laughs, "I'm not quite an officer yet. I'll pass out in April, all being well." She smiles up at him.

"Are you enjoying the course?"

"I don't know that *enjoy* is quite the right word. They certainly keep us at it. There's a lot of studying and physical activities. But it'll all be worth it."

"It certainly will. I'm sure your parents are very proud of you."

Gladys gestures for him to help himself from the drinks tray, shakes her head when he offers to mix something for her first. Not for the first time does his charm strike her. He has an easy, honest air about him which she has liked since she first met him. He pours a measure of Martini, tops it up with soda from the syphon.

"Here. Have this armchair by the fire. And I'll put this little table by your chair for your drink." She carries over the table and an ashtray and settles herself further away from the fire on the settee.

"You spoil me."

"You menfolk need looking after. And," she adds mischievously, "I haven't got a son of my own to spoil so I have to borrow you."

He feels in his pocket to hide his embarrassment, brings out a packet of Senior Service.

"Put those away, Basil. There's no need for you to smoke your own. Help yourself from the box. Bring that table lighter over too."

She takes the cigarette he offers from the silver box and he lights it for her. She blows out little puffs of smoke, holding it at a careful angle away from her face.

"That's reminded me. We must fill this box up. Perhaps you could do that for me later. Everyone will be wanting cigarettes, even the ones who don't usually smoke."

"Except my mother. I don't think she's ever even tried a cigarette."

"That's a shame. I don't have many, but I do think the odd one is very nice. Now, you sit down and enjoy your drink. I don't know what time

Beryl will be in. She's supposed to finish at eight tonight, but if they need her for longer she just has to stay on."

"Is she cycling back?" He frowns at the thought of the wet, dark roads.

"No. Not in this weather. I've arranged for Mr Jones to collect her. She'll telephone when she's ready."

"I'll have time to go down to De Greys before she arrives."

"No need. I've invited your parents up here for supper."

"That's so kind of you. I'm sure they will appreciate it."

"I thought it would be a fine start to the holiday for us all to be together and it will save you having to decide where you should be, up here with us or down at De Greys."

"I do sometimes feel when I'm on leave that I ought to be in two places at once."

"I know. That's why I asked them. You have such a short time with us all. And it's always nice to see your mother and father."

"That's very thoughtful."

"It'll be a cold meal tonight. We've got a big ham. It's all cooked and ready." Basil knows better than to look surprised.

"It sounds marvellous. I shall look forward to it."

"Tomorrow there's church for anyone who wants to come, and then we'll have drinks and the presents back here."

"That all sounds good."

"We'll be twenty-two for lunch. In the afternoon we'll be at Barnsley Hall for the entertainment."

"That sounds interesting. Who's performing?"

"Hasn't Beryl told you?"

"No."

"We all are!"

* * *

Boxing Night. The wind and rain has carried on through Christmas Day and now, at the end of the holiday, when the curtains have been drawn for hours and people have gone to bed and the weather no longer matters, the rain stops and the wind dies down. Gladys puts her head round the drawing room door and Basil gets to his feet.

"I've just come to say don't forget to put the guard in front of the fire when you come up, Beryl."

"I'll remember."

"And Basil, make sure you get the front door properly closed when you go. Give it a good slam."

"I will, Mrs Watson."

"And when you get down to De Greys, try not to wake people up as you're going upstairs."

"I'll take my shoes off. I always do. And thank you again for everything."

"It's all gone very well."

"The best. The best Christmas ever."

* * *

Gladys closes the door on the two young people. She supposes they're all right, left there huddled together on the sofa.

It would never have done in her day. She and Harry hardly got a moment alone until they were married. Her mother was always making sure there was someone hanging around them. Heavens knows what she thought they'd get up to. You'll need a chaperone, Elizabeth used to say, if you're going out with Harry Watson. And more often than not it was Ralph. They didn't mind. Harry and Ralph. They got on.

In her bedroom she switches on the kettle, starts to undress. The rows of steady little flames on the gas fire hiss gently. She sits at the dressing table, massages night cream into her face. Not that it'll stop these lines from getting any deeper, she thinks. Nothing will do that.

She picks up the silver framed photograph of Harry with her and the girls. He hadn't liked the photo, she remembers, hadn't thought the photographer did a very good job on them all.

He'd have liked Basil. They'd have had a drink together in the evenings. It would have been very congenial. They wouldn't have had much in common though. Except Beryl. Harry would have been pleased to see her with a steady young man, even if Harry had never been steady himself.

Downstairs Basil and Beryl are going over the day.

"Do you really think it's been the best Christmas, or were you just making up to my mother?"

"No. I meant it. It's been so different from the sort of Christmases my family have. They've always been nice, but nothing like this. Twenty-two for lunch. I don't know how your mother does it."

"Don't forget she did pay a lot of money to lure Mrs Harper up here to cook for us all today. And the organising has been going on for ages. I think the best bit was this afternoon."

"It brought a lot of pleasure to those sick men. And the way all the patients struggled in from the other wards to join in."

"I thought I'd resent having to go up to the hospital when I wasn't on duty. But it was fine. It was so different, with us all sitting around on the beds. Sister would kill us normally if we sat on the beds."

"They loved the singing. Mrs Lancaster is amazing when she is playing the piano."

"And she composed those songs herself."

"She's very clever. But you and Zena, doing that duet on the piano. That went down very well."

"And the stories you told them. You really made them laugh. You're a born storyteller. I hadn't realised." She heaves a sigh. "It was all so different from when I'm up there working. I wish I wasn't back on duty tomorrow."

"So do I. But look, we've been lucky to have had Christmas Day."

Beryl shrugs irritably. "You're always trying to look on the bright side. It hasn't been long enough. I don't want to be up at the hospital when I could be here with you for your last day."

"Only half a day," he reminds her. "I'll be back on the train after lunch. And I ought really to spend some time with my mother and father. That's what I plan to do in the morning."

"I suppose so." She gets up and gives the fire a stab with the poker. A couple of embers flicker into life. He watches her turn her back to the fire, stretch her arms in the air.

"Are you tired?"

"Quite. But I don't want to go to bed yet. I want to stay here, with you."

"Come and sit down again. There's something I want to say."

"That sounds serious."

"It is, in a way."

She pushes a plumped cushion into a corner of the sofa and settles against it with her legs curled.

"I'm not sure where to start." He's usually so relaxed but now he looks awkward, his long legs hunched uncomfortably on the edge of the sofa. "You know in April I'll be passing out."

"All being well."

"OK. All being well."

"You'll be Lieutenant French."

"And I'll get a pay rise."

"That'll be nice."

"But also, a married officer's wife gets an allowance too."

"That won't affect you."

Basil takes a deep breath, decides he'll just say what he wants to say and hope for the best.

"You're right. It won't affect me when I pass out in April. But if you and I were to get married, well, that would be different."

She stares at him, her eyes wide open in shock or amazement, he doesn't know which, looking as if she wants to speak but she stays silent. He has no idea what she is thinking.

"You see, you'd then have the allowance. We could save it up so that at the end of the war we'd have something behind us."

She speaks slowly, trying to fathom what he is trying to say.

"Are you suggesting we get married?"

He takes her hand, fiddles with the charm on her bracelet.

"Yes. I mean no. I'm not suggesting it, I'm asking you."

"Asking me to marry you? So that we can claim the officer's wife's allowance?"

"No! I'm sorry. I didn't mean it to come out like this."

"You're not just asking me because of the officer's wife's allowance then?"

"Is that what you think!" He looks up from the bracelet. "I've made a real hash of this. I'm asking you because I love you. And I think you love me."

She bursts out laughing.

"I'm teasing you." She throws her arms around his neck, buries her face on his shoulder. "The answer's yes. Of course the answer's yes!"

"You're crying."

"It's because I'm so happy."

"Your mother wouldn't like that."

"I know. She'd kill me. Don't tell her. And don't let's tell anyone yet about us."

"We'll wait until April. Then we can be properly engaged."

"Our wonderful secret."

* * *

Saturday 24 July 1943

The music swells and two hundred guests get to their feet.

The wives crane their necks for a first glimpse.

Beneath her veil she walks unruffled on the arm of Eric and the aisle is filled with the scent of her bouquet, long arum lilies and ferns trailing over the lace of her dress. Her hair is swept back from her forehead in soft waves and crowned with flowers. Denise and Zena and Basil's cousin Hazel follow, in lilac organza with long white gloves and wide picture hats.

She has never been so sure of anything as she is of marrying Basil. He stands with Maurice, in full officer dress, at the top of the aisle.

Ralph sits in the pew behind Gladys, wondering what is going through his sister's head.

Two hundred guests is not a problem for her. Today is different, of course, her family, her friends and the people who surround her in business, those who need her and those who are useful to her.

If she's not thinking about the staff back at Mount Pleasant putting the finishing touches to the buffet in that great big marquee, maybe she is remembering Mother and Dad. Mother should have been here today. And Harry, of course.

Afterword

2018

In the photographs they are grouped in their finery on the lawn at Mount Pleasant, captured forever on that sunny wartime day, looking so sure of themselves, my father and mother setting out on what was to become sixty-seven years of married life.

Basil died in 2011 and Beryl, now 96, lives on. Theirs was a love match but she attributes the strength she has had to survive widowhood and old age to her childhood experiences when she had to learn independence and resilience in the face of the loss of her father.

Maurice stands back in the photograph, next to Zena, and Denise, on the far right, was no doubt wishing she could be next to him. Nine years later, her dream that one day she would marry him came true and they were together until he died in 2002.

Gladys brazenly invited Mr and Mrs Manning, the local Food Inspector and his wife, to Beryl's wedding. They were only too happy to accept, to be counted with the doctors and lawyers of the town as Mrs Watson's friends. She kept Mr Manning happy throughout the war with a constant supply of gifts for his wife and lunches at De Greys for which he never paid, all of which played a significant part in her emerging safely with an unblemished reputation at the end of the war.

After the war, Pip and Eric parted company. Neither remarried. Their unhappy marriage and the death of Beverley cast a lifetime's shadow over Zena. Gladys kept in touch with Pip but her loyalty first and foremost had to remain with Eric.

Tragedy struck when Nancy Gordon took her life. The shock to Gladys was huge. She kept in touch with Ian and their son Bunny, who was still at school, and she used to have Bunny to stay at Mount Pleasant in his holidays.

Dora did not come to the wedding but happily her estrangement did not last for ever. In the mid 1960s Eric was diagnosed with cancer and it brought Dora and Gladys together. They took it upon themselves to share his care and, after his death, the two sisters became closer.

After her wedding at Coughton Court, Ann Throckmorton accompanied her new husband, Baron von Twickel, to Germany and they had two children. He was killed in action in 1945 and she returned to Coughton where she lived until her death in 2007.

Babs Luce divorced her husband and then had an affair with one of the residents at De Greys. At the end of the war she became his wife and moved with him to Wales where they had a long and happy marriage.

Maud died at Mount Pleasant. Gladys ensured that, sick and bedridden, her final months were comfortable and Denise, forever Maud's favourite, would clamber up to Maud's bedroom in the attic with dainty dishes of food to tempt and comfort her old nurse.

After she was widowed, Daisy England made her home in Bromsgrove where she lived for the rest of her life.

In Nottingham, Fred left his wife, cruel Auntie Gertie. Beryl never forgave her aunt for the terrible things she had said to her on that visit to Nottingham.

Emma Watson lived on and used to make an annual visit to Mount Pleasant. Gladys always gave her a loving welcome, knowing that she and Beryl and Denise were Emma's precious link to Harry.

In 1945 Gladys was obliged to engage a new secretary when Prim married and, with her share of the wartime bookkeeping at De Greys, set up a successful business with her new husband. It is difficult after all these years to work out exactly what Prim and Gladys did to cheat the authorities, but it is more than likely that the numbers of people staying at De Greys and Mount Pleasant were overstated and rations were being claimed for fictitious residents. Ralph and his contacts in farming were also heavily involved and accounted for the whole pigs hanging in the alley next to Prim's office that Beryl remembers would appear overnight. Eric was never involved in the Bromsgrove comings and goings but was, when called upon for Beryl's wedding, able to turn up plenty of decent champagne.

After the war, Gladys returned to being a law abiding citizen. She was a pillar of the community in Bromsgrove and didn't consider the fearless subterfuge in which she had played a part as anything more than survival. She never forgot the time she'd spent in Nechells and, as far as she was concerned, in participating in the Black Market in wartime, she was merely grasping a God given opportunity to secure her future.

In 1943 it was difficult to know where to go for a honeymoon, the seaside out of bounds to civilians and petrol shortages keeping people nearer home. So, Stanley French lent Basil his car and after the wedding my parents drove the twenty odd miles to Stratford-upon-Avon where they stayed at The Dirty Duck, a popular riverside pub to this day. Each sunny day Basil rowed his new wife along the Avon and in the evenings they went to the theatre. It was a glorious week of freedom snatched from duty before Beryl was back on the wards and Basil, by the autumn, was on his way to Burma.

The war in Europe came to an end in 1945 but for Basil, in Burma, the fighting continued. In September he was given a week's leave. The troublesome Sister on Beryl's ward refused to give her any time off, but Gladys contacted Andrew Shepherd who overruled the decision. An unprofessional way to carry on by today's standards, but this was wartime and you will recall that the Chief Medical Officer and his wife were grateful recipients of Gladys' gifts and one good turn deserved another.

The nurses on Beryl's ward rallied round and relieved her of all her shifts, which she subsequently spent weeks repaying with no time off. Fifty years later Basil wrote down his wartime memories and this is what he said of that leave.

The end of the war is, of course, almost the end of my story. We have reached September 1945 and from Taunggyi, about this time, we moved to Meiktila, the scene of much fighting which I mentioned earlier. And here I received yet another stroke of luck – my name came out of the hat for a month's leave home to England. The journey was by RAF Air Transport Command in Dakota aircraft and converted bombers, mainly Mitchells and Stirlings.

It was a wonderful leave – we got some extra petrol for the 1937 Morris 8HP belonging to Beryl's mother and toured the Cotswolds, visited relatives and in fact enjoyed our first real taste of married life together. But all good things come to an end and by Christmas Day 1945 I was back in a transit camp in Rangoon waiting for transport back to the Regiment.

Jayne, my sister, was born nine months later, heralding the end of Basil's Burma days. He was home in time for the birth, thanks to Dr Eades' urgent telegram to the War Office. There was nothing wrong with Beryl, but the telegram worked and Basil was despatched to England.

And what of the good doctor and his wife?

The friendship remained steadfast. During my childhood a family Sunday lunch or afternoon tea with Dr and Mrs Eades in Birmingham or Bromsgrove was always followed by Albert and Gladys retiring to Gladys' bedroom to see if he could do anything for her headaches or back pain. This continued well into the 1960s, long after he had ceased to be her doctor, and we children and my mother and father took it for granted as part of the visit. Mrs Eades, remaining downstairs with us, never showed the slightest perturbation.

Gladys was a great correspondent, especially in later years when she had more time, and although none of her letters to Dr Eades and his wife have survived, several written by them to her did. The letters from Mrs Eades are warm and affectionate, mainly letters of thanks for visits to Bromsgrove. Her letter following Basil and Beryl's marriage has survived and is worth a mention. Miss May, of course, is Vi, who helped to organise the wedding.

In such pleasant company – and with such a sumptuous spread – we forgot the worries and anxieties of the times. Barbara was greatly thrilled, for she has been studying very hard indeed and has had no break from it whatsoever.

Beryl looked a picture bride and Basil a film-star bridegroom didn't he, and I hope life will continue for them in the delightful manner they set off on it. You and Miss May must have been terribly tired the day after.

It was lovely and thank you so much for asking all my family.

The wartime letters from Dr Eades start in 1939 and finish in 1943. In 1941 he wrote a lengthy letter to Gladys about his experiences in the city as a medical officer and the destruction of part of his house and in my story the letter is the basis of the experiences he tells to the startled residents at Mount Pleasant when he and his wife visit for Sunday lunch.

On 23 December 1942 he sent Christmas wishes to Gladys and Vi. The first paragraph suggests that he was aware of Gladys's Black Market activities and there are several letters in which she is thanked by Mrs Eades for sending over fruit cakes and other treats.

Dear Mrs Watson and Miss May

I am writing on my Lass's (his wife's) *behalf and my own, to wish you both a very Happy Christmas and lots of prosperity and all good things in 1943. May your troubles – and pains – grow less, and your food supplies more!*

I wish I could see De Greys at Christmas. I am sure it would look and feel beautiful with just the nicest atmosphere that exists in any place in the country (ie that is psychological atmosphere!), a just reflection on the minds that run it. I expect that you will have all sorts of parties and games and all sorts of happy times both there and at Mount Pleasant.

Well good luck and more power to your elbow. Give my love to the girls, that is, your own, and all best wishes.
With very kind regards.
Sincerely yours.

The letters from the late 1950s start very differently with *My dear Glamorous Glad* and *My very dear Gorgeous Glad*. He sends her tablets, for headaches and sleeping and for gastric problems and, on one occasion, after having given her advice on taking some new medication he adds: *If I had hold of you I would quieten you down!*

One thing shines through the letters, that Albert Eades was a man of great sensitivity and kindness who always did the right thing by his family and friends. He inspired confidence and affection in his patients and was a gentleman in the truest sense. And maybe, for all these reasons, that is why Gladys just might have loved him a little.

But Harry, of course, was never forgotten and, although I was born nearly twenty years after his death, Gladys brought him to life for me and told me much of what I have written in this book. And now, in her old age, my mother has added her own memories to the story.

Time has not been kind to Bromsgrove. It stayed much the same throughout the 1950s but in the following years change started to take a hold, as it did for so many market towns across Britain. The fields surrounding the town have gone to be replaced by the homes of thousands of people who travel daily to Birmingham. The town is a less cohesive and distinctive place altogether, with a pedestrianised high street lined with shops whose names are replicated throughout the country.

The building which was De Greys, now renumbered as 22-24 High Street, houses a pizza and pasta restaurant on the ground floor which belongs to a popular Italian chain, and in recent years, incredibly, planning permission was obtained for all the windows on the remaining three floors to be blocked up, giving a startling impression to the front of the old building, as though it has been blinded.

Developers have demolished Mount Pleasant at the top of what was Alcester Road and is now Stratford Road, and over two hundred flats and houses have been built on the site which has been renamed Stratford Gardens. The long lawn on which Gladys stood with Victor Powell and made her decision to buy the house and where croquet was played on long summer afternoons is now the residents' car park.

AFTERWORD

In Birmingham, on the corner of Corporation Street and St James Street and opposite the Victoria Law Courts, the building that was The Court has fared much better than the building that was De Greys in Bromsgrove. Much of it has been given over to offices and, with the help of a kindly and interested concierge to whom I told Gladys' story, I was able to visit the top floor of the building which would have been the flat.

It is now an open plan office space, a hive of commercial activity, busy people who hardly registered my presence as they worked at their screens, oblivious to the ghosts of the family who once lived there, of the man who died there and of my grandmother who, out of that tragedy, went on to make another life in another place for herself and her daughters.

THE END

References

ARMSTRONG Eric, *Birmingham Between the Wars*, Tempus Publishing, 2004

BELANGER GRAFTON Carol, *Shoes, Hats and Fashion Accessories 1850-1940*, Dover Publications, 1998

DOUGLAS Alton & Jo, *The Birmingham Scrapbook*, Brewin Books Ltd, 2006

DOUGLAS Alton & Jo, *Birmingham in the Thirties*, Brewin Books Ltd, 2002

DRAKE Peter, *Birmingham Shops and Shopping*, Tempus Publishing, 2007

GARNETT Oliver, *Coughton Court*, The National Trust, 2012

HOLLOWAY David ed, *The Thirties – A Chronicle of the Decade*, Simon & Schuster Ltd, 1993

McGREGOR-SMITH Jenny, *From Bromsgrove to Aston Fields*, Brewin Books Ltd, 2009

PUGH John, *A Walk Through the Town – The Bromsgrove That I Knew*, The Bromsgrove Rousler nos 21 and 22

THOMAS Donald, *An Underworld at War*, John Murray (Publishers), 2003

TWIST Maria, *Saltley, Duddeston and Nechells*, Tempus Publishing, 2006

UPTON Chris, *Back to Basics*, The National Trust, 2008

Obituary: Harry Watson Snr, Newspaper cuttings from *The Nottingham Evening Post* (undated)

Obituary: Harry Watson Jnr, Newspaper cuttings from *The Birmingham Evening Despatch* (undated)

Various family correspondence – local newspaper cuttings